BEYOND BEYOND

Jon Traer, M.D.

Jon Traer 2010

TO: Art & Jeannie
From one NFHS
grad to Another
Enjoy!

Published by Jon Traer, M.D.
2382 Julienton Drive, N.E.
Townsend, GA 31331-5021
USA
www.jontraer.com

Publisher's Note
Beyond Beyond is a work of fiction. Characters, names, places
and incidents mentioned are the product of the author's imagination, or are used
fictitiously. Any resemblance to persons living or dead, or to businesses,
establishments, and locales is entirely coincidental. The local and U.S. law
enforcement entities mentioned in this book actually exist; however, their functions
and interaction as portrayed here, should be considered fiction.

Cover Design
With the exception of the cannabis leaf image obtained in public domain from the
Internet, photos, drawings, and cover design are by the author.

ISBN 1-4505-4202-6

Pagination by
Darien Printing & Graphics
Darien, Georgia
USA

Printed by CreateSpace
Charleston, South Carolina
USA

Available at:

www.jontraer.com

Also by Jon Traer, M.D.

Going to the Gradies

Beyond the Gradies

ACKNOWLEDGMENTS

I found writing *Beyond Beyond* more of a challenge than I had initially anticipated. The principal reason, I think, is that I had largely run out of the abundant autobiographical elements that served as the basis for many of the fictional accounts found in the first two books of this trilogy. My hobby of boating on the Georgia coast, plus a newer retirement hobby of kite aerial photography, were the main personal experiences I had left to fictionalize. I certainly used those hobbies here. There are also a number of law enforcement entities mentioned, and that's an area where I have little personal experience and no expertise. Running out of self-experienced events meant I had to do some "research" to loosely understand the basic fundamentals of the law enforcement components mentioned in this book.

In the spring of 2003, as a part-time retirement job, I began working as a role player at the Federal Law Enforcement Training Center (FLETC) located in Glynco, Georgia. During the course of that role-playing activity, I've interacted with many very experienced federal officers (mostly instructors) who have diverse backgrounds within our federal government's various departments, divisions, services, agencies, et cetera. Through conversations with these federal officers, I've gained some insight as to how things work. I thank all those officers who took their time to explain unclassified details of inner workings; however, because I have so fictionalized their explanations, a true "federal insider" will probably be quite amused by my fictional warping of how things actually work on the "inside." I won't mention those federal officers by name; *they know who they are,* and I certainly thank them all.

A book, *WITSEC: Inside the Federal Witness Protection Program* (Pete Early and Gerald Shur, 2002), also provided me with nonfictional "insider information." I have fictionalized some of that information for my own purposes here. I recommend that book for readers who want a more accurate nonfictional picture of how WITSEC actually operates.

I thank those who have helped with the technical side of

publishing a book. Wendy Johnson at Darien Printing & Graphics has again done a great job with pagination and getting everything ready for print. To Gene Wesolowski, Jerry Cummings, Ron Fleury, Dr. Daniel Good, and Susan Brown: My thanks for your hours spent proofreading the *Beyond Beyond* manuscript, one that had about as many errors as words! To Miguel A. Cruz-Lopez, a fellow role player at FLETC, my very special thanks for his region-specific translations of the Spanish language elements scattered in the text of this book.

Last but not least, I thank my hazel-eyed sweetheart, my wife ... for putting up with the many hours I "disappeared" into the "Bat Cave." (That's what she calls my loft office where I write!)

AUTHOR'S NOTE

I am a retired surgeon, one who writes as a hobby. I've attempted to write the three books mentioned below in such a manner that each title could be read independently; however, I think most readers will find them much more enjoyable if read in their *chronological sequence*. Dr. Mark Telfair, and his nurse-wife Anne, remain as central characters in all three books, and the continuity of events in their lives evolves sequentially over a multiyear timeframe. That timeframe begins in the 1960s for the first book, then progresses through the 70s, 80s, and early 90s for the second book, then moves on to the mid-90s in the third book.

Third book: The title you're about to begin, *Beyond Beyond,* is the last book in the trilogy. *Beyond Beyond* begins in 1993 as the doctor and his nurse-wife are first entering their retirement years. Disheartened by the stressful and litigious environment evolving in their chosen fields of surgical work, Mark and Anne Telfair mutually agreed to quit their respective Middle Georgia small-town practices located in Statesville, Georgia. The professional couple decides to retire to Georgia's McIntosh County ... a rural coastal setting they'd *assumed* would be very relaxed and tranquil. Initially their retirement spot had seemed to be exactly that—a very laid-back environment, free of obvious crime, and filled with ample stress-free time for their mutual hobbies of photography, boating, fishing, shrimping and crabbing. While developing a new retirement hobby of kite aerial photography, Mark Telfair accidentally stumbles upon illegal activities almost within sight of their humble retirement home. The Telfairs soon find themselves in the position of being asked to bring their surgical and nursing skills out of retirement to administer surgical treatment to a U.S. Border Patrol officer, one "trapped" in the Federal Witness Protection Program. The professional couple subsequently discover they, too, are "trapped," and fear for their own lives as they get deeply involved in solving a unique drug-smuggling scheme.

Second book: Beginning in the early 1970s, *Beyond the Gradies* is a humorous look at Dr. Mark Telfair's many years of private surgical practice in the small town of Statesville, Georgia. In Statesville, Mark Telfair and his nurse-wife find exactly what they'd mutually sought in life: a comfortable place to live and enjoy life while carrying out one's chosen professional work. Totally unexpected, however, was the abundance of Statesville's humorous happenings and its endless bounty of riotous characters ... all of whom were found among patients, their medical colleagues, or other local folks swimming around in small-town social undercurrents.

First book: Set in the 1960s, *Going to the Gradies* is a humorous politically incorrect account of Dr. Mark Telfair's surgical training at Atlanta's huge inner-city Grady Memorial Hospital. Recall the 60s were an era filled with racial tensions, a rapidly changing sexual morality, and very mixed feelings about the war in Vietnam. To this, add the fact that Dr. Telfair had grown up in the very sheltered environment of Atlanta's Buckhead, a moderately affluent neighborhood in Northeast Atlanta. At Grady he learned to use M*A*S*H-like humor to shield his psyche from terrifying events experienced during training ... and he becomes quite familiar with harsh life in the real world, one that existed on the other side of Atlanta's tracks. Somehow, amid the turmoil, he still manages to fall in love with a beautiful OR nurse.

CONTENTS

PROLOGUE

*The secret to retirement is to
appreciate the pleasure of
being terribly deceived* — Oscar Wilde

A couple of years into their early retirement, the professional medical couple were enjoying their martinis and each other's company from side-by-side chaise lounges. Their comfortable recliners were located on the stationary portion of their dock, one situated at the rear of their property. More so than talking, they were just *looking* ... observing the natural beauty before them. The early October sky slowly threatened to turn crimson as the sun eased toward its set, the diminishing rays now slowly painting the marsh a brilliant golden color that always reminded them of ripe wheat. This was their most-liked time of day, the comfortably warm time of year, that Mark and Anne Telfair cherished the most about their chosen retirement spot ... but more than their retirement spot itself—despite some 25 years of marriage—they still cherished each other like hormone-saturated teenagers first in love.

Mark turned on his chaise, and noted the incoming tide was now almost fully in; it had swelled the Julienton River, along with its small previously unnamed tributary creek that traversed the expansive marsh before them. Somewhat pretentiously, and on a whim, they'd chosen a name for it: "Telfair Creek." Their neighbors—the few that they had—now also delighted in using that same name for the creek, and they'd done so since the hot July day in 1993 when Mark and Anne had first moved into their new home at Dunham Point.

Telfair Creek came directly to the floating portion of their dock, which rose and fell with each tide cycle; a short gangway connected the stationary dock to its floating portion, where Mark stowed one of their two boats. Their smaller craft, presently hauled on the float, was a 14-footer made of aluminum, and had a small outboard motor. *Creek Boat,* they'd unimaginatively named the little one. For ventures out in the open sound and offshore, their 25-foot Seahawk (*Fanta-Sea*) was at the ready and moored at Dunham Point's modest community dock.

That dock was only a short walk away. Silently, reclining on his chaise, Mark turned and stared at their namesake creek. Without warning its mirror-like surface exploded. A cloud of small fish leapt from the creek's surface.

Mark sat up, immediately turning toward Anne. "Wow! Did you see that, honey? I bet a big spot-tailed bass is having his dinner of menhaden. Right here in our creek! Think I should get a fishing rod?"

"No, Little Man," nurse-wife Anne replied, using her favorite pet name for her retired surgeon-husband. "We don't have any more room in our freezers. Besides, we've already got all the fish, shrimp, and crabmeat we'll need for the entire winter. But maybe we could catch a couple of fresh trout tomorrow, then enjoy them for supper tomorrow evening. I'll really look forward to that. Yeah, fresh trout ... I really like them broiled the way you do it."

"Glad to cook them for you, Anne. But you're probably right ... about the freezer space. You are *almost* always right, you know."

"Shall I write that down, then have you sign and date it?" Anne replied teasingly, to her husband, one who rarely remembered details *he* considered trivial. She smiled as she spoke, but then frowned when she noticed the first sting of a sand gnat that had made its appearance since the breeze had stilled.

"I don't think a written note will be necessary," Mark replied, smiling as he marveled at his wife's intuitive ability to be right about most things, and recall even the most frivolous of details, ones he'd long forgotten or didn't care to remember in the first place.

Now in silence, and swatting the occasional gnat, they continued waiting for the birds. It was time for them to come: sunset. And they did moments later. The long undulating string of white ibis were approaching from the west, flying low over the marsh. The Telfairs knew this was their evening return to their overnight roosting spot at the Harris Neck National Wildlife Refuge. It was so quiet, the whispering noise created by their hundreds of wings was clearly audible, yet the nearest string of birds was at least several hundred feet away from their lounges on the dock. Mark knew the refuge was only a mile or so north of the birds' current position, so they didn't have much farther to fly before they'd get a good night's rest. He and Anne knew the refuge was indeed a blessing, not only for the birds, but for themselves as well. The 2,800 acres of federally owned and protected saltwater marshland, grassland, and its mixed deciduous woodland would not be opened to residential development, at least not in their lifetimes.

The gnats weren't very bad yet, nor was it very dark. Anne sighed. "Little Man, are you ever sorry we left Statesville ... just up and quit surgery and nursing? I guess what I mean is, do you ever regret we elected to retire so early?"

"I really don't think so, Anne. Well ... now I do miss the technical side of surgery, but not the threat of litigation that goes with it. I'll always miss interaction with patients, especially those who were so grateful for my surgery improving their longevity or quality of life. And I think I'll always miss the doctors and friends we had there in Statesville, especially my Grady-buddy and partner, Jerry Bacon ... who I left behind. And of course Snake Holton, our senior partner who died way too soon. Heck, I even miss old Willie Lee, our yardman."

"Do you miss the *Luci?*" Anne asked, referring to their previous 20-foot wooden fishing boat, one jointly built by Mark and his Statesville fishing buddy, Roy Partridge.

"In a way I do miss *Luci,* but I think I did the right thing by selling my half-interest to Roy. Wooden boats can become a maintenance headache if they get year-round exposure to the saltwater environment we've got here. Roy's told me he uses it a lot up on Lake Sinclair near Statesville, and he knows he's certainly welcome to fish here without the hassle of hauling *Luci* down here on her trailer. I think Roy is planning to come down in late November, and I told him *not* to bring *Luci.* I told him we can use either *Creek Boat*, or the *Fanta-Sea,* depending on where we want to fish. And, believe it or not, another thing I miss is Big Orange," Mark said, referring to his old bright orange 1966 F-150, one that had been his "personal ride" almost the entire time he'd practiced in Statesville.

"Mark, selling Big Orange when we left Statesville was simply the right thing to do. She had almost 300,000 miles on her—and burned about as much oil as gas! And we both agreed we'd support only *one* vehicle, and possibly *two* boats on our retirement budget. Remember?"

"Yeah, yeah," Mark groaned. "I knew it was time for a full rebuild on the truck's 27-year-old engine, but I still miss it. I definitely don't miss your LTD wagon, though. You really didn't drive that monster wagon, you just sorta 'aimed' it ... but it was a good tow vehicle for *Luci.* Now that we're down to one vehicle, I think our Ford Explorer was a good compromise. It's not a bad driving car on a road trip, and it makes a good tow vehicle when we need to haul *Fanta-Sea* to put her in storage, or get her bottom painted."

"Well I miss Burena. She was such a delightful maid, and I'm glad the folks that bought our home up in Statesville decided to keep Burena and Willie Lee working for them there. And I do sometimes miss the Surgical Intensive Care Unit nursing I did in Statesville … but not the stress and risk of litigation that goes with it!" Anne replied, the last sun rays reflecting in her hazel eyes, and off her pretty blond hair, now developing a few streaks that were a delightful shade of white. "Mark, what do you think is ultimately going to happen to our little rural coastal paradise here … this little Dunham Point Subdivision in McIntosh County, the place we've chosen as a parking place for our retired butts?"

Pausing a moment in thought, Mark smoothed his short dark brown hair. It was beginning to gray a bit at his temples, but the majority hadn't grayed yet, and matched his brown eyes. "Well, I like Dunham just the way it is … even the 26-mile drive to the nearest grocery store. But I do know Georgia's 100 miles of coast—especially right here midway between Savannah and Brunswick—is going to have a lot of pressure from developers in the future. I'm thankful that Dunham Point is largely undiscovered, still has unpaved roads … and we've only got how many houses now?"

"Eight homes," Anne answered immediately, extracting the information from her brain's trivia-bank. "But perhaps even more important, no new ones are under construction!"

"Suits me," Mark replied. "But you know Dunham is laid out for 170 homes at full development. You can bet I'll do what I can to keep development as slow as possible, for as long as possible. The federal wildlife refuge northeast of us will protect us from residential development in that direction; the 900 acres of land north of our road is still zoned agricultural-forestry and owned by Interstate Paper Company, I think. And it's all planted in pines that are still way too young to harvest … and that land has *no* water access. So, it won't be attractive to a developer. Southward, this marsh and Julienton River we're now looking at is owned by the State of Georgia, and won't be developed."

"We can only hope," Anne replied, leaning from her chaise enough to give him a kiss on the cheek."

"Is that all I get? Just a little peck on the cheek?"

"For now, yes. The gnats are getting pretty bad and the sun's down … and it's getting a little cool. Want shrimp for dinner?"

"Yeah! But what's for *dessert?*" Mark asked, smiling in a way that let her know he was *not* talking about food.

"'Dessert' is the same thing it's been for the last 25 years," Anne smiled seductively. "Race you back to the house, Little Man."

They walked briskly up the 100-foot-long wooden walkway connecting their dock to the rear deck of their home.

1

THE SAND GNATS

After their carnal "dessert," and a delicious boiled shrimp dinner that followed, they enjoyed a "food dessert" of vanilla ice cream, then slept soundly through the night in their king-sized bed.

The next morning, Mark got up at six, the time he usually awoke naturally. Gingerly, he got out of bed wishing not to disturb Anne's final hour of sleep. He walked quietly to the living room's sliding-glass door, one that opened onto their home's rear deck. He didn't open the door, only peered out. It was dark. He flipped on lights that illuminated their dock and the walkway that led down to it. Dense fog greeted his eyes. About 150 feet away, the lights on the dock itself were barely visible halos, but he knew the fog would burn off in an hour or two. The weather radio in the living room indicated there'd be no significant wind for the day, and a high of 68 degrees was predicted. A glance at his tide chart told him high water would be about 10:00 a.m. Recalling Anne's request made yesterday for fresh trout for today's supper, he thought: *Perfect. We'll still be able to fish in the creek today.*

With Anne still sleeping, Mark put on a pot of coffee. Waiting for it to perk, he started reading an article about sand gnats. He'd had the article for quite some time, just hadn't gotten around to reading it yet. In a way, Mark and Anne detested the noxious insects, yet were uncertain in their minds about their place in the environment. Early in their coastal-living experience, they'd learned the local gnats were decidedly different from their relatives that inhabited their prior residential area in Statesville, Georgia. The coastal gnats were of a *biting* kind; the inland gnats only offered the nuisance of swarming in your face, and seemed especially attracted to one's eyes. Their nearest neighbor, George Benton, a retired USPS employee, felt coastal gnats were a blessing in disguise. In fact, George's old Chevy pickup sported a bumper sticker: PRESERVE OUR SAND GNATS … THEY SAVE US

FROM YANKEES!

Mark poured himself a cup of coffee, then moved to the breakfast table and continued reading the article given him by a U.S. Fish & Wildlife Service biologist, one who worked for the nearby Harris Neck National Wildlife Refuge.

Culicoides furens was the scientific name for the most common species of the sand gnat that inhabited the local area. Commonly they were referred to as "biting midges," the article stated. But Mark had also heard the locals call them "sand fleas" and "punkies." "No-see-ums" was another common local name, but his Statesville fishing buddy, Roy Partridge, had his own special name for them: "Gall-a-napers." But Roy used that term to refer to either mosquitoes *or* sand gnats, and when trying to elude their noxious bites, the frantic fanning and slapping motions folks made with their hands Roy had given a special name: the "McIntosh Salute."

"How long you been up, Little Man?" Anne asked, walking into the kitchen.

"Not long. Coffee's ready," Mark replied.

"Whatcha reading?" Anne asked, as she sat down beside him.

"An article about sand gnats. One I got from that Dr. Spencer Roberson, the Ph.D. biologist over at the refuge. Remember him?"

Anne yawned, then spoke. "Yeah, I sure do. It was awhile back. That program he gave on local area plants was great. I think he is a very knowledgeable fellow. Don't you?"

"Sure is, Anne, but he said he didn't actually write this article on gnats. He told me one of his entomology buddies did."

"So, what does the article say? Just summarize," Anne replied, taking a sip of her coffee.

"Well, it seems gnats have a definite place in the food chain."

"Yeah! Like you and me ... when we're sitting on the dock, or when we're out in *Creek Boat,* and there's no wind and the fishing is at its best ... and the temperature just right for us humans!" Anne laughed.

"Anne, did you know that only the *female* gnat bites?"

"Well, then, in my book she's a total bitch!"

Mark laughed. "Just doin' her job, honey. Seems it's essential for her reproductive cycle. A blood meal for the female is necessary for the development of her eggs. Says here she uses her cutting teeth to rip the skin and get the blood flowing, then sucks it up through a straw-like structure called a 'proboscis.' Seems she squirts an anticoagulant chemical into the open wound to inhibit blood clotting.

The amount of blood lost is insignificant, and not even visible without magnification … but most human victims have allergic reactions to that chemical, the anticoagulant. And that's what produces the intense itching and the red spots, or even welts in some folks."

"Mark, let me ask you a question. What if all the sand gnats just up and suddenly disappeared … like mass extinction? You really don't think our beautiful ecosystem here would collapse, do you?" Anne asked, trying to make a point about what she considered the only objectionable thing about the area where they lived.

"Don't know for sure, Anne. Have you seen that bumper sticker on the back of George Benton's truck?"

"Do you mean the one about preserving sand gnats?"

"Yes. I know it's intended to be a joke, but there may be some truth to it. If we didn't have gnats here, you can bet a lot more folks would want to live here—and development would boom!"

"Well, maybe," Anne allowed. "But other than keeping Yankees away, what other value do they have?"

"They feed bats, gnatcatchers, purple martins … and fish, or so this article says. Eggs are laid spring and fall in moist areas that have decaying vegetation—like the marsh we love. Also it says the larval forms move around by wiggling and they feed on microscopic aquatic organisms until they become 'pupa,' which float like a cork. Then they become food for small predators," Mark explained.

"*Small* predators? Like what, *Little* Man?" Anne teasingly asked her husband, who at five-six was shorter that she at five-nine."

"Like birds, frogs, insects, crabs … and small *fish!*" Mark shot back, not the least sensitive about his short stature. "But I'm sure I've accidentally swallowed hundreds of the adult flying gnats … after I'd inhaled them!"

"Oh well, just a little extra protein," Anne laughed.

"Seriously, just be glad they are there," Mark said. "And just be glad the five million eggs female gnats lay per acre don't all make it out of their larva and pupa stage to become the flying ones that bite us! Only ten percent make it to flying adults, or so this article claims."

"Enough of the biology lesson. Want some breakfast? Fog's beginning to lift, and I thought you were going fishing today."

"No, I thought *we* were going fishing today. To catch trout for supper. You change your mind, Anne?"

"Mark, there's no wind and it's gonna be warm today. So, I think I'll let *you* feed the female gnats all alone … and after breakfast I'll do a little grocery shopping. I'll pick up some Deep Woods Off bug spray while I'm at it. And I'm still looking forward to some fresh broiled trout for supper tonight."

After their unhurried breakfast Anne departed for the grocery store. Mark, using a small spray bottle kept on the kitchen counter, applied an insect repellant containing Deet to areas of his skin not covered by his shoes, jeans, flannel shirt and knitted cap. A tackle box, small cooler, and fishing rod in hand, he walked briskly to their dock. The fog was now gone. Not a breath of air stirred and the sand gnats, as expected, were on a feeding frenzy. Immediately, they found even the smallest bare skin spot where he'd missed applying repellant. He loaded the items he'd carried with him, then slid *Creek Boat* off the floating dock; rollers beneath the hull at dock's edge made the task a quick and easy one. The15-horsepower Johnson sprang to life on the first pull, and he quickly got underway. He exited Telfair Creek and entered Harris Neck Creek, a larger tributary of the Julienton River. Mark headed north up Harris Neck Creek with enough speed that the sand gnats couldn't follow. Now approaching Dunham's community dock, he slowed and came alongside *Fanta-Sea,* his larger boat. He retrieved a bucket of live bait shrimp he had tied to a cleat on her gunnel, then transferred the container to his smaller boat. *Glad to have that part behind me ... hope the gnats won't find me where I plan to fish,* he thought.

Gnats now out of his mind, he continued going up Harris Neck Creek at three-quarter throttle, dodging the creek's many sandbars he knew like the back of his hand. He also maneuvered around multiple numbered spherical Styrofoam floats, ones that marked not only his own crab traps (he had only three), but also a dozen more that belonged to the few respectful commercial crabbers that also used Harris Neck Creek. Mark's traps were presently unbaited; he left them in the creek year round, simply to "claim" his territory, something all crabbers—recreational or commercial—seemed to respect as unwritten law. *Why do the Yankees insist on calling them crab pots? Pots are for cooking, traps for catching,* he pondered. *Need to pull my own traps ... make any repairs they might need before crab season next spring,* he thought, making a mental note while en route.

In less than ten minutes, he arrived at one of his favorite creek-fishing spots. That spot was located in a sharp bend, at a point where Harris Neck Creek was only about 50 feet wide. The currents there made a peculiar eddy, part of which flowed in a direction opposite that of the still-incoming tide. *Maybe it's the deep water and crazy current here that trout like ... confuses the shrimp and little fish they feed on, and makes them easier to catch,* his mind concluded.

Though it had taken two attempts, he finally got his little boat positioned and anchored to his liking. *Gnats haven't found me yet,* he thought as he baited up and made his first cast into the center of the eddy. His float went down immediately. He could tell that the fish was a relatively small one by its "feel." When he got the 15-inch spotted sea trout alongside the boat, he reached over the gunnel, submerging both his hands. He gently unhooked it without the fish ever breaking the water's surface. "Go back home and grow some more," he said aloud as the little fish swam away.

The next cast was a different story. Setting the hook, he smiled and knew *this* one was a keeper. When he landed the fish, he estimated it to be about 18 inches long. *Two to three pounds,* he thought. He'd boated another fish identical in size when his hands started stinging. *Well the gnats have finally found me!* he thought. *Just need to put some fresh repellant on my hands. Musta washed it off when I released that little one.*

"Shit!" he said aloud, as he searched his tackle box, finding only an empty can of spray. *Oh well, I've already got enough for our supper… and yesterday, Anne said we're out of freezer space,* he thought as he pulled anchor and headed back home.

Once underway, the gnat problem was again solved. He now dreaded stopping at the community dock to return the remaining live bait shrimp to *Fanta-Sea* … or the gnat exposure he'd surely get when he winched *Creek Boat* back onto the floating dock in his own backyard. After he rounded the creek's last bend before the community dock, he saw something strange: *a man standing in Fanta-Sea.* He was not a neighbor, or anyone else Mark recognized. Mark slowed to an idle as he cautiously approached his larger boat.

"Hey you! What are you doing in *my* boat?" Mark yelled at the large fat man in a dark expensive-looking three-piece suit. The stranger clinched a large unlit black cigar in a corner of his mouth, and he was frantically fanning and scratching his bald head with both hands—while executing perfect "McIntosh salutes" between his spells of clawing. Though Mark was now only 50 feet away, the fellow didn't answer him, just stepped quickly out of *Fanta-Sea* onto the dock, then scurried up the gangway to the community lot where a strange car was parked. Mark quickly secured *Creek Boat,* and pursued the fleeing mystery man.

Again, Mark spoke just as the man was preparing to get into his car. "Hey mister, exactly what were you doing in *my* boat?" Mark loudly demanded, while noting the metallic gray Mercedes had a New Jersey plate on its front bumper. Mark also noted a middle-aged big-haired woman in a fur coat sitting silently in the front passenger's seat.

"Uh … just looking," the man finally grumbled as he continued swatting at biting things he could not see. He paused long enough to light his cigar and exhaled a big cloud of blue smoke, which swirled around his shiny bald pate, temporarily dispersing the gnats that were giving him hell.

"Mister, you're *not* from around here. You've got a Jersey plate on your car. And I don't appreciate you getting in my boat without my permission. That's *private property,* you know."

"Private property? Little Guy, do I look like I really give a shit?" the stranger replied, with an attitude and thick Jersey accent that immediately pissed Mark off.

The gnats were giving Mark hell, too, but he was determined not to let the rude Yankee stranger know he'd even noticed them.

"Hey, sorry," the man said as he extended his hand to Mark. A gold pinkie ring on the fella's right hand with a diamond the size of a grape caught Mark's eye. "Uh, that's my wife, Stella, in the car. My name is Anthony Graziliano, but my friends call me Tony."

The gnats were still biting Mark, especially on the backs of his hands, where the repellant had been washed off. *Maybe I should try to be civil … need to find out what this guy is really up to,* Mark thought.

"Well, Tony, this community lot and its dock, and my boat, are all private property, but—"

"I'm well aware of that," Tony cut in. "That's why the wife and me are down here. I could get a better view of the riverfront by getting in that boat you claim is yours. That put me a little farther out in the water. Ya see, I own a development company in Jersey, Graziliano Development, Inc., and I was tryin' to estimate how many docks we could put on this stretch of the river. I gotta contract to buy all the remaining lots here in Dunham Point …162 lots left, if the records at that hick-filled courthouse in Darien are correct."

"Why would you do that?" Mark asked, still fighting the urge to claw his own stinging hands.

"Spec housing. We build 'em cheap and fast. They'll sell like hotcakes to folks from up North … and we'll make a bundle. If my company owns the majority of lots in here, we'll get one vote for every lot we own, or so the covenants for this place say. That means we're in control. We can change covenants and architectural review requirements, or anything else my company wants to change. So, are you from around here? Wanna buy into my deal?"

"Yeah, I'm from around here … lived in this area all my life," Mark lied, noting the very slight breeze that had just developed. It soon dispersed the "protective envelope" of cigar smoke that enshrouded the get-rich-quick shyster's head. Needless to say the hungry female gnats attacked his shiny scalp with a vengeance, and the man immediately began to claw his scalp. His manicured nails actually drew a little blood in a place or two.

"What the fuck! Some kinda little flyin' shits are biting the crap out of me again! Started out in that boat," he said in near panic. "What the fuck are they?" the man demanded.

"Gosh, Tony. I'm not sure, but I'd guess it must be the *sand gnats*. Yep, I'll bet that's what it is. The sand gnats, Mr. Graziliano," Mark answered, using all his willpower to remain stone-faced, while fighting the almost overpowering urge to claw his own hands to shreds. "Ya see," Mark explained, "I'm a retired doctor. I specialized in immune disorders," Mark lied again. "And if you weren't born and raised in the area, then you haven't developed the antibodies in your system that neutralizes the chemicals they inject when they bite. Takes a number of years to build up your sand-gnat immunity. Usually 15 or 20 years. So, that's gotta be what's buggin' you, Tony—*sand gnats!*" Mark said, his face expressionless. He experienced a smile he didn't let show when he noted the woman in the fur coat had just gotten out of the car to determine what was driving her husband so nuts. She remained out of the car a mere ten seconds, then began clawing her hair-sprayed beehive hairdo to shreds as the gnats homed in on her scalp. Like a rocket, she shot back into the car, slamming the passenger's door loudly.

"Shit! I can't stand this!" Graziliano exclaimed. "Doc, are they this bad *all* the time?" he asked, preparing to also retreat to the safety of his Mercedes.

"Nah," Mark replied, "gnat season is only the months that *don't* have an *r* in them … so it's really not their peak season," Mark informed, as the man shot into his car, slamming the door.

Graziliano cracked the driver's window about an inch, then spoke to Mark. "This place sucks! I'm cancelling the fuckin' purchase contract. Even the stupid Yankees I'd planned on sellin' th' homes to are smart enough to avoid this kinda shit. I'm haulin' ass outta here," he yelled just before fully closing his window and starting his car.

Mark smiled in thought: *Just get your fat ass out of here, Mr. Tony*

Graziliano ... so I can scratch my fucking hands!

As though he'd read Mark's mind, the developer revved his car, but accidentally slammed it into reverse, then crashed immediately into a two-foot-thick pine tree ten feet behind him. Mark was pleased to see the grossly deformed New Jersey tag on the rear ... and the deep dent in the center of the expensive car's rear bumper; it was deep enough that the trunk lid of the Mercedes was also substantially buckled. Mark innocently smiled, then casually waved as the driver finally found a forward gear and tore off up the dirt road in a cloud of dust. Mark laughed aloud when he saw about a foot and a half of the wife's expensive fur coat sticking out of the crack at the bottom of her door ... and dragging in the sandy road, stirring up its own little "personal" dust cloud.

When the Mercedes disappeared from sight, Mark screamed at the top of his lungs: *"Thank God! And thank you, lady gnats!"*

Sprinting up the road and clawing his hands as he ran, he quickly covered the 200 yards back to their house. He found Anne was not back from grocery shopping. Still out of breath from the sprint to the house, he immediately plunged both his hands into the cold water that was filling the kitchen sink. *I'll go get the damn trout and bring the little boat back later,* he thought, just as he heard Anne drive their Ford Explorer into the carport.

"Mark, I hope you're not cleaning fish in the kitchen sink ... *again!*" Anne exclaimed, wearing a frown as she entered the house carrying a sack of groceries. "You know how I feel about that ... those scales fly everywhere, then stick to everything within five feet of the sink." Though it rarely happened, she was obviously quite displeased with him.

"Honey, there're no fish in your precious sink," he replied as he removed his hands from the cool water, and showed them to Anne.

"Oh my God! What happened?" Anne asked. "Looks like you have a bad case of measles."

"I almost wish that was the case. This is totally the result of gnat bites ... damn little bitin' bitches!" Mark growled, as he returned his hands to the soothing water, the stinging now subsiding.

"So, you forgot to spray, didn't you?" she accused.

"No. I sprayed before I left, then discovered the can of repellant in the tackle box was empty. I think I washed it all off my hands when I released a little trout."

Her attitude softened. "Honey, is it still stingin' bad? Want me to get some Benedryl out of our medical kit?"

"No. It's about quit now," Mark replied, as he started draining the sink, then dried his hands.

Anne removed assorted groceries from the bag, then placed two cans of Deep Woods Off on the counter directly in front of Mark. "Here, put one of these in your tackle box. Do it now, before you forget. No amount of fish is worth going through this. And you should have known better! And speaking of fish, where the heck are the ones we'd planned on having for supper tonight? Didn't you catch anything?"

"Yeah, two nice trout," Mark replied defensively.

"So where are they?" Anne demanded, arms akimbo.

"They're still in a cooler in *Creek Boat,* down at the community dock," Mark replied.

"Why'd you leave the little boat down there?" Anne asked, knowing his usual routine was to return *Creek Boat* to the dock in their own backyard, and clean fish at an outdoor sink located there.

Better tell her the whole story… before she really gets pissed off, he thought. And he did. Every last little detail about his encounter with Mr. "Tony" Graziliano. Anne sheepishly smiled after he'd finished his "gnat saga," then she kissed the back of his hands, then his mouth, then other parts while they showered together prior to "dessert" served in their king-sized bed.

A NEW HOBBY

A brief nap followed for them both. Their phone's ring brought them both fully awake.

Mark answered. It was his Statesville fishing buddy, Roy Partridge, calling to say he regretted he would not be able to come down in November. "Got a dang three-week business trip to England, to the home office of my kaolin company there. Margie is goin' with me 'cause th' company's payin' all the expenses. And she's never been to Europe before. So I'm gonna have to pass this time," Roy explained.

"Call when you and Margie get back. Y'all have a good time. Maybe we can set up some fishing in January or February," Mark said before clicking off.

Mark relayed Roy's disappointing message to Anne.

"That's too bad, Mark. I was looking forward to seeing both Margie and Roy."

Anne soon had a light lunch prepared, then she reminded him that *Creek Boat* was still down at the community dock and had uncleaned fish aboard.

"Thanks for the reminder, Anne. But I'm not quite that forgetful yet. They're on ice in our little cooler ... and they'd be fine, even if I didn't clean them today."

"But I was looking forward to fresh broiled trout for supper tonight, Little Man."

"Me, too. I'll be back in a little while," Mark said, leaving their house. Now protected with a fresh layer of insect repellant, he walked to the community dock. He retrieved his little boat, piloted it up Telfair Creek, and winched it onto their dock. A nice breeze had started, which made the repellant he'd applied a redundant precaution. Mark knew a breeze over three or four miles per hour kept the little suckers "grounded." Using the dock's sink, he quickly cleaned the two nice trout he'd caught earlier in the day. For some reason, he felt a little saddened: *Fishing season for the creeks will soon be beyond its peak. Roy and Margie aren't going to be able to come down in November. Crabbing won't be worth a flip till spring. Shrimping won't be good again until early fall next year. Need to find me a new hobby... one to take up the slack,* he thought while carrying the large trout fillets to the house.

* * *

Winters at Dunham Point were usually mild and short. January and February were the only two months Mark Telfair actually considered "winter" months, ones that limited his usual boating, fishing, shrimping, and crabbing activities. December was usually quite tolerable, but he and Anne usually went south for Christmas for visits with her brother, Thom, who lived in Orlando, or to Tampa to be with Anne's sister, Susan, and her husband, Alan.

Late December found the Telfairs driving south to Orlando, Mark at the wheel of their Ford Explorer. Anne, working a crossword puzzle in the front passenger's seat, seemed completely content as the miles clicked leisurely by. Despite the holiday season, the traffic on the secondary roads they'd chosen remained light. Mark's mind pondered possibilities for a new hobby: *My classical guitar playing is coming along fairly well ... but that's an indoor hobby. I want something I can do outside. But what? Photography? I've already done plenty of underwater photography earlier in my life ... and on land I've shot photos of about every scene and creature they've got in the local wildlife refuge. But what about aerial photography? Too expensive!* his mind concluded. Even though he (while in the Air Force) had obtained a private pilot's license, and had logged a low number of hours in a Cessna 180, he continued thinking: *Aerial photography... but how? Planes are just too expensive, at least on our retirement income. Balloons? Helium? Hot air? How big a balloon would I need to lift a camera,* his mind kept prodding. *Kites? Yeah, that's it. Maybe a big kite ... like the one we built when I was a kid growing up in Atlanta,* he thought, just before his mind shot back some 45 years in time ... to his boyhood while growing up in Atlanta's Buckhead.

* * *

As a ten-year-old, Mark Telfair's experience with kites started in a typical way. It was just a short bike ride to the stores in Buckhead; twenty-five cents would buy him the largest premade kite sold by F.W. Woolworth's, Buckhead's five-and-dime. They were made of brightly colored tissue paper in many colors, and used thin wooden sticks as their spars. Regardless of the kite's color, each had "High Flier" plus a cloud scene printed on the side that would face the flyer. For another 25 cents, you could even buy a ball of cotton string about 1,000 feet long. With an allowance of 50 cents a week, he almost always knew exactly where he'd spend it: at Woolworth's, to replace the previous week's High Flyer that had fallen victim to a tall un-climbable tree, or drifted off to God knows where when the flimsy cotton line snapped.

Without doubt, Jerry Bieger, Bill Carson, Timothy Reese, and Robert Anderson were his four closest childhood kite-flying friends. They knew they were fortunate in that their neighborhood on Acorn Avenue had something most other Atlanta neighborhoods lacked: a large cow pasture that abutted their backyards. In the pasture they'd frequently joined forces after school, or on weekends, to go fly their kites together. The pasture was well over 100 acres in size, and had a number of grazing milk cows owned by Atlanta's R. L. Mathis Dairies. Other than a few scattered 100-foot pines (and abundant cow pies on the ground!) it really was a great place to fly kites.

Jerry Bieger was the oldest, but still a couple of years too young to get a driver's license. At the end of a kite-flying day, and speaking to the group of his buddies, Jerry had spoken his mind about their poor mutual experiences with High Flyers bought at Woolworth's.

"Ya know, three of us have lost our kites this afternoon. I think we should just start building our *own* kites, fellas. These High Flyers are just too flimsy," Jerry said with a frown. "Those that don't come apart in the air, fall apart with the slightest touch of a tree limb. Or that sorry Woolworth's line snaps."

"Jerry, I'm not sure we could make one that would fly," Timothy (the timid one) allowed. "But we could measure a High Flyer, and make a tougher kite exactly the same size. We could even use that brown paper, like they put around my dad's suits he gets back from the drycleaner. And use tougher sticks. Maybe like bamboo."

Mark recalled it had been Timothy's childhood statement that had first caused wheels to spin in his own child's mind. "Well," Mark said to the group, "why don't we make a *really* tough kite? Make it *really* big, too! Use cloth, like silk maybe. And use metal, like aluminum, for the sticks?"

Robert Anderson chimed in: "Mark, you're the youngest and smallest one here. I think your brain is the smallest, too! Just where do you think we could get that silk and metal shit? Huh?"

Mark puffed up like a toad. He didn't mind being called the "smallest" in the group, but he sure didn't like Robert's insinuating he had the smallest brain, and thus was the dumbest one in the group. Now angry, Mark replied, "Your momma know you use words like 'shit,' Robert? Besides silk and aluminum aren't 'shit.' But that cow pie your dumb ass just stepped in ... well, that's what *I* call shit!" Robert glanced down, to discover he'd accidentally planted the new navy-blue Ked on his left foot in the middle of a decidedly green odoriferous cow pie. Shaking his foot, then rubbing it on the grass, Robert blushed in embarrassment, as Mark continued: "Robert, I assume your big brain can read. You ever read the *Atlanta Constitution*? You ever look at all those ads in the back? War's over Robert, if you'd bother to read ... and they've got all kinds of military surplus stuff for sale in downtown Atlanta."

Bill Carson, the quiet chubby one, finally spoke up. "Hey fellas! That's enough of the insults between Mark and Robert. I don't want the rest of us to have to break up a fight between you two. But I happen to like Mark's idea. We could pool our allowances, and catch a trolley to downtown to look at military surplus stuff. If Jerry went along, our parents would probably let us go by ourselves. He's the oldest. Heck, he's even almost old enough to drive."

* * *

In the passenger's seat of their Explorer, Anne cleared her throat. Mark's mind snapped back to the present.

"Little Man, you're mighty quiet. Whatcha thinking about?"

"Not much of anything, Anne," he said, not wanting to tell her he was half-daydreaming about his childhood in Atlanta.

"Well, I'm still working this darn crossword puzzle. And a simple little four-letter word has me stumped. Begins with a *k* and ends with *e,* I think, if I've got the other words right."

"What's the clue?"

" 'Ancient Asian ceremonial item,' it says."

"Try the word *kite*. Would that fit?" Mark asked.

Anne quickly penciled in Mark's suggestion. "You're a genius, my Little Man! That'll work. I'm afraid it was so simple I didn't think of it.

And I need to pee. How about you?"

"Yeah, me too. We're on State Road 35, coming up on Wildwood, Florida. We'll make a pit stop there, get gas, and catch a bite to eat, too."

After their brief gas, food, and potty stop in Wildwood, Anne turned to a new page in her crossword book. She immediately started working on a fresh one. Mark's mind again returned to his childhood and kites.

* * *

Though it took about a week, the Buckhead Boys finally talked their parents into allowing them to take the trolley to Five Points in the heart of downtown Atlanta. Several provisos: Jerry Bieger, the oldest, was to be in charge of the rest of the kids, and all their parents had indicated they had to mind Jerry and be home by dark. Jerry was also to be in charge of their money; between piggy banks and pooled allowances, they had put together the great sum of $21.55. About noon on a Saturday, they walked to the trolley stop at the corner of Lindberg Drive and Peachtree Road. After waiting only a few minutes, the familiar red electric bus arrived. Jerry paid the 50-cent fare for the five of them. When the trolley stopped at Five Points, they all got off. Mark had the latest military surplus ad page from the *Atlanta Constitution* neatly folded in his hand. Mark passed the ad page to Jerry, who studied it briefly, then said, "I think we should first look at Buck's Army Navy. It's only about two blocks away, on the corner of Pryor and Decatur."

When they entered Buck's, they were all flabbergasted. Mess kits, collapsible shovels, tents of all kinds, sleeping bags, spools of cable, helmets, ammo belts, uniforms both Army and Navy, all greeted their eyes. Mark was the first to notice something they would subsequently purchase: a 30-foot-diameter white silk parachute. They mutually agreed the parachute silk would be more than large enough to make a great sail for their proposed "monster kite." An hour later, they finally located a 1,000-foot spool of small aircraft cable. "It's braided stainless steel, 2,000-pound test, and only one-eighth inch in diameter. Three bucks, including the steel spool it's wound on," the store clerk said.

"How much for that parachute?" Mark asked the clerk, pointing at one suspended from a steel girder high in the roof structure of the cavernous building.

"I'll have to go check with the boss," the clerk said to Mark. "Ladies have been buyin' the heck out of them to make dresses and stuff. Not really silk. They are made of nylon, just feels like silk. Be back in a minute."

The clerk soon returned with the sad news: "Boss says the parachute is $15. But that includes all the lines, plus a free duffel bag to stow it in."

Jerry Bieger, their leader and "banker," stepped up to the clerk. "Look mister, we've only got $21.05. If we buy the parachute and the aircraft cable, that means we've spent $18 ... leaving us with only $3.05 left. We also need some aluminum for spars in a big kite we wanna make, and we'll need 50 cents to get the five of us back to Buckhead on the trolley. Have you even got any aluminum? Stuff that might work for kite spars?"

The clerk was quiet for a full minute, closing his eyes in thought. "Tell you what," he finally said, "how about you guys follow me out to the backyard of this building. We just got in a bunch of aluminum blimp ribs and longerons. Might be something in that stuff that would work."

The boys were soon sorting through an amazing pile of scrap aluminum tube, each about one and a half inches is diameter. The clerk quickly explained: "These are all tempered aircraft aluminum. Very strong, but light. The pieces that have gentle curves are actually the blimp's ribs. The ribs with the sharpest curve are from the nose or tail of the blimp, where the diameter is smaller; the straight pieces are longerons. They're parts of the blimp's frame that ran front-to-back. Nickel a pound, either curved or straight. I'll get a hacksaw and cut stuff to any length that you guys want."

After a "group consultation" the guys decided they wanted a straight piece 30 feet long, and a curved piece 20 feet long. The clerk soon returned with a scale, tape measure, and hacksaw. Mark selected the pieces. He finally found a curved piece that he felt would match the curve in the transverse spar of a High Flyer, should one ever "grow" to such huge dimensions. The clerk stood on the scale, first noting his own weight of 165 pounds. Mark held his breath when he handed the salesman the two pieces of cut aluminum; the scale jumped to 195 pounds, meaning they had 30 pounds of aluminum. They all breathed a sigh of relief when the salesman announced, "That's 30 pounds at a nickel a pound ...so you guys got $1.50's worth here! Need anything else?"

Jerry Bieger shook his head indicating they needed nothing more.

It hit all the boys about the same time, but Mark was the one to ask their leader a question: "Jerry, how in the heck are we going to get a 30-foot piece of aluminum back to Buckhead on a trolley? The parachute's in a duffel, and the cable's on a spool. So they won't be a problem."

"Mark, just pray we have an understanding trolley driver ... and some understanding passengers on that trolley," Jerry added.

They paid Buck's cashier the $19.50 they owed, and Jerry doubled-checked the $1.55 change, then stowed it in the pocket of his jeans. Jerry spoke to the cashier: "You don't reckon you've got about ten feet of binder's twine you could give us, do you?"

"Sure," the friendly cashier replied, then reached beneath the counter and presented a ball of twine to Jerry. "Take what you need. On second thought, take the whole ball of twine. But exactly what are you kids gonna do with all that stuff? The parachute, those aluminum tubes and cable?"

Jerry smiled. "Would you believe we're gonna try to make a huge kite, then fly it on that aircraft cable."

The cashier's smile faded into a frown of concern. "Any grownups gonna help y'all? I guess you know that cable will conduct electricity. I don't want to be reading about any electrocuted kids in the paper. Just stay away from any power lines, OK?"

"We got a great place to fly. No power lines, just a few trees," Jerry replied. "Say, could you let us tie those aluminum tubes together ... do it on the floor of that aisle over there?"

"Sure," the cashier replied. "Just don't let any of our customers trip over it while you're doing it. OK?"

Jerry checked his watch, the only timepiece in the group: 3:00. He knew it would be dark in a couple of hours ... so everything had to go smoothly for their promised "before dark" return to their Buckhead homes. All knew if they were late, it would not go unnoticed by angry parents. They quickly had the 20- and 30-foot aluminum tubes lashed together and headed out the door of Buck's Army Navy to face the next challenge: a cooperative trolley driver. Amid stares from pedestrians on the busy sidewalk, the fivesome hauled their purchases to the trolley stop at Five Points. Minutes later an *empty* trolley arrived. Jerry quickly boarded, and explained their dilemma. "That duffel and spool of wire are OK inside, but not that long tube stuff you've got!"

"See if he'll let us tie it to the *outside* of the bus," Mark urged Jerry.

Jerry made the request. The driver initially shook his head, then smiled before he finally said, "OK ... but it's gotta be on the left side, so it won't block the curbside doors. And hurry. The cars behind me are getting impatient, blowing their horns. I don't want to get reported to the company."

Amid honking horns from angry car drivers behind the trolley at Five Points, they worked feverishly. In less than two minutes they used the remaining binder's twine, and had the aluminum securely lashed to the left side of the trolley they'd take home. They had to open four trolley windows to do it, so they could use the pillars between the windows as their "anchor points." Their ride to Buckhead was uneventful, though a few newly boarded passengers near the open windows complained. Bill Carson and Robert Anderson both shed their jackets to give to two old ladies who complained the loudest about being too cold. Finally they reached their destination stop at Peachtree Road and Lindberg Drive. Quickly, they cut the aluminum free with Timothy Reese's pocket knife, while Jerry Bieger profusely thanked the driver, and offered a tip in the amount of $1.00. The driver shook his head, refusing. "Believe it or not, I was a kid once myself, too. Besides, tips are against company rules. Y'all be safe, and have fun while you can. You'll be grownups before you know it."

Bill and Robert retrieved their jackets, closed the trolley windows, and hurried off the bus. Jerry checked his watch: 4:45. Only 30 minutes till dark, and they had to carry their stuff some three miles. They actually jogged home, two runners supporting the 30-foot aluminum at its ends; the rest took turns with the parachute-containing duffel bag and spool of aircraft cable. As they turned onto Acorn Avenue, it was five 'til five, getting dark, and all were out of breath. They stopped at Jerry Bieger's driveway. Mr. and Mrs. Bieger were standing there! Mr. Bieger had his arms wrapped around his barrel chest. At first he looked mad, but then smiled. "I'll help you put your stuff in the garage ... and thanks for keeping your word to us parents about getting home before dark."

* * *

"Where are we now?" Anne asked looking up from her new crossword puzzle.

"We're on State Road 91 ... about 55 miles from Winter Garden. So that puts us about an hour from your brother Thom's house in Ocoee."

"You've sure been quiet this trip, Little Man. Something bugging you?"

"No. Just enjoying the near-zero traffic, and thoughts about my childhood while growing up in Buckhead."

"Anything you want to share?"

"Just kid stuff," Mark allowed, not wanting to delay the return to his trip down memory lane.

"What's a three-letter word for fun? Don't have any other letters yet," Anne asked, knowing he was keeping his current true thoughts to himself.

"Sex. Try that as a three-letter word for fun," Mark said, laughing.

"Honey, you're a horny nut case ... but I love you anyway! I'll shut up, you drive. I'll try to finish this crossword myself before we get to Thom's house."

* * *

Mark immediately returned his thoughts to his childhood, and the "B-29"—the name they'd chosen for the large kite they were planning to build. Well, it was actually Timothy who'd come up with the name; he was also into building model airplanes, and had actually built a model of Boeing's WWII vintage heavy bomber that carried the same "B-29" name. But Tim insisted the "B" stood for "Buckhead," the "29" for the 29-foot height the finished kite would have if scaled to match that of a giant High Flyer. Timothy also did the math, figuring their finished diamond kite should end up exactly 29 feet tall and 19.33 feet wide. It took them two weeks of after-school work, and all their free weekend time to finish it. Several moms, especially those who wanted the leftover scrap nylon, were enlisted to do some sewing machine stitching of a perimeter hem. That hem would create a perimeter "pocket" around the large diamond, and through it they'd feed a perimeter line. The perimeter line (inside the hem) was made from the strong nylon shroud lines that came with the parachute, and would anchor the massive sail to the tips of the crossed aluminum spars, ones that were proportionally spaced exactly as if they were on their familiar High Flyers. The shorter 19.33-foot curved aluminum spar was the horizontal one, and Timothy said its curve was a perfect match to what you'd find on a giant High Flyer.

The following Saturday left them disappointed; it rained all day, and the wind was nil. It rained on and off on Sunday, too. But the following Monday seemed perfect. They thought school would never end that day. At three o'clock, they all raced home on their bikes. The steady March wind and clear skies told them today was the "perfect" day to give the B-29 its first test flight.

Most of the construction had been done in Mr. Bieger's large garage. Actually it was a two-car garage combined with a workshop. For storage, they'd had to suspend their B-29 horizontally from the garage rafters; this allowed Mr. Bieger to park his car beneath when he returned home from work.

On that "perfect" March Monday afternoon, they carefully lowered their suspended B-29, backed it out of the garage, then cautiously carried it horizontally to the large cow pasture. One boy was assigned to each "corner" of the huge diamond. Jerry Bieger functioned as their "commander" as they carried it several hundred yards deep into the pasture. Jerry also carried the spool of aircraft cable they had connected to the B-29's bridle; in his other hand, Jerry carried an 18-inch piece of a baseball bat, one that had a 60-foot piece of aircraft cable attached at its center and the excess carefully wound around the bat. "Stop right here," Jerry ordered. "No cow pies here! Now carefully keep it level, guys. Wind's about ten miles an hour, so don't let it get cockeyed. If we get it cockeyed it may take off before we're ready. Remember, *level!* On the count of three. One … two … three," Jerry counted aloud. The B-29 was now safely flat on the ground. Each "man" remained at his "corner," just to be sure the wind didn't get beneath the kite. Mark Telfair had been assigned to the "tail" or bottom corner of the diamond. "Mark," Jerry ordered, "take this and tie the free end of the cable to the tip of your spar. Use that hole we drilled in the aluminum. Pass the wire through the spar several times then use a good knot. And don't get that 60 feet of cable wound around the bat all tangled up. That's going to be our temporary tail."

Jerry turned and walked away, then hollered back to his crew. "Everybody stay in place!" Jerry ordered, as he walked farther into the wind. He walked and walked, wire spooling off the reel behind him. When he estimated only a few hundred feet of cable remained on the spool, he made about 20 wraps around the base of a convenient pine tree, one that was about two feet in diameter. He then fashioned a good knot. Feeling that it was securely anchored, Jerry jogged back to his "ground crew."

"OK guys, I think we're ready. Except for Robert at the nose, I want everybody else to go to the tail. Unroll that wire wound around the bat, straighten it out, but whatever you do, *don't let go of the bat!*" Timothy, Mark, and Billy were all now in position, firmly gripping the

19

bat, with Mark in the center.

"Ready guys?" Commander Jerry asked his crew.

"Yeah," the tail-holders hollered in unison.

"OK," Jerry barked. "Robert, you raise the nose into the wind!"

It all happened so quickly the tail-holders were caught off guard—except Mark Telfair, who first saw Timothy, then Billy lose their grip on the bat, and fall to the ground when they were only about six feet in the air. Neither seemed hurt and they were screaming at their commander, and pointing to the lone tail-holder. Mark suddenly found himself at least 300 feet off the ground ... scared to death, *and all alone!*

His companions were screaming up at him, but the wind, distance, and flapping of the nylon on the aluminum spars made understanding a single word impossible. *How long can I hang on?* Mark's mind questioned, as he looked down at his companions, who now looked like little ants. He studied the white knuckles of his hands that gripped the bat on either side of the wire. *I know I won't be able to hang on until dark, when the wind normally dies. Maybe if I could pull myself up and let the wire go between my legs, I could sit on the bat, like a swing ... just hold on to the wire, and let the bat carry my weight on the cheeks of my butt,* he thought.

It took him several attempts, and he suffered some superficial cuts to his hands from the wire, but he finally pulled up and positioned himself so he was actually sitting on the bat. One at a time, he pulled his hands back inside his jacket sleeves, then regripped the wire using the sleeves as protective padding for his hands. The kite was fairly stable. He even relaxed a moment to survey his neighborhood from on high. He could even see Peachtree Road and a trolley and cars moving along it. Every house on Acorn Avenue he could identify. All the while his companions on the ground were still yelling unintelligible words up to him.

His moment of relaxation was brief. The wind began gusting and B-29 started darting left, then right. Like a clock's pendulum he began swinging side to side suspended on 60 feet of thin aircraft cable. His swing motions seemed to exacerbate the erratic kite's behavior, and with each swing the wire cut into his crotch. *Oh God! What if the kite actually loops,* he thought, knowing that was something High Flyers did in gusting winds, especially if they didn't have a tail that was long enough or heavy enough.

He didn't know how long he'd been airborne, but it seemed like forever. He kept watching the sun, attempting to estimate the time, but knew his body couldn't take it much longer ... especially his sensitive private anatomy that now felt completely raw. He glanced down at the severely frayed crotch of jeans, expecting to see blood, but there was none.

Then a thought struck him: *I'm not over any trees. They could hand-over-hand walk the kite down. Surely the combined weight of Jerry, Robert, Timothy, and Billy would force the kite down ... if they'd all just grab the cable and walk toward me. How can I tell them to try that?* he wondered. He made "walking motions" with the fingers of a free hand, but he was so high they probably couldn't see his attempt at hand language. Besides, his companions were all in a tight huddle, looking down and hopefully thinking about a solution. Their huddle on the ground suddenly broke up, and all four of his friends began stripping off their jackets. They gathered as a tight group, each wrapping their jacket around the cable. The group then began slowly walking toward him, letting the cable slide through hands that were padded by their jackets. The walk-down had progressed about 500 feet toward him, and he could see that his altitude was now diminishing. On the shorter tether, however, the kite's flight sometimes became even more erratic. The ground crew temporarily stopped their walk-down, waited for the next wind lull, then advanced toward him again. By then, he noticed the flapping sound of the nylon was slackening overhead, and over the next ten minutes the wind slowly died at dusk. Mark Telfair and the B-29 made a perfect gentle landing. The B-29 suffered not a scratch; holding himself through the shredded crotch of his jeans, Mark was not sure he'd ever be able to have sex ... even when he got old enough.

* * *

Mark's inexplicable raucous laughter stopped Anne's concentration on her current crossword puzzle, her fifth or sixth. From the Explorer's passenger seat, her hazel eyes peered over her reading glasses, to discover her husband with one hand on the steering wheel, the other holding his crotch, and still uncontrollably laughing.

"Little Man! What's so damn funny? You thinking about the first time you got laid? Or have you gotten bored and decided to fondle yourself? Need to pee again? Or what!"

"None of the above. Just recalling a childhood injury. The one that left me with those scars on my balls," he explained.

21

"Yeah, I've noticed them. Real faint. Minimal. You told me you ended up straddling a wire as a kid. Remember?"

"That's exactly how it happened Anne. End of story."

"Mark, I could care less about those faint scars. The 'main attraction' seems to still be working just fine! And exactly where are we now?" she asked, as Mark's laughter ended.

"Uh … we're still on 91. About 35 miles from Winter Garden. About 45 minutes to go before we get to your brother's in Ocoee."

Anne shook her head, exhaled audibly, and quietly resumed her crossword. *Men,* she thought. *They get the strangest moods … and don't have PMS to blame it on!*

They rode in total silence the next 20 miles. A question popped into Mark's head, one he shared aloud with Anne. "Honey, do you think anyone has ever tried to put a camera on a kite to take aerial pictures?"

She didn't answer his kite question, just asked one of her own. "I need a seven-letter word for 'obscene.'"

Mark thought a long moment. "Have you tried 'raunchy.' That's seven letters," Mark offered.

"I'm not sure where your mind is today, Little Man. But 'raunchy' won't fit, at least not for this puzzle!"

Silence returned, and remained, until they pulled into Thom's driveway in Ocoee. Thom, who had apparently gotten off work early, cordially greeted them in the drive, then helped them with their luggage. Anne retreated to a bathroom to freshen up.

After they were settled in, Thom offered Mark a drink. "Want your usual? A martini with a capful of vermouth and olive brine, and one olive?" he asked.

"That'd be fine, Thom. But just make the vodka two ounces. The drive was easy. We took the chicken way out, used back roads most of the way, and traffic was light. Your sister worked crosswords the whole way down, and it was a relaxed quiet trip."

Anne was still in the bathroom. "Done your Christmas shopping yet?" Thom asked Mark.

"Yeah, all done. I got Anne one of those new digital cameras. And a little digital photo printer. It's probably gonna commit me to buying a computer soon. I want one for myself anyway. And I want one of those new parafoil kites … one made out of nylon. Just a small one, about 16 square feet … or four feet by four feet in size."

Thom laughed. "No offense, but aren't you getting a little old to fly kites?"

"Not for what I've got in mind. I want to use a kite to carry a camera up for aerial pictures," Mark replied, taking a sip of his drink.

"Looks like you guys have settled in," Anne announced as she returned from the bathroom and entered the living room. "Sorry, I just had to brush my teeth and fix my makeup. So what's the game plan, bachelor brother Thom?"

"Dinner here tonight. I'm cooking prime rib on the grill, and shish-kebab veggies. Tomorrow, we can do any last-minute Christmas shopping you guys may need to do, then next day we can drive over to Tampa, to be with sister Sue, Al, and their grandkids to open all our presents. Sound OK?"

"Perfect, Thom," Anne said, and gave her thoughtful brother a peck on the cheek. "But maybe tonight, or tomorrow night, we could drive around your neighborhood and look at all the Christmas lights. When we came in, I noticed your unlit lights are all blue and orange bulbs. For the Florida Gators, right?"

"Go Gators!" Thom enthusiastically responded. "But I guess it's 'Go Dogs' where you guys live in Georgia. Kinda hard to have red and black lights ... never seen a *black* light bulb!" Thom laughed, then went to the patio to start his grill.

Following Thom's excellent meal, Mark showered and prepared for bed; Anne and Thom watched TV and chatted, catching up on the latest family news. In the process of their talking, Thom asked Anne a question: "Is Mark acting a little strange, or is it just me?"

"Thom," Anne replied, "Mark has always marched to a slightly different drummer. But what makes you ask that question?"

"Well, I think it was when you were in the bathroom. Right after y'all first got here. But he mentioned something to me about putting a camera on a kite for aerial pictures. Doesn't that strike you as a little strange?" Thom asked.

"Not really ... at least not for him. In fact, he mentioned that while we were driving down here. Just told me he wondered if anyone had ever put a camera on a kite for aerial pictures."

"And ...," Thom prompted.

"I didn't answer, and the subject got dropped. But now that you mention it, Mark was mighty quiet the whole drive down here. He gets that way when he gets something on his mind."

"Well, he told me he wants a small nylon parafoil kite. I think I know where we could get one, if you'd like to give it to him as a gag Christmas gift. On the way home from work today, I saw a vendor selling kites in a vacant lot on a street corner," Thom explained.

"So let's get him one tomorrow," Anne said. "And maybe one of those new disposable cameras. Mark really hates to grocery shop, so we'll just tell him we're going to do some quick grocery shopping. I guarantee he'll be glad to stay here and watch TV or read. Or he'll be on your computer hunting for stuff on the Internet. As you know, we don't have a computer yet. And Mark doesn't have the slightest idea, but we've got a neighbor who's in the computer business, and he's going to build him a custom computer when we get back home. So a computer is his real Christmas present. The kite and camera would just be a gag-gift."

The next day went exactly as planned. Mark stayed home at Thom's, while Anne and her brother went "grocery shopping." The friendly kite vendor had several parafoil kites, and indicated a Sutton FlowForm kite should easily lift a camera. "It's made of ripstop nylon and has no spars to break. It's 'almost indestructible,' and has a lot of lift for its size of only 16 square feet," the kite salesman quickly explained. At the vendor's suggestion, Anne also bought 1,000 feet of 200-pound-test Dacron kite line, plus a little plastic hoop spool to wind it on. A quick trip to Eckerd's Pharmacy produced a couple of disposable 35mm Kodak film cameras. Another brief trip to a local Publix produced the few groceries that Thom actually needed. When they returned to Thom's house, Mark was neither reading, nor watching TV; he was at Thom's computer, surfing the net for parafoil kites.

On Christmas morning, Thom, Anne, and Mark drove to Tampa to be with Anne's sister, Susan, and the rest of the family. Anne's real Christmas present to Mark consisted of an envelope containing a note and a photograph of a computer: "Built to your specifications, when we get back home. Merry Christmas! Love, Anne," the enclosed note read.

Of course Anne was delighted with Mark's gift to her: a little point-and-shoot Canon digital camera. "Mark, you've got one more present," Anne announced, her new camera at the ready. She handed him a package about twice the size of a shoebox, and smiled in a strange way.

Mark cautiously opened his remaining present. As he sorted the parafoil, kite line, and disposable cameras, he could feel his face turning red. Pretty soon his face matched the bright red color of the kite … especially after reading Anne's note stuck in the bottom of the box: *"Go for it, Little Man!"*

Anne immediately took multiple pictures of her red-faced

husband. Mark was at a loss for words, but not for thoughts: *I don't care if I get hair-lipped in the process … by God, I'm gonna show her I can make aerial pictures using this damn kite!*

THE OYSTERMAN

The drive back to their home at Dunham Point was uneventful. Anne worked a number of crossword puzzles while Mark did the driving ... and thinking about how he was going to execute his mental promise to take aerial photos with his gag-gift kite. *Gotta learn to fly that kind of kite first,* he reasoned. He'd never flown a parafoil-type kite before.

Fortunately, the Harris Neck National Wildlife Refuge had a large parking lot at its little-used Barbour River Landing. It was used almost exclusively by a few local black men, who, depending on the season, used the landing to bring to shore their harvest of cast-netted shrimp, crabs caught in commercial traps, or hand-pulled oysters. They'd then load their catch into their raggedy trucks and drive to nearby wholesale buyers in the county. Even before they'd gotten home, Mark had decided Barbour River Landing would be his "test flight area." He'd chosen it for several reasons: First, the site would have very few observers to witness his screw-ups. In addition, there were very few obstructions, such as electrical wires and trees. On multiple visits there, he'd noticed there was almost always a good breeze at the landing.

For over a month, he didn't go much further with his thinking about the kite. He'd been distracted ... sidetracked, deciding about the specifics of the computer his neighbor would custom build. Anne's only request had been quite simple: "Just be sure I can use it to look at my digital pictures on the monitor ... and send e-mails!"

In early February, at Barbour Landing, he finally got around to attempting to fly the kite. Having no spars or rigid structure, it had to first be "inflated" by the wind in order to fly. Though discouraged, he finally figured out a system where he could launch it solo. He was too proud to ask Anne to assist him, by holding the kite "open" into the wind, while he held the flying line. He found he could tie off about 100 feet of kite line to any fixed object, then go downwind and hold the kite "open" until it inflated, and took off like a rocket. Without any tail it was highly unstable, darting left and right, even looping, and occasionally collapsing in the air, only to crash to the ground in its deflated state. The little red kite was indeed tough; after several dozen crashes no visible damage was apparent.

It took a few days, but with the aid of his new computer he found a solution. A company named IntoTheWind had tails specifically designed for parafoil kites. He learned they were called "drogue tails," resembling a small parachute. Online, he ordered one that was recommended for a parafoil kite the size of his. It took ten days, but it finally came in the mail.

The next day, he told Anne he was again going to Barbour Landing to fly the kite. He didn't tell her he'd not yet had any real success flying it. "Need any help?" she innocently asked, trying to be helpful.

"No! I can do it by myself," he replied not wanting to admit he'd failed thus far.

"Be careful, honey. You're pretty isolated over at that landing. Even though it's on federal property, I've heard rumors of some real bad characters over there ... folks that use the landing to bring in illegal drugs."

"I've heard those rumors too, Anne. But all I've ever seen there is either nobody, or an occasional oysterman or crabber. Anyway, I've got my pistol under the seat of the car. So relax," he said in parting.

Five minutes later, when he arrived at Barbour Landing, he saw a familiar pickup: a half-rusted-out blue Chevy truck. He'd seen that same old truck on most of his trips to the landing, but its owner usually was nowhere to be seen. If Mark happened to be at the landing when the old black man arrived in his boat laden with crates of oysters, he'd offer a friendly wave, one the old fella had yet to return. Making no effort to communicate with Mark, he'd just quietly load oysters into his truck, then leave. In his mind, Mark had already decided he wasn't very friendly, and had chosen a name for him: *Oysterman.*

But today, Oysterman was apparently still out on the river gathering oysters when Mark first arrived. He attached the newly acquired drogue tail and launched *Little Red,* his chosen name for the kite. Once *Little Red* got out of the turbulent air near the ground, it was stable as a rock. *Looks like it's nailed to the sky!* he thought, as he spooled off almost all the 1,000-foot flying line. *Still stable, and it's a good 800 feet up,* he estimated in his mind.

Smiling, and observing that *Little Red* was now just a tiny dot in the sky, he saw Oysterman approaching the landing in his boat. Mark quickly tied the kite line to the trailer hitch of his Ford Explorer, then sat on the ground trying to observe the stability of a kite he could barely see. He waved to Oysterman down on the dock, and, for the first time, he waved back. Mark pointed to the tiny red speck in the sky, and Oysterman directed his gaze in the direction Mark was pointing. The waterman smiled, and after securing his boat at the landing, he began slowly walking toward Mark. The man had both hands in the pockets of his bulky jacket. *Hope he doesn't have a knife or gun,* Mark worried while sitting on the ground, and leaning against the rear bumper of his Explorer.

"What's dat you got up on dat string?" the old black man asked, when he was about 25 feet from Mark.

"It's a kite. Been trying for days to get it to fly right. And today, I *finally* got it to work right!" Mark explained, allowing his excitement to show.

"Mind if I pulls on th' string?" the old fella asked.

"Well, I guess not," Mark replied, worrying that the man might, for some strange reason, want to *cut* the line.

Oysterman grabbed the line with his work-callused hands, and gave a tug, then repeated it several times before speaking. "She sho pull strong, don't she? And the wind she be only 'bout eight today, th' radio say. But now dat you got it flyin' lak you want, watcha gonna do next?"

"Well, I'm trying to develop a system where I can put a camera on that kite, then take pictures from up in the air," Mark explained.

"Sho 'nuff?" Oysterman asked, a smile developing on his face.

"Yeah, sure enough I'm gonna try," Mark replied, also smiling.

"You ain't been a drinkin' today, is you?" the old fella asked, now laughing, showing perfect white teeth that matched his close-cropped snow-white hair.

"Not yet," Mark answered. "But I may go to drinking before I get this thing figured out!"

"I seen you a buncha times befo'. Jus' figured you wuz jus' some crazy ol' white guy. But what your name is, and where you stays at?"

"I live just down the road, at Dunham Point," Mark explained. My name is Mark Telfair. I'm a retired doctor, and live here full time. Where do you live?" Mark asked.

"Up on Harris Neck Road. Just about a mile after you gets to th' road what go into where you lives at. My name is Oscar. Oscar Dunham. My family goes way back to slave times … slaves what worked on Dunham Plantation. My peoples is been livin' here and workin' these waters lotta years. We all usta live out on Harris Neck, but back durin' th' big war, th' gov'ment run us black folks off to make 'em a Army base for airplanes. Gov'ment then gived it back to th' county, county gived it back to th' gov'ment, then turn hit into dis wildlife place after dat. Don't much lak what they did to my peoples, but least they lets us use dis landin' an' dis dock fo' free."

"I'm sorry to learn that history, Oscar. But at least you can still use the water to make a living. Looks like you got a boat full of oysters. Need any help getting them to your truck?" Mark asked.

"You lak oysters?" Oscar asked.

"Love 'em!" Mark replied. "How much for a bushel?"

"I gets seven-ten for mine."

"Only seven dollars and ten cents?" Mark asked, surprised.

Oscar chuckled, then explained Mark had misunderstood his dialect. The real price was seven*teen* dollars per bushel. "I give you a free bushel, if you hep me get 'em to my truck. Kinda down in my back today," Oscar said, rubbing his low lumbar area.

"Well, I'd be glad to help you," Mark offered.

"You sho is nice … fo' a *white* boy," Oscar beamed.

"Well, you're nice, too … for a *black* man!" Mark shot back, a little incensed. "But Oscar, you need to understand something about me. I can't speak for all us 'white boys,' but you need to understand this right up front: I grew up in Atlanta. Got plenty of black folks there, some even worked for my family. And I did most of my surgical-doctor training at Grady Hospital in Atlanta. At Grady, we had a lot of black patients. As a surgeon, it didn't take me long to discover *all* my patients were exactly the *same* color when I looked at their insides. Outside color didn't make any difference. They all hurt the same, got sick the same, even healed the same … and when they were beyond our help, they even died the same. So, have we got this black-white thing straight now?"

There was a long awkward pause before Oscar replied, "Well, Doctor, I reckon we is got dat straight!" The old fella first laughed, smiled, then sincerely extended his hand to Mark.

It took about 30 minutes to unload Oscar's boat, an old work-worn 24-foot Carolina Skiff. The radio on its center console was softly blabbing about the weather as Mark helped Oscar. Unloading the boat was indeed back-breaking work, and Mark didn't know how a fellow he estimated to be in his 80s did this kind of work all year long. By pointing, Oscar would indicate exactly which crates he wanted Mark to handle and carry to his truck. As for the crates Mark handled, they all appeared to contain nothing but beautiful select oysters; however, a few of the crates Oscar personally carried appeared to contain something in addition to oysters: brick-sized cubes wrapped in cloudy black plastic. When the last crate was in Oscar's truck, he asked Mark a question: "Ain't you forgettin' somethin', Doctor?"

"Forgetting what, Oscar?"

"Your oysters! Let me get some papers out my truck. I'll put 'em down in th' back of your fine car. They's still drippin' a little mud and saltwater. And you kin see what that salt has did to my old truck!"

Mark opened the hatchback of the Explorer. Oscar carefully spread multiple layers of newspaper on the carpet in the back of the car. Dodging the kite line Mark had earlier tied to the trailer hitch, Oscar carefully transferred a weathered wooden crate of oysters to Mark's car. "Jus' bring my box back next time you comes over here. If I ain't here when you is, jus' leave hit on th' dock. Hope you enjoy them oysters," Oscar said in parting.

Mark profusely thanked Oysterman for the gift, and after his truck disappeared from sight, Mark started the long and laborious task of retrieving his 1,000 feet of Dacron kite line. It now exerted an almost-constant 20-pound pull. Mark finally got the little red parafoil kite back down to Earth. It had taken him about a half-hour, and his hands felt raw on the steering wheel as he drove back to Dunham. During the short drive, Mark found himself in deep thought: *There's just gotta be a better way to do this. A better way to rewind this line on the hoop spool. Use a hand-cranked mechanical reel instead? Maybe a big electric fishing reel? Doing it this way, I really need some gloves … this line is eventually going to cut my hands. Wonder if Oscar uses gloves when he gathers his Oysters? Wonder what Oscar had in those plastic-wrapped cubes?*

DON'T GIVE UP

"Honey, how'd it go?" Anne asked immediately upon his arriving home at Dunham.

"Went great! Best flight so far," Mark said, not wanting to tell her this was his *one and only* successful flight to date.

"Did you take any pictures yet?" Anne asked immediately.

"Uh … not just yet. Still working on that part. It'll be awhile because I gotta figure out some way to attach the camera, then aim it and fire the shutter."

"Mark, I was beginning to worry a little. You know, your being there all by yourself. You see anyone else over there? What took you so long?" Anne asked.

"Honey, it takes quite awhile to get the kite back down … there's a lot of tension in the line, and it takes a long time and a lot of effort to wind 1,000 feet of it back in. You really need gloves to protect your hands. I think I'm gonna make a mechanical hand-cranked reel, or possibly get an electric fishing reel … a big one." Mark paused a moment. "And I did meet a nice old black fella over there this morning. I'd guess he's in his 80s. Anyway, I helped him unload his oysters. He told me his name is Oscar Dunham. I think he's possibly a slave descendant, one whose ancestors worked on Dunham Plantation. The other night I was reading about the history of this area in that new book you bought, *Early Days on the Georgia Tidewater*. I think our subdivision is also named Dunham Point, because it was once a small part of the Dunham Plantation that existed here back in the 1800s. Anyway, the fella I met is an oysterman and he gave me a free bushel of oysters!"

"Uh … Mark, at Christmas when I gave you that kite and the cameras, I did it purely as a joke! So don't feel obligated to make it work."

By God, I'll make it work! I don't give up, Mark thought, deepening his resolve even more.

"You said 'Dunham' was the old man's last name?"

"Yes, Oscar Dunham. Lives nearby, off Harris Neck Road. So?"

"So have you read the latest *Darien News?*" Anne asked.

"No. But what's your point?" Mark replied.

Anne located the paper and handed it to Mark. "Look on the second page. There's an article about suspected illegal drug traffic at Barbour Landing, and several other landings in our area. The title of the article is 'Under Our Noses.' See it?"

Mark read the short news article, and was pleased to find no mention of Oscar Dunham's name among the several that had been arrested. "Anne, I don't see any mention of the 'Dunham' name, or any other name that I recognize. Most of the arrests were made at the dock in Valona, others in Crescent, and that was at night. I think a smuggler would have to be crazy to use a federally owned dock in broad daylight!"

"Agreed," Anne replied. "Just keep it in mind. And as for the free oysters, let's roast some tonight for dinner, and shuck what we don't roast to save for oyster stew. Don't worry. I'll make room in the fridge!"

* * *

March morphed into April, then into May. He was now spending almost all of his time at Barbour Landing, experimenting, and frequently failing. Despite the frequency of his visits, he hadn't again seen Oscar Dunham since the day he'd been given the oysters. Mark had returned Oscar's oyster box the very next day, and placed it on the dock. It still was unmoved from the spot where Mark had left it. Oscar's boat also appeared not to have been moved since the day he'd helped him unload the oysters. Questions entered Mark's mind: *Could he be sick? Has he possibly died? Or has he been arrested, even though his name was not listed in the news article Anne showed me?*

Mark also questioned himself: *Have I become obsessed with making this kite-aerial-photography thing successful?* He'd finally gotten a very large electric fishing reel, a 12-volt Penn Senator. He'd located the reel on the Internet using the computer Anne had given him at Christmas. He'd attached the reel to a hand truck that also carried the required battery. He'd even rigged up a brake system that would lock the wheels of the hand truck, and keep a hard-pulling kite from causing it to accidentally roll. Launching and retrieving the kite was now effortless. But mounting the camera remained a vexing problem. He'd already crashed several times, destroying the Kodak disposable cameras Anne had originally given him at Christmas. Mark purchased an Olympus point and shoot 35mm film camera, and he first tried mounting that camera directly on the kite's bridle, then to the spars in a newly acquired 11-foot-wide delta kite, one he'd purchased from IntoTheWind on the Internet. The larger kite could easily lift the camera in a gentle five or six mile per hour wind. After trying more than a dozen different methods, he finally resorted to suspending the camera in a custom-built "cradle" or "pod," one that hung down from the kite line like a pendulum. Radio-controlled electronics, similar to those used by model airplanes, controlled the cradle and the camera mounted in it. He could now place the camera at altitude in just a few minutes, and control the camera's tilt, pan, and shutter release by using a handheld radio transmitter on the ground.

* * *

Mark hadn't seen Oscar in months, but on the morning of his first successful radio-controlled flight, the old man had mysteriously arrived in his rusted-out Chevy truck, and was his sole witness at Barbour Landing.

"See ya gotta new kite, Doctor," Oscar said, walking to the spot where Mark stood next to his cart-mounted electric reel.

"Yeah, Oscar. I got me a new one. But this one is for low winds ... winds like we've got today. Still use that little red one when the wind gets strong," Mark explained.

"How high up you reckon you is now?" Oscar asked, squinting and pointing at the new kite.

"Oh, I'd guess it's about 800 feet, for the kite. But that little black dot you see hanging from the kite line is the camera. And I'd guess it's about 500 feet off the ground."

"Don't see no black dot, but maybe I ain't lookin' in th' right place," Oscar allowed.

"Well, I'm bringing it down now. When it gets a little closer to the ground, you'll be able to see the camera. I'll show you how it works when it gets close enough to see."

"And what's that thing you got in yo' hand?" Oscar asked, pointing at the radio transmitter Mark held with its three-foot telescoping antenna extended. "Sho look lak a radio to me. Do it play music?"

Mark chuckled. "No. It's just a radio transmitter that controls the camera."

"Sho 'nuff. I ain't never heard of such!" Oscar chuckled, apparently amused by the crazy things white folks did.

Mark flipped the switch that started the electric reel. The reel made a soft whirring sound as it wound in line, and in a few minutes the kite and camera were close enough for Oscar to see them clearly. Mark turned the reel off to stop the retrieval process when the camera was only 300 feet away, and about 100 feet off the ground.

"Can you see it now, Oscar?" Mark asked, feeling the old waterman's vision might be impaired by cataracts, or possibly the need of eyeglasses he couldn't afford.

"Yes, suh. I sees good. I kin see hit just fine now. Jus' didn't know e'zakly what to look fo' befo'."

Mark turned the pan control on his transmitter; the camera turned. "You see that, Oscar?" Mark asked again.

"I seen it turn, Doctor! So you showin' me you can point that camera any which a way you wants. But how about makin' it look down? Lak straight down? Kin you do dat, too?"

"Sure," Mark replied. "Or any place between straight ahead and straight down. Just keep watching it." Mark turned a transmitter control that controlled the camera's tilt.

Oscar broke out with laughter, then spoke. "Well if dat don't beat anythin' I ever seen befo' in my life. Lawd, dat is somethin' else! But how do you tell th' camera to make a picture?" he asked, pronouncing the word "picture" as "pitcher."

Mark pointed to a third control on his radio. "If I push this button on the radio, the camera will take a picture." Mark panned the camera and adjusted its tilt. Oscar could now see the camera's lens was aimed directly at the two of them standing side by side on the ground next to the electric reel.

"Is you gonna take our pitchers?" Oscar asked, smiling, his teeth resembling perfect white piano keys.

"'Fraid not, Oscar. When I sent the camera up, the roll of film in the camera had only 24 shots on it. If I didn't count wrong, I've already taken all the pictures when I had it up real high."

"Hummm," the old fella mused. "Uh … you don't never show any them pitchers to the sheriff, does you?"

Mark fell silent in thought: *Anne showed me that article in the paper about local drug smuggling. Haven't seen Oscar in several months. Has he been in jail? That day I helped him unload oysters, he did have something in some of his boxes besides oysters … something wrapped in black plastic.*

"Well, does you?" Oscar asked again, a hint of impatience in his voice.

"No Oscar. These are my very own pictures. They aren't any of the sheriff's business!"

A smile slowly formed on the oysterman's weathered face. "I sho lak th' way you thinks … not too bad for a *white* boy!"

"Oscar, the first day we met we discussed the black-white thing. I thought we'd put that behind us. Why do you bring it up again?"

"Jus' wanna be sho you ain't changed yo' mind … and you still one of th' peoples I kin trust."

"Oscar, I can keep my mouth shut, and I keep my word. I did bring your oyster box back the next day, didn't I? And I thank you again for the oysters. They were great. Me and the wife really enjoyed them."

"Well, I appreciate you bringin' my box back, but if you's been a comin' over here much, I think you's already noticed … I ain't been around," Oscar explained.

Mark figured now was the time to ask some questions: "You haven't been sick, have you?"

"Naw suh. Well, now, maybe jus' a little bit, but I's doin' fine now. Jus' been away … mostly doin' somethin' for th' gov'ment … somethin' I ain't ev'n allowed to talk about."

Mark's curiosity was getting the best of him, and he decided to bluntly push the envelope of his relationship with the old fella. "Oscar, are you in trouble with the law? Have you done anything illegal?"

Oysterman's reaction was immediate. "Naw suh! I's churchgoin' and honest as they is. Jus' ax around. *Never* had no trouble with th' law, but some folks around here …." Oscar closed his eyes, apparently pausing in deep thought. He kept his eyes closed a full 30 seconds, before opening them again and continuing: "Doctor, I sho wish I could tell you where I been at … but I can't."

Though Mark felt Oscar was probably being honest with him, he still had unvoiced questions he wanted to ask the old fella. *Is Oscar really working for the government? Especially something he can't talk about? Guess I best get my kite and camera down, and not press for more answers, at least not now,* Mark thought, as he flipped the toggle switch on the electric reel.

Oscar stood by and quietly observed until Mark had the rig back on the ground, and ready to be packed in the back of his Ford Explorer. Mark did not attempt to start another conversation with the old man; he just waited for Oysterman to speak.

"Doctor, I still think you OK … for a white boy!" Oscar chuckled, smiled, then extended his hand to Mark. They shook hands, and Oscar continued: "Please don't say nothin' to nobody 'bout me workin' for the gov'ment. Could be bad for us both if you did. Don't you worry, I be goin' back to work on the water tomorrow, or day next … be catchin' crabs this time of th' year. You want some?"

"Sure!" Mark replied. "How much for a dozen?"

"They's free, to you. It'll take me a day, maybe two, to get my old boat runnin' again … and get all my traps put back out. So, if you be over here about ten in the mornin' day after tomorrow, I'll give you a mess. Just bring a empty five-gallon bucket with you."

In parting, Oscar explained that later today he was going to take the batteries out of his boat and recharge them at his house, then return bringing his crab traps and recharged batteries to the dock. Without further words, Oysterman got in his truck and quickly drove off.

No sooner than Oysterman was out of sight, and while Mark was carefully packing his kite aerial photography gear in the back of his car, a late model gray F-150 pickup quickly drove up. Mark noted the U.S. Fish & Wildlife Service logo on the doors of the truck. A dark-haired well-tanned uniformed man in his late 30s or early 40s promptly got out of the truck. Mark noted he was armed with a pistol holstered on his right hip. He rapidly approached Mark.

"Mind if I ask you what you're doing here?" the man asked, his right hand casually resting on his holstered pistol while he froze, standing about 20 feet away.

"Sir, I was flying a kite a little while ago. Is that against the rules?" Mark asked.

"No. At least not in this particular area of the refuge. I was over at the wood stork pond—the one we call Woody Pond—trying to do nest counts, and I happened to look up. I saw what I first thought was a strange gigantic bird. Then I looked with my binoculars. I saw it was not a bird, but a delta-shaped kite. Is that what you were flying?"

"Yes sir," Mark replied, pointing to his kite that was now collapsed and rolled up, looking somewhat like a colorful beach umbrella stowed in the back of the Explorer. "Want me to assemble it? Won't take but a minute."

"Sure!" the officer smiled. "And by the way, my name is Dr. Spencer Roberson. I'm a biologist with U.S. Fish & Wildlife." Roberson seemed to relax, moved closer to Mark, and removed his right hand from the vicinity of his gun's holster. "But haven't we met before? Weren't you that fella who came to one of my lectures on native plants? It was a number of months ago."

"Yep, that was me and my wife, Anne. We live just down the road at Dunham Point. I'm Dr. Mark Telfair, a retired surgeon. And my wife is a retired surgical nurse. You're the fella that gave us an article about sand gnats … said it was written by one of your entomology buddies. Remember that?"

"Sure do," Dr. Roberson replied, then laughed. "You're the fella who asked more questions about gnats than about plants!"

Mutually laughing now, they shook hands. "Just call me 'Doc.' That's what most folks call me anyway."

"Well, just call me 'Spence.' But are you going to put that big kite together?"

Mark nodded a "yes." In 30 seconds he had it assembled, flight-ready.

"Yep. That's it. That's exactly what I saw through my binoculars from Woody Pond," Spence replied, studying the assembled 11-foot-wide nylon kite resting flat on the grass. "And I understand the purpose of that battery and electric reel I see in the back of you car … but what are those other things? That radio and camera gear?"

Feeling a demonstration was worth more than words, Mark handed Spence the entire camera rig, camera still installed in the cradle. "Spence, you're holding the entire device. Weighs only 19.9 ounces. As you can see, there are four basic components: the camera, the camera's cradle, the line clamp, and the pendulum that suspends everything from the kite line."

"Can you show me how it works? Like, here on the ground?" Spence asked.

"Sure. Just grab it by that aluminum bar at the upper end of the pendulum. That bar is actually a clamp, one that connects directly to the kite line. As you can see, the pendulum is a quarter-inch carbon-graphite tube about 18 inches long, and is connected to the clamp in a way that allows the pendulum to swing either forward or backwards. That allows the rig to always hang plumb, no matter what the angle of the kite line may be at the time."

Spence seemed to immediately understand, and gripped the rig by the line clamp that would normally be connected directly to the kite's flying line. When actually using the rig, Mark explained, he connected the rig to the line only after the kite was airborne, and flying in stable wind well above ground turbulence. "I usually connect it to the line about 100 feet below the kite." Mark first turned on the radio transmitter, then the camera's cradle while Spence held it at arm's length. Using the transmitter controls, he first made the camera pan, then tilt, and activated the shutter button.

"Pretty darn neat!" Spence replied. "You take any pictures today?"

"Yeah. I made 24 shots, Spence. They're the very first shots I've ever made using this device, so I have no idea what they are going to look like until I get the pictures developed."

Spence paused a moment, then asked a question. "Is there any way a digital camera could be put in this camera cradle you are showing me? I see that your little Olympus is a 35mm *film* camera."

"Yes, with some modification of the cradle. But I don't plan to use a digital just yet. The small digitals are certainly light enough, but way too expensive for me to risk putting one in the air. I'm sure I'll ultimately go digital when they get a little cheaper … and I have more experience at doing this!"

"What if I could talk the Fish & Wildlife into supplying a digital camera?"

"That would be great … but I don't even want to risk using someone else's camera until I have more experience. Anyway, I first need to see what the film images look like."

Spence handed Mark the camera cradle. They chatted while Mark disassembled the kite, turned all the electronics off, and stowed the gear back into the rear of his car.

"Doc, would you mind showing me those pictures when you get them developed?"

"Not a bit. But how do I get back in touch with you?" Mark asked.

"I work on several different coastal refuges." Spence retrieved a business card from his uniform's shirt pocket, and handed it to Mark. "My office phone numbers are on that card. I'm over here at Harris Neck about two or three days a week. Do you know where the refuge office is here? It's the same place where I gave that talk about native plants."

"Yes I know where it is. So …?" Mark questioned.

"Just call the office. I stay in contact with them by radio," Spence explained, pointing to a radio clipped to his belt on his left side. "They'll know exactly where I am. We can arrange to meet somewhere. I sure want to look at your pictures. If they are any good, we might find a use for low-level aerial images right here at Harris Neck. I might even be able to talk 'em into *paying* you to do some work for us. I'm especially thinking aerial images might help us count wood stork nests at Woody Pond. The regular use of planes and helicopters is far too expensive for our budget, plus their engine noise might disturb the adult storks and make 'em get off the nest. That might let the young chicks get too cold to survive. The body heat of an adult parent is essential for incubation of eggs. It's also essential to the chick's survival in the early part of their lives."

"Spence, I'll get these pictures developed as soon as I can, and let the office know. It's been nice to meet you again ... and thanks for that article about sand gnats."

They shook hands again, got in their respective vehicles and left Barbour Landing. On the short drive home, Mark's questioning mind was in overdrive: *Wonder if my pictures are going to be any good? Wouldn't it be great to have a retirement hobby that I got paid for? Why would a U.S. Fish & Wildlife officer, especially a biologist, need to carry a gun? Does Spencer know Oscar Dunham? Is Oscar's government work somehow connected to Dr. Spencer Roberson's work?*

5

I THINK I DID IT

"Honey! I think I did it!" Mark excitedly told Anne the instant he entered their house at Dunham Point.

"Did *what?*" Anne replied, not looking up while making shrimp salad in their kitchen.

"Made 24 pictures, from about 500 feet up. That's what!" Excitement rang in his voice like a youngster at Christmas receiving his first bicycle. "And Dr. Roberson came up just as I had finished. He seemed very interested in the process and mentioned they might want me to do some aerial pictures for them—and *pay* me for it!"

"Dr. *who?*" Anne asked, while spooning generous helpings of shrimp salad onto the beds of chilled Romaine lettuce covering their lunch plates.

"Dr. Spencer Roberson, the Ph.D. guy over at the refuge. You know, the one who gave that talk on local plants ... and gave us the article about sand gnats?"

"Oh, yeah. I remember him now. Want some iced tea?" Anne asked as she placed their lunch plates on the table.

"Tea would be fine, honey. But after lunch I want to drive to Brunswick. I want to find one of those one-hour film developing places. I know I'm acting like a kid, but I'm real anxious to see the results," Mark admitted, but felt Anne didn't share his enthusiasm.

Following lunch, despite her seeming lack of equal anticipation, Anne agreed to ride to Brunswick with Mark. They quickly located Glynn Camera, a single-owner photo shop that offered a one-hour developing service. They dropped the film off, and jointly did some grocery shopping while waiting for the photos to be developed. An hour later, when they returned to the shop to pick up the prints, the shop owner approached them wearing a frown. Apologetically, he said, "I'm very sorry to tell you this, but it seems I've somehow screwed up. About six of your images have a thin white line on them. I've checked their negatives with a magnifying lens, and there are no scratches on the film's emulsion. I cleaned my processing equipment, and even made a second set of prints I'll give to you at no cost. The same six images still have the white lines on them. Otherwise, they're absolutely beautiful aerial images."

Mark burst out laughing, feeling he knew exactly what the "white lines" were. Mark, Anne, and the shop owner jointly looked at the pictures. Still a smile on his face, Mark replied, "Sir, there is absolutely nothing wrong with your processing equipment! The white lines are pictures of the kite's line. I'm now using 300-pound-test Spectra."

"*Kite* line?" the owner asked, his facial expression indicating he felt Mark may have a mental problem.

"Yes, *kite line*. You see, this whole set of photos was made using a kite to lift the camera. When I've got the camera panned so it's shooting directly back toward me on the ground, the kite line will be in those pictures. That's the only direction where the kite line will be seen in the picture. In fact, if you look closely with a lens, I bet you'll be able to see me standing there on the ground with a radio transmitter in my hands."

The owner said nothing and stepped into a back room in the store. He returned promptly with a hand lens. He studied intently the half-dozen prints with white lines. "Well I'll be damned!" he exclaimed. "There you are! Blue shirt and all. I even see your radio and its antenna, and a little cart that looks like it has a very large fishing reel attached to it. And maybe a car battery, too."

Silently, Anne continued studying the photos while Mark and the store owner continued to discuss his technique, one Mark had decided to call Kite Aerial Photography, or "KAP." His enthusiasm bubbling over, Mark even stepped out to their car and returned with his KAP rig to demonstrate it for the second time that day. The shop owner remained intently interested, but was also trying desperately to sell Mark a small $600 digital camera. "If you'd used a digital, it would be very easy to 'remove' the white lines by using a computer program like Photoshop."

"I'll have to think about it," Mark allowed. "I've got a new computer, but I'm going to refine the technique using the inexpensive little Olympus film camera I already have."

When the shop owner resorted to mentioning several less-expensive digital cameras, Anne came to the rescue. "Honey, we have hamburger and ice cream in the car. We need to head on back home and get things refrigerated."

* * *

Anne was quiet during the first few miles of the 45-minute drive back home. Finally she spoke to Mark, who was still smiling. "Little Man, I was beginning to think you had gone a little nuts on me—with this kite-and-camera thing! I do apologize for thinking that. I thought you'd never get it to work. Even though I just gave you that stuff as a joke, I've gotta admit those pictures are almost perfect."

"What do you mean, *almost?* Shit, even the ones with the kite line in them are perfect!" Mark exclaimed, still feeling so proud of himself he could burst.

"I'm not talking about the 'white lines.' The guy at the camera shop told you how you could fix that," Anne replied. "But before you ask, don't you even *think* about it ... about asking to use *my* digital camera, the one you gave me for Christmas!"

"No, I don't want to borrow your camera. But what's wrong with the pictures other than the white lines?" Mark shot back, briefly turning his head to look at her in the Explorer's passenger seat.

"Mark, it's the shots you made when the camera was aimed downward over the water. The whole picture is almost nothing but water and marsh. I assume the water is the Barbour River, just below the landing. That correct?"

"Yeah. So?"

"So did you notice those dark spots in the river, the ones showing mostly water?"

"No, I didn't notice that," Mark replied. "Maybe they are a shadow of the kite."

"No, Mark. There are *three shadows* in each picture, if that's what they indeed are. I've never heard of something having a triple-shadow. In those same pictures I also noticed two white dots in the water, but I finally figured out what they are."

"Like what?" Mark asked.

"I think they're floats marking someone's crab traps in the river."

"You're probably right, Anne. We'll look at all the pictures more closely when we get back home."

* * *

The phone was ringing when Mark and Anne entered their house. Along with the two packets of his photos, Mark hurriedly placed one

42

bag of their groceries on the kitchen counter, then grabbed the ringing phone while Anne brought in the rest from their car.

"Hello," Mark briskly replied to the caller.

"Hello yourself, my old Grady buddy!" said the familiar voice on the line. It was unmistakably the voice of Dr. Jerry Bacon, his former surgical partner in Statesville, his Grady-in-training buddy, and certainly among his dearest of friends.

"Mark, I really wish I was callin' to tell y'all I'm comin' down for a visit. Heck, the way things are goin' here, they're workin' me and your replacement, Dr. Joe Steel, to death. We're up to 60 majors a month now."

"Wow!" Mark replied. "Want me to come out of retirement, Jer?"

"Not unless you want to ... but the real reason I called is ... well it's to give you some very bad news, some news you may not have heard yet."

"We don't get much news here. Only got a few TV stations we can get by antenna, and *The Darien News* only comes out once a week. But 'bad news' like what, Jer?"

"Like both Roy and Margie Partridge have been killed in a plane crash. I know you guys were real close, and fished and vacationed down there on the coast. Apparently they were on another European vacation, and goin' from Cornwall, England to Paris in one of those little commuter jets. I heard about it only this morning. Happened late yesterday, our time. Seems the plane went down in the English Channel, shortly after takeoff. No survivors. They hope to eventually identify all the bodies, but they've already positively identified Margie and Roy. I'm sorry, old buddy."

Mark felt tears forming in his eyes. He knew Jer would not be joking about something this serious. Stunned, Mark did not know what to say to Jer. He found himself unable to speak so he simply said nothing. Anne walked to her silent husband with a phone in his hand and tears in his eyes.

"Honey, what's wrong?" Anne asked, with concern in both her eyes and voice. Mark still said nothing, just handed the phone to Anne, then walked to the sliding-glass door that looked out over the beauty and tranquility of the marsh and river behind their home. Through tear-glazed eyes he removed his Saint Christopher medal from the key pocket in his wallet, then stared at it while gently rubbing it. While he considered himself an agnostic, he'd kept that medal with him for years as a substitute for any secular faith. *I think it's just the feel and sight of this medal ... that gives me inner calm*

... almost like hypnosis, he thought, not really hearing the words Anne was exchanging on the phone with Dr. Jerry Bacon.

Anne, too, had immediately recognized Jer's voice. She received again the same bad news that had left Mark speechless, in tears ... and staring at a medal jokingly given him by a Jew when he was in the Air Force some 25 years ago.

Anne and Jer talked another ten minutes. She remained relatively composed while Jer gave her additional details she'd later relay to Mark.

STATESVILLE REVISITED

Anne gently hung up the phone. She went to Mark, who still stood at the sliding-glass door. He blankly stared out at the marsh and river, while rubbing Saint Christopher between his right thumb and index finger. He handed her the medal. Anne also rubbed it behind Mark's back while her arms encircled him. Both remained that way for a long moment, sharing not words, but tears.

Finally feeling somewhat composed, Mark was the first to speak. "Well, I thank you for taking over on the phone. I didn't want Jer to hear me crying."

"Little Man, crying is not a weakness. It simply means you're expressing human emotion. That's nothing to be ashamed of."

"OK, Anne. But I still don't like to cry in front of another man. Somehow I don't mind crying in front of you ... because our minds are so inner connected. Know what I mean?"

"Yes. Our bodies, too, Mark. We both know that. But Jer told me something that may make us both feel a little better about Roy's death."

"Like what?"

"Like Roy would have died in about three years anyway," Anne explained.

"Died from *what?*" Mark asked, knowing Roy was quite healthy for a 62-year-old.

"Jer told me it was like this: Dr. Joe Steel, the Grady-trained surgeon who replaced you, saw Roy in the office about three weeks ago. He'd been referred by an internist who was trying to track down the cause of Roy's chronic anemia. The internist had found traces of blood in several stool samples, but had been unable to locate the source of bleeding using conventional GI X-rays. Long story made short, Steel and Jer did a full GI workup on Roy. A repeat colonoscopy revealed a very flat two-centimeter-diameter tumor in his transverse colon, one not safely removed using a colonoscope because they didn't know how deeply it penetrated into the colon wall. Colonoscopic biopsy revealed a high-grade invasive tumor, an adenocarcinoma. It definitely was not present when Roy had had a routine colonoscopy done only two years earlier, nor was it seen on the barium enema X-rays the internist had ordered several weeks ago. So, Jer and Steel decided to do an open colon resection. Unfortunately, at the time of the surgery Roy already had multiple small metastatic tumor implants in his liver. After recovering from surgery, Jer said Roy felt fine."

"Did they consider doing any postop chemo?" Mark asked.

"Yes. They gave Roy that option, but he declined. Jer said Roy understood the current chemo drugs would only slow the process, not cure him, and that the chemo would have very substantial side effects. So, he and Margie both elected to retire from their jobs in Statesville, and spend the rest of his days traveling and doing the things they enjoyed doing together ... while Roy still could. Jer told me he felt Roy had about two good years left, before the liver metastasis seriously impacted his health. In fact, Jer told me Roy had said after they got back from Europe, he was going to give us a call ... and see if it was OK if he and Margie came down here to stay with us to fish the entire months of October and November."

"God, they'd have been more than welcome!" Mark exclaimed, feeling the urge to cry building inside himself again. Anne handed the Saint Christopher back to Mark, then gave him a long kiss. One or the other seemed to have worked. His composure returned.

"So I guess there'll be a funeral, or some kind of memorial service ... when they get the bodies back to the states?" Mark asked.

"Jer said to call and he'd keep us posted," Anne replied. "He suggested we watch the TV news, but said there probably won't be much, especially since Margie and Roy were the only Americans on the plane. The other passengers were all apparently from either France or the UK."

* * *

Needless to say, Mark's joy over having made his first successful kite aerial photos was completely overshadowed by the loss of great friends and fishing buddies. And he wondered how Jer was going to replace the irreplaceable—Margie Partridge, the able office manager for the Statesville practice.

Speaking to either Jer or Jer's wife, Sylvia, Mark or Anne phoned

Statesville daily regarding funeral arrangements. It took some ten days to get the bodies back to Statesville. In talking with Jer, Mark learned there had been no fire associated with the plane crash, but both bodies were severely traumatized, almost beyond recognition. Investigators felt the small jet's engines failed after encountering a flock of birds, then crashed into the Channel. Jer indicated there would be no funeral, only a 10 a.m. memorial service to be held in two days at the First Baptist Church in Statesville.

Anne and Mark set their alarm clock for 4:30 a.m. on the day the service was to be held. In a somber mood, they drove to Statesville for the memorial, one arranged by Sam Langly, a prominent Statesville funeral director. Evelyn Holton and her two sons, Judge Harkin, Popeye Gillette, Patti Ann Norton, Tom Holton, Dr. Jerry Bacon and his partner, Dr. Joe Steel, "Deddy" Smith, and about 100 additional Statesville folks were in attendance at the First Baptist Church. Before the service started, the director whispered to Mark and Anne that he needed to talk to them *privately,* following the service.

Mark was relieved he had not been requested to give any words in eulogy. He felt he would again cry in front of many grown men friends. The crowd slowly dispersed at the end of the 40-minute service. Mark and Anne hugged or shook hands with many of their old friends, and almost all begged them to come out of retirement and return to the Statesville medical community. Following the service, after the last of the attendees left, Sam Langly approached Mark and Anne: "Good to see y'all again, and I'm very sorry it took the tragic death of two fine Statesville folks to get you two back up here."

"Sam, it's a trip we both dreaded making. We were close friends with the Partridges, even vacationed and fished together down on the coast where we now live," Mark replied.

"I know, but I've been instructed to give you these," said Sam, pulling two sealed envelopes from inside his suit's jacket. "I think they're unofficial codicils to the Partridges' wills. Their attorney, Bert Avant, gave them to me with instructions to personally deliver them to you and Anne ... along with their ashes, which I have over at the funeral home. Bert said these codicils don't change or override any provisions in their recorded wills, and they simply represent the Partridges' last requests made to two great friends."

"Since these codicils aren't legal, is there any way Anne and I can get in trouble?" Mark asked.

"No. At least Bert Avant says not. Bert drafted their wills. He is fully aware of their provisions. And he assured me their official wills specifically requested 'cremation and scattering of ashes at sea.' And it is to be done solely by the individuals specified in the two envelopes I just gave you and Anne."

THE WHALES

Before leaving Statesville, the Telfairs went to Langly's Funeral Home to pick up the ashes of Margie and Roy Partridge. Mark had never in his life dealt with any "cremains," as Sam Langly respectfully called the two labeled black plastic boxes of ashes he gave the Telfairs. *Strange, how human bodies can be reduced to something that'll fit in boxes the size of ice cream cartons. But why are they so heavy? Must be the calcium in the bones,* Mark's mind thought and questioned.

Mark wrapped the two cremains boxes in his suit's jacket, then placed them on the seat behind the driver's, and secured them there with the seat belt.

Anne smiled, then said, "Little Man, that's kinda redundant, don't you think? The seat belts are to help protect the *living!*"

"I know, I know. But the contents of those boxes are still very much alive in my mind. Just humor me, Anne." Mark started the car, and without further words began driving home.

They both remained largely silent until they got on I-16, heading for the coast. Traffic was extremely light, and they began to chatter like kids at a pajama party.

"Little Man," Anne said, "you want me to open the envelopes and see what they say?"

Mark thought a long moment before speaking. "No. Let's wait till we get home. I can do a better job of driving if I'm not upset by something those letters may tell us to do."

"I agree," Anne said. "So let's change the subject, and talk about your kite pictures."

"Fine with me. We never did really study them closely after we got the bad news about Margie and Roy, did we?" Mark asked.

"No, But I've looked at them a couple of times since," Anne admitted. "And those dark spots in the water still puzzle me. Have you had any thoughts about that?"

"Yeah. I think they may be whales."

"*Whales?*" Anne replied, a questioning look on her face.

"Yes, *whales!*" Mark shot back.

"Come on, Little Man! You ever see a whale when you've been fishing offshore in the *Fanta-Sea?* Have you ever seen one when we've been out in *Creek Boat?*"

"No, Anne, but that doesn't mean it's *impossible!* And I've read that right whales do come this far south ... as far as Georgia and Florida, for calving, as best I remember."

Anne thought a moment. "Mark, how big do they get?"

"Don't know," he admitted. "But I know they get really big. Much larger than the bottlenose dolphins we see all the time in the waters at home."

"So what's the biggest dolphin you've ever seen at home?" Anne asked.

"I know I've seen some that would probably be about 12 feet long."

"And how long do you think those 'shadows' in the water are? The 'dark spots,' whatever they are?" Anne probed.

Mark pondered her question for a beat or two. "Well, we'll just have to figure out some way to estimate the length from the photograph."

They rode in silence about five minutes. Anne finally resumed their conversation. "You remember us talking about the 'white dots' in some of the photos? And how we said they might be floats marking someone's crab traps?"

"Yeah. And so?"

"So if we can measure the distance between those floats, then we'll have some idea of scale. You following me?"

"Brilliant idea, Anne. But what if some crabber has *moved* his traps. Moved them *after* those photos were taken?"

"Hadn't thought of that," Anne admitted. "That would certainly throw everything off, wouldn't it?"

"Yeah, it sure would. But you've given me an idea. What if you and I could go to the area where I took the pictures? Then we could put out some crab trap floats—just the floats—but *not* connected to an actual crab trap, only to a line connected to a weight on the bottom of the river."

"A weight? Like what?" Anne asked

"Like a concrete block. We could even use DayGlow-yellow floats, something that would be easily spotted in an aerial image. We could put that stuff out using *Creek Boat,* and I've got some extra floats we could paint a bright color. And I've even got a couple of old concrete blocks in the shop."

"Well and good, but here's the real question: Could you put your camera in the *same* spot? I mean put it exactly where you had it when you took the first set of photos?" Anne questioned.

"Well, not *exactly* the same, but pretty darn close to the same. I've marked the kite line with a black Magic Marker where I attach the camera rig. That's at a point 100 feet down the line from the kite itself. When I took those over-water pictures I had let out all the kite line and that's 1,000 feet. So, minus the 100 feet where I actually attach the camera, that would mean the camera was 900 feet up the line. In a little notebook, I recorded my estimate of the angle of the kite line when I took each picture. I've even got a little plastic protractor I take with me. Using geometry, that should be enough information to allow us to calculate the altitude of the camera and distance I was away from the actual spot I photographed in the river. The only problem would be that we'd need a northwest wind, exactly like I had on the day I made those pictures. That should put the camera in almost exactly the same position. Wanna give it a try?"

Anne didn't answer, at first. She loosened her seat belt enough to give him a kiss on the cheek, then said, "I've got something else I want to try first ... when we get home ... in bed! I bet you'll be able to get *that* in exactly the right position," she added, lightly patting his groin before tightening her seat belt again.

"Anne, you're an absolute tease, and you know it!"

Anne smiled. "You complaining?"

"No ... and you don't complain when I sneak up behind you when you're washing dishes at the sink ... and I grab your stuff!"

"*Stuff?* Little Man we're both professionals, and we know the correct anatomical terms ... but despite the years of marriage, I still like it when you mess with my stuff!"

With all that has happened, I know I've gotten a little behind in the lovemaking process, Mark thought. Instantly, he burst out laughing.

"What's so darn funny?" Anne asked.

"Oh, it's just something I was *thinking* about ... a pun-like thought, I guess you'd call it."

"A pun? Like what?" Anne asked, grinning.

"Getting a *little behind* in the lovemaking process. That's what I was thinking!"

Anne joined him in hearty laughter that lasted several miles.

Finally, Anne spoke. "Well, 'getting a little behind' is easy enough for us to fix. We'll fix that right after we eat our supper tonight. Then we'll open those letters, and see what they say ... read exactly what they tell us to do."

Mark smiled, then started laughing again. When he stopped laughing, he said, "Anne, I can't remember when I've ever looked so forward to getting back home again! And over the next several days, it looks like we've got a bunch of other things to look forward to as well."

"I know," Anne added, "but only *after* 'my stuff' plays with 'your stuff' tonight!"

"I think we can self-discipline, and wait that long. Then we should see exactly what Roy and Margie put in those envelopes ... and deliver their ashes to God knows where. Then, as I've already talked about, we need to put some marker floats out in the Barbour River ... and make some new aerial pictures when the northwest wind is right. We'd then need to study the first set of aerial pictures some more, and show the results of everything to that Dr. Spence Roberson over at the refuge."

"Sounds like a plan to me, Doctor. But did you realize what just happened to us? To *both* of us?"

"Happened to us? Like what? I've been driving 70 miles an hour and following the same damn semi for the last 40 miles. That's not much of a 'happening' in my book," Mark answered, puzzled by her question.

"Just think about it, Little Man. Remember how depressed we both got after our dog Peewee died, then a dear patient, then our friend Spud Smith and Dr. Holton, your senior partner? Then the malpractice suits? Remember how we lost our appetites for both sex and food? Remember all that? Remember how close together all those things happened? Remember how depressed we both got?"

"Well, now that you mention it, Anne, this time we are both obviously still horny, and we've even managed to laugh together after leaving a memorial service."

"You got it, my Little Man. I think that's exactly how Margie and Roy would want us to be. Think you could drive a little faster without getting caught?"

RETURN TO DUNHAM

Mark smiled as he eased down on the accelerator until the Explorer's speedometer hit 85. He began chuckling as he quickly passed the truck he'd been following for miles.

"What are you laughing about now?" Anne asked after they'd passed the trucker, who was running the legal limit.

"Anne, do you remember that time a trucker passed *us* on I-75 while we were heading for Detroit? Back when we were in the Air Force in Michigan, and you were assisting me in my urgent and frantic efforts to pee in an empty Coke can—while I was still driving! Remember?"

"Never forget that! You don't urgently need to pee again, do you?"

"No," he replied.

"Good. I'm sorry, but we have no empty Coke cans this time," she replied, grinning.

"No problem. I'm OK. I can wait this time," Mark replied as he took I-16's Old River Road exit that would lead him to U.S. 17, then south to home.

Some 40 minutes later Mark pulled into the carport at their Dunham Point home ... happy that he'd avoided getting a speeding ticket, happy to again be inhaling the intoxicating air found only adjacent to saltwater river and marsh environments ... happy that he and Anne would soon be messing with each other's "stuff."

Anne, scurrying into their unlocked house, announced that she was going to get a quick shower. Mark smiled in anticipation, but remembered he needed to retrieve the belted-in ashes he'd wrapped in his jacket. "Oops! Sorry you guys!" he exclaimed. While unwrapping the cremains wrapped in his suit's jacket, he'd accidentally dropped both "Margie" and "Roy" on the concrete carport floor. The sturdy plastic boxes remained intact. With caution and respect he quickly carried the containers inside. He decided to place them on the mantel over their fireplace for safekeeping until they could be distributed as the Partridges' letters possibly directed. He returned to their car, removed the letters from the Explorer's glove box, then placed them on the mantel alongside the boxes of ashes.

Mark heard Anne turn off the shower in the master bedroom, and he quickly went there to take his own. He stripped off his clothes. Just seeing her nude while drying her hair stirred his desire even further. "Wanna mess right now?" he asked over the noise of her dryer.

Anne turned her dryer off, then gave him one of her special grins. "Little Man, there's gotta be something wrong with *both* of us. I know I'm 49 and you're 55 … right? But just look down at yourself. You're already hard as a rock, and I'm wet … and it's *not* from the shower!"

Needless to say, Mark's shower, and their evening meal, got delayed about an hour while they messed with each other's 'stuff' to the point of total exhaustion. Mutually awakening from their nap that followed, Mark glanced at his watch to discover it was after midnight.

Both still in bed, Anne yawned a question. "You hungry?"

"Yeah! We kinda forgot all about our supper, didn't we?" Mark replied. "But first let me ask you a question: Why do you think medical folks seem to get so horny?"

"I don't know, but I've got my own theory," Anne replied.

"A *theory?*" Mark asked, his eyebrows arched in doubt.

"Yes, a theory, my Little Man. I think it has to do with working around death … like we did at Grady. Just seeing death on a daily basis makes medical folks realize it is also an inevitable reality for themselves. They need to do something to actually *prove* to themselves that they are still very much alive. And sex certainly lets you know you're still among the living!"

"You've got a point, Anne, but I'm not sure I buy all of your so-called 'theory.' At Grady, we were both a lot younger and under a lot of stress. We also had periods of stress when we were in private practice in Statesville. I've read that stress increases androgenous hormone levels in *both* men and women, and it's a proven fact that high androgen levels increase the sex drive in *both* sexes. Maybe the knowledge of Roy and Margie's deaths figures into it. Who knows? I've also read the number of rapes go up in a war zone, but maybe that's a combination of seeing both death and the stress of combat. But then why did we get so depressed, then lost our libidos and appetites, when we experienced that string of deaths shortly before we retired from Statesville? One, two, three, four. Just like that!"

"Mark, we'll never figure it out. But we're definitely blessed with a good loving relationship, irrespective of cause … and we'll just 'use it till we lose it,' as the old saying goes."

"Agreed," Mark replied. "Are you as hungry as I am? We didn't even eat lunch today, you know."

"Honey, I don't have enough energy left to fix anything complicated. I don't know about you, but I'm fucked flat! So, how about a couple of PB & J sandwiches each, and a glass or two of cold milk?"

"Ditto on the peanut butter and jelly … and being 'fucked flat' myself. But where did you ever come up with that term?" he asked.

"Don't really know," she replied. "It just sorta popped into my head … after we finished that final time. You know I rarely use the f-word, but that's exactly how I actually felt."

"Ditto again. You fix the sandwiches and I'll shower."

"No, Little Man. We'll shower *together*. I think we can now do it without risk of further hanky-panky. I got so worked up, so hot and sweaty, I really need another shower … and time to dry my hair fully. Then we'll eat some PB & Js and decide what we're going to do after we read those letters from Roy and Margie."

They showered together without event, then gobbled their sandwiches and split a quart of cold milk. While Anne cleared the table, Mark brought the Partridges' letters and cremains to the table where they'd just eaten.

Both now fully awake at 1:45 a.m., Mark spoke. "OK, I guess we start with the letters," Mark said, handing Anne the one labeled "Anne Telfair." His was labeled "Dr. Mark Telfair." The envelope labels were typewritten, but the short handwritten letters inside were in the respective and readily recognized handwriting of their deceased friends. They both read in silence, gently shedding tears, otherwise remaining composed. They then swapped letters and read them.

"Well," Mark said, "that's about the nicest thank-you for a friendship I've ever read."

"And the instructions about their ashes are quite simple," Anne added.

Mark dried his eyes with his napkin. Reading aloud and pointing to the first sentence in Roy's letter, Mark spoke: "'If you guys are reading this, you'll know I've gone to the bone-yard carnival without you, and my life's story is now permanently out of print.'"

Anne smiled. "Sounds just like something Roy would say. We'll sure miss his crazy ways of putting things."

Mark continued: "And he also said if I want the *Luci,* just tell his attorney, Bert Avant. He'll transfer the title to me. Otherwise, she'll be sold when they liquidate their estate. Half their estate will go to the American Cancer Society for research on colon cancer. The other half will go to their church."

"Mark, do we really want the *Luci* back?"

"No, I don't think so. Every time I'd get in her, I'm sure I'd turn around and expect to see Roy standing there. I think l just want to remember the many fun hours we spent together building her in my shop in Statesville ... and the many more hours we enjoyed fishing from her down here on the coast at the Two Way Fish Camp. Besides, we don't need three boats, and wooden ones are harder to maintain."

"Well," Anne said, "let's get back to their ashes. That part certainly seems simple enough. Just thoroughly mix them together, and deposit about half of them at the Two Way exactly where Margie and I caught that 42-pound catfish ... and the rest go to Little Egg Island, exactly where you and Roy fished for trout that very first time you guys took the *Luci* out at the Two Way."

Mark yawned and felt relieved. "Yep, simple enough. So let's go back to bed and just *sleep*. Then we'll plan our ash-delivery day about midmorning tomorrow."

ASH WEDNESDAY

Mark had always been an earlier riser than Anne. Wednesday July 12, 1995 was not an exception. Though they'd gone to bed only a little over three hours ago, he found himself fully awake at 6:00 a.m. Beside him, Anne still slept soundly. He eased out of bed, went to the kitchen and prepared coffee for himself. With his cup of steaming "joe," as Roy Partridge would have called it, he climbed the stairs to the loft area that overlooked the great room area below. He turned his computer on, and patiently sipped his coffee while the dial-up connection slowly connected to the Internet. Mark couldn't remember if he'd read it, dreamed it, or if someone had actually told him the EPA and DNR had "regulations" about disposing of human remains. Finally locating the appropriate websites, he was shocked at the volumes of regulations about putting a person's ashes in freshwater or the ocean. Getting angrier by the moment, he focused on "TITLE 40" currently displayed on his monitor screen:

TITLE 40—PROTECTION OF ENVIRONMENT Sec. 229.1 Burial at sea. Cremated remains shall be buried in or on ocean waters without regard to the depth limitations specified in paragraph (a)(2) of this section provided that such burial shall take place no closer than 3 nautical miles from land. (b) For purposes of this section and Secs. 229.2 and 229.3, "land" means that portion of the baseline from which the territorial sea is measured, as provided for in the Convention on the Territorial Sea and the Contiguous Zone, which is in closest proximity to the proposed disposal site. (c) Flowers and wreaths consisting of materials which are readily decomposable in the marine environment may be disposed of under the general permit set forth in this section at the site at which disposal of human remains is authorized. (d) All burials conducted under this general permit shall be reported within

30 days to the Regional Administrator of the Region from which the vessel carrying the remains departed.

"Damn! What's this world coming to!" he screamed aloud. Then he heard Anne's footsteps as she ascended the stairs to the loft.

"Morning, my Little Man. But what's got you so stirred up this early in the day?" Anne asked, having yet to actually read what was displayed on the computer's monitor.

"This shit!" Mark said jabbing his finger at the computer screen. "This absolutely total bureaucratic bullshit! Just read what I've now got on the monitor. It says 'no closer than three nautical miles from land,' then mentions 'general permit,' and we have to do some kind of report to the 'Regional Administrator of the Region from which the vessel carrying the remains departed.'"

"And do it 'within 30 days,'" Anne remarked, while standing and reading over his shoulder. "Just calm down, Mark!"

But he was not about to calm down. "Just how in the heck are we going to comply with the last wishes of our two dear friends without breaking some damn law? Just tell me, Anne!"

"Quite simple. We're going to *ignore* the law—any knowledge of it—and if we get caught we'll simply play dumb and ask for forgiveness," Anne calmly remarked.

"Anne, you and I both know those ashes are sterile. Totally harmless. Hell, you could even dump them down an open well, then drink the water from that well with no ill effects!"

Still standing behind him while he was seated at the computer, Anne began gently massaging Mark's neck and shoulders. She could feel his tension slowly melting beneath her fingers. She spoke to him softly: "Little Man, the folks that write this stuff are probably not microbiologists. Neither are we, but I doubt a single writer of these rules has had the in-depth medical training we've had. So let's just relax. We'll get it done."

She's right, Mark thought as he turned the computer off. "Anne, I guess that means we've got a full day ahead of us."

"So?" Anne asked, curious about his plan for their "full day."

"First, we'll go to Kip's Fish Camp at Shellman Bluff and get a full load of fuel. We do that before going to Little Egg Island to distribute half the ashes. Then we'll go back in Altamaha Sound and on up to the Two Way to distribute the other half of the ashes where you gals caught that monster catfish. I think we should use our big boat, *Fanta-Sea. Creek Boat* is too small to deal with going outside in the ocean, or crossing the sound, or outrunning the DNR if we have to. After leaving the Two Way, we'll go put out those marker floats we've talked about … put 'em in the Barbour River and set them about 100 feet apart. And I'll paint some crab floats a bright color, be sure I've got enough line to anchor them, and put two concrete blocks and my 100-foot tape measure in the boat."

Anne chuckled. "Well, it is a Wednesday, you know. But it's *not* the real Ash Wednesday, which I think was back in early March," she replied, her Catholic upbringing not totally forgotten.

Following a quick breakfast, Mark and Anne opened the cremains boxes, and thoroughly intermixed the ashes, then placed the "Roy-Margie mixture" into separate unlabeled one-quart Ziploc bags. Anne followed Mark to his little workshop, and they quickly settled on a bright yellow latex paint left over from the original painting of their master bathroom. The paint on the two eight-inch-diameter Styrofoam crab floats dried rapidly. Mark quickly located suitable anchoring lines and two concrete blocks. Using an indelible Magic Marker, he wrote "A-2383" (his crab license number) on the yellow floats. Along with the 100-foot tape measure, they placed everything in a little cart and rolled it to their dock.

"Tide is fully in, Anne," Mark said. "I think I'll just walk down to the community dock and bring the *Fanta-Sea* back to our dock. We'll load everything right here. That would be simpler than using *Creek Boat* to take all this stuff to the *Fanta-Sea.*"

"Sounds like a plan. While you're doing that I'll fix us a snack lunch, and bring a large tackle box and a couple of fishing rods to put in the boat."

"Tackle box and rods? For what?" Mark asked.

Anne smiled. "You never know. They just might come in handy."

* * *

Forty minutes later, the *Fanta-Sea* was fully fueled and they'd already cleared Sapelo Sound. Now in the open Atlantic, Mark made a southwesterly turn that would head them in the general direction of Little Egg Island.

Anne rarely accompanied Mark when he went offshore, and preferred the creeks and sound. She had a tendency for seasickness that made most offshore trips miserable for her. Seeing sites not familiar to her, Anne had a question: "Where are we now, honey?" she asked, over the synchronized hum of twin 150 horsepower Mercury Black Max engines bracket-mounted to the stern of the *Fanta-Sea.*

"We're about halfway there," Mark told her over the whine of the boat's two engines, now turning 3,500 revolutions per minute according to the helm's twin tachs. To be sure he'd told Anne the truth about their position, he opened the overhead electronics compartment in *Fanta-Sea's* T-top. He turned on both the loran unit and the marine radio mounted there. "We're running about 38 miles per hour, and if the ocean stays this flat, we're only about 20 minutes away. Next loran waypoint will be for the southern side of Wolf Island. It's on the north side of the mouth of Altamaha Sound," Mark said, pointing at the loran's LCD display. "We'll be able to see both Little Egg and Big Egg Islands from there."

"Honey," Anne said, looking aft, "I think there's another boat following us."

"Strange, we've not seen another boat," Mark replied, but on weekdays (and it was a Wednesday) he'd not expected to see much boat traffic other than the occasional commercial shrimping vessel.

Mark glanced aft. Sure enough, perhaps a mile back, Mark spotted a smaller boat of a gray color. It was out of trim, bobbing porpoise-like and struggling with the light chop *Fanta-Sea* was handling with ease. "Oh shit!" he exclaimed.

"Oh shit *what?*"

"Anne, they just turned on flashing blue lights. Must be a DNR boat." *What to do?* Mark thought. *I know flashing blue is the standard for lights on law enforcement boats in this area. But we haven't broken any laws ... yet. I know I've got all the required safety equipment and registration papers on board.* Then it hit him: "Anne, where are Margie and Roy's ashes?"

"I put them in the bottom of that big tackle box," she replied, pointing to where it rested on the floor near the starboard side of the transom. "It's between the concrete blocks and crab floats, and the little blue cooler where I put our lunch."

The boat with the blue lights still remained about a mile off their stern. Mark eased the throttles forward, increasing his speed to 45 miles per hour. *That should buy some time,* he thought. He reached up, increasing the volume of his radio and verifying it was set on Channel 16. He grabbed the mike from the electronics locker: "*Fanta-Sea* to Kip's ... *Fanta-Sea* to Kip's. Request radio check. Radio check. Over."

"Gotcha five bars on 16. Where're you at, Doc? Over," the familiar voice of Sans Stryker, the proprietor at Kip's, replied immediately.

"I'm not lost. Repeat, I am not lost. Please standby on our *usual* alternate channel. I'll change to that channel now, but don't radio me. Repeat, do *not* radio me on our usual alternate channel. *Fanta-Sea* clear." He changed the radio to Channel 10, one reserved for commercial communications.

"What was all that channel-changing gibberish about?" Anne asked.

"Explain later," Mark said. "But go ahead and stick those two rods you brought in the two stern holders. We'll make it look like we're planning on fishing if they board us." He thought a minute then said, "Oh shit!"

"What's the problem now?" Anne asked. "We can certainly make it *look* like we're fishing."

"What! With *no* bait? Either artificial or natural?"

Anne smiled. "We have plenty of bait."

"Where?"

"Frozen squid, in a Ziploc in the bottom of our lunch cooler," Anne smugly replied. "And I left an assortment of tackle, including some artificial lures, in the top tray of that big tackle box … and some other fishing stuff on top of the ashes in the bottom of the box."

Mark opened the throttles fully, tachometers now reading 5,500, and loran indicating a speed of some 54 miles per hour. The smaller boat that was apparently following them, rapidly became just a small speck several miles back, but the flashing blue lights told him they had not given up pursuit. He made an abrupt turn westward when he came to the loran waypoint at Wolf Island. Thirty seconds later, he throttled down and idled up to Little Egg Island. Anne was two steps ahead of him, and had retrieved a single bag of ashes from the big tackle box. She crawled up on the foredeck to the point of the bow, then quickly emptied the Ziploc when Mark told her they were at the exact spot where he and Roy had caught so many trout the first time they'd taken the *Luci* out fishing.

Mark backed some 50 yards away from the little island, and when his depth finder told him he had 12 feet of water under the hull, he instructed Anne to drop the bow anchor. Anne climbed off the foredeck, while Mark set a stern anchor and turned the engines off. In the shade of the T-top they briefly hugged, then shed a few tears. Mark, though not Catholic, or by any measure a "formal religion" guy, took his Saint Christopher medal out of his wallet. They each quickly rubbed the medal before Mark put it back.

Anne sighed. "That boat with the flashing lights is not that far away now. But I feel like we should have at least said special words … or something. Don't you?"

"No. Words can't describe the feeling we both have … the memories say it all, Anne. I'm just happy we could carry out this much of their final wishes. It's the least we could do for the two friends who gave us those memories."

"That boat's *still* coming!" Anne observed.

"Yeah," Mark replied. "But they have now slowed to idle. They are probably going to check us out. Just act normal. Let's pretend we're actually fishing."

Anne and Mark quickly baited the two rods with squid, and cast their baits about 75 feet off the stern. They reset the rods in the stern holders. Ignoring the DNR boat and the two armed uniformed officers aboard it, Anne gave Mark a long kiss in the shade of the T-top. The blare of the gray boat's bull horn interrupted their staged tender moment:

"DNR. Remain where you are. We are going to come alongside and inspect your vessel."

"Permission granted," Mark yelled back, breaking their embrace. "But you'll find I'm legal. I have all the proper safety gear. You're wasting your time."

As the 18-foot gray Boston Whaler with a single Mercury 150 came alongside, Mark smiled and silently helped them secure gunnel-to-gunnel. He estimated one of the well-tanned DNR officers to be in his 20s, the older one in his 40s. Both were clean-cut and polite as they went through their routine inspection: Class I Registration Certificate; validation decal and bow-side numbering; PFDs (personal flotation devices); Type B fire extinguisher; pyrotechnic visual distress signals (flares); navigation lights; flashlight and many other things were inspected. *They're determined to find something wrong,* Mark thought as the inspection continued.

"Where's you HIN?" the younger of the officers asked Mark.

"My *what?*" Mark asked seeking clarification.

"Your Hull Identification Number," the younger officer smirked, feeling sure he'd found at least *one* thing wrong.

"Oh that … it's attached to the transom, on the starboard side. On the outside. It's on the metal plate the manufacturer installed. Just check it, if you don't believe me."

The young officer did indeed check. He precariously leaned over the transom, his boot clad feet firmly planted on each side of the ash-containing tackle box. *A gentle shove would put his ass in the drink,* crossed Mark's mind. "OK mister, you've got it," he replied as he returned to a standing position "This your tackle box? Between my legs here?" *Shit! He's gonna want to look inside there!* Mark thought while thinking about some plausible explanation for the cremains. *That remaining Ziploc is unlabeled … they'll probably think it's some type of illegal drug, and confiscate it for chemical analysis,* Mark's mind worried.

Then a stroke of luck: The rod in front of the younger officer suddenly bent over, then the reel's drag started screaming as some sizable fish tried to swim away with the bait.

"Hey, mister! You gotta fish on. Better set the hook!" the excited younger officer yelled.

"Why don't *you* catch this one for me!" Mark shot back.

"It's against regulations. Heck, they won't even let us keep any fishing stuff in a DNR boat!"

"You're *not* in a DNR boat right now, so have at it!" Mark said, trying hard not to burst out laughing.

While remaining in the shade of the T-top, Anne and the older DNR officer softly talked and chuckled. But the younger officer could resist no longer. He snatched the rod out of the holder, aggressively set the hook, and for a full ten minutes skillfully played a four-foot blacktip shark. Fortunately, after Mark had netted the shark it immediately came unhooked while still in the net. *Thanks, Saint Christopher … no need to open the tackle box for tools to get the hook out,* Mark thought.

"You wanna keep it?" the younger officer asked, now drenched in sweat, more so from excitement than exertion.

"Nah," Mark replied. "Neither the wife nor I much care for shark meat." Mark released the shark, and the officers got back in their own boat. The older officer cranked their engine, but almost immediately turned it off again. He then spoke: "I've just a couple of questions before we leave."

"So ask," Mark replied.

"We heard you call Kip's for a radio check on 16. We then tried to call you on 16, but you wouldn't reply. Why?"

"I'd changed channels. Just following the rules about keeping Channel 16 open as much as possible," Mark answered.

"I'll accept that, but we had our blue lights flashing … and you just kept pulling away. Why'd you do that?"

"Sir, when I'm driving my boat I try to look where I'm *going* … not where I've *been!*" Mark replied.

The older officer laughed, then replied, "Makes sense to me. But let me ask you a final question or two. Are y'all in a real big hurry to get back to fishing? Think you could spare about ten minutes to let us do something?"

Mark checked his watch. Five 'til 10. "Sure, but what?"

"We'd like to untie and approach your boat again, but with a video camera running the second time. We'd go through the same safety equipment inspection routine your boat just passed. Our Enforcement Division is in dire need of a training video … one we could show the students training at the Federal Law Enforcement Training Center in Brunswick and elsewhere. We'd let you view it before we used it, and you'd have to sign some papers giving us your permission to use it. Your *Fanta-Sea* is the only vessel we've boarded in months that has had *all* the proper equipment."

"Sure, no problem," Mark answered, trying to seem casual, but then worried they might actually open the tackle box the second time around. As promised, the training video was completed in ten minutes and the tackle box not opened. Preparing to depart for good, the older officer asked a question: "Y'all ever do any fishing in the Barbour River?" Mark nodded an affirmative. "Well keep your eyes open when fishing there. We've got a drug-smuggling problem … and we think the Barbour River is possibly one of the links we can't quite figure out." The older officer then handed Mark a business card with his name and contact information on it. "Call me if you see something suspicious … and good luck with your fishing."

Thank you, thank you, thank you … Mr. Saint Christopher, Mark thought, as the DNR boat pulled away, heading back north, "And thank you, Anne," he said aloud.

"For what?" Anne asked.

"For bringing the bait and the fishing rods. Without them they probably would have looked inside the tackle box. You heard what the older guy said. Granted, they may be just checking boats for required equipment … but I think they are keeping an eye out for drug smuggling as well."

"Could be," Anne allowed, "but I think maybe old Mr. Saint Christopher is still working for us down here on the coast, just as he did in Statesville."

"We'll never know, so let's get going on the rest of the stuff we need to do," Mark replied.

They quickly stowed the fishing gear, hauled anchors, and headed up the Altamaha Sound and on to the Altamaha River. In 20 minutes they were at the Two Way Fish Camp. They tied up, then walked to the bait house/store. There, they instantly saw a familiar face: Scooter Culpepper, the camp's proprietor. He was sitting in a rocking chair on the porch, his bald head topped with a green fedora, and a big cigar occupied his right hand.

When Scooter saw the Telfairs, the recognition was instantaneous: "Well how th' hell are ye! Where ye been a missin' to. Ain't spied ye since four or three year ago," Scooter said in his familiar but strange dialect ... a blend of Cajun, Elizabethan English, and coastal redneck. Scooter got out of the rocker to shake their hands, then asked, "Where's ye friends, them Partridge folk what usually come with ye? From way up the hill ... Statesville, I think it was. Margie and Roy, right?"

Mark paused for a long moment. "Uh, Scooter ... I'm very sorry to tell you, but both Roy and Margie Partridge were killed in a plane crash. Happened in France, about two weeks ago."

"God! I'm sorry ye had to learn me that. They was fine folk. Mighty fine. And I tell ye that Roy was quite a funny fella, with his funny sayin' words for things and such. I'll never forgot 'at time when th' ladies caught 'at big'un ... that cat*fash,*" Scooter continued, his speech running true to form, still pronouncing the word "fish" the way he always did: *fash.* "And I'll never forgit 'at time lightning, run in on ye and blowed up ye TV. Was 'at same day a tornadda come up th' river. Remember?"

"Scooter, we'll never forget that day or any other day we stayed at your rental house," Mark said, turning to reminisce and look at the house that still stood in the middle of the sandy parking lot. Then Mark noticed: The FOR RENT DAY/WEEK sign had been taken down. "Scooter, did you quit renting out the house?" Mark asked, pointing.

"Yeah, Doc. 'Fraid so. I sold the whole fash camp. Sold 'er 'bout two week ago. Sold it to some fellas what gonna make 'em a restaurant ... say it'll be right were the bait house and store is now, and gonna call it 'Mudcat Charlie's,' or somethin' such. And then they'll build some of them condos on the back side," Scooter said, pointing to the other side of the parking lot. "And the rental house will be a comin' down week next, when they pave the parkin' lot."

Mark glanced at his watch. It was now 12:30, and they needed to eat lunch, deposit the remaining ashes, and get over to the Barbour River to finish their mission. They bid Scooter Culpepper farewell and walked back to the dock. Anne selected a seat on a dock bench at the spot where she and Margie had caught the huge catfish; Mark went to their boat, and moved the remaining ashes from the tackle box to their lunch cooler. Carrying the cooler, he rejoined Anne. Being a weekday, few others were present. Without incident, they opened the Ziploc, and tearfully emptied it into the swift-running Altamaha River below. They again gave Saint Christopher a few rubs, then returned it to Mark's wallet. They dried their eyes on paper napkins Anne had thoughtfully placed in the lunch cooler. The squid were now fully thawed, and the napkins smelled fishy ... but neither cared. Fond memories of two great friends, and of the Two Way itself, overpowered all their other senses, including their sense of smell. Each drank their semi-cold Cokes, and ate the sandwiches.

"Need to pee before we take off again?" Mark asked Anne.

"Not a bad idea, and you?"

"Guys can pee anywhere, Anne, but I'll be polite and do it here."

"Yeah, I know. Like peeing in a Coke can while driving 85 on an interstate highway!"

They went quickly to the store to use the restrooms. Scooter was no longer in the rocker, and had apparently left the camp.

They exited the restrooms at the same time, both laughing. "What's so funny, Mark?" Anne asked.

"Still got that same graffiti in the men's room: OLD BUCKS WITH SHORT HORNS AND LOW WATER PRESSURE PLEASE STAND CLOSE. It's been partly scratched out and replaced with DON'T PISS ON THE FLOOR!"

"The women's had I MISSED MY PERIOD, and beneath it someone had written, I DON'T MISS THAT SON OF A BITCH THAT CAUSED ME TO MISS MINE!"

In a lighthearted mood, they departed the Two Way. Because the wind had picked up, Mark knew it would be too rough for Anne if they returned to the ocean. He elected to go down the Altamaha to Little Mud River where he turned north and soon entered North River. Now approaching Doboy Sound, Mark warned Anne it was going to get a little rough. She tolerated the Doboy crossing better than he'd expected, but she again visibly relaxed only while progressing north in the smooth waters of Old Teakettle Creek, then Mud River which took them to Sapelo Sound. Mark was pleased that Sapelo seemed a lot flatter than Doboy. Mainly to give Anne something to do, other than worry, he handed her a pair of binoculars he removed from the console locker. "Here, take these. Stand back close to the transom. You won't bounce around as much." Pointing in the general direction of a marker, Mark said, "See if you can read the numbers on that marker."

Anne finally confirmed: "It says '138.' That what you want?"

"Yes, that's the mouth of the Barbour River." He replied.

"Why do we have to go to that marker? Looks like it would be much shorter to go to the left of it," she replied.

"Not unless you want to get stuck on a sandbar. Right now there's only about a foot of water on that side. I know. I tried that shortcut last year."

"Was that the time you were so late getting back in, and I was worried silly?"

Mark blushed. "Yep, that was the time," Mark said, making a left turn just after they'd passed Marker 138.

Fortunately the Barbour River was so flat it looked like a mirror. He increased his speed, and in no time they were at Barbour Landing. Oysterman's Carolina Skiff was secured at the federal dock there, but the old fellow was nowhere to be seen. No cars or trucks were in the parking lot. *Perfect,* he thought. Then it hit him: *I didn't see a single crab float in the area where I took the pictures. Shit! No reference point.*

He explained the dilemma to Anne. She replied, "Honey, I've studied those kite pictures, perhaps more than you have. In the several that have the white dots and long dark spots, there is a good bit of marsh showing on one side. A single palm tree was visible. Think we could find that tree?"

Mark gave her a kiss. "You're a smart cookie! That's why I'm so glad I'm married to you."

"And I thought it was because I can be sexy!" Anne said, blushing.

Mark didn't answer, only thought: *God, am I lucky … to have it all wrapped in one package. Bright and sexy. Folks telling those dumb-blond jokes need to meet my wife!*

"Anne, let's get it done. I know exactly where that lone palm is. I use it as a marker for one of my favorite trout-fishing spots."

Mark turned the *Fanta-Sea* around, heading slowly south down the Barbour. After he'd gone about 1,000 feet, he spotted the lone palm on the west bank.

"Anne, exactly where was that palm tree in relation to the white floats that have now obviously been removed from the river?"

She closed her eyes in concentration. "The palm tree was about midway between those two white dots we thought were crab floats."

"That's about as accurate as we're ever gonna get," Mark said. He prepared one marker, affixing the line to both the concrete block and the float, adding about five feet to the line length so the float would still be visible at a full normal high tide. He tied one end of the 100-foot fiberglass tape measure to the line where it attached to the float. With a splash, he dropped the first marker off the stern, and instructed Anne to firmly hold the tape measure's case and let tape peel off while he very slowly progressed downriver. "Stop!" Anne yelled when the tape went tight. Mark backed up a couple of feet, and dropped the second marker. Anne rewound the tape as they slowly backed the 100 feet to the first marker they'd placed. Mark then disconnected the tape from the first marker float they'd dropped.

"Remind me to soak that tape measure in fresh water when we get home. The saltwater won't hurt the fiberglass tape itself, but it'll probably cause the steel case to rust," Mark said, as he throttled up for a quick run back to Kip's. He'd burned about 50 gallons, had about 25 left, and wanted to top off.

While putting fuel in his boat, Sans Stryker asked Mark a question or two: "Did you guys catch anything?"

"Just one shark that we didn't keep," Mark told him.

"And why'd you want to go to Channel 10?" Sans asked with a knowing smile.

"Well, Sans, it was like this: A DNR boat was on our tail. Turned out all they wanted to do was a routine safety equipment check. But if I'd needed to have a private conversation with you, I could have done it. They would have had to hunt through over 50 radio channels to find which one I was using, and before they'd have found our 'secret' alternate, I could have told you what I needed. And we never had this conversation. OK?"

"Sure, Doc. You and the wife are one of us locals now. Gotta stick together when it comes to the DNR and the outsiders."

* * *

In 20 minutes they were back at Dunham, and had secured the *Fanta-Sea* to Dunham Point's community dock. Walking hand-in-hand on the dirt road, they both felt exhausted when they reached their house.

Entering the house, Anne said, "I'm totally whipped, and it's only five o'clock. How about a grilled cheese sandwich for supper?"

"Honey, I'm whipped too. The grilled cheese is fine. A day on the water will do it to you every time. But this wasn't just an ordinary day, was it?"

"No, my Little Man, it certainly wasn't … but it will be one of our most memorable."

10

MORE PICTURES

Like a child waiting for Christmas morning to arrive, Mark impatiently listened to his weather radio several times daily. He was hoping for a wind coming from the northwest. It needed to come in the mid part of the day when the sun would be high overhead. That would give him the best photographic lighting for the task at hand: taking pictures of Barbour River's water at their marked spot. He felt he understood the normal sea breeze/land breeze cycles, and knew he'd need a weather front—an inland high—that would override the usual cycle. A week later it happened. Hauling all his kite gear, he and Anne rushed off to Barbour Landing in their Explorer. Upon arrival Mark spotted Oscar's skiff immediately. Apparently he was just returning from somewhere downriver to empty and re-bait his crab traps. He had about a dozen boxes of blue crabs aboard.

After spotting Anne with Mark, Oscar at first seemed a little hesitant to greet them. Anne broke the ice. "Hi, I'm Anne Telfair, Doc's wife," Anne said, smiling and extending her hand to the old black man.

Oscar hesitated briefly, then spoke as he accepted Anne's soft hand: "I's Oscar Dunham. Met the Doc a little bit back. Nice to meetcha, lady. But whatcha hepin' him do today?"

After briefly shaking Oscar's hand, Mark returned to their car and busied himself preparing his kite gear. In the interest of time, he decided to let Anne continue her conversation with Oscar alone.

"Oscar, I'm just going to help Doc fly his kite and take some pictures with it," Anne explained. "And we really did enjoy the oysters you gave him the first time y'all met."

The old man didn't acknowledge her "oyster thank-you," but mentioned the kite: "Yeah, he done showed me how that kite work. That's somethin' else I tell ya," Oscar said, beginning to relax. "Where he gonna make he pitchers at?"

"Just around that bend in the river," Anne explained, pointing southward downriver.

"Somethin' funny goin' on down there. 'Round th' bend. They's a new crabber on th' river, and old one he now be gone," Oscar informed.

"Something funny, like what?" she asked.

"It's them num'ers on some new crabber's traps … A-2383. He floats be yellow, not white. He ain't from 'round here. Ain't never seen them num'ers befo'. Old traps that was 'bout that same place was white, an' didn't have no num'ers a'tall."

"Those yellow A-2383s are Doc's traps," Anne said not wanting to disclose the fact that the floats for the "traps" were connected only to concrete blocks. "Doc has a commercial license so he can use commercial traps … but we have only three traps. We usually put some of them out in the Julienton River, or Harris Neck Creek. But crabbing has not been too good there this year. But don't you worry, Oscar, we just catch for ourselves. We have no intention of going commercial."

Oscar smiled, seemingly relieved that no new "competition" was coming to *his* river. "When he get through messing with he kite stuff, tell 'em that part of th' river don't catch too good no way. He need to move to th' next bend down … on th' insides of th' curve."

Oscar walked away and began loading boxes of crabs into his old Chevy pickup, then left the landing when done.

Mark already had his 11-foot delta kite airborne, camera rig attached 100 feet down the line, and was spooling out more line hoping to place the camera over the area they had marked a week ago.

"Mark, you did that so quickly I'm afraid I didn't give you any help."

"That's all right. You kept old Oscar occupied. He'll talk your ears off if you get him wound up, and I want to take advantage of this perfect wind while it lasts." Mark withdrew something from his pocket and handed it to Anne.

"What in the heck is this thing?" she asked, holding the plastic-encased device about the size of a package of cigarettes.

"It's something that reads wind speed. It's called an anemometer. Slide the cover off, and hold the flat side into the wind."

"Neat!" Anne said, as she looked at the LCD screen. "Says 8.2 mph."

"Perfect for this kite. I've got all the line out. I'm going to start taking pictures now. The camera is aimed straight down for all shots," Mark said, showing her the knob on his radio that controlled the camera's tilt function.

"Honey, the kite slowly drifts sideways, back and forth. Will that make any difference?" Anne asked.

"Not really. I doubt it's moving more than 25 feet, either left or right. I'll make plenty of shots. At least one of them should be centered on the river."

Mark flipped the switch on the electric reel and started the five-minute retrieval process. When the camera rig was at hand, he noted the LCD on camera indicated all shots had been taken. He reloaded fresh film into the camera and let the line out again, but took several shots before he had the entire 1,000 feet of line out. He retrieved the kite a second time, and felt pleased that all shots had apparently been made the second time as well.

Mark checked his watch: two o'clock. They quickly packed the gear into their car, then left Barbour Landing, heading for Brunswick to the nearest one-hour film processor.

* * *

Their 45-minute ride to Brunswick would normally have been boring, but anticipation about what the photos might reveal made it seem longer than usual. To fill the driving time, they started a conversation.

"Anne, I don't see how we could have missed at least getting a few good pictures of our markers."

"The proof will be in the pictures themselves. Just be patient," Anne urged.

"If we'd been using a digital camera, we'd already know," Mark replied.

Smiling, Anne replied, "Honey, the answer is still 'no' … about using the digital camera you gave me for Christmas!"

"Well, let's change the subject. Do you have a feeling something is not quite right? I mean, like, are we on the 'outside,' and just looking 'in' on a serious issue? Maybe discovering something that will lead to trouble for us?"

Anne thought a second before speaking. "Honey, I think you might be getting a little paranoid. I'll admit that article in *The Darien News*—that 'Under Our Noses' article I showed you—indicates there is probably at least *some* drug traffic in the area, but it's certainly not obvious to me."

"Anne, maybe my thinking is a little paranoid. But consider these bits and pieces: The first time I met Oscar Dunham, I helped him transfer some oysters from his boat to his old truck. In addition to oysters, some of the oyster crates contained what appeared to be small boxes wrapped in black plastic, and he alone handled those particular crates. He subsequently disappeared for a couple of months and when I finally saw him again at the landing, he told me he'd been 'away' doing some work for the 'government' ... doing something he 'couldn't talk about.' I quizzed him about serious illness or trouble with the law. He denied both. After Oscar left the landing that day, Dr. Spencer Roberson, the biologist, suddenly showed up. He approached me with caution, his hand on his gun. Do I look *that* threatening?"

"No," Anne admitted. "But maybe he's had bad experiences when walking up on strangers before. Who knows?"

"I certainly don't know. But just this last week, what happened?" Mark questioned. Before Anne could answer, he spoke again: "Remember what the older DNR guy told us when they finally left the *Fanta-Sea* after their inspection?"

Anne thought a moment. "Yeah! He did say something about drug smuggling, and the Barbour River being a 'link' they couldn't figure out. He told us to keep an eye out when we were in the Barbour. Remember?"

"Yeah," Mark answered. "And he also gave me his card. Maybe after we look at these pictures, we should contact both that DNR officer *and* Dr. Spencer Roberson with Fish & Wildlife. But let's decide what we're gonna do *after* they look at the pictures," Mark said, parking the Explorer in front of Glynn Camera.

11

STUDY HALL

"Your pictures are ready," the proprietor of Glynn Camera said, as Mark and Anne returned to the store after doing a little shopping while their photos were being processed. The shop owner studied his watch. "You're just in the nick of time. I close at five, you know." He continued: "This time your pictures don't have any white lines … just some small yellow dots that I think are something actually floating in the water."

"Great!" Mark replied, relieved.

"I'd say they are technically perfect, and probably the best you can do with that little small-format Olympus film camera you're using. But to be honest—and please don't take this as adverse criticism—they all look pretty much the same." *Sorta boring is what you really wanted to say,* Mark thought, but felt confident he had achieved exactly what he had hoped to accomplish.

Mark paid the proprietor without even looking at the pictures. He was as anxious as the store owner was to leave, and wanted to avoid another sales pitch about digital cameras.

Now on their way back home, Mark commented: "Sounds like we've done exactly what we hoped to do."

"Want me to look at them now, or shall we wait till we get home?" Anne asked from the passenger's seat.

"Wait," Mark replied. "Don't cheat and peek!"

* * *

Their evening meal of rare grilled sirloin steak, English peas, salads, and baked potatoes, as 'sides,' was virtually inhaled. No mind-dulling alcohol was consumed, only black coffee. While Anne cleared their dining table, Mark made a quick trip to his shop to get a mechanical drawing set he'd had since high school.

Anne had loaded their dishwasher and cleaned the glass-topped table where they'd just eaten. "Study hall" was now in session.

"OK," Mark began. "Let's lay out my very first set of photos—the ones of last month—left to right. We'll do it according to their exposure numbers on the backs of the images. Then we'll put out the two rows of photos we've made today. OK?"

"I need my glasses. Need yours?" Anne asked.

She quickly went to their master bedroom, returning with their reading glasses they each kept on their respective bedside tables. They both remained silent for several moments while scanning the rows of photos before them.

"Well," Mark commented, "I think old Oscar was right about the floats being recently changed. The white ones are gone in the second set of photos, replaced by our yellow floats that we know are set approximately 100 feet apart."

"And there's that palm tree again," Anne said, pointing. "So we got our markers in the right place."

Using dividers from his old mechanical drawing set, Mark set them to span the distance separating their yellow marker floats. "OK, so that's the distance that equals about 100 feet." Using a scale rule, Mark quickly figured out each inch on the recent photos equaled about 100 feet. He then used the dividers to measure the length of the "shadows" seen only in the very first set of his kite photos. While Anne looked intently on, Mark said, "According to this scale rule, those three shadows are each almost a perfect 30 feet in length. I still think they are whales."

"Little Man, I think you have a big imagination—and other things too! But I'm certainly no expert on whales. I think it's time we show these pictures to someone who might know more about whales than we do."

* * *

It took a week to set a time and place for a meeting with both the DNR and Fish & Wildlife. In two days, at 2:30, a meeting was to take place in the office at the Harris Neck National Wildlife Refuge. The biologist, Dr. Spence Roberson, would represent the U.S. Fish & Wildlife Service; Victor Timmons, the older officer who'd done their *Fanta-Sea's* safety inspection, represented the Georgia DNR; the Telfairs would simply represent themselves as "citizens," a retired local professional medical couple.

On the short drive to the refuge for the meeting, Anne asked a question: "Mark, why do you think it took them so darn long to set up a simple meeting? I mean, like, all we're gonna do is look at some pictures, right?"

"You need to remember we're dealing with bureaucrats, both federal and state. But maybe they can help us figure out what those shadows are."

When the Telfairs arrived at the office, a secretary quickly ushered them to a small private conference room in the rear of the building. Dr. Roberson and Officer Victor Timmons were already there, both talking on separate odd-looking phones. Mark noted a tape recorder placed in the middle of the conference table. Spencer motioned the Telfairs to seats at opposite ends of the table; Victor and Spencer sat opposite one another on the long sides of the table.

"Thanks," Spence said into his phone, then hung up.

"You sure they're *both* clean?" Victor asked on his phone. "Thanks, I appreciate the check. Bye now," Victor finished.

"Clean?" Spence asked Victor.

"Yeah," Victor answered. "And on your end?" Victor asked Spencer.

"Clean, too," Spencer replied.

Dr. Roberson stood, reaching to shake hands with the Telfairs. "I'm sorry you guys caught us conducting a little business … but thanks for coming," Dr. Roberson said, reading the puzzlement apparent on both the Telfairs' faces, but not commenting on the nature of the phone conversations. "I understand you've already met Vic," Roberson said smiling.

Mark paused a long moment looking at Anne, who seemed just as puzzled as he was. "Yeah, I've met Victor … during the course of a boat inspection. But look, Dr. Roberson, all the wife and I want to do is have you guys look at some aerial pictures I made using a kite. And I'm a little uncomfortable about us being kept in the dark. It's obvious you and Victor know each other on a first-name basis. So how about telling us what the heck is going on."

Victor and Spence looked at each other across the table for a long moment, seemingly ignoring the Telfairs altogether. Victor was the one to speak first: "Spence, let's just look at their pictures … then decide if there's a need to know more."

"I'll go along with that," Spencer replied, then turned his attention to the Telfairs. "So, you guys have some photos you want us to look at?"

With reservations about "being in the dark," Mark arranged the pictures as he and Anne had earlier done at home. He quickly pointed out the three dark shadows seen only in his very first set of photos, then explained in detail how they had been able to "scale" the shadows to a length of approximately 30 feet by using their yellow marker floats anchored with concrete blocks. "I think the shadows are whales, possibly right whales," Mark finally told them. Spencer first chuckled, as he and Victor both looked and listened intently, then stared at each other, smiling. Spencer first broke the long silence: "Vic, I think it's time we tell 'em something."

"Agreed. You do it," Vic said to Spencer.

"OK, but I want to record the conversation," Spence said, now standing. Turning to the Telfairs, he requested they sit side by side on the long side of the table where he'd been sitting. He then went to the opposite long side of the table and stood next to Vic, who remained seated. "Do I have your permission to record this conversation?" Spence asked the Telfairs.

Anne and Mark looked at one another, then said "yes" in unison. Spencer turned the tape on, gave his full title and name, time, date, and asked that others in attendance do the same. He again individually asked Vic, Mark, and Anne if he had permission to record their conversation. All agreed.

"OK, now that we've got the preliminary stuff out of the way, let me first answer Mark and Anne Telfair's question: No, these are *not* right whales. From your high school and college biology, I'm sure you know right whales do inhabit the Atlantic Coast, and are endangered mammals of the order Cetacia, genus *Eubalaena,* species *galacialis.* They can grow up to 55 feet in length, and weigh up to 70 tons. So if these should be whales—and they are not—they'd be immature, and swimming alone isolated from their pod. Besides, the overall shape of the head is wrong, and there are *no flukes."*

Spencer paused to retrieve a hand lens from his briefcase, handed it to Mark, then continued: "Look closely, Dr. Telfair, and I think you'll see your 'shadows' have *no* dorsal fin, which is a characteristic that would certainly fit with them being right whales. But what else do you see there?"

Mark studied all three "shadows" on several different pictures. No flukes. Then he saw something with the lens: "You're right, Spencer. Instead of a dorsal fin they do have something sticking out of their backs. Looks like a pair of small greenish-black pipes to me," Mark said.

"Bingo!" Spence said, taking the lens and verifying Mark's observation.

"But what in the heck are those pipes?" Mark asked.

"The forward one is an air intake snorkel, the one aft is the SS's exhaust pipe for their diesel engine," Spence explained.

"Spencer, you've gotta talk my language if you expect me to understand what's going on," Mark replied.

"Uh … sorry. 'SS' is an abbreviation we use for 'semisubs,' or 'semisubmersible' boats used to smuggle drugs. Some folks call 'em SPSSs, for Self-Propelled Semi-Submersible. But I use 'SS.'"

"So you think they are now being used here, on the Georgia coast?" Mark asked.

"I think your photos prove we've got at least three. We've never spotted one on the North Atlantic coast before. We've known for years SSs have been manufactured in the jungles of Columbia, and are being used to smuggle cocaine and other illegal drugs to our coast on the Pacific."

"So," Mark responded, "you think they are now bringing cocaine to the Atlantic Coast?"

Spence glanced at Vic. "Whatcha think, tell 'em more?"

"OK by me," Vic replied. "We both know their NCIC is clean. So are their state records … not even a traffic ticket. Just tell 'em they have to first sign a legally binding NDA before we go further."

"Whoa!" Mark exclaimed, suddenly standing up, blushing. "I could talk to you guys in medical jargon you'd never be able to figure out. I feel the wife and I are getting in over our heads. All I wanted to know was if I'd photographed whales. You've answered that question to my satisfaction."

Silence fell all around the table. Anne finally spoke: "Honey, let's hear them out. We don't have to sign anything if we don't want to."

Then Spence said, "Sorry about the language, Doc. NCIC refers to a National Crime Information Center, a federal computer database. We've checked both your backgrounds, and we know you two are 'clean' law-abiding citizens with nothing to hide. We've checked some state records as well. The NDA Vic mentioned refers to a nondisclosure agreement. I do appreciate your letting us look at your pictures. As a personal favor to me, I'd appreciate your not discussing this meeting with anyone. I cannot legally force you not to talk to others, but if you do, you might be putting yourselves in danger from the criminal element we think is already here. I really can't tell you more until you two sign the NDA. Here's a thought for you to consider:

You and your wife obviously love this area, the one you selected for your retirement years. Do you want to help us keep the criminal element out of this paradise of an environment? If you don't care to help us, just say so now."

"Spence, let us think about it overnight at home. We'll get back in touch tomorrow," Mark said, and hurriedly began gathering his pictures in a way that kept them in order. "We know our way out," Mark added. He and Anne rapidly departed the conference room to go get into their car.

12

GETTING IN DEEPER

In five minutes they'd made the short drive home, both remaining amazed and silent. Once inside their home, they began chatting. Anne spoke first:

"Mark, it looks like your kite hobby has opened a can of worms, don't you think?"

"Well, *you* started it ... by giving me that damn first kite!" Mark replied loudly.

"Don't get testy with me! It was *your* crazy idea in the first place," she responded equally as loud. "But let's not get in a fuss over it. I think we're both just upset to learn things might not be quite what they seem around here. We're either going to get involved or bail out. We're either going to help them fight the problem, or ignore what's going on around us, or possibly leave here and go somewhere else to retire."

She's right ... almost always is. Those are our basic options, Mark thought. "Anne, I agree on the number of choices we have. But there's no way we could possibly make an informed decision unless we know what we're getting into. When you think about it, we really don't know much about Dr. Spencer Roberson, and even less about that Victor Timmons, the DNR guy. Today, we gave them information in the form of photographs, and they gave us virtually nothing except to say my so-called 'whales' are actually what they called 'SSs.'"

"Can't you get on the Internet, and check that Dr. Roberson out?" Anne asked.

"I'm sure I can. I don't doubt that he is a real biologist. He did immediately spit out the order, genus, and species of right whales. What doesn't fit is a biologist being so deeply involved in trying to solve some drug-smuggling issue. Does this make any sense to you?" Mark questioned.

She thought a moment. "No. Not unless his role as a biologist is being used as a cover for who he really is ... who he's really working for."

Anne began preparing their dinner; Mark went to the loft to get on the Internet. Though Spencer was a number of years younger than Mark, he was a little surprised to learn Dr. Roberson was a graduate of his alma mater, Emory University in Atlanta, and had later earned his Ph.D. in biology there in 1975. He'd published numerous scientific articles, including one on a simple field test for THC, or tetrahydrocannabinol, the active ingredient in marijuana. One article mentioned that the Drug Enforcement Administration, or DEA, had adopted a field test—one developed by Dr. Spencer Roberson—as their "gold standard" for testing suspicious plant material. Mark found virtually nothing about Victor Timmons, other than the fact he was with the Coastal Resources Division of the Georgia DNR, and worked in "enforcement and special assignments." Mark turned his computer off, and went downstairs to join Anne for a shrimp and grits dinner.

They talked throughout their meal, and continued chatting another several hours while trying to make a decision about getting involved, or not getting involved. During the course of their discussion, they went to the loft, where Mark even researched nondisclosure agreements on the Internet. They soon learned an NDA could be a powerful legal document, violation of which could result in fines, imprisonment, or both.

Several additional hours passed as they vacillated between "yes" and "no." "Honey," Anne finally sighed, "it looks like we're getting nowhere. Damned if we do, damned if we don't."

"Well," Mark began, "I think we should go as far as signing that NDA. That's the only way we're gonna get enough information to understand the problem."

"Little Man, when we were in practice in Statesville, we were both told a lot of things in confidence. The doctor-patient-confidentiality thing, you know. And to this day we haven't talked about those secrets. If you and I decided we ever wanted to blab about things told to us in confidence, all hell would break loose in Statesville ... and I don't know how many divorces would happen!"

"Point being ...?" Mark asked.

"The point is we both *know* we can keep our mouths shut when it comes to secrets."

"I agree. That's not the problem. The problem is we haven't even decided a 'yes' or 'no' about being privy to the information."

"So?" Anne yawned, despite her coffee overload.

Mark paused a moment. "Anne, do you remember how we finally

decided whether or not we wanted to have children?"

"Sure. And it was probably one of the craziest things you and I have ever done! We flipped Mr. Saint Christopher ... heads meant 'yes,' and tails, the blank side, meant 'no.'"

"Wanna do that again?" Anne asked.

"Yes ... I guess ... but I want to be the one to flip it this time," Mark said. "Last time I let you flip it because you'd be the one getting all swelled up ... assuming you got pregnant."

Giddy from their caffeine high, they both laughed. Mark got his wallet out and removed Saint Christopher. He moved to the center of their great room for the toss. With great fanfare, he gave Saint Christopher a mighty flip. The medal first hit the 18-foot cathedral ceiling in the great room, bouncing down on top of a rapidly spinning ceiling fan, and ricocheted to another area of the room and bounced off a wall. Thirty minutes later, and resorting to a flashlight, they finally located the old fella. He was resting, *faceup,* in the dark ... beneath their skirted sofa.

13

LONG MEETING AT THE HEAD SHED

They slept fitfully through the night. When mutually awake, they'd refused to discuss the matter again, feeling Saint Christopher's decision was "final," and not to be questioned further.

At 9:00 a.m., Mark called the office at the Harris Neck National Wildlife Refuge. He explained to the civilian secretary that he and his wife wanted to set up a joint meeting with both DNR Officer Victor Timmons and Dr. Spencer Roberson with Fish & Wildlife. He told the secretary who he and Anne were, but did not discuss the purpose of the meeting. She indicated she would have to contact Dr. Roberson and Victor Timmons by radio, and said she'd call back when a meeting could be arranged.

Anne had eavesdropped on Mark's side of the conversation. "Well, what did they say?"

"The secretary at the refuge indicated she'd contact them by radio, then call back when a meeting could be set up. Fat chance that'll happen anytime soon."

"Bureaucrats have a way of taking their time, honey," Anne said, as she began preparing their breakfast.

Ten minutes later, the Telfairs' phone rang. Mark answered: "Speaking ... What time? ... Two o'clock *today?*... Where? ... That's One Conservation Way, next to the bridge over the Brunswick River. I know where it is. We'll be there ... Yes, we'll bring the pictures ... And, yes, the negatives, too ... Thanks," Mark said, and clicked off.

"Well so much for the *slow* bureaucrats," Mark said to Anne. "The refuge secretary said they want us to meet at the DNR's Coastal Regional Headquarters in Brunswick at two o'clock *today!*"

* * *

Promptly at two o'clock, the Telfairs arrived at DNR headquarters. Mark carried nothing except his photos, car keys, and his wallet in his hip pocket. Anne had only her purse. A receptionist took them to an elevator that stopped at the third floor. They were promptly escorted to a closed door labeled "Conference Room." For some strange reason, a very fit man in his late 20s or early 30s stood next to the closed door. He was dressed in a dark suit and necktie, and had a star-shaped pin on his left lapel indicating he was from the U.S. Marshals Service. After checking the Telfairs' driver's licenses, the packages of pictures Mark carried in his hand, and the contents of Anne's purse, he opened the conference room door for the Telfairs, and immediately closed it after they'd entered. *Strange,* Mark thought. *This conference room has only one door ... and no windows. And, presumably, there's a marshal outside guarding that only door.*

Dr. Roberson, Victor Timmons, and a short black-haired stranger wearing a tasteful dark suit and tie, were already sitting there. The stranger appeared to be Hispanic. Vic and Spence were in uniform, but were not wearing their side arms as they usually did. *Strange,* Mark thought. Again, a tape recorder had been placed in the middle of the conference table. Mark promptly placed the packets of pictures on the tabletop next to the tape machine.

All three men then stood. Dr. Spencer Roberson spoke: "Roberto, this is Dr. and Mrs. Telfair. I do appreciate their coming on such short notice and bringing their pictures with them. I hope their visit means what I think it does ... that they've decided to sign the NDA, and we can quit keeping them in the dark."

Turning to the Telfairs, Roberson continued: "Doc, you and your wife already know me. You already know Victor, too. But this 'stranger' here actually is a former U.S. Border Patrol officer. His 'assumed' name is 'Roberto Gonzales,' so *always*—unless instructed otherwise—refer to him by that name should you ever meet again under different circumstances."

"Pleased to meet you, 'Roberto,'" Mark said, extending his hand to the short Hispanic-looking man in his 30s. "I'm Dr. Mark Telfair, and this is my wife, Anne," Mark replied, pointing to her. Mark desperately tried not to stare at the birthmark in the very center of Roberto's right cheek. In coloration, it resembled one on the scalp and upper forehead of Mikhail Gorbachev, former Soviet Union president. But Roberto's mark, though smaller, was much more obvious. It was a very deep purple in color. The mark would have fit inside a three-inch-diameter circle, and resembled an odd-shaped and tilted Christian cross. *At least his olive complexion doesn't contrast so sharply with the deep color of the birthmark ... but his natural skin color makes it only slightly less obvious,* Mark thought.

Everyone seated themselves. Dr. Roberson was apparently heading the meeting and was first to speak. "OK," he began, "I don't like formal meetings. As far as I'm concerned we can use our first names, except for the first part of the tape where we'll give our full names, titles, and individual permissions to record. After that it's Spence, Vic, Roberto, Mark and Anne. Any problems with that?"

No objections were voiced. Spence went to the door, opened it, and whispered something to the U.S. Marshal that still stood outside. A moment later, the marshal returned with two sets of papers; one he handed to Anne, the other set to Mark. The marshal quickly stepped out of the conference room and closed the door. *The NDAs,* Mark thought, and he was right.

Referring to Mark and Anne, Spence said, "Please take whatever time you two need to read those nondisclosure documents. If you have questions, just ask. If neither Vic nor I can answer them, we'll find someone who can."

Mark and Anne read in silence for about ten minutes. Mark finally had a question: "Can these things ever be 'revoked,' or whatever you call it?"

Spence answered: "Yes. It may take some time, even several years, depending on the circumstances. It's not possible on your behalf to 'revoke' until the information is no longer considered sensitive. But did you notice that *we*—I mean Roberto, Victor, and myself—*also* have to sign those papers?"

"That was my next question. So why do you guys have to sign them, too?"

"For your and your wife's protection. We can *never* 'revoke' our end of the agreement. That is, our agreement *not* to disclose what we've told you and your wife. Should we ever disclose that you and Anne have been given certain information, and if certain criminal elements learned that, you'd possibly be in great danger. Believe me, the cartels behind all this have no qualms about 'eliminating' those outsiders that have knowledge of the inner workings of their organizations."

"*Eliminating? As in killing* them?" Mark asked Spence.

"Yes. I guess I was trying to soft-pedal ... and not scare the wits out of you both. But to be honest, that's the way it is. Just ask Roberto. He'll tell you," Spence said, pointing at the short Hispanic.

Spence turned the recorder on, stated the time and date, then had all present "sign in" by giving their individual permissions to record, as well as their full names and professional titles.

"OK, Roberto. You may begin," Spence said.

"Doctor Mark, it is like this: I was born in Hermosillo, Mexico. When I was a child my father moved our family to the border town of Nogales, Arizona. He became an LPR of the U.S."

Mark loudly cleared his throat. "Your father became a *what?*"

"Sorry, Doctor ... that is Lawful Permanent Resident of the U.S. He did that in the search of better work. Eventually my family all became LPRs, then in time, U.S. citizens. All of the family then lived on the Arizona side of the city. Later, as a young man, I got married, and moved out of the family home after I'd become a United States citizen. I build a brand new home in Nogales, Arizona, for my wife and two children. Hoping to find even better work for myself, I went through special training at a government facility located near here in Glynco, Georgia. After my training, I joined our U.S. Border Patrol. After serving six years with them, I had a very wrong turn in my life. Like the back of my hand, I knew which areas of the southern land border were easy to penetrate, especially using tunnels. Also, I knew those areas where it was virtually impossible to penetrate the border. While patrolling the border, I was ambushed and captured by members of the Sinaloa Cartel, a drug cartel. During the ambush, they shot and killed my patrol partner. They threatened to kill me, my wife, and two children ... unless I joined them, and gave to them U.S. Border Patrol's information about weak points in our border's protection. To convince me they were serious, they burned my new home in Nogales. I had happily lived there with my wife and children for only two years when it happened. By mistake, at the school for my children in Nogales, the Sinaloa even shot and killed a child, one that looked almost identical to my youngest son, Pepe. Sinaloa then get word to me that next time they would not make such a stupid mistake again!"

"Oh my God," Anne and Mark muttered in unison, as all color drained from their faces.

"Hold up just a second, Roberto." Spence interrupted. "I don't think you should go any further until we and the Telfairs sign the NDA."

Anne piped in: "Spence, what is the real risk as far as Mark and I are concerned ... the risk of us learning this information?"

"In my opinion, your personal risk is quite minimal. You do not currently have, and will not be given, any information that's of much interest to the known drug elements we have here on the Georgia coast. Most of them here are 'little fish,' ones mainly involved in small-scale trafficking, not large-scale accumulation and distribution. But large-scale ... well, that's what we're dealing with on our southern border. We simply want to keep our peaceful Georgia coast the way it is ... and not let it grow into the monster that now plagues many areas of our border with Mexico. So, are you guys 'in' or 'out?'"

Mark and Anne stared at each other for a long moment. Anne noted Mark's face was now red, his fists clenched, the way he usually got when he was really mad about something. *The bastards killed his partner, burned his house ... even tried to kill his kid!* Mark thought.

"Count me in, Spence!" Mark finally blurted, then he looked at Anne.

"Me, too!" she replied. "Mark and I love where we live, and I'm *not* going to stand by while the drug people wreck it."

"Good!" Spence exclaimed. He turned the recorder off, then walked to the door and opened it. He again whispered something to the U.S. Marshal that still stood there. Moments later the marshal entered the room, accompanied by a woman identified as a notary public. All present signed the NDA, the marshal signing as a witness. Both the notary and the marshal then left, taking the papers with them.

Spence spoke: "Now that we've got most of the legal stuff squared away, let's let Roberto continue his story. Roberto?"

"Doctor Mark y Señora Anne, as you can see, soy un hombre marcado," Roberto said, slipping a bit to his native tongue.

Mark replied, "Entiendo que eres un hombre marcado. You have told me you are a 'marked man.' I know only bits and pieces of Spanish remembered from my high-school days. So please speak to us in English only."

Roberto nodded and apologized, then continued: "The Sinaloa Cartel that captured me, simply call me 'Marcado.' They like the fact that I have this birthmark that is so obvious here on my right cheek," Roberto said, pointing. "I once tried to grow a beard to hide it, but hair will not grow where the mark is. When I was rescued by Border Patrol, the Sinaloa knew they would have no trouble identifying me on sight, should they ever see me again. If I am ever again recaptured by Sinaloa, most likely they would kill *me* on the spot! My family, too, if they could find them."

"Roberto," Mark informed, "the birthmark you have is a fairly common one, called *naevus flammeus* ... a vascular malformation."

Roberto suddenly broke out in infectious laughter, soon to be joined by Victor and Spence, then by Mark and Anne as well. Roberto finally contained himself, as did the others. He then spoke: "Doctor Mark, you earlier request I speak to you in English only. I now make the same request to you!"

Mark chuckled and apologized to Roberto, then explained: "Your birthmark also goes by another common name ... 'port-wine stain.' The mark consists of abnormally large blood vessels in your skin. It will not go away with age. In fact, that type of birthmark usually gets darker and more bumpy with age ... and hair will never grow in the area of the birthmark. Fortunately, you have a relatively small mark. I know doctors are now experimenting with different types of laser treatments, but in your case I think simple surgical removal would give the very best results. Using plastic surgical techniques, you should be left only with a very fine scar. It should be visible only if you used a magnifying glass."

"That is very good to know, Doctor Mark," Roberto replied.

"But exactly why are you here today?" Mark asked.

"It is a long story," Roberto began. "During the two years Sinaloa had me in captivity in Mexico, I learned many facts about their organization. I was tortured over and over until I agreed to 'join' them ... and I'm ashamed to admit it, but I did disclose a few true facts our U.S. Border Patrol has about weak points on the southern land border. I tried to use vague and misleading answers, and give them as little truth as possible."

"I'm sure that was an extremely bad time for you, Roberto. But how did you ever get back into the U.S.?" Mark asked.

"Through the good work of U.S. Border Patrol officers. They 'caught' me during a raid in Nogales, on this side of the border. They immediately recognized me as a former Border Patrol officer. For awhile I was in their protective custody, but now I am in the U.S. Witness Protection Program. My wife and children are with me. I cannot disclose where we now live, or give any details."

"My God, Roberto!" Mark said. "You must live in constant fear ... even in Witness Protection."

"It is a combination of fear and *isolation.* Especially the isolation. As a family, our travels are very limited. My children will now grow up having only a very small circle of friends, and they will have little knowledge of our world. If I could only get this birthmark removed, I would have much less fear. When I was growing up in Nogales, my parents took me to several different Mexican doctors who said they couldn't treat it. Doctor Mark, you need to know we were a poor family, and they could not afford to take me to more specialized doctors here in the United States. I understand that you are a surgical doctor. Is that correct, señor?"

"Yes," Mark replied. "I am a retired surgeon, but some of my training involved plastic surgery."

"Would the surgery need to be done in a hospital?" Roberto asked.

"No," Mark answered. "Any well-equipped surgeon's office would be fine. It could be done in stages using local anesthesia."

Spencer Roberson cleared his throat, then interrupted the conversation that had been largely dominated by Roberto and Mark. "I'm going to let that U.S. Marshal join this meeting for a minute. OK by you Vic?"

Victor Timmons nodded a "yes."

Spence turned the recorder off and opened the door. The marshal was still standing there at parade rest, jacket unbuttoned and gaping a bit. Mark could not help noting he was armed. "Marshal, would you mind stepping in for just a moment."

"Certainly, Dr. Roberson. What can I do for you?" the marshal asked.

This whole meeting is getting bizarre, Mark thought. *Anne and I have come down here to show them some aerial pictures, then sign an agreement, then I talked about birthmarks with a former Border Patrol officer who's in the Witness Protection Program ... and I can't figure out jackshit. And now we've got an armed U.S. Marshal in the room ... and Spence didn't even bother to tell us the marshal's name. Strange ....*

Spencer's words to the marshal interrupted Mark's thoughts: "Can the Service arrange to have the birthmark surgically removed from Roberto Gonzales?" Spence pointed to Mark. "And I prefer that Dr. Mark Telfair be involved in the process."

"Has Telfair been checked out?" the marshal asked.

"Yes. Completely. So has his nurse-wife, Anne," Spencer replied.

"I'll see what the Marshals Service can do. A doctor's office, or a hospital—either civilian or military—are probably out of the question. Give me a day or two. I'll contact you, Dr. Roberson."

"Thank you, Marshal. Please resume your post outside," Roberson said, then reached to the table's center and turned the recorder back on.

Anne saw Mark getting redder by the second. She knew he was mad, and getting even more angry by the nanosecond. He suddenly stood up and faced Dr. Spencer Roberson.

Spence tried to speak. "Look, Dr. Telfair, I understand you're—"

"Pissed off!" Mark finished. "And I'm gonna be the most uncooperative little son of a bitch you've ever dealt with … unless you let me ask *you* some questions—and *I* get some damn straight answers!"

"Doctor, this conversation is being recorded. A transcript could end up in a court of law," Spencer reminded Mark.

"I don't give a shit! That's s-h-i-t … just so the transcriptionist won't misspell it!" Mark yelled. And my last name is T-e-l-f-a-i-r, not T-e-l-f-a-r-e, as some try to spell it!"

Anne hung her head, utterly embarrassed, but she knew Mark's anger would have to run its course.

Roberto chuckled. "I like this little man with such large spirit … he reminds me of Chihuahua dog!"

Victor said nothing, but smiled at Mark's outburst.

Spencer, too, was wearing a smile. "Doctor, you have legitimate reasons to be angry with us. So, I will now let *you* ask the questions."

"Good! It's about time," Mark replied, his anger now quelling. "First of all, Dr. Roberson, I want to know exactly why you, a biologist, appear to be in the middle of all this?"

Spence immediately replied. "Spencer Nelson Roberson is my full real name, and I am a real biologist with a Ph.D. I earned it back in 1975 at your alma mater. My first permanent work was, and still is, with the U.S. Fish & Wildlife Service. My main interest was, and still is, in plants, as opposed to animals. I got involved with the Drug Enforcement Administration in 1976, a few years after it was first formed. That happened because I had developed a quick chemical field test for THC, the active ingredient in marijuana. So, to answer your question, I work undercover for the DEA; my cover just happens to be who I actually am in real life … a biologist."

Now it's beginning to make some sense, Mark thought, while formulating his next question: "Who is Roberto Gonzales?"

Spence explained: "Roberto Gonzales is not his original name. It is a new name he chose to give the U.S. Marshals Service, which oversees the U.S. Witness Protection Program. I personally do not know Roberto's original name, and I will never know it. What Roberto told you about his work with Border Patrol is all true, including his two years spent as a captive of the Sinaloa Cartel. Roberto told you he is a 'marked man.' The cartel now simply calls him 'Marcado.' His picture is now widely circulated among the cartel's members. They are actively searching for him. If spotted, they would kill him in a heartbeat, and that is why he is still in the Witness Protection Program. Doctor, you need to understand Roberto has extensive knowledge about the inner workings of several Mexican drug organizations, especially Sinaloa. We want to put him back in the field working with DEA, our Drug Enforcement Administration. That would not be possible because his birthmark makes him so easy to recognize. In short, he is an 'encyclopedia' of drug-cartel knowledge … but he's also a 'walking target.'"

"OK," Mark said, "I know where you and Roberto stand. But how does Victor Timmons, here—who's supposedly with DNR—fit in?"

"A logical question, Doctor. Victor is actually with the Georgia Department of Natural Resources. His primary function is exactly as it appears: enforcing marine laws where DNR has jurisdiction. On the day he inspected your boat while you and your wife were fishing at Little Egg Island, he had a rookie DNR officer with him. So, in a way, he is an instructor. It was also a training exercise for the younger officer. But Vic's function that is not so apparent, is his connection with the DEA. He serves as 'eyes and ears' for that portion of the Atlantic ICW that's located in the State of Georgia. Specifically, Vic keeps an eye on that portion of the Intracoastal Waterway located in McIntosh County, Georgia … and he reports his observations directly to me. Any more questions, Doctor?"

"I've several. While developing my kite aerial photography system, I ran into an old black man over at Barbour Landing. He told me his name is Oscar Dunham, and said he was an oysterman and crabber. What's his connection to all this?"

"Oscar Dunham is his real name, and he is an honest hard-working old man that is helping us, but in no official capacity. He's signed a nondisclosure, just as you and the wife have today," Spence said. "Oscar already knows everything we've talked about in this meeting, with one exception: Oscar has no knowledge of Roberto Gonzales, and really has no need to know."

"Well," Mark began, "I certainly will not tell Oscar about Roberto. But I noticed Oscar had been missing at Barbour Landing for awhile, and when I questioned him about his absence, he indicated he'd been doing some work for the government, but would not tell me more."

Spence smiled. "Oscar's just honoring the NDA he signed."

"But what does he actually do that helps you?" Mark asked.

"Several things, Doctor," Spence began. "We took Oscar to Atlanta to work with our map guy, a cartographer. He's been trying to update

DEA's nautical charts for all of the McIntosh County waters, including the ICW and literally hundreds of no-name creeks in that county. Nobody—I mean *nobody*—has the knowledge of the local waterways like that old Oscar Dunham fella has. Anyway, Oscar worked with our Atlanta cartographer for about two months. Together they reviewed satellite images of the local coast. We now have a topnotch chart, one showing several obscure pathways that a surface drug boat, or even a semisubmersible, could possibly be using in McIntosh to avoid detection. For the first time ever, we now know the approximate depth and width, at both low and high tides, for every damn little 'no-name' creek in that county!"

Mark laughed, and said, "Spencer, you're being recorded. You want to retract that 'damn' you just said … before a transcriptionist gets a hold of it!"

Everyone, including Anne, enjoyed the "laughter break" that seemed to ease tensions, especially Mark's.

"No," Spence said. "Let my 'damn' stand. Any more questions, Mark … or Anne?"

Mark had one. "On the first day I met Oscar, I was helping him unload some oysters from his skiff. Some of the oyster boxes had brick-sized things in them that appeared to be wrapped in black plastic. What were those things?"

"They were watertight 'bricks' of high-tech marijuana buds, each weighing about a pound. Street value per pound on the West Coast would vary from $4,000 in Seattle to about $6,000 by the time it reaches Los Angeles. Then smaller street-sellers would push it for about $600 to $800 an ounce," Roberson explained.

"Wow!" Mark exclaimed. "It sure wasn't that way when I was in college in the 60s. I admit I tried pot a time or two, but it was quite inexpensive back then. Didn't like the stuff anyway, just preferred a good drink of booze instead."

"Me too," Roberson admitted. "But you need to understand this pot is genetically altered, and it's up to 100 times more potent than the stuff you and I grew up around. We're almost positive this high-tech stuff is coming across our *northern* land border, and is being grown in underground Canadian labs that use artificial lighting."

"Well, I thought Roberto's knowledge was about the *southern* land border, not the northern," Mark said.

"Doctor Mark," Roberto said, "my knowledge is *mostly* about the southern border. But while I was in captivity by Sinaloa, I often pretended to be asleep … but I listen carefully to their words among themselves and when they talk on their phones. But believe me, they *are* growing in labs in eastern Canada, and now they're somehow using the ICW to smuggle their product southward along our Atlantic Coast."

"Any more questions, Doctor?" Spence asked, looking at his watch.

"Only a couple more," Mark said, also looking at his watch to discover it was after four o'clock. "What did Oscar do with the marijuana he had in his oyster boxes?"

"He brought it directly to me. He discovered he could find those packets in crab traps, but *only* in the ones with floats that had *no numbers* on them. It seems he found each packet had been tightly wrapped in black polyethylene plastic, then dipped into paraffin to make it completely waterproof. Through the paraffin coating and plastic wrap, I'd simply make a very small puncture hole using a Vim-Silverman surgical biopsy needle. You familiar with that needle?" Mark said nothing, but nodded a "yes." "So, in that way, I obtained a small 'biopsy' of each package, field-tested for THC to confirm, and I'd send the rest of the biopsy to a plant genetics lab in Atlanta. Using the same needle, I'd then inject into each package a small amount of a harmless fluorocarbon chemical, one that would serve as an invisible 'marker.' If the package should be recovered after distribution, a simple lab test would confirm it came from crab traps in the Barbour River, or one of its various tributaries. Then, using paraffin, I'd reseal the needle holes and return them to Oscar, who'd put them back exactly where he'd found them—back into the same unnumbered crab traps."

"Time for one more question?" Mark asked.

Spencer again checked his watch. "Yes, a short one."

"What do you foresee as my, and my wife's, role in this whole scenario?"

"Doctor, yours is a short question, but the answer to it is not. I want you to leave your photos in my custody, including their negatives." Spencer quickly removed a form from his briefcase. He made some quick notes on it, then signed it, and handed it to Mark. "I'm sorry, but I now have to close this meeting to tend to other matters," Spence said, again glancing at his watch. "You, Anne, and myself will have a private meeting in the refuge office soon. I'll keep you posted. Don't worry, you'll get your pictures back. Just remember both of you signed the NDA. Thanks for coming," Spence said, as he turned the tape recorder off, and prepared to leave.

14

GETTING READY

Without conversation, but with their heads filling with thoughts, Anne and Mark walked briskly to their Explorer parked in the lot in front of the DNR building. They had driven about five minutes toward home before either uttered a single word. Anne broke the silence:

"Mark, didn't you think that was odd?"

"What part are you talking about? I think the whole damn thing was odd! Especially the way they ended the meeting."

"That's what I'm mostly talking about, too, Little Man. The abrupt ending. Dr. Spencer Roberson just saying 'I have to close the meeting now to tend to other matters,' or something close to that. Granted, he did give us a receipt for your pictures, but it does not specify the process for us to get them back," Anne said. She was in the passenger's seat reading the single-page receipt hurriedly handed to Mark at meeting's end.

"I agree about the abrupt ending," Mark said. "Kinda like we got the brush-off at the end there. And another thought just struck me."

"What?"

"We do not have personal copies of the nondisclosure agreements we signed ... nor do we have the negatives anymore. They were in the packages with the prints," Mark said.

"I know," Anne said. "But you really embarrassed me in that meeting when you got so mad. I thought you were going to explode. I'll bet your blood pressure was off the charts! Let's plan a little 'relaxation therapy' this evening. Make a pitcher of martinis, go to the dock, watch the birds come in ... and—"

"Play with each other's 'stuff' after dinner!" Mark finished.

* * *

Anne had been right. The "relaxation therapy" had worked wonders. *The combination of martinis, bird watching, evening meal, and lovemaking ... a perfect stress-reliever combo,* Mark had thought immediately before going soundly to sleep. Upon awakening the next morning, they continued pondering the peculiarities of their own behavior as well as the meeting at the DNR building in Brunswick.

While eating breakfast, Mark commented: "We really got wound up there for a bit before going to sleep, didn't we? Sorta confirms my theory about stress making folks horny."

"Doctor, you have your theory, I have mine. But who cares? It certainly got our minds off yesterday afternoon, and we both slept well."

Mark smiled and took a sip of his coffee. "I still get the feeling they are hiding something from us. Don't you?"

"I'm not sure," Anne answered. "You've always had a bit of a paranoid streak. Remember how you got when we were first looking at Statesville as a practice location? You felt quite sure there just had to be something wrong with the place because it all seemed too perfect."

"Yeah, I remember ... and it turned out I was wrong. It was a perfect small town for our surgical practice. I thought Dunham Point here in rural McIntosh would also be the perfect retirement place ... but now I'm beginning to wonder."

Anne sighed. "Well, we know Dr. Spencer Roberson is who he says he is. Your check on the Internet proves that, including his being an Emory graduate with a doctorate in biology. He openly admitted to us he was working undercover with DEA. Your Internet check on Victor Timmons also proved he's a real DNR officer, and they admitted he feeds information to Spencer, who then feeds it to DEA."

"What do you think about Roberto?" Mark asked.

Anne chuckled. "Well, the little guy has a great sense of humor. Remember him saying you reminded him of a Chihuahua? Roberto said it right after you got so pissed off! But I think 'little pit bull terrier' would have been more accurate. And I think Roberto's cute as a bug! He'd be downright handsome if he didn't have that horrible birthmark."

"Really?" Mark asked, a tinge of resentment in his voice.

"Mark, I've never figured out why I'm attracted to shorter men ... uh ... I'm talking about their parts you see with their clothes on."

Mark chuckled. "I'm glad you seem to appreciate my God-given personal anatomy. You certainly seemed to appreciate it last night!"

"Do I detect a hint of jealously?" Anne asked, now laughing.

"No! Well, I guess I really *don't* know ... I've never seen Roberto with his clothes off! Birthmark aside, he does have beautiful olive skin, the type that leaves minimal surgical scar. I agree he is a good-looking man, and I honestly feel sorry for him if what he told us is true."

"Mark, I think we're getting sidetracked here. Do we really have any reason to doubt Roberto's story?" Anne asked. "And how about old Oscar Dunham? That explanation seems to fit."

"Well, I don't have any concrete reason to doubt their stories. At least nothing I can prove, nothing I can put my finger on. I just can't help but feel the real reason they want to get us involved is they need a surgeon. It's like they want to have the surgery done, yet leave absolutely no record of it ever being done."

"I think you may be right about that one," Anne said. "Maybe their interest in your pictures might not be quite as keen as we were led to believe. I think they've already suspected those semisubmersibles, or SSs—or whatever they called those things—were being used here on the Georgia coast. They just had not been able to *document* it. That is, until they saw your so-called 'whale' photos."

Mark paused a moment. "And now they have my pictures ... perhaps the only concrete proof of SSs in this area. At least we left the meeting with the ball in *their* court."

"Like how?" she asked.

"Spencer said he'd be back in touch with us 'soon,' if I recall correctly. I don't feel like just sitting around the house waiting for him to call," Mark explained.

"Why don't we go shopping. We've been wanting an answering machine for our phone ... so let's get one and hook it up, then do whatever we want."

"Sounds fine to me," Mark said, while helping with after-breakfast cleanup.

An hour later they had driven to Circuit City, an electronics store located in a mall in Brunswick, Georgia. They spent about an hour looking over more options than they ever imagined existed for something as simple as an answering machine. Finally, they selected one. Mark then started looking at digital cameras, but still found them too expensive for something he planned to 'trust' to a mere kite flying over water and marsh. When a knowledgeable salesman demonstrated a digital image program for his computer he became quite impressed. Needless to say, he ended up buying Photoshop Elements 3.0, a software program that would allow him to manipulate images Anne made with her digital camera. Feeling they'd spent enough of their month's retirement budget, they finally left the store and headed home, but stopped at Archie's, a popular inexpensive seafood restaurant in Darien. When they arrived at their Dunham home, the phone was ringing. Mark answered.

"Hello," he said, and listened for a moment or two. "We'll be there. Bye," Mark said and hung up.

Anne raised her eyebrows. "Well that was short and sweet. Who called, Little Man?"

"It was Dr. Spencer Roberson. He wanted to know if we could possibly meet him right *now* over at the office in the wildlife refuge. He said he'd tried earlier to call three times, but got no answer ... and he has some equipment he wants to show us, plus he's got several questions to ask."

"Well?" Anne asked.

"I think we should go. I've still got a lot of questions I want to ask him, too," Mark answered.

When the Telfairs arrived at the refuge office, the secretary promptly escorted them to the same conference room they'd used there earlier. This time, Spencer was alone. His briefcase, two blue plastic cases, and several small cardboard boxes were on the conference table. *There's no tape recorder this time,* Mark noticed in thought.

After warmly greeting them, Spencer said, "Please have a seat, and let me start by apologizing for the way that meeting at DNR abruptly ended yesterday. I was up against a timeline. I'd had a chopper waiting for me at the Brunswick Golden Isles Airport. A pilot had been waiting since four o'clock to fly me over the Barbour River from its beginning to end. And the guy charges the DEA $100 per hour, either on the ground or in the air."

"I thought you said Oscar Dunham had helped your cartographer guy create great charts of the area. Did you find they're not good enough?" Mark questioned.

"Doc, the new charts Oscar helped us create are very good. I just wanted to get a mental aerial image of the Barbour River in my own head, especially at high tide. Specifically I was looking for *any* connection between the headwaters of the Barbour and the South Newport River. I could find no navigable connections an SS could use, even on a spring tide like we had yesterday afternoon. And I wanted to see exactly where you and Anne had put out those yellow marker floats, the ones you two used to scale your kite images. The chopper had a digital belly camera. We took some more shots of those floats. We took them at exactly 500 feet, according to the chopper's radioaltimeter. The pilot said knowing his exact altitude, plus knowing the view angle of his camera's lens, would permit a precise calculation of the exact distance between the yellow marker floats you guys used as your reference scale."

Somewhat defensively, Anne spoke up. "So you don't trust our estimate that those SS things are about 30 feet long?"

Spence smiled. "You guys did great! Your marker floats were almost a perfect 100 feet apart. Using our high-tech measurements from the chopper, and repeating the same scaling process you guys used on the first kite photos, we now feel the SSs are exactly 32 feet long. All three of them, identical." Spence then looked only at Mark. "Doctor, you and I both know finding three identical-length immature 'whales' separated from their pod would never happen. I do trust you still believe me when I told you the 'shadows' definitely are not whales."

Mark laughed. "Spence, I never doubted your conclusion. So it looks like you've gone to a lot of trouble, and expense, to prove what I've already accepted as fact."

"Well," Spence began, "we could try to use well-instrumented motorized aircraft to patrol the area … and possibly spot more SSs. But here's the problem: They would spot us first, then duck under completely."

"I thought you said they were 'semisubmersible,'" Mark said.

"We've acquired a couple of abandoned larger SSs on the West Coast, but we've yet to capture a single crew member aboard. It seems they always detect our approach, and simply abandon their boat along with its drug cargo, be it marijuana or cocaine. The crew seems to disappear into thin air. The two West Coast subs we have in custody are some 60 feet in length, diesel/electric powered, and can run about 12 miles an hour. Using only a single load of diesel fuel, we estimate their range is about 2,000 nautical miles. Here's the important part: We think the ones we've got on the West Coast can *completely* submerge for short periods of time, at least up to a few hours. They even have compressed oxygen cylinders and carbon dioxide scrubbers that would allow them to submerge for several hours without suffocating the crew. We think the 60-foot jobs probably have a crew of three or four men. On the center of their topside they even have a very low-profile 'cabin' and radar dome. Our tests indicate their radar can scan a full 360 degrees, but only from the horizon to a few degrees above it. That would mean they would miss detecting most aircraft at close range, but do a good job of spotting watercraft and other near-surface objects. We think most—if not all of their aircraft detection—depends on modified aircraft-type transponders they carry. Electrical engineers are still trying to figure out the transponder modifications, but we think they can *receive*, yet don't emit a *return* signal that would disclose the SS's position. Their snorkels and periscopes are completely retractable, as are radio antennas and GPS gear."

"So," Mark commented, "they've really gone high-tech, haven't they?"

"Not completely," Spence explained. "The hulls of the two we have in our possession are rather crudely made of fiberglass, and our folks don't think they can dive very deep without crushing the hull. But their electronic gear, except for their radar, is all state-of-the-art stuff. That's the scary part."

"So, you've never captured any of the crew *after* they abandon ship?" Anne asked.

"No ... not yet," Spence admitted. "So, if the 32-foot versions we have here on our coast are anything like their larger West Coast cousins, they'll probably have all the same bells and whistles. I'm talking radar, sophisticated radio, hydrophones, sonar, modified aircraft-type transponders, periscopes, even the latest in loran and the newer GPS technology. In other words, they'll still spot us before we spot them. The SSs have such a low profile in the water they are not readily visible using conventional watercraft-based radar. They leave no wake, and unless sea surface conditions and lighting are perfect, it's almost impossible to visually spot them from patrolling aircraft."

"Oh my God!" Anne exclaimed. "Just how *expensive* are these things? They certainly can't be cheap."

"We estimate the larger ones we've got cost about one million dollars a copy," Spencer answered.

"Well, just how do they ever manage to—"

"Pay for them?" Spence interrupted, anticipating Anne's question. "I think I've told you some of this before, but you do the math. We know the bigger SSs can carry 10 tons of cargo, so that's 20,000 pounds. In L.A., for the big-time accumulators, their cost of high-tech pot is around $6,000 a pound. So, that's about $120 million right there. You can safely figure the SS runners get about half the accumulator's cost ... say $60 million, for each successful run. And, as I said earlier, on the street the sellers are getting $600 to $800 an ounce!"

Anne and Mark were stunned. After a long awkward silence, Mark finally spoke. "Spence, we've already proved they are here. At least on one occasion. How the heck do you think kite images are going to help further?"

"I'm not sure additional conventional kite aerial photos will help. We definitely could use your method of aerial imaging for biological research here in the refuge. As far as using your method for SS detection goes, I've a couple of things in mind … but we first need to do some tests."

"Such as?" Mark asked.

Dr. Roberson began: "We need to determine if your kites and the camera rig are visible on radar. Judging by the type of on-board radar equipment the larger SSs carry, anything like a metal airplane or chopper would be easily detected by their radar, provided that aircraft was approaching from a great distance, and thus very low on the horizon. In other words, their radar does *not* do a good job of 'looking overhead' close to the SS, but does a great job of looking sideways at almost any distance, until the curvature of the earth becomes a factor. Are you following me, Doctor?"

"I think so Spence," Mark answered. "You are saying the SS radar can 'see' line of sight, like a human, but they can't turn their 'eyes' upward, or tilt their head, to look much higher than level."

Spence laughed. "You understand the principle, and I like your explanation of radar horizon better than my own!"

Mark thought a moment, then said, "But what if conventional aircraft flew high over the area with their transponders turned off?"

"We've thought of doing that. Because of FAA regulations, and the amount of local civilian air traffic, and military planes from Fort Stewart, we think that's a dangerous if not an illegal option. Then there is another problem," Spence said.

"Like what?" Mark asked.

"We don't even know if the SSs have a heat signature that's detectable from the air."

"*Heat signature?*" Mark asked, seeking clarification.

"I'm talking about infrared radiation, or IR," Spence explained. "Just like a whale's spout, a diesel's exhaust is obviously warmer than the surrounding air. Aerial infrared photography should pick up that difference in temperature. We tried testing that out on the West Coast, but there was too much clutter from warm-blooded marine animals … mostly seals and whales. Here, on the Atlantic side, there are fewer chances of false positives because we have fewer warm-blooded things in the waters."

"When do we get started?" Mark said, now anticipating the undertaking.

"Tomorrow, early afternoon," Spence replied. "I've gotta go to the reserve at Wolf Island early in the morning to retrieve data from our unmanned weather station there. I also need to replace some batteries and graph paper inside it."

Mark thought a second or two. "Mind if Anne and I tag along?"

Spencer paused a moment in thought. "This weather station data is all boring stuff ... and I'm sure you know the only way to get to Wolf Island is by boat. Vic Timmons is supposed to meet me at Barbour Landing at six tomorrow morning. He's going to be in a larger DNR boat that has conventional marine radar, similar to that on the West Coast SSs. After I've checked the weather station on Wolf, I'd planned to use the DNR's radar to see if it can detect your kite gear in the air. Winds are supposed to be eight to fifteen tomorrow ... so it could be a rough boat ride, but great for flying a kite."

"In that case, I think it best Anne and I remain on the hill," Mark said. "When you guys get back, we'll figure out how we're gonna do the radar test. OK?"

Anne sighed, and Mark knew the reason for her apparent relief: her fear of seasickness.

Spence said, "Sounds like a plan, Doctor. But let me go over several other things, and see what you think." Spencer opened his attaché and removed several eight-by-ten color photos. "These are high-resolution digital shots we made about 5:30 yesterday afternoon. We used the chopper's permanently mounted belly camera. What do you think of these images?"

Mark and Anne studied them for a full minute. Finally Mark spoke: "They're shots of my yellow floats—the markers Anne and I placed in the Barbour. I can even read my 'A-2383' numbers on the floats!"

Dr. Spencer Roberson smiled. "The wonders of digital technology. Now what do you think about this?" Spence asked, pushing one of the cardboard boxes on the conference table toward Mark. Quickly, he opened it to discover a digital camera about the size and weight of a brick.

"How much does this sucker weigh?" Mark asked.

"Look under 'specifications' in the manual. It's in the bottom of that box," Spence said, pointing.

Anne was reading over Mark's shoulder, when he finally found the weight: *31 ounces.* "That's more total weight than my current camera rig—with its cradle included! I don't know if my kite can lift that much weight. If I adapted my current camera cradle to carry this new camera you've got here, we'd be talking about at least three pounds total, I'd guess."

"Could you use a 'dummy weight?'" Spence asked.

"You mean put a 31-ounce weight in my cradle, then test fly?"

"Exactly, Doctor. I need to be sure it'll fly, too. That's a $10,000 camera you're holding there. I had to sign my life away just to borrow it from DEA. When you read the manual completely, I think you'll see why it's so expensive. It'll shoot both regular and infrared images, depending on the mode you select on the camera."

"Wow!" was the only word Mark could muster.

"Mark, I need your permission to do something."

"Like what?" Mark asked, having no idea what Spence meant.

"I'd like to remove your numbered yellow crab trap floats from the river."

"Well, Anne and I can certainly do that, Spence."

"No, I don't want *you* to do it personally. I'd rather not chance anyone seeing you, or your boat, associated with those floats," Roberson explained. "I'll get Oscar Dunham to remove them at night. He'll then give them to me. I'll return your floats to you personally."

"Spence, the floats are not that expensive, and I don't care about the concrete blocks that anchor them. So don't make a big deal out of getting them back to me," Mark replied.

"I realize that," Spencer answered, "but you need to remember something: Oscar has found the contraband only in *unnumbered* traps, ones that aren't being used by our legitimate crabbers. Most local fellows follow the DNR's regulations requiring a license number being displayed on their floats, and they realize they could lose their license if they fail to display their numbers. Our locals know if they lose their crabbing license, they lose their livelihood. I doubt the smugglers even know or care about our crabbing regulations, but they've probably figured out locals won't disturb anyone else's traps, even the unnumbered ones. We want to give the criminals a lot of space on the river ... space free of crab floats, as a kind of 'bait,' one that will encourage them to use the same technique again. Who knows? Maybe we'll be lucky enough to capture one of their SSs, including its crew and cargo."

Anne, who'd been silent, finally spoke: "Spence, why all this secrecy?"

"It's like this, Anne. We don't want the Telfair name, nor your boat's name, *Fanta-Sea,* connected in anyway to this investigation.

I've told you two a number of details during this meeting ... details that could put you guys in danger if criminal elements learn of your insider knowledge. So, do you now see where I'm coming from?"

"I think so, Spencer. But yesterday you said our personal risk would be 'minimal,' if we got involved."

"I think it's still that way ... minimal. I just want to *keep* it that way. All you've got to do is keep your mouths shut about what you two already know, or may learn in the future. Don't write down anything you've learned, or may learn in the future. Don't write or record it *anywhere*." Spencer paused a moment and withdrew some papers and Mark's photos from his attaché. "Before I forget it, here are your original pictures, their negatives, and photocopies of the NDAs you guys signed yesterday at the DNR building in Brunswick. I strongly suggest you put these in your safety-deposit box at your local bank. We already know you use the Southeastern Bank's branch in Eulonia, and have a safety-deposit box there. I suggest you keep your NDAs as well as your present and selected future kite photos there ... especially any images that might show SSs." Spencer paused, embarrassment obvious on his face. "I should confess that last night I took the liberty of having your kite pictures—only ones showing the SSs—scanned, to get them into a digital format. I had a DEA digital photographer enhance the images for maximum clarity. Other than being a darker greenish-gray in coloration, the visible top structures on the shorter SSs we have here are identical to the larger ones out on the West Coast. Using a secure electronic Internet communication, we sent your digitized SS images to our appropriate aerial-observation assets. All that work may have been for nothing," Spence concluded, frowning.

"But why?" Mark asked.

"Because we think the SSs can detect conventional aircraft well in advance, then submerge completely. But we wanted our people to at least have an idea about what the smaller SSs look like from the air, especially their coloration."

A long uncomfortable silence followed. Anne finally said, "Dr. Roberson, Mark and I had a long discussion last night about getting involved. We decided to get involved, but the main issue for me—and I assume Mark, too—is our personal safety."

"Our personal safety is my main concern, too," Mark chimed in. "To be honest, I somewhat resent your intrusions into our private lives. You even know where we bank and that we have a safety-deposit box! What else do you know about us?" Mark asked, a tinge of anger in his voice.

Spencer actually blushed, then paused. "Granted, we have more information about you two than we actually have need to know. We know you purchased a little Smith & Wesson Airweight .38 revolver through a licensed gun dealer, about two years ago. We know you have a permit for that gun, but don't have a conceal-carry permit. We know you do not have a home security system installed at your residence. But we know virtually nothing of your personal medical histories, which is the most difficult database for us to lawfully penetrate. We know, as a surgeon, you've been sued twice for malpractice in Statesville, Georgia, and that both frivolous claims were thrown out, and that you got a couple of shitty lawyers permanently disbarred. We know you have no pending legal actions against you, malpractice or otherwise. We know, upon retirement, you have requested the Georgia State Board of Medical Examiners to place your license in an 'inactive' category. We know—"

"*Enough!*" Mark shouted, his face turning beet-red. "I was very worried that Anne and I would never be able to have anything that resembled a private life in the small town of Statesville where we practiced. And now we retire to the rural Georgia coast, and we run into *you!* You know more about us than anybody in Statesville ever did!"

Spencer seemed to realize he was treading on very thin ice. A slip here would mean he could kiss any cooperation from the Telfairs good-by. He saw Anne's fearful facial expressions, and knew Dr. Mark Telfair was about to explode emotionally.

The silence lingered.

"Doctor," Spencer began softly, "we had to meddle into your private life for several reasons, but mainly for our mutual safety. We needed to be positive you two were low-profile law-abiding citizens that had no criminal connections … connections that could compromise our investigation and put everyone involved in danger. I've signed the NDA. So has your wife, Officer Victor Timmons, Roberto Gonzales, and even old Oscar Dunham. I'm sure you know a lot about your patients in Statesville, things you will never disclose. Right?"

"Right," Mark replied, his anger slowly resolving while Anne gently massaged the back of his neck. "But for us it was a matter of professional ethics … the doctor-patient confidentiality, something drilled into us while in med school and training. You guys seem to need nondisclosure agreements. Why is that?" Mark asked, now calm again.

"Doctor," Spence said, "I agree law officers shouldn't need NDAs. Unfortunately, we have a few bad apples among us. The temptation for a law officer to disclose critical information can be tremendous ... especially when they're tempted with sums of money far greater than they'll ever make in their legitimate lifetime career in law enforcement. Or in the case of Roberto, you find yourself captured, tortured, and your family threatened."

"Speaking of Roberto, my assumption has been that you want me to remove his birthmark so he can come back on line working for DEA. Is that correct?"

"Yes, Doctor. I spoke at length with DEA last night," Spence admitted.

"But I can't legally do Roberto's surgery," Mark explained.

Spence smiled. "Yes you can, Doctor ... in international waters. We know your Georgia license is inactive, but according to DEA, you can legally do it aboard a ship, or on an island, in international waters, or anywhere our state and federal laws do not apply to you. That, in no way, would be breaking any U.S. law. We realize your breaking the law would compromise your ability to reactivate your license with the Georgia State Board of Medical Examiners ... should you ever choose to do that at some future time."

"I'll agree to do the surgery under those conditions, with Anne assisting. It's a simple operation, but I'd need to have all the right equipment," Mark explained.

Anne nodded agreement.

"Tomorrow," Spence began, "give me a list of the instruments and supplies you need, and we'll arrange to have exactly what you need aboard a ship, or at some location where U.S. law won't apply to you. It may take a little time to set that up, but I'll keep you informed."

Anne had largely been silent, but had several questions building in her mind. "Spence, can I ask you some questions?"

"Sure. Fire away."

"Why do you carry a pistol? Looks to me like that's something your average refuge biologist wouldn't do."

"You never know, Anne. Other visitors at the Harris Neck National Wildlife Refuge have asked me that same question. So far, I've had to shoot a couple of rabid raccoons that tried to bite me ... and one alligator that tried to get into the boat with me at Woody Pond while I was counting wood stork chicks! But I've never had to use my gun against threats from humans ... but I'm prepared. Before I went undercover with DEA, they required that I go to Brunswick to receive proper firearms training, and I did that. They sent me to the Federal Law Enforcement Training Center, which they call FLETC, pronouncing it as 'flet-sea.' Have you ever fired a gun, Anne?"

"A few times, Spence. Mark's little pistol. He wanted to be sure I knew how to use it, especially when he leaves me at home alone while he's offshore fishing."

Speaking to both now, Spencer smiled. "I call that being prepared for the worst case scenario. That little Smith & Wesson revolver you have is a good personal self-defense weapon up close. But like you medical folk do with your crash carts for CPR, or just like the spare tire you carry with your car, I want you to consider preparing for something I think will never happen. Even Oscar Dunham, old as he is, is a damn good shot with what I'm about to show you. Oscar is certainly the civilian who is most likely to address the criminal element one-on-one. So, please allow me to show you something better than the little revolver you have," Spencer said, opening the two blue plastic boxes on the conference table. "These are the same gun I carry. They are Sig-Sauer P226s. The P226 is a safe-handling, dependable, accurate, easily maintained, fast 9mm semi-auto with a 15 round magazine."

"Look, Dr. Roberson, I don't want to shoot one of those things!" Anne said, pointing at the P226s.

Mark yelled, "Me neither! I've spent too darn many hours in ORs trying to fix the damage these things can do to the human body!"

Spencer held both his hands up, as if in surrender. "I'm not suggesting you two get training with these guns *now!* At the moment, you two are as involved in this drug-smuggling case as you'll probably ever be. If our radar tests tomorrow show the kite rig is visible on radar, then it's all over for the two of you ... at least as far as using kite images to try to catch drug boats. If you're agreeable, I'd still like to use your imaging technique for my bird counts at Woody Pond. OK?"

"You can definitely count me in as far as the bird photography goes. The wife and I will have to think about the rest. By the way, what's in those other two small cardboard boxes?" Mark asked.

"Something just as important as the two guns I just showed you." Spencer carefully opened the remaining boxes and handed one device to Anne, the other to Mark. The Telfairs studied the multiple buttons on the devices about the size of a small Band-Aid box.

"Are these phones?" Mark finally questioned.

"Yes, of sorts," Spencer explained. "They are secure satellite phones, or satphones. You can securely talk to anyone anywhere in the world. With the touch of a button, you can even send a coded distress signal that will pinpoint your exact GPS location anywhere on the face of the planet." Spencer cleared his throat, looking totally exhausted. "I guess what I'm trying to do is convince you two there are ways of obtaining equipment and training needed to ensure your safety in a worst-case scenario. Old Oscar has both a P226 and a satphone, and he's been taught how to use them both. They go with Oscar wherever he goes ... until this is finally over."

Despite Roberson's apparent tiredness, Anne couldn't resist a final question: "Spence, when you retire what do you plan to do?"

"I'm going to become one of your neighbors. That's going to be about ten years down the road ... I hope."

"One of our neighbors?" curious Anne asked.

"Yes. Check the courthouse records in Darien. You'll find I own lots in Dunham Point, where you guys live now. They are adjoining marsh front lots at the west end of the subdivision. I, too, feel this is a paradise of a retirement environment. I'm making my own personal effort to keep it that way. I hope you both will join me, if need be."

"Well, Spencer," Mark said, "you've certainly given us a lot to think about today."

15

TEST DAY

The Telfairs spent another restless evening at home discussing the new knowledge gained during their meeting with Dr. Spencer Roberson. About 1:00 a.m., and getting weary of discussing the same things over and over, they finally trudged off to bed. After they'd turned off their bedside lights, Mark had a few final thoughts before sleep finally came: *We're damned if we do ... damned if we don't. I hope my kite is highly visible on their radar, and we can forget this whole mess.* He then thought about their toss of Saint Christopher, their "decision-making system," one that hadn't led them astray thus far in their lives together. *Ah shit, I'll worry about it tomorrow,* he thought as his mind finally went blank.

It was not the best sleep the couple had ever had, but they simultaneously awoke about 9:00 a.m. Amazingly, they felt rested. The moment they'd finished breakfast, the phone rang. It was Dr. Spencer Roberson:

"Hope I didn't wake you up," Spence said.

"No, we've been up awhile. Already had breakfast. So, exactly where are you now?" Mark asked.

"Vic and I are just now leaving Wolf Island. I'm calling you on my satphone so expect a short delay between parts of our conversation. I've got the weather station stuff squared away, and we should be back at Barbour Landing in about an hour. Just be glad you two didn't come along today. It's pretty rough out here ... even in this 26-footer Vic borrowed from DNR. I'll call you again when we're about 15 minutes from Barbour Landing. Have you got your kite equipment ready for the radar test?"

"No, but I'll have everything ready by the time you get here," Mark replied, amazed at the clarity of the conversation despite the satphone's slight transmission-reception delay.

"See ya soon," Spencer said, then clicked off.

* * *

The couple quickly scurried off to Mark's workshop located between their home and the sandy road that served their rural subdivision. Anne had looked a little puzzled when he'd requested she bring alone a large Ziploc bag and their kitchen food scale.

Once in the shop Mark said, "Honey, please take your scale and little garden trowel, and go out to the road. Scoop up exactly 31 ounces of sand to put in that Ziploc bag."

"Is that going to serve as the 'dummy weight' you plan to put in the camera cradle ... something that's exactly the same weight as that fancy expensive digital camera Dr. Roberson showed us?"

"Exactly," Mark replied. "I have no idea if the sand will show up on radar ... don't know if my kite will lift that much weight, nor do I know if any part of the camera cradle, or the kite, is visible on radar. We'll just have to wait and see."

Anne quickly returned with the required weight of sand. Mark reweighed it: exactly 31 ounces according to the kitchen scale. He then weighed his entire camera cradle with its Olympus film camera installed: 19.9 ounces. "I don't think this is going to work!" he said to Anne. Mark removed the Olympus from the cradle, and stuffed the bag of sand into the cradle's space normally occupied by the little 35mm film camera. The sandbag really didn't fit well, so Mark reached for some duct tape to hold it in place.

"Honey," Anne said, "do you think that silver duct tape may have metal in it ... something that might reflect radar?"

Mark gave her a quick kiss. *Brilliant and sexy ... all in one package!* he thought. "Anne, I honestly don't know, but I'll use paper masking tape instead. Other parts of the cradle have aluminum and carbon-graphite composite, so it might show up anyway, and the sand and tape might not make any difference."

After he'd secured the dummy weight to his satisfaction, he again weighed it. "That's exactly 41.5 ounces," Mark announced.

"So that's 2.59 pounds," Anne instantly replied.

"Are you sure?" Mark, the mathematically impaired one asked. He then reached for a calculator he kept in his shop. "It's actually 2.59375 pounds, smarty," Mark replied, then kissed her again.

"I know," Anne said, "but you being a non-math guy, I just rounded it off in my head to two places. Wanna kiss me again like that?"

"Hell yes! But you and I both know what that could lead to ... and we'd never make it in time to meet Dr. Roberson at the landing."

"How about a raincheck? Good for this evening, after we finish all this stuff?" Anne asked, wearing one of her special grins.

Mark snatched a Post-it note from his workbench top, then quickly scribbled a note: "One raincheck, good for today." He initialed and dated it, then handed it to Anne. She stuffed the note into a hip pocket of jeans that were totally ineffective at concealing her scrumptious curves that had teased his mind for years. Mark sighed, "I think we should go back inside the house—*and sit apart*—and wait for Roberson's call."

Less than five minutes later their phone rang. It was Roberson indicating they were on schedule, and he should arrive at Barbour Landing in about 15 minutes. They quickly placed the kite gear in the Explorer and headed to the refuge. The only other vehicle at the landing was a gray Fish & Wildlife Service truck, a Ford F-150, one Mark knew was used by Dr. Spencer Roberson. In a few minutes they spotted the 26-foot Grady White rounding the river bend south of the landing. Its radar, a Furano unit, was conspicuously mounted to the top of the boat's T-top. Less than a minute later, the Grady White dropped to idle speed as it approached the dock. Except for the area affected by windshield wipers, Mark noted the boat's entire windshield was coated with dry salt spray. *It sure musta been rough as a cob out there,* Mark thought, as he caught a bow line tossed to him by Victor Timmons, then a stern line subsequently tossed by Roberson after he'd stepped away from the helm. Without words, Mark secured both lines, and Spence shut down the boat's twin Yamaha 225s.

"Got everything ready, Doctor?" Spence asked, stepping to the dock and extending his hand first to Mark, then Anne.

"We think so," Mark replied. "But exactly how are we going to do this test? You want me to fly the rig off the dock here, then look for it with your radar?"

"Wind's coming from the southeast," Victor butted in, as he also stepped to the dock. "If you fly it from here, the kite and camera will go northwest over land. Besides, the river bluff here is about 20 feet tall. That would put the boat's radar dome *below* the surface of the ground at the top of the bluff. All you'd see in the direction of the kite would be riverbank itself. We need to be out in the open somewhere, maybe even fly it out of this boat. Have you ever flown your rig out of a boat before?"

"No I haven't, Victor," Mark replied. "But I don't see why that wouldn't work. My electric reel, its 12-volt battery, camera stuff, even my kites rolled up inside PVC storage tubes, are all stowed and secured to a hand truck. It's in the back of our car. It's pretty heavy, mainly due to the battery. I'd need some help getting the hand truck into the boat. We could put it on the aft deck, but we'd need to tie it down somehow to keep it from sliding around. Vic, these kites pull like heck, and the wind's pretty strong today."

Spencer nodded approval of the "fly-from-the-boat" idea. In ten minutes they had Mark's entire rig secured in the rear of the Grady White, and were slowly motoring south downriver. When they came to the spot where Anne and Mark had placed the yellow marker floats, a thought struck Mark: *My floats ... they're gone!*

"Spence! This is where Anne and I placed the marker floats ... and they are now gone!"

Spencer smiled. "They're behind the seat of my pickup that's in the landing parking lot. Oscar Dunham picked 'em up about two o'clock this morning. You'll get 'em back."

"How far downriver are we going?" Anne asked, fearing if they approached Sapelo Sound, the water would start to get rough, and seasickness might well become an issue for her.

"We can anchor right here," Vic said. "This area is open enough for the test."

Anne breathed a sigh of relief, but didn't speak. In just a few minutes, Mark had his 11-foot delta airborne, and had the dummy-weighted camera rig attached at its usual point, 100 feet downline from the kite. To Mark's amazement—despite the added weight—the kite flew perfectly. He handed Anne his anemometer. "Says it's 12.5 mph," Anne reported. Mark mentally filed the information away: *With a 12.5 miles per hour wind, this kite can lift 2.5 pounds with ease.*

Over the next hour Mark and Anne continually listened to Vic and Spence jabbering about "megahertz this" and "megahertz that." They constantly tweaked knobs on the radar's controls. Mark adjusted the kite and camera cradle's altitude and distance from the boat as instructed. When the officers started discussing the radar's "X-band" and "S-band," Mark and Anne felt they may well have been eavesdropping on a conversation in a foreign language.

Spencer pulled out his satphone, and walked to the bow of the boat to have a private conversation. He talked to someone about five minutes, then returned aft to give Mark and Anne the news: "The radar units on the West Coast SSs are, we think, identical to the Furano radar we've got aboard this boat. Same model number. Same adjustable modes. Plus their SSs have no way of raising their dome as high as the one mounted on this boat. Also, from the digitally enhanced versions of your original pictures, we can make out the word 'Furano' on one of the domes. So, bottom line, in the Furano's X-band mode, there is so much clutter they'd never pick out the kite rig amid the other 'noise' being displayed on the screen ... and in S-band they'd never see it at all!'"

Mark smiled, mainly because he knew Dr. Spencer Roberson was elated ... excited about having a possible way to spot SSs without them spotting him first. Mark had mixed thoughts: *I bet I'll be flying kites for hours ... over any stretch of water where new unnumbered crab floats appear. God, I hope Anne doesn't forget about that raincheck. I need to get my mind on something else for awhile.*

Vic pulled anchor, and Spence started the engines. Thunder in the distance let Mark know a storm could be approaching. The Grady White's marine radio warned of a large slow-moving weather front slowly approaching from the southeast, and was currently located about 12 miles from their own position. Spence moved back upriver at idle speed toward the dock. As they slowly motored along, Mark retrieved his kite rig using the electric reel. In five minutes he had all his gear aboard and stowed. In another few minutes, the boat was secured to the dock at the landing, and Mark's gear placed back inside the rear of the Explorer. Anne had already retreated to the passenger seat of their car to "fix" her hair that had been seriously windblown asunder. Victor stayed with the boat, indicating he'd remain aboard, and return it to whomever he'd borrowed it from at DNR ... "I'll take it back when I see what this weather is gonna do," Vic had explained.

"Thanks for all your help today," Spence said, approaching his truck in the parking lot. With a smile he reached behind the truck's seat, then handed Mark the two yellow floats Oscar had faithfully retrieved during the night. "I think these belong to you. And I think we learned a good bit today. Don't you?"

"Well, yeah. First, it seems the kite and camera won't be visible on radar, at least the type radar they're apparently using. I learned that a boat is a good platform to fly from. It doesn't make any difference which way the wind blows. In this area you can always position the boat so the camera will be over almost any target area you choose. But it's gonna be a two-man job, Spence. You'd need one man to drive the boat, another to fly the kite and control the camera."

"Doc, that same thought struck me, too. How'd you feel about teaming up with Oscar Dunham? Let Oscar drive his boat to position it as needed ... and you fly out of it?"

Mark paused a full moment in thought: *I think I recall Spence saying Oscar was the one most likely to contact the criminal element one-on-one … and I'm now going to team up with Oscar?* Spence cleared his throat, apparently to remind Mark to answer his question. "Uh, Spence, didn't you say earlier you thought Oscar was the one most likely to have a face-to-face confrontation with the drug folks?"

Spence paused, apparently choosing his words very carefully. "Yes, I did say that. But I don't think that is likely while you are aboard his boat. I think the real danger of a confrontation is when Oscar is alone, and he's either removing contraband from traps, or when he's putting it back after my testing and chemical marking of the material. Oscar does that *only* at night, usually between midnight and two o'clock in the morning. Under no circumstances would I suggest you be out on the water with Oscar at night. And unless there's a front moving through, there is usually not enough wind to fly your kite at night. Remember Oscar is armed, shoots quite well, and has a satphone. All I'm asking at this point is that you *think* about it."

"OK. At home tonight I'll think about working with Oscar. I'll let you know something tomorrow. I'll still help you with your bird photos at Woody Pond, no matter what. And I'll still agree to do Roberto's surgery to remove his birthmark, provided I can do it without breaking the law." Mark explained.

"Which reminds me," Spence said, "have you got that list of the surgical stuff you'll need for Roberto's surgery?"

"No, not yet. I'll try to do that tonight, too. Or tomorrow. Has that guy from the U.S. Marshals Service picked out a place to do the surgery yet?" Mark asked.

"He's still working on it. You're not afraid of helicopters, are you?" Spence asked.

"No. Not in good weather with an experienced pilot," Mark replied. "Flew in a bunch of 'em myself when I was in the Air Force … and Anne has flown on Life Flight choppers several times. She's not afraid of 'em."

"Good," Spence said. "I'd guess the Marshals Service will probably recommend using a chopper to take you two to a place that's in international waters."

"Spence, you know you're sure keeping an older retired surgeon very busy!"

Dr. Roberson chuckled, made no reply, just smiled as he started his truck and drove off.

* * *

It started misting as the Telfairs prepared to leave the refuge for their short drive back to Dunham. Anne had "repaired" her hair in the car while Spence and Mark had chatted briefly in the parking lot.

"Seems to me we learned a lot today," Anne said, glancing over at Mark as he eased into the driver's seat of their car.

"Well, it seems to me I've now got more questions than answers," Mark replied.

Anne pondered a moment. "Like what?"

"I *still* feel like we've got only fragments of the whole picture. Granted, we learned it's easy to fly out of a boat and position the camera over a target. We also learned that my kite rig is difficult—if not impossible—to detect on the SS's radar. But how do the smugglers do the actual transfer? How do the local drug distributors pick the stuff up? How do the SSs put the drugs into the crab traps without being spotted? How often do they do pickups and deliveries ... and on what schedule, if any? What are my chances of ever getting another photograph of an SS again?"

"I see what you mean, Mark. I think your catching those SSs on film that first time is a one-time stroke of luck. Maybe we should just forget about all this stuff ... at least for today. Let's just go home, have a martini or two, fix dinner, and retire early. Tomorrow *is* another day, you know."

Mark smiled in thought: *We're obviously at the leading edge of this weather front that's coming our way. Hope it moves slowly, and it rains all night ... and we can leave the bedroom windows open, and listen to rain ... while we use that raincheck.*

And they did.

16

MORE DECISIONS

At seven the next morning the sun was already up. Neither Mark nor Anne knew exactly when the rain had stopped, but knew they felt refreshed when they awoke. Still in bed, Anne turned toward Mark and was first to speak. "Little Man, in a way yesterday was fun … especially last night, during that delightful rain."

"Yeah, *especially* that!" Mark replied. "But today it looks like we've got to make some more decisions, and get back to things less fun."

"Such as?" Anne asked, getting out of bed and stretching.

"Decisions," Mark answered.

"Such as?" Anne again prodded.

"I need to decide on that list of the surgical supplies we'll need to remove Roberto's birthmark. But that's no big deal. That won't take long, maybe ten minutes at most. Yesterday I think you were already in the car fixing your hair when Dr. Roberson discussed the possibility of us teaming up with Oscar."

"Teaming up? Like how, Mark?"

"We'd use Oscar's boat to fly kites from. I expressed my reservations about perhaps placing us closer to the drug folks, but Roberson downplayed the risk. I told him I'd have to think about it overnight."

"Well?" Anne asked. "What do you think?"

"I'd certainly feel like a chickenshit if I don't do it. Spence said it would be only in the daytime, and he thinks the actual drug transfers occur at night. Plus, I'd be a good distance away … in Oscar's boat, at the end of the kite line. Up to 1,000 feet away, in fact. And, push come to shove, Oscar's boat can certainly outrun an SS."

"Well," Anne replied, "if old Oscar has the guts to get that close to the bad guys, maybe you and I should have the courage to get a little closer."

Mark sat on the edge of the bed and reached for his wallet resting on a nightstand at his bedside. He removed Mr. Saint Christopher, then flipped it so he'd 'land' on their bed. It did: *faceup,* meaning a "yes."

"Are you just getting a 'second opinion' about us working with Oscar?" Anne asked, now laughing.

Mark began laughing, too, but finally spoke: "Never hurts to check. You fix breakfast, and I'll start making out the list of the surgical stuff we'll need. After we eat, I'll call Dr. Roberson and tell him we've definitely decided to work with Oscar."

"Sounds like a plan, Doctor," Anne said, putting on her bathrobe while heading for their kitchen.

Immediately following breakfast, Mark called the Harris Neck National Wildlife Refuge office. The secretary indicated Dr. Roberson was available only by radio at the moment, and she'd contact him and have him return the call.

After removing the camera cradle from the gear stowed in their Explorer, he took the rig to his workshop. There, he removed the sand-containing Ziploc from the cradle, and began thinking about the best way to modify the cradle for a different camera. *I really need to have Spence's camera in hand before I can figure out exactly what to do,* he finally thought.

"Mark," Anne said, bursting into the shop, "it's Dr. Roberson. He's on the phone right now! Quit messing with that camera stuff. Come inside and talk to him."

"Hello," Mark said, accepting the phone handed him by Anne.

"Hi, Dr. Telfair. It's me, Spence. You called?"

"Yeah. Anne and I have definitely decided to work with Oscar … fly out of his boat."

"That's great!" Spencer replied. "But there are still a lot of details to work out. I think you, me, Anne, and Oscar all need to have a meeting—a 'strategy session'—for lack of a better term. Roberto Gonzales will definitely *not* be there, nor a U.S. Marshal. Please remember Oscar does not know about Roberto, so don't even mention that name when Oscar is present. Witness Protection has very strict rules."

"I think Anne and I understand that. But when do you want to meet with us?" Mark asked.

"I wish I could do it today, but I can't. But how about very early tomorrow?"

"Sure, Spence. What time, and where?" Mark asked.

"Five o'clock tomorrow morning at the refuge office. Is that too early for you folks?"

"No. We'll be there," Mark said. "Spence, is there any way I could get my hands on that fancy camera of yours today? I need to have it in hand before I modify my current camera cradle to carry it. And I'll need the camera's instruction manual, too."

"No problem. It's all in the safe at the refuge office. I'll personally deliver it to you at your home in about an hour. That OK?"

"Sure, but do you know exactly where I live?" Mark asked.

"Certainly! Our background folks do excellent work. In fact I probably know more about you than you know about yourself," Spence replied, laughing as he clicked off.

Anne stood silently by as Mark paused a long moment holding the phone while thinking: *I know Roberson is using his satphone ... wherever he is at the moment. The conversation delays are a dead giveaway. But he can't be too far away if he's going to be here in an hour. Why such security about the simple conversation we just had? Why didn't he just use a regular phone?*

Anne cleared her throat. "Mark, are you just gonna stand here in this kitchen holding the darn phone ... or are you going to tell me what Dr. Roberson said?"

"Uh ... Sorry, Anne. It looks like Spence is stuck in fast forward! He wants to have a 'strategy session' meeting early tomorrow morning—just you, me, him, and Oscar—at five o'clock tomorrow morning in the refuge office. And he says he's gonna come to our house in about an hour to bring me his camera, that fancy one he showed us earlier."

"Wow!" Anne exclaimed. "His sense of urgency does seem a little weird."

"And the *secrecy* ... that's what caught my attention. Spence was on his satphone, yet he's apparently somewhere nearby," Mark explained. "Oh well, guess I better finish getting that list of surgical equipment together. He'll probably be wanting that also, by the time he gets here!"

Mark had just finished the list of surgical items needed for Roberto's surgery when he heard a vehicle drive up. It was Dr. Spencer Roberson, driving a silver four-door Nissan Altima. Mark stepped outside to greet him. Dressed in business casual clothes, Spence quickly got out to greet Mark. "Camera stuff's in the trunk. I brought all the accessories that go with that camera ... owner's manual, charger for its batteries, and a USB cable that allows you to connect it to your computer."

"Thanks, Spence. I must say you look like a civilian today," Mark casually remarked.

"No, I'm still with U.S. Fish & Wildlife, undercover DEA. I went home to change clothes and vehicles before coming to your house. I don't want to take any chances that the local bad guys, or your neighbors, will see me at your home in a government vehicle ... or as a government officer in any capacity."

Spence quickly opened the trunk and handed Mark a box containing the camera gear. "See ya tomorrow morning at five." Spence promptly got back in his car and immediately started to leave.

"Hey! Wait a minute, Spence! I've got the list of surgical stuff we'll need for the surgery. It's inside the house. I'll get it for you."

"Just bring it with you tomorrow morning. Gotta go now!" Spence said, immediately driving off, churning the white lime rock gravel in Mark's driveway as he vanished.

Talk about brief visits ... I think I just had one! Mark thought, still standing in the drive, holding a box filled with expensive camera gear.

He hurried to the house and showed Anne the items delivered by Roberson, then told her he'd be in his workshop. As instructed by the manual, he plugged in the camera's charger, then placed the camera in the charger's base while he began reading the rest of the complex instructions. For some reason the instructions indicated the camera should always be turned off while charging; otherwise, damage to the camera could occur. As he read the manual further, he learned the camera was made by a British company, Structure Diagnostic Solutions Ltd. *Never heard of it,* he thought. "SDS 6500" was the only manufacturer's logo he could find on the camera body. Unlike Anne's little point-and-shoot digital camera, he soon learned the SDS 6500 had no "memory card" at all, nor did it have an LCD display. Instead, it had only an optical viewfinder, but had an unbelievable one-gigabyte built-in "internal memory" that could be uploaded to view on a computer screen. A number of the camera's buttons and knobs were labeled and self-explanatory; others had abbreviations and icons he did not yet understand.

After a couple of hours of reading instructions, and a brief trip back to the house for a little Internet research, he finally developed a fairly clear understanding of how the camera operated: Basically it was a "normal" five-megapixel digital camera that had an internal filter that permitted it to be used as an infrared (IR) camera as well. A slide switch on the camera body allowed selection of either standard (STD) or infrared (IR) modes, and the operator could alternate between those two modes during the same shooting session. In addition to being "water-resistant," it also had a fully adjustable time-release shutter capability. This allowed the camera to be set to continuously shoot pictures at intervals from one second apart, up to two hours apart. Once set, and the shutter button pushed one time, it would keep shooting until the internal battery was depleted, or the internal memory completely filled. The manual indicated a fully charged battery should allow about two hours of continuous operation.

Upon return to the shop, LEDs on the charger indicated the camera's battery was fully charged. He removed the camera from the charger and made a number of test shots inside his shop. He switched between STD and IR modes as he made them. *Now I know why Dr. Roberson seemed so interested in this particular camera,* Mark thought, while walking back to the house, carefully carrying the camera and the cable needed to connect it to his computer.

"Lunch is ready," Anne announced the minute he stepped inside the house.

"Can't lunch wait a minute? I want to look at some pictures before I eat. They're some test-shots I made with Roberson's camera. You can't view them on the camera itself. His camera has no screen, so it has to be connected to a computer to see the images. Interested in looking with me?"

"Sure! All I fixed us is two chef salads. I'll put them in the fridge."

Moments later they were in the loft staring at thumbnails of the dozen test-shots displayed on Mark's computer screen. "Yuck!" Anne said when she saw the first IR image displayed full size. "Looks like artwork done by someone on an LSD trip! The regular pictures look normal … just like ones I take with my own little digital camera."

"I agree," Mark replied. "But just look at how even a slight temperature difference changes the object's color: black is cold; blue hues are warmer; purple tones slightly warmer still; orange shades even more warm; yellow is hot, and white is even hotter still," Mark explained.

"So is that why the red iron vise on your workbench, looks black, the wood of the workbench top is in shades of blue and purple, and why the fluorescent lights over the bench look a yellowish-white?" she asked.

"Exactly. That transformer that charges my cordless drill appears orange, indicating that it is warmer than the wood of the workbench top, and that's why the cool concrete floor of this shop looks black, the same color as the iron vise."

"Neat stuff, I'll admit," Anne said. "You want me to take *your* picture with Roberson's camera ... so I can see where *your* 'hot spots' are, Little Man?"

Mark burst out laughing, then said, "No! That would be redundant. You *already* know exactly where my 'hot spots' are ... and you've known about 'em for years!"

* * *

Following his chef-salad lunch, Mark returned to his shop to face an additional task: adapting his current camera cradle to carry Roberson's camera aloft. Most of the conversion went smoothly, with one exception: switching the camera's mode between STD and IR while airborne. *Shit, I'm stumped,* he thought some four hours later. Frustrated, he went to the house for some iced tea.

"Got if figured out yet?" Anne asked.

"No!" Mark growled.

"Mind if I look at it?"

"Be my guest, Anne. I've mounted an additional servo but I can't figure out how to connect it to the damn STD/IR slide switch. I definitely want to be able to change modes when it's in the air."

Anne poured two large glasses of iced tea which they both carried to the shop. Mark showed her the problem. Using the tip of her index finger, Anne activated the slide switch several times. "Sure slides easily. With your radio on the ground, you can cause the arm on that little 'gizmo' [servo] to move side-to-side ... either left or right, correct?"

"Yeah. But I already know all that, Anne! The problem is the slide switch has such a low profile on the camera body. I can't figure any way to connect to it without first gluing some 'projection' onto the switch. And I'm not about to do that with someone else's $10,000 camera!"

"Why connect anything to it? Why not just cover the hard plastic on that gizmo's arm with soft rubber of some kind ... something that would simulate a soft fingertip pressed up against the slide switch ... and then let the gizmo move it either way, right or left?"

I've been searching for the answer for over four hours ... and she comes in here and solves the problem in less than four minutes! he thought, feeling like a mental midget. Visibly chagrined, Mark

120

searched through odds and ends in his shop, and finally found some soft rubber tubing of appropriate diameter. He cut a short segment, and slipped it over the servo's plastic arm leaving just enough length protruding that would allow only soft rubber to press against the slide switch. He turned on the battery power to the cradle's radio receiver and transmitter. Using controls on the radio transmitter, he cycled the slide switch between "STD" and "IR" modes a dozen times or more. It worked perfectly!

"Do I get a prize?" Anne giggled.

"You bet! But maybe not tonight. Remember we've got a meeting with Dr. Roberson and Oscar beginning at five in the morning."

"That's OK, Little Man ... I'm still running on yesterday's 'raincheck.'"

17

FLYING WITH OSCAR

After their supper, Anne retired early and was now sleeping soundly. Mark, still awake, was 'tweaking' things in his workshop. He yawned. Checking his watch, he discovered it was well after midnight. *I'm just wasting my time,* he thought as he obsessively checked, and rechecked, all his gear. He'd put fresh AA alkaline batteries in the cradle's radio receiver, as well as the handheld radio transmitter he used on the ground to control the camera while in the air. He'd even recharged the SDS 6500's internal battery, though it probably didn't need it. *Gear-wise, I'm as ready as I'll ever be,* he finally thought, while placing the equipment back in the Explorer. Finally, he locked their car, something neither he nor Anne routinely did at home.

Their master bathroom connected directly to their master bedroom. Only a louvered door separated the two rooms. Mark elected to shower in the guest bath so he wouldn't disturb Anne's sleep. He eased into bed around 1:00 a.m. without awakening her. Knowing the alarm would sound at 4:00 a.m., he tried his best to fall asleep quickly. Defeating his efforts at sleep were thoughts; each kept tumbling in his mind. He finally eased out of bed and fixed himself a stiff martini in their kitchen. Mark drank it quickly, and returned to bed. Sleep ultimately came.

The alarm faithfully signaled at four. Grudgingly, he shut it off. "Good morning my Little Man," Anne said cheerfully, reaching over and touching his leg with her foot.

"What's so good about it?" Mark asked, wishing he could just turn over and go back to sleep. "It's just another day … and another damn meeting with Roberson. That guy seems to 'run on meetings' … and little or no sleep!"

Anne realized Mark was in a sour mood. She knew her husband got that way when he was frustrated, but felt it best to let him vent his frustration during the meeting they'd soon be having with Dr.

Roberson.

Following a quick breakfast, the Telfairs arrived at the refuge office a few minutes early. Dr. Roberson's truck was already there. Walking past it, Mark, for no particular reason, touched the hood of Spencer's vehicle; it was cool. *He's been here awhile,* Mark thought. Oscar arrived in his old Chevy truck moments later, its loud rusted-out muffler a now-familiar sound to Mark's ears. They attempted to enter the front office door, but found it locked. Oscar knocked loudly on the door several times. In stocking feet, Dr. Roberson finally unlocked the door from the inside, and invited them in. "Sorry I locked you guys out. The secretary doesn't come in till eight, and I was catching a catnap on a sofa in the back."

"Is our meeting still on?" Mark asked.

"You bet!" Spence said, sounding more chipper than he looked. "I'll go put on a pot of coffee while you guys settle in the conference room."

Mark, Anne, and Oscar walked down the short hall to the conference room, finding it completely dark. "I knows e'zakly where dem light switches is at," Oscar volunteered, entering the dark room and turning on two rows of bright fluorescent fixtures recessed into the conference room's ceiling. Mark noted an empty coffee cup and a facedown legal pad resting on one end of the conference table. *No tape recorder this time,* Mark noted. Spence soon appeared with a tray bearing a pot of coffee and four cups. He placed everything in the center of the table and said, "Help yourselves ... if you like it black. Seems Fish & Wildlife is too stingy to provide cream and sugar!"

Everyone chuckled and helped themselves to coffee. In the bright light, Mark noted Dr. Roberson had his weapon holstered at his side. His uniform was a little wrinkled, the whites of his dark brown eyes reddened, perhaps from sleep depravation. Dark beard stubble indicated he'd not yet shaved for the day.

"OK," Roberson began, seeming a bit more perky now. "It looks like we're *finally* getting ready to start *doing* something, rather than just *talking* about it. I've already talked to Oscar about using his boat for kite flying. Mark, you've agreed to fly the camera stuff from Oscar's boat. Correct?"

Both Mark and Oscar nodded an affirmative. Roberson continued: "I've spent hours thinking about what our ultimate objective should be." Roberson reached for the legal pad, and flipped it faceup on the table. Reading from his own handwriting on the pad he said, *"Capture one or more of the SSs and its live crew."*

Silence dominated the conference room for a period seeming longer than a freight train. Mark finally said, "Spence, I don't think you're being realistic."

"How so?" Spence responded.

"Well," Mark replied, "to do that, we've got to know *exactly* where they are, and when they'll be there. We need to know their schedule."

Spence smiled. "We're on the same page, Doctor. On this pad I've also written both 'location' and 'schedule' as essential steps beneath my ultimate 'capture boat and crew' objective. I've also written 'establish heat signature.'"

Mark shook his head. "Spence, I still think all this is a total shot-in-the-dark ... a one-in-a-million chance we'll ever photograph another SS again."

"You never knows, till you tries," Oscar piped in.

Then Spence spoke: "Doctor, let me ask you a question. Did you ever give up on a patient that had a more-than-likely fatal illness or injury? Did you ever give up because you knew the odds were very highly stacked against you and your patient at the very outset? Like, maybe those patients with only a one-in-a-million chance you could save them?"

Mark blushed, while Anne spoke defensively. "Dr. Roberson, Mark is definitely not a quitter! He's like a little bulldog. He won't turn anything loose until he's positive the fight is lost or won. We trained together at Grady Hospital in Atlanta, and we often worked against a low probability of a patient's salvage. We worked many years together in private surgical practice in Statesville, Georgia ... and not *once* ... not even a single time, have I ever known him to give up, even when working against very long odds."

"OK, OK, OK!" Mark finally blurted. "When and where do we get started?"

Oscar smiled and spoke: "'Bout ten o'clock dis mornin', Doctor. Ain't gonna be no wind till 'bout dat time. An' we's got two pieces of the Barbour what's got new traps ... an' ain't none of 'em got no num'ers on they floats! Found 'em late yesterday, an' they's still empty rat now ... least they wuz 'round two dis mornin'."

"Oscar," Roberson asked, "do you mean you think nobody has put any drugs in them yet?"

"Dat's my meaning, sir," Oscar replied. "So maybe we kin get lucky, get a pitcher of 'em while they's puttin' they stuff in 'em."

Roberson next asked Mark a number of questions regarding the camera. "Where is the camera I brought to you yesterday?"

"It's in the back of our car out front," Mark replied.

Roberson frowned. "Doc, is your car locked?"

"No."

"Well go lock it. Or, better yet, bring it in here if you don't mind."

Mark made a quick trip to the Explorer, and returned with his radio transmitter and the expensive SDS 6500 installed in the modified cradle. Walking back to the office he felt his shirt pocket to be sure he also had the envelope with the list of surgical instruments needed for Roberto's surgery. *Somehow, I've got to get this instrument list to Roberson without Oscar's knowing about it,* he thought. *I assume Roberson still wants Oscar to be kept in the dark about Roberto Gonzales.*

When Mark returned to the conference room, Oscar was standing, obviously preparing to leave. He quickly explained to Mark: "Doctor, I needs to run my own traps an' get 'em baited back up befo' we gets started today. So I'll meetcha at my boat, 'round ten."

Mark checked his watch to discover it was only 5:45.

After Oscar left, Roberson smiled while shaking his head. "That old Oscar is 82. He's still sharp as a tack. I really don't know how he works as hard as he does."

"Doesn't his work for you hurt him financially? Mark asked. "I know he certainly must burn a lot of extra fuel just doing stuff for you guys."

"Doctor, we try to take good care of Oscar. I already told you we took him to Atlanta to work with our DEA cartographer for a couple of months. What I haven't told you, is that during that same time we also arranged to have Oscar's prostate cancer treated by a renowned specialist at Emory University Hospital. The urologist thinks his prognosis is excellent."

"Is the urologist's name one I'd recognize?" Mark asked.

"In all probability. He was there while you were in training in Atlanta. But I'm not going to disclose any further details ... like I wouldn't disclose to Oscar any of the background details we know about you and Anne. In fact, I probably shouldn't have even mentioned Oscar's health issues to you folks."

"Well, I really don't have a need to know. Just curious, Spence," Mark said. "But what about all the gas he burns running up and down rivers just looking for stuff?"

"We permit him to use fuel from the refuge's own storage tanks," Spence explained. "And by using 'informant funds' from DEA, we compensate him well enough to make up for his loss of time and revenue from his crabbing and oystering business. I think Oscar would help us even if he didn't get a dime. I think he's just that committed to keeping our area's communities safe, peaceful, and crime free. Oscar has seen firsthand what drugs have done to several communities … not so much his own local black community here on Harris Neck, but those located nearby, like over in Crescent and Jones."

"Spence, you don't need to convince me further. I'm looking forward to working with Oscar. I think I can speak for my wife, too," Mark stated, as Anne nodded agreement. "But let's get back to the camera."

"Mark, you've read the manual. I haven't. I'm sure you understand that camera far better than I do. So why don't you explain how you think we should use it," Spence said, pointing at the complete rig now resting on the conference table.

Mark began: "I've done a little Internet research on this camera. It's made by a British company, 'Structure Diagnostic Solutions,' and was originally developed to evaluate heat changes in various structures, including buildings and bridges."

"The guy at DEA who got it for me told me it was actually an 'industrial camera,' one used because it had good infrared capture capability. So, Doc, have you made any test shots with it yet?"

"Just a few in my shop. Anne and I've looked at them on my computer at home, and it seems to do a very good job of detecting even subtle temperature differences."

Dr. Roberson paused, thinking a moment before speaking. "I'm sure there's nothing in your shop that we'd classify as 'sensitive information' … but when you take surveillance pictures over the river, and then look at them, please be sure your computer is not connected to the Internet. Specifically, don't ever store the images on the hard drive in your own computer at home. Just transfer them to disk, and we'll store them in the fireproof safe here at the office. That way we don't have to worry about loss in a fire, or the images flying off into cyber space and getting into the wrong hands."

God, Roberson seems almost paranoid about information leaking out … but maybe there's a reason for his caution, Mark thought.

"Spence, getting back to the camera, and what I think we should do, let me first explain this: I can set up the camera to automatically shoot images at intervals. As a starting point, I'd recommend 30-second intervals. I also recommend we begin by alternating the image mode … do it every 30 seconds, alternating between the camera's standard and infrared modes," Mark said.

"I'm not sure I follow," Roberson said, yawning.

"Shoot first a standard ... then infrared ... standard ... infrared ... standard ... infrared ... and so on. Do that the whole time the camera is airborne. You can thank Anne for giving me the idea of how to connect a servo to the camera's mode switch, permitting mode changes on the fly." Anne smiled, but remained silent. "All images would be taken about 30 seconds apart. That would let us first know what the human eye could see, and then what the infrared sees ... all in a near-simultaneous time frame. Didn't you earlier tell me you were interested in knowing if the SSs had a 'heat signature'? I think that's what you called it."

"Yes, I did say that ... and that our tests on the West Coast were lousy. So, let's start by doing exactly what you suggest. I'll let you, Oscar, and Anne have at it for the rest of today. I'm bushed, and need to get some more sleep."

"Spence," Mark said, "I know you're tired. But since Oscar is not here, let me give you this list of things we'll need for Roberto's surgery. How are plans for that coming along?"

"I spoke at length with the U.S. Marshals Service last night. They've got some firm plans for about two weeks from now. I'll give you details later. I'll have all the surgical stuff you need by then."

* * *

Driving back to Dunham, Anne indicated she'd let Oscar and Mark work alone today. Mark glanced at his watch. "It's going to be several hours before it's time to meet Oscar at his boat. You sure you don't want to go with us?"

"Not today, Mark. I really need to do some washing and ironing, make a grocery list, and do other not-so-fun stuff around the house today."

"Well, OK. That would give us a little more working room in Oscar's boat. I sure hope he's got most of the 'junk' out of his skiff. Those crab traps and oyster boxes take up a lot of room."

Anne began her housework as soon as they got home; Mark fiddled with camera gear, checked the charge of his electric reel's battery, mostly killing time before meeting with Oscar. At 9:45 he gave Anne a quick kiss good-by while she was running their vacuum cleaner. She paused, went to the fridge and withdrew a brown paper sack. "Lunch," she explained, as Mark left to drive back to the refuge landing. When he arrived, Oscar was already there, moving extra oyster boxes and traps to the dock.

When the old waterman spotted Mark, he waved and said, "I's 'bout ready, now. Is you?"

"Reckon so, Oscar. You want me to roll my cart down to the dock now?"

"Yes, suh. I'll hep you get hit over into th' boat."

Effortlessly, gear was placed in the boat aft the small center console. Oscar started the four-stroke Honda 90. It was barely audible at idle speed. Mark scanned the bare essentials that remained in the topless 24-foot workboat: two anchors and lines; four six-gallon fuel cans; a small canvas duffel stuffed beneath the console on a shelf; a wooden paddle; a gaff hook; twin 12-volt marine batteries, and a canvas-hooded square 'something' mounted to the top of the small center console.

"Where should we go first, Oscar?" Mark asked.

"Tide, she be full in now. We goin' upriver first. They's six new traps, 'bout three mile up, and they ain't got no num'ers on 'em."

Mark cast lines and Oscar eased the throttle forward. The boat easily planed at about one-quarter throttle. *A 90-horse motor planing a 24-foot boat at quarter-throttle? Unbelievable! Must be the flat bottom,* Mark thought.

In a few minutes, the connecting side creeks became unfamiliar sights to Mark's eyes. He quickly realized he'd never been that far up the Barbour River before. He stood beside Oscar because the boat had no seating. Asking questions, Mark realized how easy it was to have a conversation over the sound of the exceptionally quiet engine.

"How much farther?" Mark asked.

"Two mo' bends, then th' new traps. We gonna go rat past 'em, then fly back dis away. Wind she be northeast today and she'll blow yo kite rat back over 'em."

Mark was amazed at Oscar's ability to grasp the whole concept of positioning the kite for aerial photography. *At the dock, I didn't even pay attention to which way the wind was blowing ... but Oscar surely had!* Mark thought.

They passed the six new numberless traps without slowing down. They were all in a straight line, set about 100 feet apart, and in the middle of the Barbour River that was only about 30 yards wide at that point. Oscar chuckled loudly when they passed them.

"What's so funny, Oscar?"

"You kin sho tell 'em fellas ain't no crabbers!"

"Why? How can you tell that?" Mark asked, puzzled.

"They's a san'bar rat out in th' middle where they's got 'em at. Dem traps be high and dry when th' tide go out ... an' all th' crabs die, warm as hit still is."

When they were 300 yards upriver beyond the traps, Oscar came to a stop and instructed Mark to put out the bow anchor.

"Reckon it's time to do your stuff, Doctor," Oscar said.

In less than five minutes Mark had the camera in the air and positioned so it would be over the line of traps in the river. Using his radio transmitter, he tilted the camera to look straight down, then fired the shutter that would start the automatic 30-second time-lapse sequence of taking pictures. All he had to do was remember to flip the transmitter's control every thirty seconds to alternate the camera's mode.

"Oscar," Mark said, "that's about as perfect as we can get it. Guess I'll just stand here flipping this darn transmitter switch for the next couple of hours while the camera does its thing."

"Well, I ain't got nothin' else I's gotta do rat now. You gets tired of flippin' dat switch, I'll flip it for awhile. But we is gonna have to move the boat over rat nex' to th' bank, in 'bout a hour. Wind, she be comin' northeast now, but she gonna move to straight north when th' tide gets a runnin'. Gotta do dat if you wants to keep yo camera straight over dem traps."

"Oscar, how are you so sure that's gonna happen? I'm talking about the wind direction?"

The old fella said nothing at first. He removed the canvas hood that covered something on the top of the console. A marine compass and radio were revealed. Oscar pointed at the compass and said, "Rat now we's got th' boat pointed dead into th' wind. That be dead northeast, right? But when th' tide gets a running, hit pull dat wind out th' north with it. Jus' wait an' see if old Oscar ain't right."

I guess Oscar got his degree in meteorology from the School of Experience, Mark thought, fully dubious that Oscar was correct.

"OK," Mark smiled, staring at the compass, and still flipping the transmitter switch about every 30 seconds. "We'll just wait and see, Oscar."

"Dat's right. Jus' wait. Now when th' wind she move more north, we ain't gonna be line up perfect, lak we is now."

"So you're saying we're going to have to move toward the westerly bank of the river to keep it all aligned?"

"Lawdy! I knowed you was smart, first time I seen you flyin' dat camera. Anyway, my lunch be a showing up rat over there ... e'zakly where we needs to go when th' wind move over."

"Your *lunch* will be showing up?" Mark asked, in complete puzzlement.

"Oysters. Some of th' best you ever did see!" Oscar explained. "Dat's what I always eats for lunch when I be on th' water way up here."

"Aren't you afraid of eating them raw? Don't you worry about contamination when the water is still this warm?"

"Naw suh. Ain't no 'tamination way up here. Safe year 'round. You wants me to flip dat thing for awhile?"

"Have at it," Mark said, handing the radio transmitter to Oscar, and showing him exactly which control to "flip." Mark took off his digital watch and placed it atop the console so Oscar could keep up with the time. *What in the hell was I thinking when I came up with this mode-change idea? That's 120 flips per hour. There's gotta be some way to automate this process,* he thought.

Taking a breather, Mark reclined on the boat's small foredeck, just watching the kite, camera, and Oscar. *What a way to spend a day. We've not even seen another boat today ... utterly peaceful,* he thought, and briefly closed his eyes.

Then it happened: *WHOOSH!*

The noise had startled him, perhaps more so than the cool salty spray that settled on his face.

Oscar screamed, "Go on now! Git! Git away from here, Nosy!"

"Who are you yelling at, Oscar?"

"Dat big ol' fat rascal dolphin! I calls him 'Nosy,' 'cause you can't put nothin' in th' water without his a messin' with hit. He nose be all scratched up from messin' with stuff."

"*Messing with stuff?* Like how, Oscar?"

"Here, you hold this radio thing and flip it for awhile ... an' I'll show you e'zakly what I means."

Mark accepted the transmitter and took over the "flipping." Oscar picked up the wooden paddle and bumped it several times on the floor of his boat. *WHOOSH!* Nosy exhaled alongside, then poked his head well out of the water, and squeaked loudly at Oscar. The squeaks were high-pitched and coupled. *Almost sounds like he's actually laughing at Oscar,* Mark thought. "Go on now! Git! Ain't got no food for you today ... and quit messin' with my traps!" Oscar demanded, and extended the paddle toward Nosy. The dolphin grabbed it in his mouth, shook his head side to side, and tried to pull it from Oscar's strong hands. When the largest dolphin Mark had ever seen decided he couldn't win the tug of war with Oscar, he finally released the paddle, "laughed" again and headed downriver toward the string of traps Mark was hoping to photograph. *Perfect!* Mark thought. *Maybe I'll see what a dolphin's exhalations look like in an infrared image.*

Oscar placed the paddle back on the floor, placed his hands on his hips and said, "That sorry rascal. He bend up most of my traps tryin' to steal th' bait out. For awhile, I even tried feedin' him, hopin' he'd leave my bait an' traps alone. Only made it worser. Now I think he know th' sound of my boat motor, and he follow me. An' if I stops anywhere 'round here, he'll finally show up, an' jus' go to beggin' lak dat."

True to Oscar's prediction, the wind began to shift to a more northerly direction as the outgoing tide accelerated. Oscar's "lunch oysters" soon appeared as the tide receded. They moved the boat next to the exposed oyster bed, re-anchored, and maintained good camera position over the string of traps. The old man deftly put on work gloves removed from his canvas duffel. Next, he removed a recycled two-liter soda bottle he used as his freshwater canteen. Using only his pocket knife, the old fella expertly shucked a dozen, swallowing them whole in a matter of minutes. "Bes' lunch in dis Lawd's world," Oscar allowed.

Mark again passed the transmitter to Oscar, and started thinking about his own lunch. He opened the brown paper sack Anne had packed as his lunch: baloney and cheese sandwich on rye bread, a banana, and a small can of V-8 juice. "You may be smart, Doctor, but you sho eats funny stuff. Jus' eats stuff what come out de water, or grows in th' ground ... you'll live a heap longer!" Oscar exclaimed, then laughed, as Mark devoured his lunch.

Mark glanced at his large-numbered digital watch on the top of the console. The camera had been in the air for two hours now, and its battery should be depleted. "Time to bring it down, Oscar."

Mark flipped on the electric reel and it began whirring, quickly retrieving the camera and kite. When everything was back in the boat, Oscar pulled anchor and they headed back to Barbour Landing. After they'd tied up, Oscar said "They's mo' new traps downriver. Is we gonna look at 'em today?"

"I don't think so, Oscar. I need to study the pictures we took today and see if there's anything I need to change on the camera's settings."

"I kin be ready 'bout same time tomorrow mornin'. 'Bout ten. Jus' call."

"Call you where?" Mark asked.

Oscar rummaged through the contents of his duffel. He quickly withdrew a holstered pistol, and stuck it in his belt. Finally retrieving his satphone and a stub of a pencil, he handed the latter to Mark. He read off a long series of numbers Scotch taped to the phone's backside. Mark wrote the numbers down on a dental appointment card retrieved from his wallet. "I keep my special phone on, jus' in case you wants to go downriver tomorrow. If you ever calls me on a reg'lar phone, don't say nothin' 'bout what we is did today. Weather, she s'pose be 'bout same tomorrow."

Oscar helped Mark get the gear back into his car. Driving back to Dunham, Mark felt exhausted. *I don't know why I'm so beat. Maybe it's just a few hours in the sun out on the water ... or my lack of sleep last night ... or that nightcap martini. I think I'll go home and upload the pictures, and take a long nap ... then look at the pictures with Anne tonight.*

18

DOWNRIVER

When Mark returned home, Anne was not there. A note on the kitchen counter explained: "Went grocery shopping in Eulonia with a neighbor. Back around 4:00 p.m. Love, A." Mark wrote a reply at the bottom of her note: "Taking a nap. Wake me about 6:00 p.m. I think things went well. Don't put the computer on the Internet. Love, L.M."

Mark uploaded the images from the camera. He discovered high-resolution images take a long time to upload, and guesstimated he had well over 200 images in thumbnail form. Despite his elation, he resisted the strong temptation of enlarging and studying them in detail immediately. Instead, he took a quick shower, and crashed into bed for his much-needed nap.

When Anne returned, she discovered Mark was sound asleep and snoring loudly. She closed the bedroom door, unloaded their groceries, and began preparations for one of Mark's favorite dishes: garlic-cheese grits topped with Cajun-spiced broiled jumbo shrimp. In the great room, she watched the early evening news dominated by the Paris-bound crash of TWA's Flight 800, killing some 230 people; it had happened shortly following the plane's departure from New York. CNN's "talking heads" were wildly speculating "friendly fire," and "terrorist's bomb." She turned the TV off at six to wake Mark.

"It's uppy duppy time, my Little Man," she whispered, and softly blew her warm breath into his ear."

Mark smiled first, then opened his eyes. "What a great way to wake up. I could use a little more of that later ... after we eat and look at the pictures."

"There's a *lot* more of that ... from where that came ... later," Anne said, grinning.

Now I've got two things to look forward to! he thought, as he got out of bed.

They ate hastily, and went straight to the loft. He booted the computer, and went to the folder where the pictures were stored. Thumbnails of the images filled the screen.

"Honey, they're all so tiny I really can't tell much about them," Anne complained.

Mark double clicked the first thumbnail and it immediately filled the entire screen. It was an extremely sharp image centered over the six crab trap floats.

"Wow!" Anne exclaimed. "That's a lot better."

"Now let me show you the next in the series. It should be an infrared," Mark said, and it was.

"That IR stuff is really weird," Anne commented.

"Agreed," Mark replied. "But you'd think water in a flowing river should all be the same temperature. But do you see how the shallow areas are warmer?"

"Subtle, but obvious if you look at it closely," Anne observed. "But it looks like the water out in the *middle* of the river, where the floats are, is a little warmer than water that's close to the bank. Why?"

"Anne, I'm not positive, but I think it has to do with something Oscar told me. He said no knowledgeable crabber would *ever* put traps there ... because there's a long sandbar in the middle of the river— exactly where they've placed their six traps! The tide was still going out when Oscar and I left, but he said at low water, those traps would be completely out of water."

"And the crabs would all die. Right?"

"That's what Oscar told me," Mark answered.

Over the next three hours, the Telfairs studied image after image. They were getting both weary and bored until Mark spotted what he'd hoped to see: *a dolphin's exhalation.*

"There it is, Anne!" Mark exclaimed, pointing to the IR image showing a little orange comet-shaped 'puff' that contrasted sharply with the following standard image showing only the vague outline of a partly submerged dolphin. "I'm sure that's 'Nosy.' Gotta be!"

"Uh ... *who?*" Anne asked, confused.

Mark explained the details of their encounter with the bottlenose dolphin Oscar had named "Nosy." A repeated search for additional "Nosy exhalations" led to firm conclusions: In an IR image taken *exactly* when exhalation first began, it showed up as a discrete bright yellow dot. If the IR was shot fractions of a second later, it appeared as a larger circular orange "puff." If shot *after* exhalation was completed, and the wind blew and cooled the exhaled air, it appeared only as a ghost-like "comet shape," one bearing a faint dull orange tint. *This is some real neat stuff! I can't wait to show this to Roberson ... and, oh shit! I forgot to call Oscar about going downriver tomorrow,* he thought, embarrassed.

Anne looked puzzled when Mark took his wallet out and retrieved a dental appointment card. "Forget a dental appointment?" Anne asked. "This is an odd time to be remembering it."

"No, just need to make a phone call," he explained, picking up their phone's extension beside the computer.

"To whom?"

"Old Oscar," Mark replied, as he started dialing 0118816, then some eight other digits Anne didn't catch.

Oscar answered on the third ring, sounding as though he'd been awakened by the call. "Yes suh, we kin go downriver in th' mornin'. I be ready, 'bout ten ... if hit be th' Lawd's will," Oscar said as they clicked off.

"Anne, Oscar will be ready to go downriver about ten tomorrow morning. You want to go with us?"

"Yeah! I think I'll bring my binoculars and little digital camera ... but I hope we'll see something besides *dolphin breath!*" Anne laughed. So did Mark, as he began the process of transferring the computer images to disk. Anne patiently sat at his side watching the procedure. "That's a boring job, isn't it?" she commented.

"Yeah, but Roberson requested we *not* keep the images in our computer."

Anne leaned in her chair, ran her fingers through Mark's hair while gently blowing in his ear. "I'm going to shower. Don't be too long, Little Man."

* * *

After a leisurely hour of delightfully slow lovemaking, they both fell into peaceful dreamless sleep. Feeling rested and relaxed they mutually awoke about 6:00 a.m. Anne was first to speak:

"Thanks for a wonderful evening, Little Man. At our age, I'm happy we can still enjoy sex as often as we do."

"Maybe we're both abnormal ... at least for our ages. But who cares? Maybe we're also abnormal because I get us involved in such kooky things. If I should ever tell someone 'I am secretly flying kites carrying an infrared camera looking for drug-running submarines,' they would probably ask me, 'Where is your spaceship parked?' ... and then strongly suggest I needed psychiatric evaluation!"

Both burst out laughing as Anne got out of bed to begin preparing breakfast. While Anne was doing that, Mark recharged or put fresh batteries in all electrical components of his aerial photography system. After breakfast, Mark deleted images in the SDS 6500's internal memory to restore full capacity for future images. Now on disk, he labeled yesterday's images with date, time, day, and location information. He placed the disks in protective sleeves. He hoped to soon be turning them over to Dr. Roberson whenever they next met.

A little after ten, the Telfairs accompanied Oscar as he rapidly headed downriver in his skiff. Today, Mark noted the wind was coming from the southeast, decidedly different from yesterday's wind direction.

"Oscar, where are the unnumbered traps located? The ones we're gonna look at today?" Mark asked, as they moved along at a good clip with Anne's blond-going-gray hair flying wildly in the wind.

"They's 'bout five mo' mile. Jus' a little bit up th' mouth, jus' befo' th' river run into Sapelo Sound. Six trap. Jus' lak yesterday. All in a straight line, rat out in th' river middle."

After they rounded the river's final curves, ones Oscar called the river's "S bend," Mark spotted the first of the unnumbered traps. As Oscar had said, they were situated dead mid-river in a straight line, again about 100 feet apart. Mark also spotted the first boat other than their own: a 20-foot aluminum-hulled pontoon boat. As a courtesy, Oscar quickly slowed to idle speed, not wanting his wake to disturb what appeared to be a harmless recreational fishing vessel. It was anchored very close to the river's west bank, bow pointing upriver into the outgoing tide, and positioned so it was about midway down the line of floats out in the river's middle. Georgia registration designation on its bow read "GA 3717 ZW." *Just what we need ... a witness!* Mark thought, desperately trying to remember the boat's registration long enough to write it down. As they idled past the pontoon at a distance of 50 feet, two bearded middle-aged white men stood up and waved. Each held fishing rods and had bottom-rigged lines in the water. Mark could not see the boat's deck; waist-high railings surrounded the perimeter of the boat, and they had been covered with blue canvas. *Privacy shield? Shield from wind? Spray shield?* Mark's mind questioned. CLANG! A loud sound came from the boat. His mind questioned again: *A bell? But where have I heard that same sound before?*

Now a respectful distance past the pontoon boat, Oscar increased his speed and headed well beyond where they should begin flying the kite. Mark again retrieved the dental appointment card from his wallet and wrote "GA 3717 ZW," before he forgot it.

"Somethin' ain't right, Doctor," Oscar said, coming to a dead stop in the water. "I thinks we needs to talk to Dr. Roberson ... befo' flyin' any kite."

"What do you think is wrong, Oscar?" Mark asked.

"Well, first off, dem fellas ain't no fishermens. River she be 'bout 20 foots back where dem traps is at. But dey fishin' on de bottom nex' th' bank in 'bout six foots water ... and where they's at be so full with little oyster heads, they's gonna get they line cut 'most ever' time they tries to pull in. An' ever'body what fishes 'round here knows you ain't gonna catch nothin' but small trash fish when you tries to fish dat spot ... ev'n if you's lucky 'nuff to get one back to yo' boat!"

"Mark, did you hear that bell ring when we went past that boat?" Anne asked.

"Sure did! But I can't place *where* I've heard that exact sound before," Mark replied.

"Well it reminds me of back when we were in the Air Force, and taking SCUBA lessons ... like when we'd accidentally let a couple of tanks bang together. Remember how upset the instructor would get?" *God, what a memory she has,* Mark immediately thought, yet didn't reply.

Now a good half-mile away from the other boat, and out in the edge of the sound and still idling, Oscar removed his satphone from his duffel. He also removed his Sig-Sauer 226, withdrew it from its holster, and rested the bare weapon on the shelf beneath the console. Using his satphone, Oscar quickly punched in about 15 digits from memory. Moments later he was talking to Dr. Spencer Roberson. Oscar quickly explained their dilemma: flying the kite with witnesses able to observe the whole process from a "suspicious" pontoon boat.

"He say he want to talk to you now," Oscar said, passing the phone to Mark.

"Hello, Spence. But before you give us a 'yes' or 'no' on flying today, let me give you the Georgia registration on that pontoon boat." Mark read it off to Spence.

"I'll relay that to Victor Timmons. I don't know if DNR has him out on the water today, but I'll find out. Before we disconnect, ask Oscar to punch in the emergency location function on his satphone. That'll give us your current GPS position. I'll relay that information to Vic, too."

"Well, I think we learned a great deal yesterday working upriver ...

about the IR signature of a dolphin's exhalations."

"I'm anxious to see what you got yesterday. Somehow, we'll meet soon. And ... uh, is Anne by any chance with you guys?" Spence next asked. *What difference does that make?* Mark thought, but didn't answer. There was a long pause before Dr. Roberson spoke again. "You don't happen to have binoculars aboard, do you?"

"Yes. Thanks to Anne. *Her* idea. Got her camera, too. She's with us," Mark finally answered.

"Then *don't* fly today. I repeat, *don't fly.* I don't want to possibly put you guys in danger ... or give away your kite-imaging technique. Just mess around in Oscar's boat on the north side of the sound. Try to look like you're actually working ... running crab traps or something. But get any information you can with Anne's binoculars and camera. I'll see if I can get some of our aerial assets to do a one-time high-altitude fly-over using your current GPS coordinates as their primary target. Bye now," Spence said, and disconnected.

Mark instructed Oscar to activate the emergency location function on his phone. They spent the next two hours going from float to float, trying to look as though they were actually hauling and baiting crab traps. All the floats they visited in the sound were numbered, obviously belonging to legitimate crabbers in the area. Oscar kept his boat positioned so the pontoon boat could not actually see what they were really doing at each float. Anne had crouched so she could steady the binoculars on the gunnel of Oscar's skiff. "Hey! Take a look at this!" Anne yelled.

Mark got on his knees beside Anne. Looking through her binoculars he said, "There's now a *third* man standing in the boat. And he's taking off what looks like a wetsuit top!" *The bastards are either loading or unloading the traps using SCUBA ... and doing it right under our noses! In broad daylight! God, I wish I could rip that damn blue canvas off their boat,* Mark thought.

While Mark continued to watch, Anne reached into her purse and removed her little Christmas-gift digital camera. Kneeling, she stabilized the small camera's extended lens on the gunnel and took several shots. "Have it zoomed all the way to 3 X, Mark. Still might not be enough to identify a face."

Moments later, the pontoon boat pulled anchor, then made a tight U-turn. Anne continued taking shots, getting one distant picture when its broadside faced them in Oscar's boat. She quickly returned her camera to her purse when it looked as though the pontoon might now be heading straight toward their position out in the sound. Oscar had seen it all; he removed the Sig-Sauer from the console shelf, holding it at arm's length down low against his left thigh. He did it in a way that the pontoon occupants could not possibly see he held a gun. Oscar's right hand rested on the throttle. *He's obviously preparing to defend ... and leave fast if need be,* Mark thought. About 100 yards from Oscar's boat the pontoon made an abrupt 90-degree turn, then began heading west up Sapelo Sound. Oscar immediately notified Dr. Roberson using the satphone, and he replied: "Roger that, Oscar. I'll have our guys look for the boat at the local marinas that serve Sapelo Sound. Do *not* try to follow that boat yourselves. We don't want them to even know we're interested in their boat. And you can now turn off the emergency locator on your phone. I've relayed your location information to both Vic and our men in a plane. I suggest you guys head back upriver. Do it *now!*" Spence urged at the very end of his conversation with Oscar.

As they entered the Barbour River, Oscar couldn't resist one small temptation: pausing on their return trip just long enough to check each of the unnumbered traps. Using his gaff hook, he expertly snagged each float's line just beneath the surface, and quickly hauled each trap for an inspection, then immediately dropped them back into the water. *Empty ... all six of them!*

19

DINNER GUEST

Their uneventful run back upriver to Barbour Landing took less than 15 minutes. *When Oscar opens up that Honda 90, this old workboat will really haul ass!* Mark thought, estimating their speed to be pushing 50 miles per hour. The boat had no windshield, nowhere to hide from wind. Anne removed a couple of rubber bands from her purse, finally securing her hair in funky "twin ponytails." She did so to keep her own hair from "putting her eyes out" if she turned her head the wrong way.

After arriving at Barbour Landing, Oscar helped Mark stow the unused kite gear back inside the Explorer. That chore quickly done, the old fella indicated he needed to go home to "straighten out" some of his traps. "It's that dang ol' Nosy, what bend up my traps that a way," Oscar explained, as he left the landing parking lot, his rusted-out muffler terminating the silence in the refuge.

Mark and Anne leisurely began driving home, their heads crammed with thoughts, both wishing they could meet with Dr. Roberson right now. Mark made a U-turn on Harris Neck Road. Anne looked at him, thoroughly puzzled. "Mark, did we forget something at the landing?"

"No, we've got everything. I'm going to the refuge office," he explained.

"The *office?* Why?"

"To have the secretary radio Spencer, and see if we can set up a meeting *today,*" Mark told Anne.

"I'm sure he has a very busy schedule ... but what if we invite him to come to our house this evening. Maybe see if he and his wife want to have dinner with us?"

"Fine with me, Anne. But I've noticed he doesn't wear a wedding band, so he might not even be married," Mark replied.

At the refuge office, the secretary quickly contacted Dr. Roberson by radio. He indicated he would call back immediately to a phone situated in the conference room. Mark and Anne went there. In 30 seconds the phone rang:

"Hi, it's me. Spence. You needed to talk to me? I'm on satphone."

"Yeah," Mark replied. "We made a lot of observations downriver today. I'd like to share them with you. Plus, I've several questions. Would you like to meet me and the wife at our house for dinner tonight, say around seven?"

"You won't have other guests there, will you?"

"No. Just you, me, and Anne," Mark explained.

"Good. I'll be alone, but can we make it around eight? Is that too late? I've got a few loose ends to deal with, and I need to shower and get into some civvies before I come. I've got the DEA aerial-imaging guy holding on another line right now, so I gotta go."

"I understand. Eight is fine with us, Spence. See ya then," Mark said hanging up.

"Well, what did he say?" Anne asked, staring at Mark.

"He's coming at eight tonight. Alone, Little *Girl!*" Mark exclaimed, laughing. "Yeah, Little *Girl*. You really need to look in a mirror at your hair. You look about 12 years old ... like a little girl whose pigtails have come undone!"

"Maybe so, but I sure like doing 'big-girl' stuff' with *you*, Little Man."

"Ditto, 'Big Girl.' But let's change the subject before we get ourselves into trouble while alone in this conference room!"

"Agreed," Anne said, smiling as they walked past the secretary, then back to their car parked in front of the refuge office.

* * *

A few minutes after eight, driving his plain-Jane Nissan Altima, Spence arrived at Dunham. Clean-shaven, jet-black hair combed to perfection, he knocked on the door of the Telfairs' modest home. His pressed blue jeans, crisp khaki safari shirt, and new-looking tan Reeboks, all made him look more like a handsome photographer working a *National Geographic* gig ... rather than the man he actually was: a U.S. Fish & Wildlife officer, a Ph.D. biologist working undercover with DEA.

"Welcome to our humble home," Mark said, greeting him at the door, and noting Spence had his attaché-styled briefcase in one hand, as well as an unopened bottle of wine in the other.

"Sorry I'm a few minutes late, but I had to download and print some large image files. I think they're something you might find very interesting. More later. And you might want to put this in the fridge," Spence said, handing Mark the bottle. "It's a Riesling, that may or may not complement your meal plans," Spence explained.

"Thanks for the wine. It'll go with what I think she's got in mind. Sorry, Anne's still primping. Mostly it's her hair that got 'destroyed' on the boat ride with Oscar earlier today. Anyway, I think she's planning to have broiled flounder. She's thawed three nice ones, and they are in the fridge. I'll let your wine keep them company," Mark said, putting the wine in to chill.

"Great! I love seafood ... almost any way you fix it. Since Cathy, my wife, died a few years back, I've lived mostly on microwave dinners and junk food," Spence commented.

So he was married ... but now's not the time for details, Mark thought.

"Spence, you look different. I've gotten so used to you being in uniform ... and having a gun at your side."

"Gun's still here," Spence said, patting his attaché. There's also a couple of surprises for you in this case."

Anne appeared moments later, looking radiant. She'd finally settled on a French braid to control her hair. Anne skipped formalities with their guest, and got right to the point: "Spence, I hope you like broiled flounder."

"Anne, broiled anything sure beats the microwaved whatever I'd be preparing for myself at my trailer!"

"Why don't you guys start discussing and looking at stuff? I'm gonna start preparing our meal. Be ready in about an hour," Anne said, as she headed for their kitchen.

"Mark," Spence said, "do you realize how lucky you are to still have a wife like her?" .

"Everyday," Mark replied.

Mark at first thought he'd detected a hint of tears in Spencer's eyes, but quickly led him upstairs to the loft to look at the shots he'd made upriver yesterday from Oscar's boat. Spence followed, carrying his attaché. Mark loaded the first of the CDs into the computer, but soon jumped to several of the last ones where he knew he'd captured "Nosy exhalations."

"Interesting. *Very* interesting," Spence allowed. "Using IR, it seems you have three distinct heat patterns: focal yellow dot, orange 'puff ball,' and dull ghost-like comet."

"That's almost exactly what Anne and I came up with. You said the West Coast SSs were diesel/electric. What did you mean by that?" Mark asked.

"Their main propulsion is by diesel engine, but that engine also powers a generator to charge a bank of batteries. They can then be propelled by their electric motor at slow speed, for a short period of time. I talked with the West Coast guys earlier today. They've done some more testing on their SSs, and found they can run *completely submerged* on battery for about 45 minutes."

"How deep?" Mark asked.

"Not very. Their engineers affixed strain gauges to the poorly constructed fiberglass hull, and feared the hull would crush if they went much deeper than 15 feet," Spence explained.

"So," Mark continued, "if the West Coast cousins have the same capability as the smaller ones here on the Atlantic, our best bet would be to try to capture an IR image while they're running on diesel with their exhaust pipes exposed. My guess is the tip of the hot exhaust pipe would appear as a white or yellow dot. If we were taking an IR *video,* we'd probably always see the white or yellow dot, like the head of a comet, but its tail fading to some tint of orange that follows wind direction."

"Mark, I agree with you. I've checked, and the lightest IR-capable video camera DEA has weighs over 20 pounds! I suggest we stick with the current SDS 6500, and settle for shooting still IR images alone. I think that's our best bet, don't you?"

"Yes, at least for now. But I still think it's unlikely we're ever gonna be lucky enough to capture that heat signature you're looking for. I think our best chances are upriver, where Oscar and I went yesterday. Up there, the river gets quite shallow at low tide, especially in the middle ... even goes completely dry at dead low water, leaving those traps exposed on a sandbar. So, I think our best chances are going to be on high tides, when the SSs are not likely to get hung-up on sandbars. I'm sure the SS drivers are aware of the tides. And if the SSs are the ones putting out the unnumbered traps, I'd also bet they are doing it at high tide. That would give us some idea of their timing, in other words, their *schedule.* And I also bet drugs are being removed from those particular traps at high water."

"You've obviously put a lot of thought into this, Doctor. At first, I thought you and Anne might 'chicken out' on me ... but now I see you folks are just as intrigued as I am!"

"Hey guys," Anne yelled from below, "dinner will be ready in about five minutes."

Mark ejected the CD in the computer, sleeved it, and handed the remaining stack of CDs to Spence. Dr. Roberson immediately placed them alongside his gun and other items in his attaché. They descended the stairs to join Anne for a dinner of broiled flounder stuffed with crabmeat. Steamed asparagus and salads were served as sides. Spence sipped his Riesling, but ate like he hadn't eaten all day long. "I haven't had a meal this fine since Cathy died," Spence commented, then went on to explain his wife had fought a prolonged and expensive battle with breast cancer. Despite good insurance through his federal job, he ended up essentially broke. In desperation, he'd taken his wife to M.D. Anderson in Texas, then to Sloan-Kettering Cancer Center located at Manhattan's Upper East Side. Spence was hoping for a miracle. Both renowned "out-of-network" research centers indicated Cathy's earlier treatments had all been exactly what they would have done for the initial stage of her disease; sadly, they had only additional experimental treatments to offer. He'd had to sell their nice home in nearby Richmond Hill, Georgia, to pay for expenses not covered by insurance. He now lived alone in a small trailer situated on one of the few RV pads available at the refuge. "I'm just glad I didn't have to sell my two lots I've got at Dunham Point. In a year or two, I hope to build a retirement home here. I really like the layout of your house here. Do you still have the plans for this house?"

"We've still got 'em, Spence. We may glass-in the screened porch one day, but other than that, there's not much we'd want to change," Mark explained.

After they'd eaten their desserts of chocolate-drizzled vanilla ice cream, the conversation returned again to the drug-smuggling issue.

Spencer began: "We did learn a lot from the information you gave us by satphone earlier today. First, that pontoon boat's Georgia registration designation is fake, or you guys possibly got the number wrong."

"Well, Mark wrote it down. And I took several pictures with my own camera," Anne volunteered. "But my camera's LCD screen is so small I couldn't tell you much. Maybe if we look at my pictures on the computer, we might be able to see more detail."

The threesome went to the loft, carrying their second glasses of wine with them. Mark uploaded Anne's pictures, selected the ones showing the pontoon boat, and imported those files into Photoshop. He zoomed the broadside image. *GA 3717 ZN was clearly visible,* but not a single face was captured in Anne's photos. Mark checked what

144

he'd earlier written down on his dental appointment card; the numbers and letters matched perfectly.

"As best I recall, that's exactly the designation I gave Victor Timmons," Spence said. "I'll have him run it again, just to be sure. We're pretty sure the pontoon boat was taken out of the water at Kip's Fish Camp, down at Shellman Bluff."

"We're quite familiar with Kip's ... and Sans Stryker, the proprietor there. That's where we buy most of the fuel for *Fanta-Sea*, my larger boat," Mark explained.

"Unfortunately, none of our folks were able to get there before it came out of the water," Spence admitted. "But Sans Stryker told one of our guys they'd earlier taken out a 20-foot pontoon, with blue canvas shields. He recalled seeing fishing tackle, several crab traps and SCUBA gear aboard. Alabama plates were on both the boat trailer and the towing pickup, but he didn't write the numbers down. Three men, ones Stryker didn't recognize, left immediately in the truck after paying the lift fee in cash."

Dr. Roberson opened his attaché, and withdrew a Manila envelope containing four eight-by-twelve color photos. "Though we missed first-hand surveillance at Kip's, we also got quite lucky today. When I called in your GPS position, DEA's aerial folks happened to be in the air at 15,000 feet over Jacksonville, Florida, and heading for Hunter Army Airfield at Savannah, Georgia. So these are ...?"

"High-altitude shots of exactly where we were in Oscar's boat earlier today," Mark guessed.

"Exactly!" Spence beamed. "Now take this and look at the aft deck on that pontoon boat. Tell me what you see there," Spence said, handing Mark a lens from his attaché.

Mark was silent for several moments. "Four yellow SCUBA tanks secured in a rack, a pair of black flippers, and what looks like a black wetsuit top spread out on the deck, possibly to dry ... and six yellow crab traps and their white floats. Even with these excellent pictures and your hand lens, I can't make out any numbers on the floats."

"Exactly, again!" Spence said.

Anne piped in: "But maybe we need to rethink the delivery-and-transfer process. I can't see a surface boat putting out traps in broad daylight ... too many chances for a witness. Maybe the SSs first set out the unnumbered traps, maybe ones *already* containing drugs. Then, they are later picked up underwater by a SCUBA diver working from another conventional surface boat."

Spencer frowned. "Anne, overall that sounds good. But enough physical space for six crab traps *inside* the small SSs we have here? Well ... that is not likely. So I don't think our local SSs do the initial placing of the traps, either loaded or unloaded. Even the large ones on the West Coast have limited residual space when loaded with cocaine and other drugs, and we know their topside manhole is way too small for a crab trap to fit through it ... at least for the standard-sized commercial traps they've been using around here."

"Maybe the SSs have a larger hatch, say like on their bottoms," Anne said.

"An excellent thought!" Spence said while punching numbers on his satphone. Moments later: "Hello Randy, it's me. I apologize for calling you after hours, but could you tell me the size of the bottom hatch on the SSs you guys have out there?" After a pause, Spence spoke again: "That big? You're sure it's thirty-by-thirty inches?" Another much longer pause, then: "I'll give you a call about midmorning, your time. We may be on to something here. Catch ya tomorrow." Spence smiled, and drank the last of his wine.

All eyes were on Spence. Anne could stand it no longer. "Well, are you going to tell us what was said ... or not?"

"Sorry," Dr. Roberson said, still smiling. "Remember me telling you folks that we've never captured a crew member? Randy's with DEA on the West Coast. He'd previously told me they think the crew always escapes through a bottom hatch, possibly using SCUBA. We know the West Coast subs have a bottom hatch large enough to exit while wearing SCUBA tanks. They've also found evidence of possible SCUBA use aboard their SSs ... like high-pressure air compressors to fill their tanks, and spare regulator parts. And they always seem to run their SSs close enough to shore for that escape method to be a distinct possibility. In other words, the crew could simply swim to land, then disappear into the general population. But in a prior conversation, he'd also told me they've found no evidence that crab traps are involved on the West Coast. So, Anne, to prove your 'bottom hatch' theory, we've got to capture one of the local SSs, hopefully with crab traps inside them."

Mark chimed in: "Space permitting, I can envision Anne's bottom-hatch theory ... just running along and jettisoning drug-loaded crab traps. Sorta like laying a string of eggs. Each jettison point could be noted on GPS, plus the unnumbered floats would serve as visual locators as well. Or, if the SSs aren't the ones actually putting out the traps, they could use SCUBA to load drugs into unnumbered traps put out by *someone else* ... like maybe that pontoon we saw."

Spencer, yawned and checked his watch: almost midnight. "I didn't intend to keep you folks up this late. Anne, I want to thank you for the fabulous meal ... and your bottom-hatch theory. Before I go, I want to give you two a satphone." Smiling, Spencer removed a phone from his attaché. "It's already programmed. Their main design flaw is that they must be turned off to charge them. So, you can't use them when charging, and that puts you out of service for about an hour. If you call a satphone that's being charged, you'll still get a ringtone, but of course you won't get an answer. When fully charged, they are good for about eight hours of active use, and up to a couple of weeks on standby. When receiving a call, the phone beeps; when making a call, you'll hear either a ringtone or a busy signal, just like a regular phone." Pointing, Spence continued: "If you want to contact me, all you've gotta do is press this button to turn it on, then enter HNNWR 1. Victor is HNNWR 2, Oscar HNNWR 3. You and Anne are now HNNWR 4. The 'emergency locate' button is this one," Spence said, again pointing. "And before you ask, the 'HNNWR' stands for Harris Neck National Wildlife Refuge. If anyone calls and asks you to 'identify,' just say 'HNNWR 4.' Old Oscar refuses to use the code for shortcut dialing, but there's little chance of mistaking his voice. He's actually proud of the 15-digits he memorized for my phone, and prefers to call me that way. If Oscar needs to call you, I'll tell him it's 466974."

As Spencer was walking out the door, attaché in hand, he spoke. "Please follow me to my car. I've got something else in the trunk for you and Anne to check." He handed Mark, then Anne, a couple of medium-sized cardboard boxes. "Those two boxes are instruments and supplies for Roberto's surgery. Check them over carefully. I'll call you tomorrow."

PREPARING FOR SURGERY

"Well, that certainly was an interesting evening," Anne commented as Spencer drove off, and she then began clearing the dining table.

Like a child at Christmas, Mark sat on the great room's carpeted floor. Anne smiled as she watched Mark begin to open the boxes Spencer had left. Other than the instrument list (each item checked off by someone), and the instructions and charger for the satphone, he was thoroughly familiar with the remaining contents. *God, I love the way surgical steel feels in my hands ... so familiar ... comforting ... so natural,* he thought, as Anne observed his childish joy while he handled—almost fondled—each surgical instrument.

Anne had loaded the dishwasher and turned it on. She then came and sat opposite her husband on the floor, assuming his same cross-legged Indian-style, but facing him. "Mark, do you remember the *very first* time we ever sat facing each other this way?"

"Honey, I'll never forget that day ... was in North Georgia, beneath a huge white oak tree, on leaf-covered ground filled of chiggers ... and lovemaking. It was during that wild weekend we spent at *Possum Trot* with Jer Bacon, and other close friends who trained with us at Grady. That was when I made the best decision in my life ... I asked you to marry me."

Tears filled Anne's beautiful hazel eyes. His brown ones, too, for that matter. Moments later, they were repeating the passion experienced beneath that great white oak in North Georgia ... right there on the great room's floor, lights ablaze, in full view, should anyone be outside the sliding-glass door to their deck.

Fully sated, they were eventually lying on their backs, catching their breath. The motion-sensing floodlight on their deck suddenly illuminated. The mid-sized doe's big brown eyes peered at them curiously, but she scampered away when Mark got off the floor to locate his underwear amid the clutter of surgical instruments, boxes, and clothing scattered on the great room's carpet. Now in his Jockey shorts, he covered Anne's nude body with a bath towel retrieved from the guest bath.

"Thanks, Little Man. I'm so relaxed I think I could sleep right here."

"Me too. Wonder if that doe will tell her deer friends she's seen her first X-rated human activity?"

While cuddling, both started laughing, but finally turned the lights off. Before they went to sleep on the great room floor, Mark placed the satphone on the counter in the kitchen. They ultimately retreated to the comfort of their bed at 3:00 a.m., and promptly resumed their sleep.

The couple almost never slept late. At 9:00 a.m., a strange beeping sound awakened them both. At first, Mark and Anne both thought it was a smoke detector, one located in the kitchen. Rushing there, they discovered the source of the sound. A red LED on the satphone blinked with each beep. Mark answered it:

"Hello," Mark first said.

"Good morning, Doc," Spence said. "I thank you and Anne again for the company and great meal last night. And if you two are not all booked up, I'd like to make an appointment for a patient named Roberto Gonzales."

"When?" Mark asked.

"Tomorrow afternoon. I'll pick you up in my car, dressed as a civilian. Is three o'clock OK?"

"Yes, but let me check with Anne."

Mark quickly explained to Anne, and she nodded an "OK," then whispered in Mark's unoccupied ear, "When will we be back home?"

"Spence, Anne says 'OK,' but wants to know when we'll be back home?"

"How long is the surgery going to take, Doctor?"

"The first stage should take only about 45 minutes," Mark responded.

"*First stage?*" Spence questioned.

"I plan to do two or three excisions in stages," Mark explained. "Roberto's birthmark is too wide to take it all out with a single procedure. The resultant skin defect would be too wide to close with stitches alone. I'd have to resort to a skin graft, and grafted skin almost never looks natural. In fact, it could end up being as obvious as the birthmark itself—or even worse! But if I do it in stages, and allow the surrounding normal skin to stretch several weeks, and relieve skin tension, no graft will be needed. The cosmetic result should be excellent if we do it that way."

"I see," Spencer said. "I'll leave the methodology up to your surgical judgment, and the logistics of keeping it secret up to the U.S. Marshals Service."

"*Where* will we be going?" Mark asked, with a slight frown.

"Doctor, I honestly do not know. When it comes to Witness Protection, they are pretty stingy with the information they give me. All I know is that I'm supposed to drive you and the wife to Colonels Island, Brunswick's deepwater port. It's a division of the Georgia Ports Authority, I think. We're to be there no later than four o'clock tomorrow, and we are to remain inside my personal car at the guard's shack until we are approached by the U.S. Marshals Service. They will take it from there. That's all I know, but my assumption is a large boat of some kind is going to be involved."

Mark scratched his head. "How are Anne and I going to get back home?"

"I've been instructed to wait there until the Marshals Service brings you back to my car. My assumption is that they may keep you and Anne several hours. We'll just have to wait and see."

"Well," Mark commented, "it looks like Anne and I are finally going to have a day off ... unless we fly my kite upriver today with Oscar."

"That won't be happening today, Doctor. Oscar called me about five o'clock this morning, heading for Atlanta. He's going to the Winship Cancer Institute at Emory. It's just a routine follow-up regarding his prostate surgery, but he probably won't be back until sometime tonight. He actually apologized for not being available to us today."

"So it'll really be a day off for Anne and me. I hope he has good news on his follow-up at Winship. And I think Anne and I might even get very bored ... at least compared to the pace you've had us working!" Mark said, laughing.

Spence warned: "Bored or not, please don't even think of taking one of your own boats upriver today. We don't want your boats linked in any way to the unmarked floats."

"We'll behave. I promise. Any special instructions before you pick us up tomorrow?"

"A few. Both of you should be well rested, and wear dark casual clothes without logos or distinct features. Eat a good lunch tomorrow. Before I pick you guys up, ask Anne to put her hair back up in that tight French braid ... like she had it last night. Double-check the instruments and supplies. Be sure your satphone is fully charged and on your person. Both of you should bring your driver's license, but no other documents."

"OK, Spence. We'll be ready," Mark said before signing off.

Mark relayed to Anne the entire satphone conversation he'd just finished with Spencer. They spent most of the day speculating about how all this would be carried out. Finally, they gave up. Both were now totally "hooked" on figuring out the whole drug-smuggling scenario ... and less fixated on their personal safety. Ultimately, both concluded, Dr. Spencer Roberson would not intentionally put them in harm's way. With dusk now approaching, Mark made them a pitcher of martinis. They went to their dock to watch the birds come in, vowing not to again discuss illegal drugs for the remainder of the day.

Both slightly tipsy, they ate a light evening meal, then went to bed at eight o'clock. They slept soundly, and awoke alert and rested at six the next morning. A hearty breakfast was followed by a heavy lunch at 1:30. Both dressed in black jeans, T-shirts and shoes. Anne, however, had a bit of a problem trying to fit her ample mammary anatomy into one of Mark's black T-shirts.

"Mark, I think I've stretched one of your black shirts to the limit, but I can live with it. Does my white bra show through?"

"In an odd tantalizing way, but change to a black one," Mark advised.

She did.

"Honey, a thought just occurred to me. Do you think we should run those instruments through the dishwasher? I know that probably won't make them completely sterile, but some of them, especially the Metzenbaum scissors, still have some residual manufacturing oil on them," Mark explained.

"Good idea, Mark. We've enough time to do it before Spencer gets here."

Less than an hour later Anne removed the instruments from the dishwasher, handling them with one of the many pairs of sterile gloves in the supply boxes. She carefully wrapped them in one of the prepackaged sterile surgical towels Spence had obtained.

"Anne, once we get on site, we'll start soaking them in Sporicidin solution to be sure they're sterile. And—"

"Honey, I think Spence just drove up." She interrupted.

Mark checked his watch. "He's five minutes early, but we're ready."

Anne opened the door for Spence. "I realize I'm a few minutes early, but I need to change the tag on my car before we leave. I need to borrow a flat-blade screwdriver. Won't take but a minute."

Without words, Mark ran to his shop and returned with several screwdrivers. Spence popped his trunk, and removed a Georgia vehicle license tag from the several he had hidden beneath the carpet in his trunk. Mark noted all the tags' stickers were for the current year. The tags, on their backside, had code numbers, apparently written with a felt-tipped marker. Looking at the backside code numbers, Spence said "This is the one I need for this trip. They are all fake, except for the one I had on the car when I first drove up."

"Why all this trouble?" Mark asked, as Spence quickly changed plates.

"Let's load the surgical stuff and get going. I'll explain on the way down to Colonels Island. Got your satphone?"

"Yes," Mark replied, palpating the bulge at his beltline beneath his black T-shirt.

Everything was quickly loaded. Anne seated herself and buckled up in the rear behind Spence; Mark did the same in the front passenger's seat. *What in the hell have we gotten ourselves into?* Mark thought, as Spence quickly drove out their driveway at Dunham. *I never noticed how deeply tinted this car's windows are ... until I actually got inside it,* Mark continued thinking.

In ten minutes they were on U.S. 17, driving the legal limit southward toward Brunswick, Georgia. The sense of intrigue and mystery had left Mark and Anne speechless for the moment. The beep of Spencer's satphone interrupted the silence. Somewhat awkwardly, due to the car's seat belt, Spence reached inside his dark blue blazer. In the process of removing his satphone from his shirt pocket, Mark noted Spence had his pistol in a shoulder holster. "HNNWR 1, over," Spence said, and, after a brief pause, he again spoke to the caller: "We're on schedule. ETA 1600, or a little earlier. We're tagged as requested. HNNWR 1 clear," Spence replied, then returned his phone to a pocket of the black shirt worn beneath his blazer.

"What was that all about?" Mark asked.

"That was just a guy from the U.S. Marshals Service. Those fellas are really anal when it comes to details and schedules," Spence explained. "The fake plates on my car are their idea."

"Surgeons are sometimes that way, too ... 'anal' at times," Mark admitted. "But let me ask you another question: Why have you got your car windows so heavily tinted?"

"To keep people from seeing the faces of the occupants. But I warn you both: You may be 'hooded' or 'bagged,' as we say, before you exit this vehicle. The hoods are made of a special cloth. You can breathe just fine, and you can actually see through the material from the inside ... but folks on the *outside* can't see your face." Spence adjusted his interior rearview mirror to give him a better view of Anne. "Please turn your head sideways, Anne." *What for?* she thought, but complied. "Great job with your hair, and the French braid! That'll all easily fit under a hood, and leave nothing sticking out. We don't want anyone to even know your hair color."

Anne finally asked Spence a question: "What about rings and watches, things like that?"

"They've gotta go, too. Just be sure you take them off before you get out of the car. Keep them in the pockets of those black jeans you guys are wearing. That'll be fine. You have to take that stuff off before surgery anyway, don't you?"

"Yeah, you're right Spence," Anne finally replied. "But a woman feels kinda naked without her jewelry and a purse!"

Spence chuckled as he readjusted his rearview mirror back to its normal position. They were now well past the City of Darien and nearing Brunswick. Traffic was light, and ten minutes later they were on the south side of Brunswick, approaching the Sidney Lanier Bridge that spanned the South Brunswick River. Spence soon turned off U.S. 17, and headed for Colonels Island. He stopped his car at a guard shack, presented his credentials, and was directed to a parking spot just inside the gate.

Dr. Roberson glanced at his watch: 3:55. "Looks like we've beat the Marshals Service," Spence said, smiling.

The words were no sooner out of his mouth when a black Suburban eased alongside his Altima. Two Marshals popped out; one approached the driver's window and knocked on it. Spence rolled the window down just enough to present his credentials. The Marshal identified himself as Todd Whitmore, and presented his credentials as well.

Mark noted the second Marshal was now behind the car, apparently checking Spence's tag number. The second man came to the driver's window alongside his partner, presented credentials, and identified himself as Sloan Stafford with the U.S. Marshals Service.

Stafford spoke to Spence: "Sir, I need to enter your car to check the passengers. I need photo ID."

"Stafford, all doors are unlocked," Spence replied. "Use the right rear. Do you want them bagged before you open that door?"

"Yes, good idea." Retrieved from his dark business suit's interior

153

jacket pockets, Sloan passed two hoods to Spence, who instructed the Telfairs to place them over their heads. They did. Stafford quickly entered the car, and sat in the right rear seat, then spoke: "You can slip the hoods off for a moment now, and show me your photo IDs." Mark and Anne simultaneously removed their Georgia driver's licenses from the hip pockets of their jeans. Spence turned on the Altima's interior light, allowing Stafford to study them closely. "Welcome to our team. Both of you will be doing a little surgery in about an hour and a half. We'll have Dr. Roberson follow our Suburban to the boat. Hoods back on now, please," Stafford said, before quickly exiting Spence's car.

Spencer followed Marshals Whitmore and Stafford for about a half-mile. The Suburban stopped alongside what looked like an unmarked ambulance, or possibly an EMT truck with heavily tinted windows.

"Dr. Roberson, pop your trunk, so we can transfer the surgical supplies," Whitmore requested, and that was quickly done. Hooded, and using the truck's single curbside back door, the Telfairs were quickly ushered to bench seats inside the back of the box-like truck. "Dr. Roberson, just stay parked right here until we bring them back. If you need a restroom, there's one over there in that guard shack," Whitmore said, pointing. "Otherwise, stay with your car. OK?"

Spence said nothing, just nodded that he understood.

Both Marshals got in the front seats of the truck, Stafford driving. In moments, Mark felt a slight bump, then realized the truck was going up a slight incline. Then another bump, and the truck stopped in a level position. Even through the black cloth hood and the truck's tinted windows, he could see they'd driven up a ramp to a large boat, and they were now parked on its aft deck. Stafford got out of the truck, indicating he was going to "catch some grub with the 'Coasties.'" Whitmore remained, and slid a hand around a curtain, one that separated the front from the back. "You can take the hoods off now," Whitmore said, as he flipped a switch that flooded the truck's back interior with bright overhead light. Anne and Mark looked around in total amazement. *This is really state-of-the-art stuff ... but where's the patient?* Mark's mind questioned.

"Like what you see?" Whitmore questioned, as he slid the curtain aside.

"You bet! But where's the patient?" Mark asked.

Whitmore replied, "Roberto Gonzales is already aboard this vessel. In case you are wondering, this is an 87-foot U.S. Coast Guard cutter. You have no need to know the vessel's name. We'll be in international waters in about 40 minutes ... that's about 12 nautical miles offshore, and the captain has said it's flatter than a pancake out there."

"Where are we going to do the surgery?" Anne finally piped in.

"Right here in this EMT truck. Before I joined the U.S. Marshals, I was an EMT for several years. I'm hoping to put enough money together to attend med school. Anyway, I'm quite familiar with this type truck. If you've got any technical questions I'll answer them."

"Mind if we call you Todd?" Mark asked. "Looks like were going to work together for awhile."

"Todd's fine, Doc. But do you remember where we first met?"

It hit Mark almost instantly: "You're the same U.S. Marshal who was at the DNR building in Brunswick ... the day Dr. Roberson first introduced us to Roberto Gonzales!"

"Good call, Doc. There were actually *two* of us at the DNR building that day. I was the only one you actually *saw*. Keep it under your hat. And that goes for your wife, too. OK?"

One, then a second large engine rumbled to life. A very slight rocking motion was felt as they got underway, but soon steadied and the engines throttled up. They'd run about 30 minutes when the boat experienced some very obvious pitching. Anne looked at Mark, her hazel eyes questioning with alarm.

Mark spoke: "Todd, I thought you said it was going to be flat. My wife has a problem with seasickness."

"It'll be flat in just a few minutes. We're crossing the bow wakes of ships coming into the port. Probably just the 'big boys,' bringing us another load of Japanese cars." Todd was right. Five minutes later they might as well have been standing on a land-based concrete slab. Anne smiled in relief.

"So, Todd, exactly what are we going to use for an OR table?" Mark asked.

"Simple, Doc. Adjustable-height hydraulic gurney ... one that's specifically designed for this truck. It locks to the floor tracks. Any other questions?"

"Yes. The electrosurgical unit we have is 120 volts AC. You got that available inside this truck?"

Todd pointed to several electrical outlets that were clearly labeled "120 VAC." *Just look around before you ask more dumb-assed questions*, Mark self-chastised in thought.

Some ten minutes later, the USCG cutter slowly throttled back, then anchored. The rear doors of the EMT-style truck abruptly opened. Two burly U.S. Marshals slid in a gurney bearing a short body wearing a black hood, and clad otherwise in a dark gray sweat suit and black socks.

Once fully inside, the 'body' reached up and slid the black hood off its head. He smiled when he saw Mark and Anne. "Again we meet señor y señora! Entiendo que usted ha venido a hacerme un hombre 'no-marcado.'"

Mark responded, "Hello again, Roberto! I get the gist of what you said, but I again request, por favour, solamente hable inglés! I've forgotten most of my high-school Spanish, and I know you're fully bilingual."

"Sí, excúseme …uh, I mean yes, excuse me," Roberto replied.

Todd chuckled. "Doc, I'm fully bilingual, too. I'll keep a lid on his language, and translate if he forgets. I'm gonna remain with you throughout the entire procedure. I'll swivel this passenger's seat so I'll be facing aft. If you need any help, just let me know. Please don't think I'm trying to meddle, but the Service requires that I observe everything you do. What are you going to use for your local anesthetic?"

"Lidocaine, two percent," Mark replied, thinking: *Is an EMT-trained U.S. Marshal now going to tell me how to do the procedure?*

"Sorry, Doc. I trust you completely. The Service requires that I inspect the vial of lidocaine before you inject it into Roberto. I'm truly sorry, Doc, I really am," Todd said, his facial expression indicating he was indeed being sincere.

Mark passed the 50-cubic-centimeter vial of lidocaine to Todd, who now sat facing those in the rear. He carefully inspected the vial's factory seal, its labeling, and the expiration date. Anne began soaking all the instruments in Sporicidin (a cold sterilization solution, also prechecked by Whitmore) and she was setting up a sterile instrument tray while Mark explained to Roberto why the procedure would be done in several stages. Todd looked on, nodding approval; he even assisted in "locking" the gurney to the truck's floor tracks, and adjusted their makeshift "OR table" to a comfortable working height for Mark.

Before starting the actual surgery, Mark found himself in deep thought: *This has just gotta be the strange shit fiction is made of! Never—not in my wildest dreams—have I ever thought I'd find myself secretly operating on a Hispanic U.S. Border Patrol officer in Witness Protection … inside an EMT truck, on the aft deck of a U.S. Coast Guard cutter in international waters … and with an EMT-trained U.S. Marshal observing my every move!*

21

STAGE 1

With the exception of "Marcado" Gonzales, everyone inside the EMT truck now wore pale green disposable surgical masks. Anne had the instrument tray at the ready and began opening disposable sterile surgical drapes. From his rearward-facing passenger's seat at the front, U.S. Marshal Todd Whitmore looked on intently.

"Prep?" Anne asked.

"Betadine," Mark answered.

"Sorry, guys, but I need to check that Betadine container before you apply any of it to Roberto's face," Todd said.

Todd is going to drive me nuts before we actually begin this simple procedure! Mark thought, yet handed the bottle of Betadine to Todd for inspection.

"Betadine's OK," Todd mumbled after checking the bottle's label and seal. He apparently also recognized the exasperation building in Mark's eyes. "Doctor, by way of apology, let me first say this: This little surgery is certainly not the first time a Marshals Service guy has been *required* to observe medical or surgical treatments given to a person in our Witness Protection Program. Nor will it be the last."

"Well, Todd, this may well be the last time for me! I have nothing against you personally, but your sitting there is worse than having a damn paranoid lawyer watch every move I make!"

Todd chuckled. Roberto and Anne remained silent, both apparently dismayed at Mark's mini-outburst.

"OK, OK, OK!" Todd responded, defensively. "Doc, I understand exactly the way you must feel. But let me ask you a couple of questions: What would happen to Roberto if that 50-cubic-centimeter vial of Lidocaine *actually* contained curare, a neuroparalytic drug? Or, what would happen to Roberto's face if the so-called Betadine prep solution was *actually* glacial acetic acid instead?"

Mark blushed, paused, then said, "Well, Roberto would certainly be dead from the curare overdose ... or horribly disfigured from the acid burn. He'd possibly even be blind from the acid fumes, should the acid be placed on his skin that close to his eye. That's what!"

"Doc, I hope that puts us back on the same page again," Todd said, now seeming to relax a bit.

Mark continued: "Todd, I could give you any number of additional hypothetical misdeeds—some really sophisticated ones, if I wanted to," Mark bragged. "I'm sure you know Dr. Roberson is the one who acquired all the supplies we're going to use here. You don't actually think Roberson wants to harm Roberto, do you? You need to get real, man! Quit being so darn paranoid and be honest with me. Has anything like that ever actually happened to someone in your custody? I mean, like, to someone in the Witness Protection Program?"

"No comment, Doctor. The Service is not perfect ... but we always try to learn from any past mistakes we may have made."

Maybe there is some basis for Todd's redundant precautions ... something that has screwed up in the past ... but he's not about to admit it! Better get going, or I'll never get the first stage done, Mark thought.

Through his surgical mask, Mark took in a deep breath. "Anne? Roberto? Are you guys ready to start?"

Anne nodded a simple "yes."

"He estado listo por años," Roberto replied.

"I understand, Roberto. 'Ready for years.' But remember your promise: inglés solamente!" Mark exclaimed.

Todd butted in. "Roberto, for God's sake, turn the Spanish side of your brain off! We need to get this done quickly, and not work around language barriers. We've gone to a lot of trouble to set this up for you, and we're out here in the water, in an expensive boat, in an expensive truck, and burning taxpayer money at over $500 a minute!"

Roberto smiled, but said nothing. Mark noted the deep "smile lines" in Roberto's right cheek as he studied the birthmark more carefully. As Mark had earlier noted, when he'd first met Roberto at the DNR building, the bluish-black mark resembled a lopsided Christian cross. The vertical portion of the cross was a fairly uniform half-inch in width, and about three inches tall. Fortunately, the vertical portion paralleled the natural "smile lines" on Roberto's cheek. Hopefully, that would make any surgical scar fall within a natural skin crease. The real problem was going to be dealing with the "side arms" of the cross. Each "arm" projected about three-quarters of an inch, but they joined the main vertical "trunk" of the cross at *different* levels. Mark quickly decided upon his surgical approach, then explained to the patient how he'd do Stage 1:

"Roberto, I'm first going to take out only the long vertical part of your birthmark. That will leave two smaller 'nubs,' that are the 'side arms.' We'll remove the remainder at another time. Do you understand?"

"Sí ... I mean yes," Roberto replied.

Mark had Roberto turn on his left side, then placed a folded towel beneath the patient's head to serve as a thin pillow.

"Comfortable, Roberto?" Mark asked.

"Yes, Doctor. How long is this going to take?"

"Hopefully, less than an hour," Mark replied. "I'm going to put some cool stuff on your face. It is to kill germs. Are you allergic to iodine or any medications that you know of? Or maybe something a dentist has used to deaden your gums?"

"No, señor. I am allergic to nothing."

"Good," Mark replied, and began prepping the area with Betadine. Mark, Anne, and Todd donned sterile gloves. A sterile drape was placed, leaving only the birthmark exposed. Forewarned of the coming needle sticks, Roberto did not flinch the least as Mark injected the lidocaine.

"What scalpel blade?" Anne asked.

"Number 15 on a Bard-Parker handle," Mark answered, as she popped its handle immediately into his waiting gloved hand. Obviously, it had already been pre-prepared. *My great gal hasn't forgotten my routines!* he thought.

Mark quickly made a full-thickness elliptical skin incision around the vertical portion of the birthmark. Bleeding was brisk at first, but Anne applied pressure with sponges, while Mark used the electrosurgical unit to cauterize the larger vessels. With bleeding controlled, he began dissecting the long ellipse from its underlying layer of facial fatty tissue. Alternating between the "cutting" and "coagulating" frequencies of the electrosurgical unit, Mark had completed the excision in less than five minutes. Todd opened a specimen jar containing formaldehyde. Without words, and using forceps, Mark deftly placed the excised portion of "Marcado's" birthmark into the solution. "Thanks," Todd said, then further contaminated his gloves by taking a pen out of his pocket to write notes on the specimen container's label. That done, Todd put on fresh sterile gloves.

Mark studied the surgically created defect in Roberto's right cheek. It's gotta be five inches long and about an inch wide at the middle of the ellipse. *Wonder if I can close that sucker primarily ... or is the skin tension going to be too much? Probably too much,* Mark thought.

"Anne, let me have a 4-0 Ethilon with a curved cutting needle, on a short straight needle carrier."

"You're not going to close with *that* are you, Doctor?" Anne asked.

"No. Just a trial central suture of the 4-0. I'll judge the tension that way." Mark placed the central suture and found it would barely bring the skin edges back together. "Too much tension. I need to undermine the skin margins to relieve the tension. Let me have the electrosurgical unit."

Anne passed it to him. Almost bloodlessly, Mark dissected the surrounding skin from its attachments to underlying facial fatty tissue. He continued the dissection laterally to a point about an inch in front of Roberto's right ear, then the same distance medially, toward the patient's nose. He again used a trial stitch. It closed perfectly without tension.

Over the next 20 minutes, Mark did a multilayer closure of the deeper tissues, and finished by doing a plastic skin closure using many fine 6-0 Ethilon sutures.

Mark removed the drape and spoke to the patient. "Stage 1 is done, Roberto. I know your face still feels numb, but give me a big smile." Roberto complied. "Perfect!" Mark exclaimed. The entire suture line fell within a natural skin crease. Unless complications arose, Mark knew the scar would be virtually impossible to find in a few months.

"Can I see what you've done to me, Doctor?" Roberto asked.

"Sure. We just need a mirror," Mark replied, looking at Todd.

Todd quickly rummaged through the truck's glove box, but came up empty-handed. "Guess no female EMTs ever used this truck," Todd said. The marshal paused a moment, then reached into a jacket pocket. He extracted a small digital camera, instructed Roberto to smile, then snapped his picture at close range. He showed Roberto the clear image captured and displayed on the camera's LCD screen.

"¡Ahora soy un hombre con solo dos pequeñas marcas!" Roberto said excitedly. He was obviously pleased, and smiled so broadly Mark feared he might disrupt his suture line.

"Roberto!" Todd exclaimed. "Uh ... didn't we discuss the language-thing earlier? ¡El doctor no quiere 'oprimir uno para inglés!'"

They all had a good laugh, Anne included. Mark finally spoke:

"Todd, cut Roberto a little slack. I basically understood what he said: 'I'm now a man with only two small marks.' I think he's pleased, and that's what matters to me."

"Doctor," Todd began, "what matters to me is that I've just witnessed some of the finest surgical work I've ever seen! Granted, it is 'minor surgery,' but you and I both know that no surgery is ever really 'minor.' First as a youngster and medic in 'Nam, then as a civilian EMT, I know good work when I see it. And I know a capable nurse when I see one, not to mention the fact she's darn good-looking. The Service thanks you both."

Stroke egos and we'll follow you anywhere, Mark thought, but then directed his attention to another matter: Roberto's aftercare.

"Todd, we need to discuss follow-up care," Mark stated.

"You're looking at it—me!" Todd exclaimed, pointing his right thumb at the center of his own chest. "Just give me your routine for care of a surgical wound of this type, and I'll follow it to the letter." Mark elaborated details, then Todd spoke again: "I've already got Percocet for pain control after the lidocaine wears off, and I have everything else you've mentioned."

Todd instructed the Telfairs and Roberto to again don their hoods, then made a quick satphone call. Moments later the truck's rear doors swung open. Two U.S. Marshals removed Roberto from the truck using the gurney that had served as their makeshift operating table. The Telfairs again removed their hoods. Todd and Mark quickly exchanged satphone numbers, writing them on the backs of U.S. Marshals Service cards Todd had in his credentials case. The marshal promised he'd give Mark daily reports, and send daily 'wound images' to Dr. Roberson using a secure Internet site, one that Roberson could access.

Marshal Sloan Stafford soon returned to the truck and plopped down in its driver's seat. The boat's engines again rumbled to life, and they were soon underway heading back to Colonels Island. In 40 minutes they were back at the port and secured to the dock there. Mark heard the EMT truck's engine start. They backed off the cutter, its loading ramp now going uphill because the tide had receded several feet. Hooded, the Telfairs were immediately transferred to Spence's waiting Altima, and the marshal's Suburban quickly escorted them back to the port's main gate. In silence, Spence was soon driving the Telfairs north on U.S. 17, heading back to Dunham Point.

"I trust everything went OK," Spence finally said.

"Couldn't have gone better," Mark replied, then yawned.

Very few additional words were exchanged on the drive home.

Mark felt exhausted, as though he'd just finished an eight-hour major surgery. He constantly fought nodding off completely. Anne seemed to be fighting the same problem.

Between 'nods' he put his wedding ring and watch back on. A few minutes after midnight, Spence entered their drive at Dunham and dropped them off.

"Thanks, you guys. I'll be in touch," Spence said, and eased his Altima out of the Telfairs' driveway.

Mark used their "hidden" house key to enter their home. Both crashed into bed, still clothed in black. "Thanks for all the help, Anne," Mark said, sleep rapidly overtaking him.

"Little Man, mark this day on our calendar ... the day we were both too tired for sex ... or food ... or ..."

She never finished the sentence.

22

THE MORNING AFTER

About eight a.m. the next morning, the Telfairs began slowly awakening from a dreamless sleep. Both were in that special blissful zone, one that separates the human states of consciousness and unconsciousness.

Was last night all a crazy dream? Why do I still have all my clothes on ... including my shoes? Mark thought, wondering if Anne felt it was all a dream, too. At arm's length, Mark lightly nudged her shoulder. She was obviously more awake than he. Anne abruptly sat up on her side of their king-sized bed, then immediately spoke: "Little Man, that was some evening, wasn't it?" she asked, beginning to take her clothes off. "Sure felt like a dream, didn't it?"

"Yeah, I thought so, too, at first ... but it wasn't," Mark replied, sitting on his side of the bed to begin removing his own clothes. "See these?"

"See what?" she asked, turning to look at the items Mark extended toward her from the other side of the bed.

Mark held his driver's license, a U.S. Marshals Service card with a number written on its backside, and a wadded-up disposable green surgical mask. He'd just removed them from the various pockets of his black jeans. Anne immediately searched the pockets of her own jeans, and retrieved her driver's license watch and wedding rings. "Glad they didn't go through the washer and dryer!" Anne said, laughing.

Anne was now down to her black panties and a sexy black lacy bra. Sultry thoughts raced through Mark's mind. His private anatomy suddenly began preparing for action. Anne smiled as she looked on ... but he began wilting as his brain processed what he was now *hearing:* the beeping satphone! He'd apparently placed the phone on his nightstand the night before. "Shit," Mark muttered, as he punched a button to receive the incoming call. It was Oscar Dunham. He was back from his prostate cancer surgery checkup in Atlanta, and wanted to know if Mark wanted to go upriver. "Needs to be up there 'bout noon today, if we goin'. That's when th' river water she be high. Be 'bout eight foots, th' radio say."

"Sure, Oscar," Mark replied, now completely limp, his mind now drifting more toward food than sex. "Did the radio say which way the wind would be coming from?"

"Dey say straight northeast, eight to ten."

"Oscar, can I meet you at the landing at 11:30? That would give us time to have everything ready by high tide at noon," Mark replied.

"That be fine," Oscar said, then hung up.

"Little Man, that beeping phone sure stopped you dead in your tracks, didn't it?" Anne asked, now laughing as they both surveyed his flaccid anatomy. "But I'll try to do a little nurse-wife CPR on it this evening. Betcha I can fix it!"

"Anne, I'll look forward to your resuscitative efforts, but I don't think it was actually the phone's beep, just the possibility of receiving bad news ... maybe something going wrong with Roberto's surgery."

"You've got Todd's number. Why don't you give him a call?"

"Good idea," Mark replied, grabbing the satphone and punching in numbers Todd had written on his card. He answered on the first ring.

"Who's calling?" Todd asked. "Identify."

"It's me, Mark Telfair."

"What's your ident code? It should have been given to you by HNNWR 1."

"Uh ... mine's HNNWR 4," Mark replied.

"Sorry, Doc. But that's the drill ... until I get use to hearing your voice over this special phone. OK?"

"How's the patient this morning?" Mark asked.

"Doing fine, Doc. He has a little ecchymosis in his right infraorbital area, but it's really minimal. It looks like a very slight black eye, involving the lower lid only. The Percocet is holding his pain just fine. As you instructed, I took that thin postop wound dressing off this morning, and applied Neosporin to the suture line after cleaning it with peroxide. Roberto keeps looking in the mirror every 30 minutes, and still can't believe how much better it already looks. Don't worry, I'll call you if I even *think* something is wrong. I've already sent this morning's wound image to HNNWR 1. So, you can look at it today, if you can catch him. Call me back if you see anything in the picture that disturbs you."

"I'll do that, Todd. But where are you now?"

"Doc, you know I can't disclose that. We're less than an hour apart. OK?" Todd replied, ending the call.

After Mark finished his call, Anne asked a question: "Feel better now?"

"Yeah. I don't know exactly why I get so concerned over something as minor as Roberto's surgery."

"Because you really *care,* Mark. Major or minor, you want all your surgeries to come out perfect. Among other things, you have a big ego. You don't accept failure well, nor should you. That's just my observation after living and working with you all these years."

"Do you think that's why we both felt so beat last night when we got back home?" Mark asked.

"Possibly. But I'm the same way you are. We're both perfectionists when it comes to surgery and surgical nursing. I think the reason I felt so tired was that it was a very *stressful* evening for me ... everything happening in a totally unknown environment, combined with all that hocus-pocus black-hooded secrecy that seems to surround this whole damn mess!"

She has a way of summarizing situations and emotions ... something I've never been able to do, Mark thought while his stomach growled. "Anyway, are you as hungry as I am? You know we've not eaten a thing since lunch yesterday."

Anne completely undressed, put on her robe, and scurried to the kitchen to prepare the large breakfast they both needed and deserved. While Anne cooked, Mark took a quick shower, dressed in fresh clothes, then checked all his kite gear.

The Telfairs sat on stools eating at the breakfast bar in their kitchen, and began discussing the prior evening. "Anne, you know it would have been a lot less expensive to do Roberto's surgery in a doctor's office, like the one we had in Statesville. Todd said—and I don't think he was joking—that it was costing $500 a *minute* to do the surgery where we did it! Figure we were there about two hours. What's that come to?"

"Little 'Non-math' Man, that's a mere $60,000. And what would you have charged to do the same thing in the Statesville office?"

"About $250, including the follow-up care," Mark replied. "And about another $250 for the second stage to remove the remainder of his birthmark."

"So why do you think our government is willing to spend that kind of money on an agent they want to work undercover for DEA?" Anne asked.

"It has got to be something Roberto *knows.* Something that no other agent knows. Remember the first time we met Roberto at the

DNR building in Brunswick? Remember how he said he was captured, tortured, and eventually joined some Mexican drug cartel?"

Anne paused a moment. "The 'Sinaloa Cartel' is what Roberto told us."

God, she's got a memory, Mark thought first. He then said, "I thought that cartel operated in Mexico, and Dr. Roberson is telling us the origin of this high-tech marijuana is in Canada. Help me connect the dots here."

"Mark, I'll bet you money the Sinaloa also controls the flow of marijuana *out* of Canada. They may not control the actual production there in Canada, but probably control the outgoing traffic. I'll also bet the Sinaloa owns and operates those Atlantic Coast SS boats Dr. Roberson seems to be so interested in."

"Makes sense to me, Anne. Maybe you should have been a detective ... instead of a surgical nurse."

"But then we'd probably never have met each other ... like our very first meeting when your scrub pants fell off in the OR at Grady ... and you had on no underwear!"

"You've certainly got a point there, Anne," Mark said, blushing, as he, too, recalled that embarrassing day. "But do you remember why we retired from private practice so early? We retired mainly to avoid *stress* ... and it looks like we've jumped right back into the middle of it!"

Anne sighed. "I don't know about you, but I'm now so intrigued I'll just have to accept the stress that goes with it. At least we don't have to worry about malpractice suits! And the quicker we get to the bottom of the drug problem here, the quicker the associated stress will go away."

Mark smiled and checked his watch: 10:45. "I'll clean up the kitchen while you get dressed. We're supposed to meet Oscar at the landing in about 45 minutes."

* * *

The boat ride upriver with Oscar took only 30 minutes. Anne had already learned a lesson during her first ride in Oscar's open boat: Ponytails work great. They passed not a single boat on the trip to the string of unnumbered floats. Nothing appeared changed, except the wind direction was not due northeast as predicted. Oscar found a convenient side creek no wider than his boat. He cautiously backed about 60 feet into the creek, one Oscar said was named "Gator Creek." Mark dropped anchor when told to do so, and tied the line to a cleat at the stern. "We now be line up with th' wind to put yo' kite e'zakly over them floats in th' straightaway," Oscar explained, mainly for Anne's benefit.

Mark had his rig in the air in a matter of minutes. He had set the camera to shoot infrared images only, with the camera aimed straight down, automatically snapping a new picture every 30 seconds. Mark found it quite boring now that everything was done by the camera.

"Nosy," the huge dolphin, paid them an entertaining visit for about a half-hour. That helped break the boredom. Oscar again demonstrated Nosy's tug-of-war trick with the boat paddle. Anne laughed ecstatically and the dolphin squealed. Using her little digital camera, she snapped many close-up pictures of "man against dolphin," with Oscar again winning in the end.

Oscar quietly stowed the paddle. "We's got company comin'," Oscar whispered, as he lowered the boat's radio antenna—the only object on the boat that projected higher than the marsh grass surrounding them at their "hiding place" in the creek.

What the heck does Oscar mean about company? I don't see a thing, Mark thought.

"Y'all jus' be real quiet an' listens. Hear it?" Oscar whispered, pointing downriver.

Both Mark and Anne cupped their ears with their hands, and listened intently. *There is certainly nothing wrong with this 82-year-old's hearing! I hear it, too. A definite humming, like a colony of bees, but lower in pitch. Small engines?* Mark's mind questioned.

"Y'all stay low in th' boat. I think it's 'em SS things Dr. Robeson been talkin' 'bout. Jus' hope they don't look up and see yo' kite stuff. I's 'fraid to start my motor an' pull out dis side creek. Bes' we stays here ... and hope we get some pitchers," Oscar said, reaching in his duffel to retrieve his pistol, satphone, and fish fillet knife in a leather scabbard. He handed the knife to Mark and whispered, "Don't worry 'bout pullin' no anchor if we gotta leave in a hurry. Jus' cut de rope."

Both Mark and Anne were hunkered down. For the first time, the Telfairs were more frightened than stressed. Oscar began quickly punching at the numbed keys on his satphone, and soon was whispering to Dr. Roberson: "We's hid back in Gator Creek, and we's got all th' kite stuff up in the air over they crab floats. I think it's 'em SSs comin', 'least I think I kin hear they motors, and it ain't no reg'lar motors." Oscar paused, apparently receiving instructions from

Roberson: "Yes, suh. I already did that." Another pause: "No, suh. We ain't gonna do that 'less we has to, an' I keep it on."

Damn! I forgot my satphone ... glad Oscar remembered his, Mark thought, angry at himself.

"Oscar, what did Roberson say?" Anne whispered, while Mark checked the sharpness of the fillet knife he'd been handed. *Like a razor!* he thought, feeling its edge.

"Doc Roberson say fo' us to stay where we is, an' push th' special button that tell where you is at, an' keep dis phone on."

The humming grew louder, though still difficult to hear unless you specifically listened for it. Moments later the humming seemed to stop completely. Mark heard something that sounded like a rifle shot, soon followed by something sounding like a car door slamming.

"They's shootin' at somethin' now!" Oscar whispered into his satphone. "Sound lak big rifle to me. One shot. Dat's all I hear." After a pause, Oscar replied, "Yes, suh. We is gonna stay hid up dis creek for rat now."

Can't see jackshit from where we are. God, I hope that camera is functioning and capturing what we are hearing, Mark thought, reaching for his wallet to locate Saint Christopher. First Mark, then Anne, rubbed the medal. Oscar observed this strange ritual, and finally joined the Telfairs by rubbing his large work-callused index finger on the medal in Mark's palm. "De Lawd is gonna hep us, y'all jus' wait 'n see," Oscar whispered, and managed a smile.

The words were no sooner out of Oscar's mouth when Mark heard the humming begin again. Slowly the sound faded. When all aboard agreed they could no longer hear anything, Oscar spoke to Roberson: "We thinks dey is lef'... done gone back downriver. Ever'thing is gone quiet. Want us to leave now?" Another pause. "Yes, suh. We do dat, an' I stay on de phone."

"Oscar, what did Dr. Roberson want us to do?" Mark asked now speaking in a normal tone.

"He say fo' us to wait here 'bout 20 minute, then leave real slow. Keep a sharp eye for anything stickin' out de water that ain't natchel. 'Don't pass hit if hit ain't natchel,' he tell me. He say they's gonna try to get a bunch of shrimp boat in th' river quick, and see if dey kin catch 'em a SS while dey is leavin'."

The color had returned to Anne's face. She finally said, "Sure is peaceful now. Just hear birds peeping somewhere in the marsh grass nearby."

"'Em ain't no birds. They's baby gators hatchin' out," Oscar informed. "Mus' be a nest close by."

Moments later all aboard heard a guttural roar that reminded Mark of a recorded lion's roar being played too slowly on a tape. All eyes were now focused on a huge alligator less than six feet behind the boat's transom. The roar came again, creating visible vibrations in the water at the gator's sides. Seconds later, the huge reptile had its entire head and front legs inside the hull, attempting to get fully into Oscar's boat. The gator opened its mouth and hissed loudly, revealing hundreds of round teeth, some missing in spots. It was trying to enter alongside the motor where the transom cuts down, affording minimum freeboard. Oscar steadied the Sig-Sauer 9mm, and fired a shot directly between the gator's eyes. It dropped back into the water and did a death roll. Oscar got off two more head shots to be sure, then casually asked, "Where's my knife I give you, Doctor?" Mark gave Oscar his knife back, and watched as Oscar expertly severed the gator's tail. *The tail alone is five feet long!* Mark mentally guessed.

"Sho gonna have me some fine eatin' tonight," Oscar casually commented, while waiting for Mark to get his kite rig down and back into the boat. Mark checked his watch. The camera had been airborne for little over three hours—beyond the "two-hour battery life" stated in the manual that came with the camera. *Sure hope I didn't miss getting pictures when we heard what we thought was a rifle shot,* Mark thought, as he pulled the boat's single stern anchor.

The tide now outgoing, Oscar allowed the boat to drift out of Gator Creek. All eyes aboard surveyed the downriver straightaway. The six crab floats appeared undisturbed. Oscar started his engine, put it in gear, but kept it at idle speed. Essentially, he was using the engine only to control his downriver heading, and wasn't moving much faster than the outgoing tide itself. All eyes were looking for *anything* that might be projecting from the river's surface.

Anne sited a few "false alarms." On one sighting, Oscar corrected her: "Miss Anne, dat's jus' an ol' snag tree limb. Live oak. Been stickin' up there many a year. Whole tree, she is up under de water." But sharp-eyed old Oscar soon spotted things that were *not natural.* "Oh Lawd! We's got company up ahead. See they things stickin' up? They's three of 'em!" He put his engine in neutral, then reverse, using just enough throttle to keep them in a fixed position against the outgoing tide. "Doctor, you come here an' run th' boat. Keep us e'zakly where we is while I talks on th' phone."

Oscar talked to Roberson for several minutes.

"What did he have to say?" Mark asked, from the helm of Oscar's boat.

"He say 'keep same distance back,' and let him know if they turns 'round. He say he knows e'zakly where we is at. Dat GPS stuff, he tol' me. And he say he's got six shrimp boat a comin' up the river now, and he wanna know if they's any side creek 'em SSs kin hide in. I tell him no ... *can't hide now!*"

23

THE AFTERNOON AFTER

Oscar replaced Mark at the helm of the Carolina Skiff, and passed his satphone over to Mark with Dr. Roberson still connected. Mark spoke: "It's me, Spence. Oscar's driving the boat now. Where are you located?"

"I'm sitting in my pickup in the parking lot at the landing. Obviously I've got my satphone, but I'm also monitoring Channel 10, on a marine FM radio I've got in my truck. I've locked the gate to the landing and its parking area … don't want any innocent visitors getting in the middle of what may soon be going down here."

Innocent visitors? Shit … what about us! Me and Anne and Oscar! Mark thought, but resumed his conversation with Roberson: "From what Oscar has relayed to us, it sounds like you're planning to catch the SSs in shrimp nets. You don't really think that will work, do you?"

"Doctor, to be honest, I have no idea. Using the shrimp boats was entirely Victor's idea. I personally think the SSs would cut right through their nets, but the shrimpers think even if they did break through the netting, they'd end up getting their props so fouled in the netting, they'd be dead in the water anyway. Even knowing they may be putting their nets at risk, Vic had no problem recruiting some six shrimp boats he's got coming. He told me he thought the 'volunteer shrimpers' probably figured if they cooperated with a special request from DNR, the DNR would possibly 'cut them some slack' down the road … when they got caught breaking some of DNR's shrimping regs!"

"Spence, I've never been aboard a commercial shrimp boat in my life. I've pulled a ten-foot bait-shrimp net behind my own boats, so I understand the basic principle of how a power-drawn net works. But that's it. We're still up river about 200 yards behind the SSs that are still moving slowly downriver. There's only one more river bend before they'll be at Barbour Landing. I'd estimate they're only 20 minutes away," Mark explained.

"Good. In a few minutes, I'll need to sign off and talk to Vic on this phone. Vic's aboard the lead shrimp boat, the first one they'll encounter. It's named *Cap'n Joe.* Vic's the 'shrimper's fleet commander,' so to speak. They are communicating among themselves by marine FM radio. They're on Channel 10, Vic said. The SSs may be listening in. Do you see any kind of antennas sticking up from any of the SSs?"

"Just a minute, Spence." Mark grabbed a pair of binoculars from Anne's purse and quickly scanned. "No, Spence. No antennas. Nothing sticking up ... except for their forward snorkels and aft exhaust pipes. Occasionally, at water level, I can see what looks like a radar dome. It's about midway between the two pipes. And I see nothing that looks like a periscope," Mark explained. "Uh ... Spence, is it OK if we listen in on Channel 10? Here in Oscar's boat?"

"I think *listening* is OK ... just do *not* transmit from Oscar's boat on *any* FM radio channel. The satphone is safe. They can't detect that frequency. But the SSs may be equipped with RDF ... a standard radio direction finder. That would tell them that you guys are tailing them down the river. If they have RDF, or they're using their radar, they'll surely detect the shrimp boats coming at them from downriver. I don't see any way the subs' detection of the shrimp boats can be avoided."

"What if the SSs decide to dive? Could they escape the nets?" Mark asked.

"From my truck, I can see that the tide is now more than halfway out. Vic tells me the Barbour won't be all that deep by the time the SSs encounter the shrimp boats. Hopefully, the SSs and the shrimpers will meet up in a few minutes. If your predicted ETA for the SSs is correct, it should all happen close to the landing. I think Vic is planning to have the shrimpers in a staggered formation, with all their nets out at various depths. At half-tide, that should cover the entire cross section of the river, top to bottom."

"Well, I sure hope it works, Spence," Mark replied.

"By any chance does Anne happen to have her digital camera with her?"

"Yeah. She's got it, Spence."

"Ask her to zoom as best her little camera can, and take lots of SS pictures. Tell her to photograph anything that seems suspicious. The SSs' radar may have already told them that you guys are following them down the river. Tell Oscar to keep following, but maintain the *same* distance separating you guys from the SSs. That way they may think Oscar's boat is just a passive object, like a fallen tree that's floating, or some other unmanned object floating behind them with the tide. I'm gonna break off now. I really need to use this phone to talk to Vic for a minute or two," Roberson said, terminating the call.

Mark quickly relayed details of the entire satphone conversation he'd just had with Dr. Roberson.

Anne smiled. "Looks like it's all about to hit the fan, fellas!" she commented, while taking pictures. "Hey, you guys! Look over the marsh grass now. I can now see the stuff sticking up from the shrimp boats. A bunch of 'em. And guess what? The SSs have just ducked under completely. There's nothing sticking up from them now!"

Shit! Mark thought. *Now we have absolutely no idea where they are. Could be coming back our way. Need to tell Roberson.*

Mark quickly punched in Roberson's number using Oscar's phone. "Spence, it's me again. The SSs have just gone under! We don't know where they are. The shrimp boats are now about 500 yards away from us ... at least we can see their outriggers over the tops of the marsh grass, and they all seem to be lowering them now. What are they doing? What do you want us to do now?"

A long pause followed. At first, Mark thought he'd lost his phone connection with Spence, but apparently he'd just been watching the action and thinking. "Uh, I've got a good view from my position here in the parking lot, and they're all putting their nets in the water. Tell Oscar to turn around and go back upriver about 500 yards, and hold that position until you hear from me again. Keep looking for any sign of the SSs coming back your way. Call me immediately if you see any evidence of that. And ask Oscar to be thinking about a side creek, one that would be too shallow for an SS to even enter," Roberson said, and signed off.

Mark again relayed Roberson's message to Oscar. When told about 'thinking about a side creek,' Oscar replied, "I done already tol' him, *can't hide now!*"

"Oscar, I think Dr. Roberson was talking about a place for *us* to hide! Just in case the SSs come back our way."

"I done already thinks 'bout dat. Dis skiff, she kin run in one foots water. Has to tilt the motor up, you know. But I sho kin hide up a side creek, an' 'em SSs thing can't!"

They all heard the multiple diesel engines of the shrimp boats throttle up downriver, and could see a little black smoke rising above their barely visible superstructures.

"Oscar, since we can't see what's happening, do you think we can listen on Channel 10?"

"Reckon so," Oscar said, raising his antenna and turning the radio on.

The timing was perfect, and FM reception completely clear on Channel 10: "This is the *Cap'n Joe*. We got something big in *both* our nets. Too heavy to lift. We're going on anchor till we figure it out." Mark recognized the radio voice as that of Victor Timmons, apparently aboard the *Cap'n Joe*.

Next: "This is *Goin' Broke*. We got something in our starboard net that's not very heavy. We're raising that net now ... ah shit! Ain't nothin' but a big-assed dead dolphin. Big sucker. Sorry 'bout that, fella."

Thirty seconds later: "*Jolly Mon*, here. Got somethin' in our starboard net. Ain't too big, whatever it is."

Another 30 seconds passed: "*Big Haul*, here. We got something in our port net ... too heavy to lift without us turning turtle. Goin' on anchor now. Catch ya later when we figure it out."

A minute later *Jolly Mon* reported: "You guys ain't gonna believe this shit, but we've got *half* a gator in our net! Three shots to the head, and his tail has been cut off! Musta been 'bout a 12-footer, before he lost his tail."

Goin' Broke soon reported again, apparently not wanting to be "topped" by *Jolly Mon's* "half-gator" report: "Hey guys, we didn't drown that dolphin in our net. He's been shot by some big-assed gun, probably a rifle. Exit wound's the size of a fuckin' tennis ball. I shit you not!"

Anne had tears in her eyes as she sorted through the shrimper's radio reports. "Looks like the gunshot we heard up river was when someone shot Nosy. And we're responsible for that 'half-gator' ... but Oscar had no other choice," Anne said, drying her eyes on a Kleenex removed from her purse.

"So," Mark said, "it sounds like *Big Haul* and *Cap'n Joe* might be the ones who actually caught the SSs." The words *bottom hatch*, then *SCUBA*, suddenly popped into Mark's head. He turned the volume down on Channel 10, then frantically dialed Spence on the satphone. He answered immediately. "Spence, we were listening on Channel 10, so we pretty much know what's happened. Remember Anne's 'bottom hatch' theory? Sounds like the shrimpers may have netted three of 'em, but could the crew have escaped?"

"Not from *Cap'n Joe*," Spence replied. "His nets are pretty much intact, and wrap the subs so tightly I don't think they can even open

174

an escape hatch. They've seen no SCUBA bubbles, so far. Right now *Cap'n Joe* is still anchored and holding both of them at the surface. They finally got both subs oriented so their snorkels are exposed. Maybe the crew won't suffocate before we can figure out how to get them out of the river. Right now we're trying to find a way to get *Big Haul's* catch to the surface. We're not even positive it's a sub yet. Vic's got a local dock-builder's barge coming, one that has a huge crane. That barge is hurrying to the scene as we speak. That's all I can tell you guys for now. Keep your phone on. I'll call back when I know more."

With the tide still going out, Mark, Anne and Oscar held their position some 500 yards upriver; Oscar was first to sound the alarm. "Look at dat! Ain't natchel See dem bubbles! Doc, you hold de boat where we is. I's gonna get my gun."

Mark quickly took the helm. Oscar removed his Sig-Sauer 226 and two extra ammo clips from his duffle. He then passed his fillet knife to Anne. In fright, she hunkered down oblivious to the fact she was sitting on a gator's tail in the bottom of Oscar's boat. She removed the knife from the scabbard, and whispered, "Saint Christopher, don't let us down."

Mark observed the pattern of bubbles. With the tide slowing, and the wind dropping, the river surface became a semi-mirror. Mark found himself in analytical thought: *That pattern of bubbles tells me there are possibly three SCUBA divers and they are all hyperventilating. I'd be breathing that fast, too. Dumbasses are trying to swim against a knot or two of river current ... and their air certainly won't last long that way.* Mark adjusted the throttle in reverse to keep the nearest bubble pattern about 25 feet off the bow of Oscar's skiff. Oscar perched himself on the small foredeck of the boat, holding his gun at the ready. "You's doin' good, Doctor. Jus' keep same distance. Don't you worry none. Whatever they is, they ain't getting in *my* boat alive ... if they tries to!"

Anne seemed calmer now. Still with knife in hand, she began taking pictures of the three intermittent strings of bubbles.

Suddenly it happened: *Three Hispanic-looking men popped to the surface near the river's east bank!* All three, standing in less than three feet of water, were still hyperventilating. Their SCUBA regulators dangled uselessly at their sides. Clad only in underwear and SCUBA gear, and spotting Oscar with his gun leveled at them, each man held his hands high over his head in surrender. Each seemed to be trying to catch enough breath to speak.

Mark could feel his heart hammering inside his chest and head. With one hand Oscar quickly tossed his bow anchor out, and the boat gently swung around, its bow now pointing upriver. As the boat swung, Oscar moved to the stern to keep his weapon aimed at the three men. They'd now huddled closely together as they sat on black marsh mud at the river's edge.

"¡Hey gringos! ¿Hablan español?" the man on the left side of the huddle finally managed to ask, though still breathing far more rapidly than normal.

"Muy poco!" Mark replied, not knowing why a little of his high-school Spanish seemed to be coming back. "¡Quitese su SCUBA—no pararse—sientase con sus manos en la cabeza!" Mark yelled, hoping he'd gotten it right.

"Doc, what you tell 'em?" Oscar asked, still keeping his gun leveled at the three men.

"I'm not positive, Oscar. I tried to tell them I speak only a little Spanish, then told them to remove their SCUBA gear and not to stand up, then sit with their hands behind their heads," Mark replied.

The men obviously understood well enough that all three removed their olive drab SCUBA tanks and black swim fins, then sat at the water's edge with their hands behind their heads.

"Well, tell 'em if dey tries to run, I gonna shoot," Oscar said. "I knows they can't ev'n run in dis black river pluff mud ... they'd sink up to they balls if they tries. But I betcha 'em mens don't know dat!"

"¡Si corren le vamous a disparar!" Mark said, not at all sure he had it right.

"Sí, entendemos," the captives' spokesman replied.

"What ya tell 'em, Doc?" Oscar asked.

"I think I told them we would kill them if they tried to run, and the one that's doing all the talking said, 'Si, entendemos,' which is 'Yes, we understand,' I think," Mark explained.

With the situation stable in Oscar's boat, Mark called Dr. Roberson on the satphone: "Spence, Oscar is now holding his gun on three Hispanic-looking men that were trying to swim in SCUBA gear against the last of the outgoing tide. They're about 20 feet from us now, and just sitting on a mudflat on the river's east bank. They do not appear to be armed, and I think they've surrendered. We're now anchored, and still about 500 yards upriver. What's going on at the landing?"

"Not much change. *Cap'n Joe* and *Big Haul* are both anchored. We're now positive we have three SSs. The three folks you've caught are probably the crew members of the sub *Big Haul* netted. His net is in shreds, but parts of the netting managed to foul the prop of that sub. That sub also had a bottom hatch that was open. A dock builder's barge has just arrived on scene. The barge has a crane we think will be capable of lifting the three subs out intact. I just hope the crew inside the two subs *Cap'n Joe* has are still alive, and we'll be able to interrogate them," Spence explained.

"Great!" Mark replied. "But what do you want us to do about the three dudes we've got sitting here?" Mark asked.

"Sit tight. I'll tell Vic to send a couple of the smaller DNR boats your way. They'll take those fellows off your hands," Spence said.

"Why not call the McIntosh County Sheriff's Department?" Mark innocently asked.

"Doc, It's still the 'good-ole-boy' system with some of the 'locals.' Not as bad as it allegedly was back during the Sheriff Poppell era, but it's possibly still with us. I think it may also be a matter of jurisdiction … seems this is all going down on federal property within the Harris Neck National Wildlife Refuge. Anyway, we'll let the lawyers sort all that stuff out. When the DNR boats get to where you guys are, let them take the three guys you've got pinned down into their custody. And, for God's sake, tell Oscar *not* to shoot a single one of them! Self-defense excluded," Roberson added, then signed off.

Twenty minutes later two 16-foot DNR Boston Whalers rounded the river bend, and headed straight to Oscar's boat. Anticipating that explaining the gator tail to DNR may be an issue, Oscar instructed Anne to cover it with the poncho he'd quickly handed her. Each DNR boat was manned by two officers. Mark did not recall seeing any of the officers before, but rapidly explained the situation. One officer in each boat drew their weapons, then instructed Oscar to put his gun away. With reluctance, Oscar complied. Soon, the "prisoners" were handcuffed and aboard the DNR boats. Even the SCUBA gear was taken aboard: "Evidence," one of the DNR officers explained.

Preparing to depart, and after spitting at Mark, the prisoner who'd done all the talking yelled a message to everyone in Oscar's boat: "¡Hey gringos! No vamous a olvidar sus caras. Sinaloa los encontrara a todos, y los mataran."

Oh shit! I hope he didn't say what I think he did, Mark thought.

"What he say?" Oscar asked, while putting his gun and ammo back in his duffel bag.

"I think he said 'I will not forget your faces and Sinaloa will find us and we'll all die!' or something close to that."

"Lawd, jus' what we needs," Oscar sighed. "But maybe they keeps 'em mens lock up where they ain't able to talk to 'em bad Sin'loa peoples."

Everyone in Oscar's boat seemed to be holding their breath when they rounded the bend and saw the clutter of boats at the landing: six shrimp boats, a dock builder's barge, and several additional DNR boats.

Mark dialed Spence: "What's happening now?"

"Well, we've another interesting development, Doc. An undercover agent radioed us that the pontoon boat with blue tarps was put in the water at Kip's Fish Camp about 25 minutes ago. You know, the one you guys earlier spotted with the bogus Georgia registration?"

"Sure," Mark replied, "and I bet I know exactly where it's headed … up the Barbour River to pick up what the SSs probably left in those traps this morning!"

"My thoughts, too, Doc. Y'all have any ideas on how we could box that pontoon in?" Spence asked.

"Hold on a minute. Let me talk to Oscar and Anne," Mark said, then explained the situation to all aboard Oscar's boat. Anne quickly came up with a possible solution.

"Uh, Spence. We've all talked it over. Anne asked if the four extra shrimp boats on site could quietly proceed single file downriver? If the pontoon approaches them coming from downriver, casually allow the pontoon to pass, maybe even give it a friendly wave. Then suddenly have the shrimp boats turn broadside in the river, and anchor."

"Brilliant!" Spence exclaimed. "An old-fashioned mechanical blockade! If they can put 'em bow-to-stern across the river, no boat of significant width could pass!"

"Spence, we also suggest radio silence on Channel 10. I'd make it *all* marine FM channels, just in case that pontoon is listening in. Have the extra smaller DNR boats *verbally* relay the plan to the 'blockade' boats."

"Mark, I can't thank you guys enough. But you're not going to like what I've got to say … what I *must* say: Quickly secure Oscar's boat, get your kite gear, and leave the area. Do it *now!* You, Oscar, and Anne!"

"OK, we'll do it. But *why?*"

"Tell you later," Spence said.

"But Spence, you've locked the gate to the landing, remember?"

"When you get to the parking lot, come to my truck. I'll give you the gate key. When you get your vehicle and Oscar's old truck out, *relock* the gate and hide the key under some sand behind the post on the hinge end of the gate. I'll let myself out later. Tell Oscar I'll double-check his boat, and be sure all is secure before I leave."

After they'd been given Dr. Roberson's "orders," the conversation among Anne, Oscar, and Mark was brief, but lively.

Anne: "I feel just like we've been told we can't even watch the end of the movie—one we all acted in—and we even helped them write the script!"

Oscar: "I feel lak I's done a heap of work for nothin', an' ain't gettin' no enjoyment pay, 'cept a good gator-tail dinner tonight ... and I ev'n had to lef' dat in my boat. Too many 'em DNR folks, 'round, you know."

Mark: "Oscar, don't feel too bad. I was counting on some 'tail' tonight, too ... but not what you had in mind. And I'm now too dang beat to think about anything else—but *sleep!*"

24

AFTER THE SHOW

Locking the gate behind themselves as Spence had instructed, the Telfairs and Oscar promptly left the landing in their respective vehicles. After traveling about a half-mile down Harris Neck Road, Mark saw two McIntosh County Sheriff's cars that were speeding eastward toward them. They had their red and blue lights flashing, but their sirens weren't blaring. *Guess they're just going to see the action for themselves ... or claim a piece of the glory!* Mark thought. He felt relieved that the "locals" Dr. Roberson seemingly distrusted had paid no attention to their Explorer, nor to Oscar's old Chevy truck. Without slowing the least, two patrol cars had flown right past them. *They're doing at least 90!* Mark estimated in thought.

Without words, Mark and Anne turned off on Plantation Drive, the road to Dunham Point; Oscar, who was behind them, continued west on Harris Neck Road. Presumably, he was heading for his own house about another mile up the road.

When they arrived at their home, Mark retrieved the infrared camera from the kite gear stowed in the back of the Explorer. He locked their car and carefully carried the expensive camera inside. Both he and Anne crashed onto their sofa with a muffled thud.

Anne finally said, "Little Man, don't you think it's time for a martini?"

"Darn right!" Mark said, checking his watch to discover it was a little after five.

With a groan, Mark drug himself off the sofa, and went to the kitchen to make their drinks; meantime, Anne used the remote to turn on their TV. Savannah's Channel 11 filled the screen. A banner moved across the bottom of the screen: "Breaking News in McIntosh County ... Unique Drug Bust in Progress."

Anne couldn't believe her eyes. She turned the sound up and called to Mark in the kitchen. "Little Man, better come in here! You're not gonna believe what WTOC has got on their Early Edition News!"

Mark was bringing their martinis to the coffee table, but momentarily froze in his tracks, a drink in each hand. The newscaster spoke: "We interrupt the evening news to bring you this breaking story. These are live images from the scene. Our Bob Corrigan is bringing you this exclusive report from WTOC's helicopter. Bob ..."

"Thanks, Dan. About an hour ago, McIntosh shrimpers apparently captured three small submarine-like boats in the Barbour River at the Harris Neck National Wildlife Refuge. As you can see, there is now a large barge in the middle of the river, and on its deck are what appear to be three submarine-like boats entangled in shrimp nets. I'd estimate the identical-looking boats are each about 30 feet long. We do not know if they are manned, and if so, we know nothing about the status of any possible crew members. We do not know if this was an accident or done on purpose, but we received a radio message from a person on the ground. That person refused to be named, but indicated he was from the McIntosh Sheriff's Department, and stated this was a 'planned ongoing antidrug operation.' That same spokesman indicated he had seen a white-hulled open workboat arrive on the scene and secure to the dock at Barbour Landing. He described that boat's occupants as a middle-aged white man and woman, and an elderly black male, and further indicated they rapidly left the scene while all this was happening. The witness declined any additional comment because 'It is an ongoing investigation,' he stated."

The chopper's camera zoomed to the deck of the barge where the three SSs were resting side by side. The barge crew appeared to be cutting nets away and securing the subs to the deck of the barge with straps of some kind. Mark handed Anne her martini, and slowly sat next to her on the sofa.

The WTOC report continued, but the chopper obviously had changed positions. "This is Bob Corrigan, continuing to bring you exclusive live images from McIntosh County, Georgia. We are covering what appears to be three drug-smuggling submarines that have just been caught in the Barbour River at the Harris Neck National Wildlife Refuge. We're 200 yards south of the barge that has the actual submarines aboard. You're now looking at four shrimp boats, either anchored or run aground. They appear to be completely blocking the Barbour River. As you can see, there is also a pontoon boat about 50 yards upriver of those shrimp boats that block the river. The pontoon boat seems to be anchored, and is being boarded by what appears to be several officers getting out of two DNR boats that have quickly come alongside."

The helicopter camera zoomed to the deck of the pontoon, and the uniformed DNR officers could be seen handcuffing three men aboard. Mark could hear radio talk in the background of the chopper's noisy cockpit, but the only word he was sure of was "immediately," spoken several times.

"Sorry folks, but this is Glynn Barden, pilot of WTOC's helicopter. Savannah Air Traffic Control has just advised us we are flying in *restricted airspace*. No unauthorized motorized aircraft are permitted in this area. ATC has just informed us we must immediately leave any airspace over or near the Harris Neck National Refuge … and we are going to comply."

In the helicopter, Bob Corrigan spoke apologetically: "On behalf of WTOC, let me apologize to our viewers for the interruption of this live coverage. I now return you to WTOC's Savannah studio. Dan Durden will continue with our regularly scheduled Early Edition Newscast. Dan …"

"Dan Durden, here at WTOC's Savannah studio. You were watching an exclusive live aerial report from Bob Corrigan in the WTOC helicopter. We thank Bob for what he was able to bring us. We must pause now for a brief commercial message before resuming WTOC's Early Edition. Stay tuned."

Anne muted the TV, then took a gulp of her martini. Mark did the same, then said, "Well, shit! It's bad enough that some 'witness' called us 'middle-aged,' but it's even worse to know there was a 'witness' that could possibly identify us … like you, me, and Oscar! On top of that, the Hispanic guy in the river said he would not forget our faces, nor would the Sinaloa Cartel. And that they would find us and kill us. Anne, I think we're into this way over our heads!"

After taking a sip of her martini, Anne said, "Maybe so, but I think we need to tell Oscar … in case he hasn't seen the news. And we need to talk to Dr. Roberson, before we panic. Let's try calling Oscar first, then Roberson."

Mark went to their bedroom and retrieved the satphone he'd forgotten to take with him earlier in the day. He called Oscar. After allowing the phone to ring a number of times, Mark said, "Oscar doesn't answer, Anne!"

"Hummm," she said. "Then try Spence."

Mark immediately dialed Spencer's secure number. He let it ring 15 times. *No answer!*

"Well?" Anne asked, staring at Mark.

"Spence doesn't answer either! I think we should just get in our car and see if we can find Oscar's house. I know which road he lives down, but I don't know exactly which house he lives in."

"You're taking our pistol, aren't you?" Anne asked.

"You bet!" Mark responded.

Their adrenalin surge seemed to have erased the crushing stress-induced fatigue they both felt when they'd first gotten home. Mark slipped on a jacket, and pocketed their little Smith & Wesson .38 revolver. Minutes later they were in their car heading for Oscar's. It was now dusk. About a quarter-mile down a dirt road, Mark located Oscar's house ... at least his old rusted blue Chevy truck was parked in the side yard. Mark pulled their Explorer in behind Oscar's truck. Someone turned the porch light on as Mark and Anne simultaneously stepped out of their car. Oscar opened his front door. Without words, he motioned for Mark and Anne to come inside. He locked the door and turned the porch light off.

Inside Oscar's house, Anne immediately spoke: "Oscar, we tried to call you on the special phone but you didn't answer. Did you happen to see the TV news on WTOC?"

"Sho did, Miss Anne. I was a lookin' fo' TV weather report fo' tomorrow, but they busted in with all that mess goin' on over at th' landin'. An' I's got my special phone turn off, chargin' up, you know."

Mark replied, "Oscar, we tried to call Dr. Roberson, but he didn't answer either. Do you happen to know where he is right now?"

"Sho does! He got he phone a chargin', too ... an' he nappin' in my extra bedroom rat here in dis house. But befo' he nap, I started to tol' him 'bout what I seen on th' TV. But he say he too tired to think good, an' say he'll see the TV later, an' not to wake him up till the gator tail is done. He were plannin' to call y'all for a meetin' a little later dis evenin'. He say we's all got a heap to look at an' talk about."

Anne took an exaggerated breath through her nose. "Oscar, are you cooking something?"

"Sho is! Gator tail. Gonna do some bake first, then some fry. Put th' rest in my freezer to cook later dis year. We ain't had us no lunch today, you know."

"Yes, I know. And it smells great! But how'd you get the gator's tail here? We left it in your boat. Remember?" Anne asked, a bit puzzled.

"Doc Roberson, he bring hit in he truck when he leave th' landin'. Ya see, I ain't got no special license, what allow me to take a gator. But he do ... an' with that mess of DNR peoples at th' landin', ain't no problem if dey catch *him* takin' a gator tail to he truck," Oscar explained.

"So, where is his truck now?" curious Anne asked.

"It be hid behind my house ... behind big stack of crab trap in de backyard. He say he don't want *nobody* knowin' he here."

"Well Mark and I are *somebody!*" Anne said, laughing.

"Miss Anne, I knowed e'zakly what he mean when he say *nobody!* He mean don't tell nobody what's not us that's here, and Mr. Victor what ain't here. He mean don't ev'n tell th' sheriff's peoples!"

God! Mark thought. *Anne's such a stickler for details, she's gonna drive Oscar nuts with her third-degree questions. But at least Oscar's story fits what we know ... so far.*

Anne quickly accompanied Oscar to his kitchen to observe the gator-tail cooking; Mark lingered in the main room. As Mark glanced around Oscar's humble living room, he found himself in thought: *Spartan, clean, functional, comfortable, and efficient,* first came to his mind. A copy of the Holy Bible rested on a small table next to a recliner that faced the turned-off TV. A gold ribbon marked a place in the Bible where Oscar apparently had been last reading. The white sheetrock wall behind the TV was covered by many—maybe 15 or more—framed photographs. The smaller pictures appeared to be of his children taken at graduation exercises. *High School? College? Both?* his mind pondered. There were two larger framed images. One was of a young woman in her late 20s or early 30s. She had high proud cheeks, an exquisite smile showing perfect teeth, and flawless light brown skin. Her shining black hair was in tight braids, her scalp visible between the symmetrical rows. *Oscar's wife,* Mark thought. He next saw an image of that same woman with white hair; she was reclining in a casket, surrounded by beautiful flowers and many of the same faces pictured in the graduation exercises. The other larger image was a picture of a generic olive-skinned Jesus on a cross. *Maybe Oscar will someday tell me about it,* his mind concluded.

Oscar and Anne entered the living room where they "caught" Mark studying the picture-covered wall.

"Doctor, that's my family you a lookin' at." Oscar proudly pointed to the large picture of the beautiful black woman. "That be Cornelia, my wife. She pass on 'bout five year ago. 'Stroke,' dey say. At least she didn't suffer none. My five chillen is all gone to college, and done move away now to good-payin' job in de city. I's th' only one lef' here now, but I be happy to spend th' rest of my natchel-born days here ... jus' catchin' crab and pickin' oyster, and tryin' to catch 'em bad drug peoples what wants to mess up our good life de Lawd is give us here."

Both Mark and Anne felt truly humbled by the black man's words.

Searching for a reply, Mark finally spoke: "Oscar, I don't think I've ever met anyone quite like you before. The only person I've ever met that reminds me of you is a black man named Mose. He was an orderly in the Emergency Room where I trained at Grady Hospital in Atlanta. He gave a lot of himself for the good of others, especially for young black kids that were headed for trouble in a big city."

"Neither have I met anyone like you, Oscar," Anne echoed. "You do remind me a lot of 'Mose' that Mark mentioned. But Oscar, how'd you ever manage to send all your children to college?"

"Hard work with my hands," Oscar replied holding both out to Anne for inspection. She felt both of Oscars callused hands with her soft smooth ones. "So you sent them to college by getting crabs and oysters out of the river ... with these hands?"

"Yes ma'am, but it's out de *Lawd's* river. No Lawd, no river. No river, no crab, no oyster. No crab and oyster, no school money. So I think it was de Lawd what send 'em to college."

Mark started to say something but didn't. He only thought: *If there is a heaven, Oscar certainly belongs there ... and if the younger black community needs a role model, Oscar should be chosen.*

"Bake gator, she should be done," Oscar said, heading for the kitchen. Fry gator won't take long. I soon needs to wake up Dr. Roberson."

* * *

A half-hour later, Oscar invited the Telfairs to join them for the gator dinner he and Spence planned to enjoy. Other than his uniform being a little wrinkled, beard stubble, and disheveled hair, Spence looked halfway presentable. He quickly awoke from his nap and seemed as alert and as focused as ever. Anne was mystified at herself, but didn't verbalize her thoughts: *I never envisioned a time when I would be in a black man's home, eating the tail of a huge reptile that today had earlier tried to kill us! And I never thought it would taste this great ... like the best baked and fried chicken I've ever had!*

As the meal concluded, Roberson glanced at his watch, then said, "Folks, it's only eight o'clock. How about we do this? First, I'll go back to my trailer in the refuge. I'll shower and change into civilian clothes. Then, I'll come back here and pick up Oscar in my Altima, then bring him to Dunham Point." Spencer next pointed to Mark and Anne. "You guys drive back home in your Explorer. Do it now, and begin uploading today's kite pictures. We can use the computer at your house to look at the pictures from earlier today. Everybody please bring their satphones. Maybe the four of us can figure out what we need to do next."

25

DETAILS

At nine o'clock Spence's Altima eased into the driveway at the Telfairs' home. He carefully parked his car so it could not be seen from the road. The home's exterior lights were all off. Dressed in casual civvies, attaché in hand, and Oscar at his side, Roberson gently knocked on the front door. Anne turned the porch light on to verify the faces of the visitors, then immediately turned the light off. After letting them in, she locked the door, pointed up their stairs, and spoke: "Mark is up in the loft still uploading pictures from that infrared camera—several hundred, I think. You guys go up and join him while I put on a pot of coffee for us."

Keeping an eye on the monitor, Mark welcomed both men to his home, and moved two additional chairs next to the computer.

"At last!" Mark said, as the final high-resolution infrared image was uploaded. "OK, let me go back to the very beginning, and we'll look at all these full-screen size."

Anne soon ascended the stairs with a pot of coffee and several mugs. Realizing they were going to be one chair short, she promptly went back down the stairs to return with a stool borrowed from the kitchen. All were now seated in anticipation, each staring at the computer's monitor as though they were about to watch an award-winning movie.

After a number of images, Spence spoke: "Whoa! Stop right there," he said, upon seeing the infrared images showing the hot exhaust of three SSs. "All three are in a perfect line alongside the crab floats situated in the middle of the river! Mark, can't you put that image in a separate file? I want to build a special file that I can forward to DEA. I think this proves the SSs have a definite heat signature ... subtle but distinct. It also proves they have been spotted within a few feet of the unnumbered crab floats."

"Sure, Spence, I can do that. In fact, whenever you see *any* image you want to put in that separate file, just let me know."

In multiple pictures they could see Nosy cavorting around the three subs.

"Perhaps Nosy was pushing at them with his nose," Anne volunteered.

"Yeah, he sho kin do dat, Miss Anne. He do it to my boat, time to time. 'Specially if I's jes' settin' still in th' water a pullin' oysters, an' I ain't payin' him no mind. I think he do it jus' to let me know he there, an' jus' hopin' I give him sumthin' to eat."

Several images later, they could see that the oval hatch on the center sub's topside had been opened, and the next frame showed a man with a rifle standing atop the sub next to the hatch. The next picture, taken exactly at the time of the rifle shot, showed the plume of hot gas exiting the gun's muzzle. The following image showed Nosy's warm blood, which in infrared appeared like an orange cloud in the water.

"Put those last four pictures in the special file. That's another charge there. It's not legal to shoot a bottlenose dolphin in any state I know of," Spence remarked.

The next frame revealed something strange for the group to ponder: The man with the rifle now had its sling over his right shoulder, and both hands pressed to his crotch. From his crotch was a discrete orange line, one that went to the river's water, where it made a little orange ill-defined plume that trailed downriver.

Oscar burst out laughing, then said, "I sho knows e'zakly what he a doin'. He a pissin' in the river! Dat ain't against no law, is it?"

"Not that I know of, Oscar. At least not where that guy is doing it," Spence replied.

"Lawd, I sho hope it ain't against no law, 'cause if hit is, I sho done broke hit a heap of times!" said Oscar.

The group had a "laughter break," something they all needed after their action-filled day, one that had been long and exhausting.

"Mark, go ahead and put that last picture in the file, too. It may give the DEA boys something to chuckle about ... when they realize 'taking a leak' also has a unique heat signature!"

The next frame showed the sub's hatch closed. "Maybe that's what caused the sound we heard ... the one that sounded like a car door slamming," Anne observed.

Subsequent frames revealed little of interest, except for SCUBA bubbles. With infrared photography, they appeared almost like dull orange snowflakes, trailed out in intermittent lines. "Bubble lines" could be seen between all the subs and the crab floats. Spencer had

Mark put a number of those pictures in his special file. "Those shots are good circumstantial evidence linking the subs' use of SCUBA to the crab trap site," Spence explained.

Dr. Roberson had Mark record all their "special file" images to a disk, then asked that the entire parent image file in the camera be deleted after putting it on multiple disks to be stored in the safe at the wildlife refuge office. Spence took over Mark's position at the computer. He went online to a secure DEA site. A number of passwords later, Spence sent their file of selected images to that website.

"Well," Spence commented, "I certainly can't thank you guys enough for all your work with the kite photos. Can we now look at the pictures Anne got with her little digital camera?"

"Sure," Mark replied. "Where's your camera, Anne?"

"In my purse," she replied, and scurried down the stairs, returning moments later.

Mark connected Anne's camera to the computer using the USB cable that came with it. The lower-resolution images uploaded much more quickly than those from the infrared camera. Spence again requested a "special file" for Anne's images that were of interest to him: Nosy, when alive and pulling on Oscar's boat paddle; several shots of SSs' snorkels and exhaust pipes; multiple shots of scuba bubbles, and several excellent "mug shots" of the three Hispanics sitting on the mud flat in the river. Spence again sent images to the secure DEA site, and had Mark place them on disk as a backup.

Spencer smiled and said, "Thanks, Anne. I think your images pretty much complete the picture of what the exposed parts of an SS look like when viewed from another boat nearby." After carefully placing all the disks in his attaché, Spence said, "What say we go downstairs and turn on the TV. Oscar had told me about it before my nap at his house, but I was too beat to critically observe any TV images the station might rerun before their late news. I'll bet we'll see some reruns on WTOC's Late Edition. I was in my truck in the landing's parking lot when it all went down. I certainly saw the chopper. It stayed around only a few minutes, but I haven't seen any of their aerial footage yet."

Anne turned on their TV using the remote. Spencer noted a VCR amid the electronics in the Telfairs' rather humble entertainment center. Just before a commercial break, WTOC announced it would open their Late Edition News with an exclusive report about "Today's drug bust at the Harris Neck National Wildlife Refuge," a tease the station felt would probably keep most of the channel-changers at bay.

"You guys have a blank VCR tape?" Spence asked the Telfairs. It took a little searching but Anne finally found one and popped it into their VCR machine. "That'll let us look at it frame by frame if we see anything that may give us additional clues," Spence explained.

Mark spoke up: "Spence, the footage Anne and I saw is probably what Oscar saw, too. I think it was indeed *live, and unedited.* But their rerun could be an edited version."

"I think I seen an' hear e'zakly what Doctor an' Miss Anne did ... 'cause dey busted in on they reg'lar program," Oscar observed.

Spence replied, "That's a very good observation, Oscar. So, if you folks who have already seen it spot any changes, let me know. I think we can arrange for a subpoena or a court order that would require WTOC to let us examine their original image footage ... and the audio that went with it."

At eleven o'clock, WTOC's newscast filled the TV screen. After welcoming viewers to Late Edition, the newscaster indicated that the Drug Enforcement Administration had contacted WTOC, and requested a public service announcement, one indicating the Harris Neck National Wildlife Refuge had been declared a federal crime scene, and no attempts by viewers to visit the refuge should be made. "That includes other nonfederal law enforcement officers who are not specifically authorized to be there. To do so will be breaking federal law. I'm sure the U.S. Fish & Wildlife Service regrets any inconvenience this may cause citizens, but we've been told they will reopen the refuge to visitors as soon as possible," the newscaster announced. "As promised, here is WTOC's exclusive report aired during our Early Edition today."

Anne had the VCR on "record." All eyes and ears scrutinized the TV station's rerun of the drug-bust images and audio. The helicopter clip lasted only three minutes, and as far as Mark, Anne, and Oscar could tell, neither the visuals nor audio had been changed with one exception: The audio where the chopper pilot admitted that air traffic control in Savannah had informed him they were flying in restricted air space had been edited out. The statement about an unidentified spokesman from the McIntosh County Sheriff's Department remained unchanged. Using the VCR, they watched the whole tape several more times. Again, they found nothing new or changed, except the pilot's audio.

Finally it hit Mark. "Run it one more time, Anne. Forward the tape to where the chopper went downriver a bit. Go to the shot that shows the shrimp boats blocking the river, then pause it just before they zoomed to the deck of the trapped pontoon."

Anne reran the tape, and paused it as had been requested. Mark got off the sofa and walked to the frozen image on the TV screen. Pointing at what had caught his eye, Mark spoke: "Y'all see this? This small *tan* boat here? Just downriver of the blockade? I think that's a McIntosh County *Sheriff's* Department boat ... not DNR!"

"Sho 'nuff is! I sees 'em a heap of times, an' knows de difference. Dat ain't no DNR boat! Ain't got dat radar thing DNR has. Wrong boat color, too," Oscar added.

"That," Spence began, "may indicate the single most worrisome situation I have: the so-called witness, who saw Oscar's boat when y'all tied up at the landing. Using binoculars from that small tan boat, I think it would be possible to look *between* the small gaps in the blockade boats, and still see the landing's dock well enough to give that general description of the occupants in Oscar's boat ... the description that was mentioned by that TV guy talking in the chopper ... 'middle-aged white male and female, and elderly black male,' I think the reporter said."

"So," Anne began, "it looks like all your efforts to keep our identity secret may have failed. And I'm scared, Spence!"

"Anne, I share your concern," Spence replied. "Even though it's a very vague description, I feel like it's a personal failure on my part. But it's even worse for Oscar, because almost everyone who works the river knows his boat ... and the color of his skin. So, I think we need to isolate Oscar now. Hide him ... where nobody can find him!"

"Like how?" Mark asked.

"Like, get his boat out of the river tonight. Then hide it. In fact, I can hide it in one of the lockable sheds we've got at the refuge," Spence explained, then asked Oscar a question: "Didn't you tell me your oldest boy worked at a bank in Savannah?"

"Yes, suh. I's been meanin' to go visit soon ... new grandbaby, you know."

"You think he'd mind if you visited him for a few days, beginning tonight or early in the morning?"

"Naw suh. He be delighted! Got plenty room in he big house."

"Well, what about us, dammit!" Anne glared as she spoke to Spencer, her beet-red face a curious blend of sheer fright and anger.

Dr. Roberson held his hand up, palm facing Anne, as though preparing to defend himself against an irate hostile woman. "Anne, please calm down! Please! I still think the risk to you and Mark is minimal. You guys are relatively new here. Other than Oscar, no one who works the river knows you two. Your personal boats have never been connected to this whole scenario in any way. Granted, you guys had a face-to-face encounter with those three Hispanics who escaped from one of the subs by using SCUBA— "

"And, if Mark got the Spanish right, *that one guy said Sinaloa would find us and kill us!*" Anne yelled at Spence.

Spence blushed but remained outwardly calm. Mark thought: *That's it for us ... I'm not sure Anne can take it ... nor myself.* Oscar remained silent, his facial expression revealing nothing.

After a long moment Spence continued: "Anne, please hear me out. There were *six* more crew members ... three in each of the other two subs. Those crew members were extricated alive from their subs *after* they'd been put on the deck of the dock-builder's barge. And that was well *after* you guys had left the scene. So, those six *never* saw your faces, and the three that did—along with the six that didn't—are *all* now out of the picture anyway. DNR promptly turned them over to Border Patrol, and they have taken them to an undisclosed secure detention facility."

"A 'detention facility,' where?" Anne asked, now a little more calm.

"I can't say because I honestly do not know, Anne. They won't even tell *me* where they took them. But you can bet it is secure. Border Patrol and DEA certainly know Sinaloa's potential to be vicious. My own bet is that it's *quite* secure," Spence explained, hoping to calm Anne further.

Anne exhaled slowly, then said, "Tell us the rest Spence."

"OK, I will. The subs themselves are being barged to the port in Brunswick. There, they will be more thoroughly searched. At the port, a study of the details of their construction and onboard equipment will go on for quite some time. By the way, Anne, all three of the subs did have a 'bottom hatch,' just as you had proposed. None of the nine Hispanics had any documents on their person, or aboard their subs, that would allow them to be here in the U.S. legally ... so possibly they're *all* illegal aliens as far as we know. Border Patrol, DEA, and other Feds will interrogate all nine of them while they are being held in custody. They will probably be deported to Mexico, eventually, but that may be years from now."

Spence had summarized at length, hoping to quell Anne's anxiety and anger.

Anne paused a long moment. She first looked at Mark, then Oscar.

Neither seemed anxious or frightened. "OK, Spence. I apologize for getting so upset. I guess I'm still 'in,' and not quite ready to hide just yet. But let me ask you some questions that are bugging me."

"Fair enough, Anne. So ask," Spence replied.

She began: "How do you think a TV station's helicopter 'just happened' to be at the right place at the right time? And why do you think a major TV station would even hire a pilot who was dumbass enough to fly in restricted airspace? Why do you think the TV reporter in that chopper would know anything about a so-called 'witness on the ground,' one alleged to be an 'unnamed' law enforcement officer with the McIntosh County Sheriff's Department? And why would that local law officer *not* give his name?"

"Wow!" Roberson exclaimed. "Let's compare notes. While sitting in my truck in the parking lot at the landing, and watching the action, I made a list of questions." Spence popped his attaché, pushed his pistol aside, and removed a small note pad. He studied his notes. "Anne, you've covered the questions I had written down ... except about the reported witness on the ground, the one reportedly from the McIntosh Sheriff's Department. No mention of any 'witness' was made in the radio transmissions I monitored while sitting in my truck and listening in on marine FM."

"So, that means what, Spence? It means *someone* was communicating with the chopper ... someone *other* than WTOC's studio in Savannah and the air traffic control folks. So that leaves us with an *on-scene radio*, either on the ground or on the water in a boat. A radio that could communicate with *aircraft,* right?"

"Or in a local law enforcement officer's car, boat, or on his belt!" Spence exclaimed. "Unfortunately, that's what I think is most likely, Anne. We could have a problem with a 'dirty' local cop here. I can pretty well guarantee you it was not the DNR nor the shrimpers who radioed the chopper, or communicated with WTOC in advance. Just like your 'bottom hatch' theory for the SSs, let me put this theory on the table for our discussion: Suppose the downriver tan boat was indeed a Sheriff's Department boat, and that the officer or officers aboard somehow knew the subs would be going upriver today. Also, suppose he knew the pontoon would be going upriver to pick up drugs delivered by the subs. And suppose a local law officer suspected the drug delivery was going bad, especially after seeing six shrimp boats and a barge going upriver. Then he sees four of the shrimp boats subsequently forming a blockade ... a blockade that trapped both the subs, and a pontoon boat that was too wide to pass between them. So what do you think that local law officer would do, Anne?"

Shit in his pants! Mark thought, but remained silent. He wanted to hear Anne's response to Spence's last question.

Anne paused for a long moment, formulating her reply: "Well, if I were a dirty cop, I'd first call the local media. WTOC would probably be my first choice for our area. I know news media folks all monitor various radio frequencies, like those used by law enforcement and aviation. That's how they get their folks to a breaking-news scene first. If I were that lawman, I'd identify myself as an officer, but if I were a 'dirty cop,' as you called him, I'd probably *not* give my name—just tell them I was a law enforcement officer. I'd do that for the sake of *credibility,* then tell them when and where something was happening."

"Wow!" Spence exclaimed, writing notes on his pad. "And exactly *why* do you think that hypothetical bad cop would blow the whistle?"

"Simple. To *divert suspicion.* Suspicion that any of our local law enforcement here in McIntosh has any part in covering it up, or financially benefiting from the drug-smuggling operations that are going on here."

Spence scribbled a few more notes, then said, "Anne, you've certainly proved to me blonds are not dumb! That's a great working theory. Anybody care to comment?"

Oscar raised one hand, as he sipped his coffee with the other.

"Oscar, you have a question?" Spence asked.

"Yes suh, I sho does," Oscar said, gently setting his cup on the coffee table. "Who's watchin' th' henhouse, rat now?"

"Watching the *what?*" Spence asked.

"Dem six crab trap up de river ... what's got drugs in 'em. We knows dat pontoon ain't never make it upriver to pick 'em up!"

"Shit!" Spence exclaimed, slamming his own forehead with his palm. "How could I have been so dumb! Anne, I apologize for my language, but I can't believe I overlooked something so obvious! And thank you, Oscar, for pointing that out."

Spence removed his satphone from his attaché case, and retreated to the kitchen to call Victor Timmons. While Spence was on the phone, Anne turned the TV volume up, checked several channels for additional news about the drug bust, but found none.

In ten minutes, Spence returned to his seat on the sofa, smiling broadly. All eyes were on Dr. Roberson as he spoke: "Well, at least one member of our team, other than Oscar, wasn't asleep at the switch! It seems Vic had the same thought as Oscar. When the tide started back in, they cleared all the shrimp boats out of the river. The pontoon was taken out of the water at Kip's Fish Camp, then hauled to the DNR building in Brunswick by trailer. It will undergo a forensic inspection there. Vic said the pontoon had a trapdoor in its deck large enough for a SCUBA diver dressed in full gear, but no drugs were found aboard. That same trapdoor was large enough to drop a crab trap through it. They did find two concealed 500-gallon *diesel fuel* tanks built into the pontoon boat's hull, and Vic thinks that pontoon may have also served as one of the refueling stations for the SSs. And—"

"Spence," Mark interrupted, "I'm positive that pontoon was powered by a *gasoline* outboard, a 125 Mercury. So I think Vic is on to something ... about refueling the subs I mean. And—"

"Hate to cut you off Mark, but let me first tell you what I'm the most excited about! At Vic's request, four DNR boats remained on site in the Barbour River until the next high tide, which would crest at about 11:00 p.m. All DNR's men were told to be prepared to spend the night. Those boats hid themselves in various side creeks upriver. They were hoping someone would take the 'bait.' And they did! About an hour ago, a small tan Sheriff's Department boat passed the DNR's various hiding places. In short, the DNR guys caught two McIntosh County Sheriff Department Deputies pulling the traps, and loading their boat with the marijuana cubes the subs had stuffed into the traps upriver— some 72 waterproof cubes! And Vic estimated the street value at a half-million dollars! At the port in Brunswick, Vic also said DEA was still counting a huge amount of drugs still remaining inside the subs. So, it appears they'd planned deliveries to a number of other spots as well. But bottom line for us here is this: 'Out-gunned and out-manned,' Vic said, 'the Sherriff's Deputies surrendered to DNR on the spot.' And as a sidebar, the Sheriff Department's boat had a radio capable of operating on aviation frequencies. He said the two McIntosh Deputies are being turned directly over to DEA as we speak. He also said there may be some 'jurisdictional issues' and 'loose ends' to be ironed out, but those guys are gonna be put away for a long, long time."

Anne slowly exhaled, then asked a question: "Are you sure of that, Spencer? 'Put away for a long, long time,' you said?"

"I'm taking Vic's word on that. They were caught red-handed. I don't see how they can beat the charges," Spence assured.

"Spence," Mark began, "I don't know if this is significant or not, but when the three of us left you at the landing, we locked the gate behind us as you'd requested. As we drove up Harris Neck Road, we encountered two Sheriff's Department patrol cars going like a bat outta hell, apparently heading for the landing. Did they ever show up on site?"

"Yes, they did. On my way out I found them parked at the locked gate, smoking cigarettes, and talking. I personally know both of those deputies well, and they are good totally honest guys. They told me they heard all the squawk on Channel 10, and somehow thought a bunch of shrimp boats had run aground in the river, or were possibly sinking, and that a dock-builder's barge with a crane was on the way to help. I told the deputies not to worry, the shrimpers were all OK. And I told 'em a white lie: I told them the gate was locked because a federal crime had been committed, and the entire refuge had been declared a *federal* crime scene. That apparently is not a lie *now*, but it was at the time I said it."

"De Lawd will sho forgive you fo' dat one, Doctor Spence!" Oscar exclaimed. "You still think I needs to hide?"

"Yes. I think you should, Oscar. Just to be on the safe side. And it certainly won't hurt you to have a week or two of rest in Savannah with your family. I don't know how you keep on going like you do at your age. Heck, I'm half your age and I'm bushed. Later tonight, I've still got a lot of communicating to do with the various agencies and services involved in all this. After that, I may take some time off myself ... or at least concentrate on the biology of the refuge. Biology is the real reason I got involved at the refuge in the first place."

"Is there anything else we can do this evening?" Mark asked.

"Yes, Doctor. *Sleep.* But everybody keep their satphones on ... just in case."

26

A TIME TO REST

A little after midnight, Dr. Spencer Roberson and Oscar left the Telfairs' home as inconspicuously as they had arrived. Mark made both himself and Anne a martini to help them unwind. As they sat on the sofa and searched for additional drug-bust information on TV, they found nothing about the event that had sapped their energy and consumed their day.

"Mark, I apologize for getting so frightened and angry at Spencer."

"I think he understood your fright and anger. Mine, too, for that matter. But I think he has objectively looked at our personal risk ... our risk of being harmed by someone from the Sinaloa Cartel, or possibly by some local lawman who's pissed off."

Beep ... Beep ...Beep ... The sound caused the Telfairs to freeze in their seats on the sofa.

"Oh shit! The satphone," Mark said, grabbing it from the coffee table, fearing the worst. Mark punched a button to receive the incoming call: "Mark Telfair," he said.

"Identify yourself," the caller replied.

"HNNWR 4," Mark said, though he'd recognized the voice as being that of U.S. Marshal Todd Whitmore, the EMT-trained marshal who'd been present during the first stage of the birthmark-removal surgery he'd done on Roberto Gonzales.

"Doc, I apologize for calling at this hour, but I tried to give you a progress report earlier," Todd explained. "Everything still looks great. I did send a picture of the wound to Dr. Roberson. Have you seen it yet?"

"No. And Dr. Roberson probably hasn't either. We've all had one helluva day here. I didn't have my satphone with me most of the day, and Roberson has had his fully occupied. We had a big drug bust here and we were in the middle of it!"

"No shit! Uh ... I mean no kidding," Todd replied, sanitizing his language a bit. "Tell me about it."

"Best you ask Roberson for details tomorrow. We're all beat here. But you said Roberto's wound looks OK?"

"Yeah. And I just figured out there's no reason to send the images to you through Roberson. I shot the images on macro mode, and cropped them in Photoshop. Only the wound itself shows, not the rest of Roberto's face. My boss said it's OK if I e-mail cropped ones directly to you … 'Just do it by ordinary e-mail,' he said."

Mark gave Todd his e-mail address, and the marshal indicated he was sending it as they spoke. "I'll send you one every day, so please check your e-mails. You cannot reply to me by e-mail because it is a secure server that allows only outgoing messages. If you have any questions or comments, contact me by satphone."

Even though they were exhausted, neither Mark nor Anne could resist a quick trip to the loft to check Roberto's wound image: *Perfect,* Mark and Anne both thought, when they saw the picture.

They quickly descended the loft stairs, stripped off all their clothes and crashed into their bed … to sleep.

* * *

Anne apparently had a dreamless night; Mark did not. He awakened thinking Spence had called him on the satphone to warn him that one of the Hispanics—the one that had mentioned "Sinaloa"—had escaped DEA and Border Patrol's custody, and the bad guy was now out looking for the "gringos" that had caught him in the river. In a cold sweat, he felt for his satphone on his nightstand. It was silent. He saw the red LED that indicated the phone was on, then realized it was all a dream. After a half-hour of listening to Anne's quiet breathing he finally found sleep, but only after having a terminal disquieting thought: *I think my subconscious mind is more concerned than my conscious one … but which one should I listen to?*

* * *

At 11 a.m. the Telfairs were still dressed only in their bathrobes and just finishing their breakfast. He did not mention his dream to Anne, who seemed rested and relaxed. *If I told her about it, that could rekindle her fear and anger,* he thought. Sipping his second cup of coffee, Mark heard the unmistakable sound: the satphone's beep. They collided in the hallway as they rushed to their bedroom to answer the phone. Mark grabbed it first:

"Morning, folks," said the familiar voice of Dr. Spencer Roberson. "I sure feel better after a full night's sleep. How about you guys?"

"We're doing fine, Spence. Any new developments?"

"I've had a long conversation with WTOC this morning. They openly admitted editing the pilot's audio they ran on their Late Edition ... said it was 'on advice of their legal folks.' Seems they wanted to minimize public admission that their pilot had broken FAA regs."

"They give you any more details?" Mark asked.

"They're going to bat for their pilot, legally that is. They think he's a great pilot, and they don't want to see him grounded. Their explanation of how it all happened is this: By land phone, the station had been notified of a warehouse fire in South Savannah, and the chopper had been dispatched to that scene. Once in the air, their pilot, Glynn Barden, said he'd received an aviation-frequency radio message about the stuff going on at Barbour Landing in McIntosh County. The pilot indicated the radio message was from an unidentified lawman with the McIntosh Sheriff's Department. Barden radioed the station, and they told him to forget about the warehouse fire, and go immediately to Barbour Landing. In his excitement, it seems Barden forgot to notify ATC in Savannah. The station also offered to permit us to review their original tapes as shown on Early Edition."

"That all seems to fit," Mark replied. "Anything else, Spence?"

"Yes. But it's something I don't quite understand. A U.S. Marshal, a fella named Todd Whitmore, sent me a couple of pictures of the face of Roberto Gonzales ... with instructions to show it to you. It came to our secure website. Since most of his birthmark is now gone, and I see some fine stitches, I assume it was made following the first surgery you and Anne did. Correct?"

"Correct. But Todd called me a little after you and Oscar left my house last night. He's now going to send cropped images directly to my computer. They'll show only the wound, without any facial features that would allow someone to identify Roberto Gonzales."

"Sounds OK to me if you guys do it that way. And I guess I should tell you we got Oscar's boat out of the river last night, then locked it in a shed in the refuge. Early today, before daylight, Oscar left for Savannah to stay with one of his sons for a couple of weeks. He took his satphone with him, and I told him I'd keep an eye on his house.

You'd never guess what Oscar's biggest concern was about his leaving. It was not arson or burglary of his home."

"Then what was it, Spence?"

"That his old freezer may crap out, and let 150 pounds of gator tail spoil!"

Mark broke out laughing; Anne, standing next to Mark at their bedside, glared with impatience, her lips stamped in a straight line. She'd heard only Mark's side of the conversation and was dying to know what Spence had said.

"Anyway, that's about it," Spence said. "I'll be busy for the next week taking samples of all that marijuana we've recovered. Then I'll send the samples to a plant genetics lab in Atlanta. So far, the previous tests they have done for me indicate it's monoclonal. In other words, it's all being produced from a single highly modified genetic plant line. I'm betting that it's all coming from a single high-tech grow lab in Canada, but that's for the DEA to figure out. My assignment in all this was to figure out how the portion of the ICW located in McIntosh County was being used. We've still got some loose ends, but I think we've pretty much accomplished that goal. The interrogation of the subs' crews by Border Patrol and DEA may tell us the rest."

"Any news about the pontoon boat?" Mark asked.

Yes. DNR has told us the pontoon boat guys all have a history of multiple drug-related felonies. Seems they are what I call 'accumulators,' the guys who supply the little dealers selling on the street. I don't have a firm dollar-value on the contents of the three subs, but Victor seems to think it's gonna be in the high multimillions, maybe even break a billion. At least that'll knock a big dent in Sinaloa's funding ... at least enough to piss them off, and maybe make them forget about using the rivers and ICW in McIntosh County again!"

"Great, Spence. Thanks for the update. I think Anne and I will just kick back ... but with our eyes open, and satphone on."

"Good! And if you're free in a couple of weeks, I could certainly use your kite-aerial-photography talents at the refuge. It's nothing to do with drugs this time. I need to get some baseline photos of Woody Pond, before the wood stork rook season begins. Also, we've got a problem with rabies in our raccoon population at the refuge. I sure could use some help searching for and darting the suspicious raccoons."

"*Darting?*" Mark asked, seeking clarification.

"Yeah. Shoot 'em with a tranquilizer dart. I have several different dart guns, both pistols and rifles. After darting, we isolate them in cages for observation. I hope to be able to prevent further spread of the viral infection. Anyway, thanks for all your help thus far ... and thank Anne, too."

When the satphone conversation terminated, Anne stood in her bathrobe, one hand on her hip, the other free. Using her free hand she slowly tugged the sash of her robe, and allowed it to fall open fully. Silently standing there, she smiled as she observed the growing bulge in the front of Mark's robe. She slowly pulled his sash. "No CPR needed, Little Man. And I don't give a flip about Roberson's instructions, or any new news right now ... just turn that damn satphone *off!*"

27

THE NEXT SIX MONTHS

The following week, *The Darien News* published a lengthy article: "Drug Bust at Local Wildlife Refuge." Strangely, despite its length, very few details were given. Except for a generic image of the Barbour Landing itself, and its tranquil river devoid of any boats, the article had no additional accompanying photographs. Dr. Spencer Roberson had been interviewed by the paper, and he'd simply indicated, "It's an ongoing federal investigation." He declined any additional comment on the subject other than to say the refuge was no longer considered a federal crime scene, and that it was now open to the general public for visitation.

A spokesman for the McIntosh County Sheriff's Department had also been interviewed. He'd indicated the Sheriff's Department would "fully cooperate with the federal investigators," and acknowledged two of their own deputies had been taken into custody by federal officials. Those two deputies were presently "suspended" pending further investigation. The Department declined any comment about the charges, or the guilt or innocence of its suspended deputies: "That is a matter for the courts to decide," the spokesman was quoted as saying.

Sitting in their living room, Mark and Anne read and then reread *The Darien News* article. Both felt quite relieved; neither Oscar nor themselves were mentioned *anywhere* in the article.

After her second-reading, Anne finally spoke: "Mark, it looks like Spence was right about our names *not* being connected to the bust."

"Well," Mark began, "the names of some of the shrimp boats are certainly mentioned: *Cap'n Joe, Jolly Mon, Big Haul,* and *Goin' Broke.* And the name of the dock-building company that had the barge on scene is mentioned."

"That's true, but when the reporter from the news tried to interview the various shrimp boat captains, and that barge captain, the answers from *all* of them was essentially the same: 'We were just cooperating with a special request from DNR,' or something similar to that."

"So, you think they all got their heads together, and decided exactly what they'd tell the media?" Mark asked.

"I think that's probably what happened. It's well known that some of the shrimpers had connections to drug smuggling here in the past. I think they don't want any of that past to be dredged up, and brought to public light again," Anne replied.

The Telfairs' regular phone rang, interrupting their conversation. With no anxiety, Mark answered it:

"Hi, it's me. Feel like flying your kite today?" Spence asked.

"I certainly don't have anything on my schedule. But are you talking about taking pictures, or just flying a kite, or what?"

"Pictures. Just regular film images over Woody Pond. Rook season will start for the storks in about two months. I still need to get those baseline images we talked about before. Remember?"

"Yes, but I'll have to modify my rig again so it will accept my little Olympus film camera. That'll take an hour or two. I've been meaning to do that anyway, so I can get that infrared digital back to you. I don't like keeping a $10,000 camera in my house or car. Especially if it does not belong to me."

"DEA has been bugging me to get that camera back to them, now that they know what the heat signature of an SS actually looks like. I'm not going to say more about that on this regular phone. My satphone is charging. We can talk more when you come over. I'm at the refuge office. What time do you think you can be here?"

Mark checked his watch: nine o' clock. "A little after noon. That OK?"

"Fine. Meet me at the office. We'll look at the refuge map and figure the best way to get your rig over Woody Pond. See ya then," Spence said, and clicked off.

"I assume that was Spence wanting us to do something," Anne said, looking up from another section of the *Mullet Wrapper,* as she fondly called *The Darien News.*

"Yep. He wants some regular pictures over Woody Pond. You interested in coming along? Might learn a little more about the so-called 'loose ends' of the bust, as Spence called them."

"Sure! It's such a nice day. Why don't we have a picnic?"

"I don't know what Spencer's lunch plans are, but I'll call him back and see if he's interested in eating with us."

Mark made a quick call to the refuge office, and Spence accepted the "picnic invitation."

Anne prepared a picnic lunch, while Mark worked in his shop. He soon had his little 35mm Olympus Stylus Epic film camera functioning in the remodified camera cradle. He loaded it with a 36-exposure roll of color print film, and fired a test shot in his shop.

A little before noon they loaded the picnic basket and kite gear in their Ford Explorer and leisurely headed for the refuge. When they arrived, Spencer's truck was parked in front of the office. He appeared moments later to greet them at the office door. Spence led them to the conference room where a large map of the refuge was already spread out on the table. "Here's Woody Pond," Spence said, pointing. "Now let's figure out the best way to position your camera over it. The tall cypress trees that surround the pond block so much wind, I doubt you'd ever be able to launch a kite at the pond site itself."

"I agree," Mark replied, as everyone seated themselves around the map. "The whole pond is ... well, it's sorta down in a 'hole' in the trees. But if we go about 200 yards east of the pond, like up to the old WWII Army Air Corps runways, that would be a good area to get the kite airborne. Wind's out of the east today. That should carry the kite over the trees and toward the pond. From the old runway, I know *approximately* where the pond is in relation to the runway, but I'd need someone at the pond guiding me ... someone telling me when they saw the camera directly over it. We need a person who could tell me to move to my right or left, or move forward or backward, to get it centered. How would we coordinate that, Spence?"

"Simple," Spence replied. "Radio. Walkie-talkie. We've a number of them. I could drive you two to the airfield, drop you off there, then come back to Woody alone. From Woody, I could tell you if you needed to change your ground position at the airfield to get centered over the pond."

"Sounds like a plan, Spence," Anne said, finally entering the conversation. "But, why couldn't we just drive our car to the old airfield, and you drive to Woody Pond?"

Spencer answered Anne: "Because I want to take you guys to a very special place for our picnic, and to get there requires a four-wheel-drive vehicle, like my truck. I think it's the most perfect spot in the refuge ... and it's off-limits to regular civilian refuge visitors."

"Sounds like you're giving us VIP treatment, Spence," Anne shot back.

"You bet! You guys deserve it. And, Mark, you're actually going to get *paid* for the aerial pictures over Woody Pond. You guys ready?"

"Yes," Mark and Anne replied in unison.

The threesome departed the office conference room with the rolled refuge map in tow. Mark's kite equipment and the picnic basket were transferred quickly to the bed of Roberson's truck. Their departure for the "perfect picnic spot" was delayed a few moments when Mark handed the expensive DEA infrared SDS 6500 camera and its accessories to Spence. He went back inside the office to put them in the safe, and returned with a couple of walkie-talkies in hand. "Almost forgot the important stuff," Spencer said, blushing.

Getting in Spence's truck, Anne noted a rifle in a rack at the cab's rear window. "Going hunting?" Anne asked, pointing at the gun.

"Hopefully not today," Spence replied.

That's a strange looking rifle, Mark first thought, then asked, "Spence, what kind of gun is that? The one in the rack?"

"Crosman .22 caliber with a good scope. Uses compressed carbon dioxide ... so essentially it's an air gun. Shoots darts to tranquilize animals."

"I see," Mark replied. "Is that what we're going to use when we look for the raccoons with possible rabies?"

"Yep," Spence replied. "I've also got a Crosman pistol in the glove compartment. It's a five-shot semiautomatic, and shoots the same darts as that rifle. But I don't plan on any coon hunting today, just do the picnic first, then the kite photos. Besides, I haven't yet received the shipment of the cages to isolate the suspicious raccoons."

Everyone got in the truck, Anne sitting center. Spence put the walkie-talkies on the dash and began driving on the paved public access road that meandered through the refuge. After the first half-mile, they passed Woody Pond, and a half-mile later crossed the remains of the old WWII airfield that nature was reclaiming with a vengeance; vegetation erupted through even the smallest of cracks in the old runway's pavement. A mile later, Spence took a hard left down an unpaved road, heading north. When the unpaved trail ended, he shifted to four-wheel drive, and again turned left, heading them west through thick underbrush. He stopped and pointed at some rectangular, barely discernable manmade ruins. "That once was the swimming pool for the Pierre Lorillard mansion built here in the late 1800s. The pool was originally fed by an artesian spring, but as you can now see, it's filled only with leaves and small trees. Artesian activity ceased here in the 1950s, largely due to industrial extraction from the aquifer."

"Spence, what's that round thing over there?" Anne asked,

pointing.

"That once was a decorative fountain for the Lorillard mansion but it's now dry and largely overgrown, too. After heavy rains it fills a bit and serves as a good temporary freshwater source for the refuge animals," Spence explained.

"What's that over there ... or what *was* that before it got so overgrown?" Mark asked Spence.

"That was part of the tabby foundation of the mansion house itself. But what I want to show you two is beyond all this," Spence said, and he proceeded west through some very boggy land, to emerge on top of a high half-acre grassy hillock shaded by a massive live oak.

Everyone got out of the truck and walked to the 30-foot-high sheer bluff, one that looked vertically down to the South Newport River which marked the refuge's north end. "This is my most favorite spot in the whole refuge ... in the whole world, too," Spence explained. "Before my wife died, this is the last spot I took her to. Just to look at the expansive beauty ... with not a manmade object in sight. For Cathy, it was her last outing before her death," Spence explained, fighting tears that never materialized.

Mark and Anne both froze: They were both recalling a picnic from hell at a "perfect" picnic spot near Statesville, Georgia; there, they had found their close friend, Spud Smith. He was dead in his fishing boat.

Anne cleared her throat, then said, "Spence, thanks for sharing this very beautiful spot with us. I think I know at least one reason why this refuge is so special to you ... and you've now made it special to us, too."

"I apologize for getting a little maudlin on you, but this picnic was a good excuse to give me the courage to come back here. I've not been here since Cathy died. But what the heck! Life goes on. Let's eat and go fly a kite!" Spence exclaimed, now smiling.

Mark and Anne had a glass of wine along with grapes, cheese, and a sandwich each; in a matter of minutes, Spence inhaled three sandwiches, along with his grapes and cheese. He gulped iced tea, but declined the wine, stating, "I'm technically on duty, you know."

The picnic lasted all of 40 minutes, and Anne felt perhaps she should have prepared more food. Spence was carrying the basket to place in the bed of his truck. He suddenly dropped it on the ground, snatched the truck door open, and grabbed the Crosman rifle, then yelled, "Get in the truck now! Both of you. Close the doors!"

Neither Mark nor Anne had noticed, but a large raccoon was approaching the truck. It seemed totally unafraid of Spencer, as it awkwardly walked toward him. From the truck's cab, Mark noted the animal appeared to have a partial paralysis of its hind legs, and was frothing at its mouth. Spence first shot it in a shoulder with the dart rifle, and in about a minute the animal quietly lay on the ground, appearing to be asleep. Spence next drew his Sig-Sauer 226 and fired a single round into the animal's head.

As Spence opened the driver's door of the truck, he instructed Mark and Anne to get out. He got a large black plastic trash bag from the glove box. From the ground, he picked up a convenient clump of Spanish moss, and used it to isolate the skin of his hand from the animal's fur while grasping it by its tail. Spence slipped the coon's body into the bag, then put it in the back of his truck along with the picnic basket he'd earlier dropped to the ground. Next, he took a dart from the glove box, and quickly reloaded the rifle before placing it back in the rack. He motioned, indicating the Telfairs should now get back in the truck.

"Why the Spanish moss, Spence?" Anne asked. "I thought you had to be bitten to acquire the virus."

"That's correct, Anne. I used the moss as a very redundant precaution. There have been extremely rare cases of humans getting the virus through small cuts or scratches in their hands ... if they accidentally contact the animal's blood or saliva."

Anne thought a moment. "We never saw a case of rabies while we were training at Grady, did we Mark?"

"No, but I think that's about the *only* thing we missed seeing," Mark replied. "Well maybe that, or someone like that patient in Statesville that had his penis bitten off by a hog!"

"Oh my God!" Spence exclaimed. "Spare me the details, and I'm so very sorry you had to see that coon go down, especially following such a nice lunch at such a beautiful spot," Spence said. "But there's little question that poor fellow was terminally ill with rabies, and probably would not have survived the night anyway. Later, I'll put that coon's head in the freezer, and send it to a lab in Waycross, Georgia. They can do a fluorescent antibody test on the brain tissue to confirm my field diagnosis of rabies. At least now another healthy coon won't come along and pick a fight with him, and possibly acquire rabies in the process."

Anne remained silent, and appeared to be fighting tears. *She's seen hundreds of humans die ... but animals, like Nosy the dolphin, an alligator, and now a raccoon seem to be getting to her,* Mark thought.

Now in Spencer's truck and heading to the kite-launch site on the old runway, Mark asked a question: "Spence, why is it so important to save the raccoon population here in the refuge? They're not exactly on the endangered species list."

"Granted, raccoons are not endangered at all ... but the wood storks *are!* Healthy raccoons help us protect the wood storks," Spence explained.

"I don't get the connection, Spence," Mark puzzled.

"It works like this: Raccoons are good swimmers and climbers. They get in Woody Pond, swim to the stork nests, then climb up to the nests to eat stork eggs, or even the chicks."

"I still don't get the connection, Spence."

"I'm sure you've noticed Woody Pond has an abundant healthy alligator population. To feed those alligators, and have them *remain* in the pond, they need a reliable food source. Otherwise, they'd wander off somewhere else. The alligator's primary source of food at Woody Pond is the raccoons that are trying to get at the stork nests. I'm sure we lose a few wading birds and ducks to alligator predation in the process, but overall, it works best for the storks to have an abundant raccoon population ... to serve as easy-picking fast food for our gators. Unless a stork chick falls out of a nest to the ground, or into the water, the alligators can't get to them at all."

Anne appeared composed now. She finally laughed, then said, "Spence, I don't think I've ever heard a more convoluted explanation that halfway makes sense to me!"

Spencer was still laughing at Anne's synopsis when he stopped at the kite-launch site. He gave Mark instructions on operating the walkie-talkies as well as the Crosman dart pistol. "I'll radio you when I get on the dam at Woody Pond," Spence said, then drove off, leaving the Telfairs alone on the deserted runway. Mark quickly had his 11-foot delta kite about 500 feet in the air, camera rig attached to the line as usual. The walkie-talkie crackled to life: "Looking pretty good," Spence said over the radio. "I can see the camera well, but you need to move your ground position north ... that would be to your right."

"OK, Spence," Mark answered. I'll start moving that way. Just let me know when I'm centered." Mark slowly started moving his cart that carried the electric reel and its battery.

He'd gone about 200 feet when Spence said, "Whoa! That's it!"

"What about the east-west centering of the camera?" Mark asked.

"As we speak, I'm walking the north side of the pond to check on that. I'll call you back in just a minute," Spence said, his voice shaking. He was obviously trying to walk, talk, and watch out for gators at the same time.

A few minutes later: "Mark, you need to let out about another 100 feet of line ... that should put your camera centered front to back, as well as side to side," Spence suggested on the radio.

Mark answered: "I'm slowly doing that now. Let me know when I've let out enough."

"Perfect! Stop there!" Spence barked on the walkie-talkie a few moments later.

Mark quickly made all his shots shooting straight down, and began retrieving the kite. Anne now had the walkie-talkie: "Spence, he's bringing it down now. OK?"

"I'm on my way to pick you guys up at the airfield. See ya in a few."

* * *

Over a number of weeks that followed, the Telfairs continued working with Dr. Spencer Roberson at the refuge. Their mutual respect, friendship, and trust of Spencer grew as Mark and Anne worked with him on various projects; their fear of the Sinaloa Cartel and the connection of their names to the drug bust melted into the background of their conscious minds. Oscar had returned from Savannah about a month ago, and was now actively crabbing again.

The baseline kite aerial photos of Woody had come out quite well. They could identify a number of stork nests under construction for the upcoming rook season. Later, during rook, the nests became quite easy to identify and count; the white "guano ring" at the periphery of each nest made them look like giant "lifesavers" from the air. *Glad they shit in their own nests!* Mark thought when he'd seen his first guano ring in a photo.

Estimating the number of stork chicks also became quite simple: Using a small aluminum boat, and dodging alligators, Spence would count only the chicks at the 25 easily accessible "artificial nesting sites." At these sites, the birds built their nests on artificial "platforms" consisting of iron rebar "crosses" mounted horizontally to the top of four-by-four pilings driven into the shallow end of the pond. Those nests would be only five feet above the pond's water level. That made them easy to inspect from Spencer's boat. A much higher number of additional "natural nests" were often located up high in cypress and other trees surrounding the pond; those nests were virtually impossible to inspect. Checking only those 25 easy-to-get-to artificial nesting sites gave Spence a "chicks-per-nest average" he could multiply by the total number of nests spotted on the kite aerial photos. The product of that multiplication gave him a good estimate of the total number of chicks produced in all of Woody Pond's 25-acre rookery.

* * *

Anne swore to Mark she'd never fired a rifle in her life, but to his surprise, a few weeks later, she proved to be an excellent shot with a dart rifle. She grew quite proficient at spotting symptoms of rabies in raccoons, and darting them. More importantly, she grew quite competent at estimating a given coon's weight just by looking at it. Before their very first darting session, Spence had explained in detail: "Look for symptoms of rabies; loss of fear of humans; attacking inanimate objects; frothing at the mouth; paralysis, especially in their hind quarters. And it's the animal's weight that determines the approximate dose size of the TKX dart that should be used. The darts contain three different drugs: Tiletamine, Ketamine, and Xylazine. I'm sure you two medical folks are familiar with Ketamine, which some anesthesiologists use on humans. The other drugs are mainly used by veterinarians. Our objective here is to tranquilize—not kill—them. We put them 'out' just enough that we can safely put them into observation cages. If they develop full-blown symptoms of rabies, we euthanize them, but still verify the diagnosis by lab testing their brain tissue. So, use the green darts on the small ones in the 12- to 15-pound range; use the blue darts on the midsize ones, say 16- to 18-pound size, and use the red darts on ones you estimate to be over 18 pounds. That covers the usual 12- to 21-pound range of raccoons we've got here in the refuge. In the glove box of my truck, I've also got some orange darts for large animals. And please be careful and don't accidentally shoot one another! Even the small-animal darts, could make you sleepy if you did."

Not very sleepy ... I weigh 156 and Anne 140, Mark recalled thinking at the time Spence had cautioned them.

At the end of their first day of darting, Anne had shot twelve, and Mark only three. Spencer had four. When they'd been placed in their observation cages in the back of Spence's pickup to wake up, all of Anne's coons did; all of Spencer's did, too. *Mark's all died.*

Better stick to what I know best ... human surgery, Mark recalled thinking at the time. But when the raccoon brain examinations (including Mark's three that died) had all proven positive for rabies, it lightened his spirits, improving his self-confidence a bit. And just in time. The second stage of Roberto's birthmark-removal surgery was to be done in about a week. Spence and the U.S. Marshals Service had insisted on the same hocus-pocus to conceal the Telfairs' (and Roberto's) identity when he and Anne did the second surgery. As with the first operation, the same two U.S. Marshals met them at the port on Colonels Island, then escorted them in an EMT truck to the aft deck of a U.S. Coast Guard cutter where the surgery subsequently took place in international waters.

Following Roberto's second surgery, Marshal Todd Whitmore had again proven to be invaluable. Mark received daily wound images via e-mail attachments. The young marshal seemed to have administered perfect postoperative wound care, including final suture removal. Mark's confidence in Whitmore continued to grow during their frequent phone exchanges, and Todd admitted his present occupation with the U.S. Marshals Service was merely 'a financial steppingstone,' one he was enjoying while trying to amass the funds needed to attend med school. *This young man should somehow become a surgeon himself! I wish I could offer to assist him financially ... but my retirement income is pretty stingy,* Mark recalled thinking several times during his multiple conversations with Todd.

Some six weeks following Roberto's final surgery, Mark's satphone beeped for the first time in a very long time. It was Todd calling. "Doc, I think it's time to return Roberto to active service as undercover DEA. As you've seen in the e-mail images, his results are perfect. I don't think there's a soul in the Sinaloa Cartel that could recognize him now. He's growing a beard and not cutting his hair. I don't think even his former Border Patrol buddies could spot him easily. I'd like your OK on putting Roberto back to work."

"Well, he's six weeks into the second wound's healing, so he should be physically OK for active duty. What I'm trying to say is the strength of his skin at the wound site is about as strong as before surgery. I'm not afraid of a wound separation. But as far as his being recognized by the Sinaloa goes ... well, that's your judgment call, Todd. I'll just have to trust *your* professional judgment on that part," Mark replied.

After their satphone call terminated, Mark had an immediate thought: *For Roberto's sake, I do hope we're not making a monumental mistake!*

TROUBLE

At 10:00 a.m. the Telfairs' satphone beeped for the first time in over a month. Anne was outside trimming some of her camellias; Mark was relaxing on their living room sofa leisurely reading the Sunday edition of the *Savannah Morning News*. He grabbed the phone from the coffee table. Dr. Spencer Roberson's voice was tense and urgent. "Mark, I'm afraid I have some very disturbing news. I just received a call from a fellow named Max Bollinger. He said as a youngster he used to be a cop in Atlanta, assigned to security at Grady Hospital's Surgical ER. Bollinger indicated he's since been with the U.S. Marshals Service for a number of years, and nearing retirement age. I've even had that verified by the Department of Justice. Anyway, Max Bollinger said the U.S. Marshals Service has temporarily assigned him to a team investigating the disappearance of one of their own men. That missing marshal's name is *Todd Whitmore*. It seems he has just evaporated into thin air!"

"Spence, this is all too weird! I do remember a Max Bollinger. He was a great ER cop when I was in training at Grady ... and of course I remember Todd Whitmore and his involvement with Roberto's surgery," Mark replied, shocked.

"When did you last see or talk to Whitmore?" Spence asked.

"I don't know the exact date, but I talked to Whitmore about a month ago. All he wanted to know was if I felt Roberto was ready for active service. I told him I thought it was OK, at least as far as his surgical wound was concerned. But I haven't actually *seen* Whitmore since Roberto's final surgery," Mark explained.

"Have you received any e-mails, or any other type of communication from Whitmore since you last talked to him on the phone?" Spence asked.

"Zilch, absolutely nothing!" Mark exclaimed.

"Mark, let me be honest with you. I sure don't like the way this smells. Marshal Max Bollinger told me Whitmore did successfully get

Roberto Gonzales inserted as an undercover agent with DEA. That happened a month ago. Two days ago, a very-concerned Roberto Gonzales called me on his satphone. Roberto said he'd been unable to contact Todd Whitmore by satphone, despite multiple attempts. Roberto said he was now working undercover in Canada near the Akwesasne Indian Reservation. In a tavern outside the reservation, Roberto said he spotted a couple of Hispanics he is *positive* are Sinaloa Cartel members ... but they did not recognize him. Roberto said we might not recognize him either. He told me he's now got a full short beard, and long hair he wears pulled back in a ponytail. Roberto also said he learned the SSs—like the smaller ones we've captured here—are being handmade in Canada on the Akwesasne Reservation by Mohawk Indians. They're building them on an island in the St. Lawrence River."

"You've gotta be kidding me, Spence. This is too bizarre. I could believe a birch-bark canoe ... but a fiberglass submarine?"

"Unfortunately, I'm not kidding. Neither Roberto, nor even his wife and children have heard from Todd Whitmore since Todd placed Roberto with DEA. We do know Whitmore was a bachelor, and rented an efficiency apartment in Brunswick. There was no evidence of forced entry. The forensic folks have gone over Todd's apartment with a fine-toothed comb. His U.S. Marshals Service credentials, service weapon, satphone, wallet, driver's license, U.S. passport, car keys, apartment key, and several credit cards were all still in his apartment. His satphone had been deprogrammed. His desktop computer in the apartment contained zero; the hard drive in it had been reformatted. Todd had a small digital camera in his apartment, but the memory card had been erased. His personal car was found parked in front of his apartment; it apparently had not been moved in a month, according to his apartment neighbors. Even his clothing and all his other personal belongings appear *not* to have been disturbed. A member of the forensic team indicated there were no items or trace evidence indicating Todd possibly had a girlfriend, or 'significant other.' Whitmore did have an account at a branch of the Southeastern Bank in Brunswick, but that bank says he had personally appeared at the bank a month ago to empty and close his account. An employee at the bank said Todd indicated the U.S. Marshals Service had suddenly given him a foreign assignment. His checking account had a little over $9,000 in it, and he took it in cash. He did not have a safety-deposit box or any other accounts with the bank. Phone company records indicate no activity on his regular phone in the last 30 days.

They can find no activity involving any of his credit cards, all of which have a zero balance due."

"Wow! Spence, it's just like you said … *evaporated!*" You don't think they've put Todd in Witness Protection … or changed his identity for some reason, do you?"

"No. I've been personally assured by some of the higher-ups at the Department of Justice: Todd Whitmore is a genuine MIA, or 'missing in action.' They've extensively questioned a U.S. Marshal, a Sloan Stafford, who frequently partnered with Todd. In fact, you and Anne have both met Stafford before; he was the guy who drove the EMT truck onto the boat, when you guys did Roberto's surgeries."

"I remember Stafford. What did he have to say about Todd's disappearance?" Mark asked.

"Virtually nothing … except that Todd was a 'loner' who never discussed his private life while they were working together," Spence replied. "The Marshals Service is now seeking *our* help. On our end, I've told them it is only Oscar who knows absolutely nothing about Roberto. And that's mainly because DEA and the Marshals Service wanted it that way. Oscar really had no need to know anyway. I've already told them if the four of us—I'm talking about you, me, Anne, or Victor—receive any communication regarding Todd, we would contact the Marshals Service immediately."

"Spence, there must be some logical explanation … something we've not thought about. Do you mind if I relay these details to Anne?"

"By all means, do!" Spencer replied.

"While we've been talking, Anne's been out in our yard. She's messing with her flowers, I think," Mark explained.

"That gal, in addition to being a darn good-looking blond, is a great outside-the-box thinker. She's the one that came up with the 'bottom hatch' theory for the subs, and she's the one that figured there had to be some radio communication from the ground to the chopper on that day we caught the three SSs. Remember?"

"Yeah, Spence. She certainly makes me feel like a mental-midget at times … and like the smartest guy in the world at others," Mark confided.

"When my Cathy was alive she did that same thing to me," Spence admitted. "When Anne comes inside, just tell her the details I've told you, and see what she can come up with. I think it best we not tell Oscar about this. And remember what you tell Anne is all covered by the NDAs you guys signed months ago. Communicate with me only in person or by satphone. OK?" Spence said, then hung up before Mark could answer.

Anne entered their house a moment after Mark and Spencer had terminated their call. She held several trimmings from her camellia bushes, ones bearing beautiful white or pink blossoms. She placed them in an ordinary water glass on the kitchen counter, then spoke: "Mark, aren't these the most beautiful things in the world?" she asked.

"The most beautiful thing in my eyes, is the gal that cut those flowers."

"Thanks, my Little Man ... but I know a snow job when I see one! So what's *really* on your mind?"

"Not what you think, Anne. I was on the phone with Roberson while you were outside pruning your flowers. Apparently someone at the U.S. Marshals Service contacted Spence ... and Spence wants *your* thoughts about what he's learned."

"*My* thoughts?"

"Yes. Let's sit down and talk. *Todd Whitmore is missing!*"

* * *

Mark spent the better part of the next half-hour explaining the details of his conversation with Spence. Anne patiently listened, not once interrupting Mark, but her facial expressions indicated wheels were actively spinning in her mind. When Mark finished talking, she finally spoke:

"OK Mark, so we've got an intelligent, healthy, young and unmarried agent with the U.S. Marshals Service, one who disappeared a month ago. Other than his money in his bank account, and the electronic information in his computer, satphone and digital camera, nothing else seems to be missing. I think robbery is an unlikely motive for his disappearance."

"I agree," Mark said. "I could see extortion or blackmail as possibilities."

"Me too, but whatever caused Todd to go missing seems to have been done professionally. My gut feeling is the Sinaloa Cartel may somehow be connected to his disappearance, but if Sinaloa is involved, Todd may well be dead ... just like another Jimmy Hoffa, never to be found. But if Sinaloa killed Todd, why'd he take all his money out of the bank? That alone says this was a planned event on Todd's part, and, for reasons unknown, he elected to make *himself* disappear. If acting alone, I doubt Sinaloa is sophisticated enough to reformat his computer's hard drive and satphone. But someone familiar with the Witness Protection Program might know how to do things like that ... then disappear so cleanly!"

"So what's your bottom line, Anne?" Mark asked.

"I think Todd did it. My biggest question is *why?*"

"I certainly don't know why, Anne. All I know is that I thought Todd was a bright young man, one whose real ambition in life was to become a surgeon. He'd even admitted to me that his EMT work, and work with the U.S. Marshals Service, were simply financial steppingstones, ones he was using until he had the money to go to med school. But I can tell you the $9,000 he took out of the bank won't even begin to be enough."

"Mark, I think we should call Roberson, and tell him what we think. We also need to ask him if Todd's disappearance changes the risk that Sinaloa will find out about us and the surgery we did for Roberto ... or maybe even our part in capturing their SSs and screwing up one of their drug deliveries."

For the next two hours, Mark repeatedly tried to contact Roberson by satphone. He tried a half-dozen times, only to find he always received a busy signal. *God, please don't let Spence now be MIA, too,* Mark worried. Using their regular phone, he finally called the refuge office. "He's been in the conference room talking on his satphone for over two hours," the secretary had explained.

"Honey," Mark explained to Anne, "Roberson is at the refuge office, and busy on his secure phone. Why don't we eat lunch here, then drive over to the office and see if we can catch him between calls."

* * *

Meanwhile, Roberson was in the refuge office conference room winding down another long satphone call. This time it was from Roberto Gonzales in Canada:

"Roberto, before we finish this call, let me be sure I've got all this straight in my head. I've made some notes after your call of two days ago. I'll add them to what we've discussed today. I will burn my notes after I relay this information to DEA and the U.S. Marshals Service. First, you told me you've successfully infiltrated the Sinaloa, working through Hispanic drinking buddies at a local Canadian tavern.

Specifically, you've been offered a position as a crew member on one of their new SSs when it is completed. You've also determined Mohawk Indians at the Akwesasne Reservation are the ones building the SSs for the Sinaloa Cartel, and they're using an uninhabited island in the St. Lawrence River to secretly construct them. They then use the St. Lawrence River to get their boats into the Atlantic Ocean, then move up and down the Atlantic ICW as needed. You've been told the SSs go as far south as Key West, Florida, and they have a number of accomplices who help them refuel with diesel, and avoid the legitimate marinas altogether. You have yet to determine how the high-tech marijuana is transported to the SSs, but you are positive it is being grown locally in Canada. Is all that correct?"

"Yes," Roberto replied.

Roberson continued: "And you've told me it is rumored that the Sinaloa is planning to acquire their own professional people—computer specialists, lawyers, marine engineers—by paying for their training at various schools in Mexico.

"Yes, but please know that is *rumor only*. I do not know that for fact yet," Roberto replied.

"Roberto, it is especially important that I have this one last thing correct: Today, you told me that Sinaloa somehow knows the exact location of Dr. Mark Telfair and his nurse-wife, Anne."

"Yes, but I do not know *how* Sinaloa learned that. Maybe they want secret surgery on one of their members? Who knows? If you see the doctor and his wife, tell them I am forever grateful. Let them know I now even drink beer with Sinaloa, and in front of me they talk about 'Marcado,' still wondering where he could be!"

"Don't push your luck, Roberto! But I'll tell the Telfairs," Spence advised. "Anything else?"

"Yes. This may be important, but maybe not. I have not heard any mention of your name, nor that of Victor Timmons. They know the nine Sinaloa men who were the crew of the captured subs are being detained in the U.S. by DEA, but they do not know *where*. It is my feeling they will not try to rescue those crew members, only kill them if they ever get the chance. They'd do that to keep them from telling more details about Sinaloa."

"Roberto, even I don't know where our government is holding those sub crew members. And I may never know."

"Spencer, I can tell you this: They are mostly pissed off about losing three of their SS boats there in your McIntosh County ... not to mention almost a billion dollars worth of drugs they claim to have had inside the captured boats!"

"Roberto, did we leave out anything important?"

"No, I think not. You have all I know for the moment, my friend. I will stay in touch with you. Do *not* call me on satphone ... it could beep at the wrong time, if you know what I mean."

"God speed your safe return, Roberto," Spence said, ending the call.

Head bowed, elbows on the conference table, covering his moist eyes with his palms, Spence sighed in thought: *Oh my God ... what do I tell the Telfairs ... and how do I protect them?*

29

THE WHITE LIES

"Dr. Roberson, the Telfairs are in the front office waiting to see you. Can you see them now?" the refuge secretary said over a regular phone connected to the conference room.

"Tell them I'm very busy on my satphone, and will be for several more hours. I'll contact them at their home later today," Spence said, hoping the quavering in his voice didn't alert the secretary to his precarious emotional state.

"I'm sorry," the secretary told the Telfairs, "but he's still busy, and said he will contact you at home later today."

Disappointed, Mark and Anne ambled back to their car. Both were wondering what could be important enough to keep Dr. Spencer Roberson busy for hours on end using a secure phone.

"He'll 'contact you at home later today,'" Anne said, repeating the secretary's words as she got into their car. "He's either truly busy, or avoiding us for some reason."

"Maybe it has to do with Todd Whitmore's being missing. I guess we'll just go home and wait and see," Mark allowed.

* * *

A knock on the conference room door startled Dr. Spencer Roberson. He opened the door to be greeted by Stella Pacheco, the elderly but very competent refuge secretary.

"Dr. Roberson, I know whatever you're working on must be very important … but you haven't even paused for lunch today. Please take these," she said, handing him a box of day-old Krispy Kreme doughnuts and a fresh pot of hot coffee. "I'm sorry, but that's all I could find here in the office to eat."

"Thanks, Stella. I know I've got to eat something, and I will. But please hold all outside calls," Spence told her, as she departed the conference room.

It took about an hour of phone work, but Dr. Spencer Roberson finally tracked down U.S. Marshal Sloan Stafford. Now talking on their satphones, Spence relayed the content of his earlier call from Marshal Max Bollinger, the one that let him know Todd Whitmore was missing.

On the phone, Sloan quickly explained: "Dr. Roberson, I'm truly sorry ... but I wasn't assigned to the detail trying to locate our missing guy. They sure questioned the heck out of me, though. I couldn't tell them much, other than Todd was a very private guy, and a stickler for details and Service protocol. True, we had often worked as a pair, but I didn't really *know* the guy, if you know what I mean. But I think I'd trust him to cover my back if we ever got into a messy situation."

"Stafford, I'll understand if you are not comfortable answering this question: Have you ever tried to contact Roberto Gonzales on his satphone?"

"No. I don't even have the number. I have no need to know. Roberto Gonzales was solely 'Todd's baby,' so to speak. I do know that Todd's assignment was to get Roberto's face fixed, and then get him inserted as undercover DEA somewhere in Canada. That's the extent of my knowledge."

"Well," Spence began, "I've recently talked with Roberto at length. I think Dr. Mark Telfair and his wife, Anne, are at risk. Roberto tells me the Sinaloa knows exactly where the Telfairs are located. In my opinion, they both are potential witnesses and soft civilian targets. I guess my question to you is this: Do you know of any possible way the Telfairs could be fast-tracked into some type of protective custody?"

"Dr. Roberson, that's a complicated issue. I do remember that medical couple very well. I'm the one who drove the EMT truck to the deck of the boat on both those evenings. I didn't actually stay in the truck during the surgeries, but Todd Whitmore did. I got out both times to have chow in the cutter's mess hall. Getting back to your question about protection, I do have some buddies with the Department of Justice. If DOJ says there's a way to do it, I'll try to get you a quick answer. Let me be sure I've got this right: The Telfairs are *not* criminals, but are potential civilian witnesses ... but exactly what have they witnessed, other than Roberto's surgeries?"

"They've witnessed Sinaloa's drug-smuggling methods and have actively participated in surveillance that led up to the recent Sinaloa drug bust in McIntosh County. Believe me when I tell you they are both highly credible eyewitnesses. They've helped me accumulate a lot of photographic evidence, and they've made many direct observations that could be invaluable at a trial," Spence explained. He hoped Stafford would realize his sense of urgency, and the value of the Telfairs as witnesses. "If you don't believe me, see if there is a way you can access DEA's secure website. That's where I've sent my reports and a lot of the image data."

"Roberson, I can't make you any promises, but I'll see what I can do. I kinda liked that medical couple, and I'm sure glad they were able to help Roberto. Let me make a few calls, and I'll try to contact you no later than 1630 today," Stafford said, then clicked off.

While nibbling on a doughnut and drinking black coffee, Spencer's mind filled with troubling thoughts: *If the government can arrange some protection, will the Telfairs agree to it? If I tell the Telfairs Sinaloa knows their location, would they just panic and bolt? Shit, this is all my damn fault! I'm the one who got them so involved … and kept assuring them their personal risk was minimal.*

Stella's knocking on the conference room door interrupted his thoughts. Spence opened the door, and Stella screamed, "Dr. Roberson, there's a boat on fire at the landing! A refuge visitor just rushed to the office and told me to call the fire department, and I did. They're on the way!"

Spence immediately ran to his truck, and sped to the landing. He could hear the fire truck's siren in the distance. Spence parked his truck at the landing, then ran to the dock and saw Oscar's boat engulfed in flames. He could see no six-gallon fuel tanks in the boat, and he knew they had probably been removed by Oscar himself, as he customarily did when leaving his boat moored at the end of a workday.

The Harris Neck Volunteer Firemen quickly reeled off hose from their truck, dragged it down the gangway, and had the open flames out in minutes. But it was too late. The fiberglass hull of Oscar's boat had burned to the waterline in numerous places, but did not sink, due to the foam flotation encased in the 24-foot Carolina Skiff's double-bottomed hull.

"I think this is arson," one of the firemen commented.

"Why so?" Spence asked.

The fireman quickly replied: "This is a fairly uniform burn, stem to stern. Some accelerant, like a flammable liquid, must have been used. I noticed there are no fuel tanks in this boat, and the battery-selector switch is in the *off* position. This type boat is self-bailing and has no straight-wired bilge pump. That means the *entire* electrical system of this boat was off! And that means no source of accidental ignition due to an electrical short circuit. I'm going to ask our County

Fire Chief to go to the State Fire Marshal and request an arson investigator. But if we're gonna leave the boat here in the water, we better put some new mooring lines on it. These are about burned through," the fireman said, pointing at the half-melted nylon ropes securing the remains of Oscar's boat to the dock's cleats.

"If you want, I have a trailer for this boat here in the refuge," Spence replied. "I can get it out of the water, and store it in a lockable shed until your arson investigators look at it. I'll leave the key to the shed at the refuge office. Wouldn't that be better?"

"Yeah, that's far better. I'll help you get it out. Just show me where the shed is so I can take the arson investigators there to examine it."

With the fireman's help, the charred hull of Oscar's boat was quickly removed from the river and stowed in a shed. The firemen and truck left, but Spence returned to the fire scene. He'd returned mainly to survey the floating dock structure itself. It was slightly scorched on the vertical part nearest the spot where the boat had been secured. Though discolored by the soot from the burning fiberglass resins, the wood of the dock never actually caught fire. The horizontal wooden platform of the floating portion of the dock had turned a dark brown because it had been thoroughly soaked by fresh water pumped from the fire truck. As the dock's wood dried, it was quickly returning to its normal weathered light silver-gray color. Something painted on the dock surface began to show up more and more clearly as the wood lightened in color. Spence jumped like he'd stepped on a snake when he first looked down at his feet and saw it: *There, spray-painted on the dock's deck was the letter "S"*... blood-red in color, about two feet tall, with a short four-inch horizontal line crossing the vertical part of the letter. *Sinaloa's sentinel mark ... I've got to tell Oscar the bad news,* he thought.

* * *

Spence returned to the conference room, mainly to think. Stella had poked her head inside the door to tell him she was leaving at four. It was now 3:55. He needed to talk to the Telfairs and Oscar, but he was awaiting a return satphone call from U.S. Marshal Sloan Stafford before contacting his "civilian helpers." At 4:30 sharp his satphone beeped.

It was Sloan Stafford calling: "Roberson, I'm sorry it took me this long, but I had to call in a lot of favors, and talk to half the folks at DOJ and their OEO, which is the Office of Enforcement Operations. They've reviewed the images and reports you've been sending to DEA's secure site. They are quite impressed, especially with the aerial infrared images that defined the heat signature of those SSs the Sinaloa is using in the Atlantic ICW. Your report indicated there were three citizens who helped you: a Dr. Mark Telfair and his wife, Anne, and a fella named Oscar Dunham, an old black waterman who regularly uses the refuge dock. Your report said the infrared images were made using a kite?"

"Yes, Sloan. Crazy as it sounds, a freaking invisible-on-radar kite! One of Dr. Telfair's retirement hobbies is kite aerial photography, which he calls KAP. But I need a bottom line here: Is the government going to help me protect these three local citizens who've risked their lives and volunteered their efforts to help us make that big drug bust?"

There was a long pause. Spence could feel his heart pounding as he awaited an answer. Sloan finally spoke: "Spence, DOJ has given me a provisional 'yes' on protecting the citizens involved."

"A *provisional* yes?"

"Yes. If the three civilians were facing criminal charges, our Bureau of Prisons could simply put them in protective custody. That not being the case here, I've been told they may be eligible for WITSEC, a witness security program available to noncriminals as well as criminals."

"I see," Spence said. "So, what's the procedure for doing that?"

"The criminal cases regarding the drug bust there at Harris Neck haven't been filed yet, but I've been told that will happen within the next 24 hours. Your civilians must agree to testify in all the cases, no matter how long the various trials may last, and to *voluntarily* enter the WITSEC program."

"How soon could we get them into WITSEC, or whatever you called it?" Spence asked.

"Have any of your civilian helpers been threatened by Sinaloa?" Stafford asked.

"Not personally … at least not yet. But a few hours ago I think Sinaloa burned Oscar Dunham's boat while moored at the federal landing here in the refuge. Oscar's the elderly crabber and oysterman I've mentioned in my DEA reports. Oscar Dunham would drive his workboat to position it so Dr. Mark Telfair could use the boat as a platform from which to fly his kites. That's how we got the aerial infrared shots of the SSs. Anyway, that boat burned about two hours ago. Sinaloa even spray-painted their trademark 'S' on the refuge dock where Oscar's boat burned."

"Shit!" Sloan blurted. "Exactly where are your three civilians right now?"

"I'm not positive, but they should be at their homes ... just a coupla miles from here."

"Is there any way you can get all three of them together very quickly, say at the refuge, in less than an hour?"

"Sloan, I guess I could concoct some lie that would get them here quickly. I just hate to lie to such fine trusting folks," Spence explained.

"Just get it done! Remember, you can't lie to *dead* witnesses ... and we never had this conversation!" Sloan exclaimed.

"I'll think of something. Where are you now?" Spence asked.

"I'm in Brunswick right now, but I could drive up there to meet you and the civilians. I could be there in about 20 minutes, if I put the pedal to the metal. Punch the emergency locate button on your satphone, just in case we have trouble finding you in the refuge. It's been a few years since I've been up there," Sloan explained.

"Stafford, you don't know how much I appreciate this. I haven't told Oscar about his boat yet, and I had earlier promised the Telfairs I'd contact them today. I was going to talk to them some more about Todd Whitmore's disappearance. That, in itself, may change their personal risk in being involved."

"I think the risk to your civvies may be far greater than you think, Spence. The Sinaloa can be a triple-A badass! They'll burn you out, kill you, or a combination of the two—then leave their special mark so there's no question about who did it. That's their usual response to those who participate in screwing up their operations. I'll be leaving Brunswick in just a few minutes. I'll be driving an EMT truck so the McIntosh locals won't try to stop me for speeding. In fact it'll be the same truck we used to do Roberto's surgery. I'll have another U.S. Marshal with me, but I don't know which one yet. See ya in a few," Sloan said, and punched his satphone off.

Spencer sat dazed for a long moment. *How do I get both the Telfairs and Oscar to drop whatever they are doing, and come to the refuge immediately? I'm going to have to lie to them, fake some emergency,* he thought.

He first called Oscar, who at first seemed a little reluctant to come immediately. "I's cooking some gator tail. Can it wait jus' a little bit, Dr. Spence?"

"I'm gonna die if you don't come right now, Oscar!"

"I's on the way, but where you at?" Oscar asked, alarm now in his voice.

"In the refuge office conference room," Spence replied.

"On the way rat now!" Oscar screamed.

His "emergency" call to the Telfairs was a little more specific: "I'm in the conference room at the refuge office. I just accidentally shot myself with one of my TKX darts for *large* animals! I'll probably quit breathing in about 20 to 30 minutes! Please help me! I've called 911, but it'll be a good half-hour before they get here. If you have any antidotes at home bring them, or give me CPR until the EMTs get here."

Oscar arrived first, and ran to the conference room. The Telfairs were only seconds behind Oscar. They all froze, not knowing exactly what to do next. Spence was seated at the conference table, head hanging down, attaché case open. He held a Crosman dart pistol in his right hand, but it was not aimed at anyone.

"Spence, can you hear me? You're certainly breathing OK. Look up at me!" Mark demanded.

Dr. Roberson did not respond the least to Mark's words. Other than slow normal breathing, and tears rolling down his cheeks to drop on the tabletop, Spence appeared to be in a catatonic state. *The effects of TKX? But his breathing is too normal for it to be TKX,* Mark reasoned.

They next heard a loud screech as the EMT truck skidded to a stop in front of the office.

Upon bursting into the room, U.S. Marshal Sloan Stafford drew his service weapon from beneath his jacket. He'd immediately realized something was not right about the whole scene. The U.S. Marshal that accompanied Sloan also had his weapon at the ready.

"Spence, remain seated and surrender your weapon immediately. Do it *NOW!*" Sloan demanded loudly.

The loudness of Sloan's voice apparently jarred Spence enough to cause him to finally respond. His fingers nowhere near the Crosman's trigger, Spence tearfully passed his dart pistol butt first to the U.S. Marshal that had accompanied Sloan Stafford. Oscar and the Telfairs remained flabbergasted, frightened and speechless, and now stood with their backs tightly pressed against the conference room wall. *The pressure of this whole thing—plus his missing meals and sleep—has finally caused Spencer to crack mentally. I should have seen it coming. I really doubt this is due to TKX,* Mark thought.

Keeping his Sig-Sauer 226 drawn, and aimed at Spence, Sloan slowly slid the open attaché (containing Spencer's 226) so it would not be within Spencer's reach. Without words, the other marshal removed

Beyond Beyond

Spencer's Sig-Sauer from the attaché and stuck it in his belt, then holstered his personal weapon. With Spencer's weapons secured, Sloan holstered his gun as well, then handed Spence a handkerchief retrieved from inside his dark suit's jacket. Still hanging his head in shame, Spence dried his eyes and blew his nose before making eye contact with anyone. Sloan finally spoke softly to Spencer:

"Spence, it's OK, buddy. I've seen good men crack before. I don't know how you took the pressure as long as you did."

30

TIME TO RUN

Mark finally found words: "Spence, I had nothing at home that would counteract TKX. But exactly where did you shoot yourself, and with what size dart?"

Still distraught, Spence leveled his gaze at Mark and said, "I didn't accidentally shoot myself with a dart. The whole thing was a horrible lie ... to get you, Anne and Oscar to come here as soon as possible."

"And why are the U.S. Marshals here?" Mark asked.

"Because I asked them to help protect you, Anne and Oscar. That's not a lie," Spence replied.

The marshals stepped into the hallway just outside of the conference room, and began chatting, first to one another, then on their satphones to unknown parties.

Spencer finally managed enough courage to look Oscar in the eye, then spoke: "Oscar, the Sinaloa burned your boat a couple of hours ago. Did it right at the dock where you had it tied up. I took what was left out of the water, but it's a total loss."

"Oh Lawd no! I knowed them Sin'loa was bad mens. How I gonna make a livin' now? Don't you worry none, Dr. Spence. The Lawd will get 'em, and if He don't, I sho will!" Oscar said, patting a pocket of his jacket.

"Oscar, do you have that pistol I gave you inside your pocket?" Spence asked.

Oscar said nothing, but nodded a "yes."

Apparently Sloan Stafford heard the word "pistol," and immediately popped back inside the conference room. Spencer spoke: "Oscar is armed. I didn't know it."

"Oscar," Sloan calmly said, "we're here to help you ... to keep Sinaloa from getting you. I'm sorry, but I've got to have any weapons you may be carrying."

Oscar sequentially stared at Sloan, then Mark, and finally Anne, who'd been silent. Finally, Anne spoke in a surprisingly calm and soothing voice. "Oscar, please do as Marshal Sloan requests. These guys are our friends."

Sloan accepted the pistol Oscar reluctantly surrendered, then spoke to the Telfairs and Oscar. "Is there anything at your homes that needs immediate attention? Maybe something you need to turn off, turn on, or lock up? Have you got your satphones?"

Mark spoke first. "No, nothing to turn on or off. Satphone's in my pocket. But we did leave the house unlocked."

Sloan replied, "We'll see that it gets locked shortly after we leave here. We have members of our team that are capable of locking or unlocking residential locks without a key."

"Leave? *Leave to where?*" Anne asked, her face a blend of anger and fright.

"A safe house," Sloan explained.

"A safe house *where?*" Anne screamed, demanding an answer.

"Less than an hour's drive from here. That's all you need to know for now. Please relax, Anne," Sloan said, speaking in a calm voice that seemed to settle her down a bit.

"Oscar, what about your house? Is everything there OK to leave? Got your satphone?" Sloan asked.

"Got my phone," Oscar replied, patting his shirt pocket. "But I was a cookin' some gator tail when Dr. Roberson called. I lef' in such a hurry, I ain't sho I turned hit off! Was slow cookin' in 'lectric oven. Be ruint now anyways," Oscar explained.

"Oscar, we'll have one of our guys be sure everything is OK at your house—but right now, we all need to *leave!*" Sloan emphatically stated.

Quickly, everyone got inside the EMT truck. They sped out of the refuge, with Sloan driving. A couple of miles up Harris Neck Road, Sloan saw flashing red lights on a fire truck that abruptly turned down a dirt side road. Sloan slipped on a headset to keep any received message private. The EMT truck's radio indicated there was a structure fire in progress down Katie Smith Road. As their EMT truck flew past the intersection of Harris Neck and Katie Smith Roads, Mark got a fleeting glimpse of the orange glow down the dirt side street. *My God, that's probably Oscar's house!* he thought. Fortunately, Oscar was seated in a position where he did not see it at all. *Best I not tell him what I think I saw ... losing his boat today is enough heartache for the moment,* Mark's mind concluded.

Marshal Sloan Stafford drove the EMT truck on U.S. 17 North, running a little over the speed limit. In the passenger's seat, his marshal partner chatted on his satphone at intervals. Mark could make out little of the conversation over the truck's noise, and the "noise" of the nonstop conversations among Anne, Oscar, and Spencer who were riding on the rear bench seats facing the truck's empty aisle, one that would normally be occupied by a gurney.

"Spencer, do you have any idea where they are taking us?" Anne asked.

"I'm not sure, but we could possibly be going to my previous home in Richmond Hill ... the one where Cathy and I lived before she died," Spence explained.

Anne spoke: "I remember on the evening you came to our house for a broiled flounder dinner, you mentioned you once owned a nice home in Richmond Hill, but said you had to sell it to cover some of Cathy's experimental cancer treatment expenses. Correct?"

"Yes," Spence replied. "But does she *always* remember details like this?" Spence asked, his question primarily directed to Mark.

"Always," Mark responded. "But why would the U.S. Marshals Service have any interest in your previous home?"

"Because, I sold my former home to the U.S. Government. They were looking for a sizable home in a gated community, one they could convert into a safe house," Spence explained. "I have no idea if they followed through on that plan."

In the center of Richmond Hill, Sloan turned right onto Ford Road and drove several miles. He made another right turn and immediately stopped at a guardhouse. Sloan presented his credentials.

The subdivision guard breathed a sigh or relief. "For a minute there I thought we might have a sick resident ... with you driving this type vehicle, you know. Some of your other government people came in unmarked cars about ten minutes ago. They had a big dog with them. I think they should already be at the house."

The guard opened the subdivision's electronic gate, then waved the EMT truck through. They'd driven several blocks in the moderately upscale subdivision before Spencer spotted his previous home site: "Wow! I sure hope they didn't put that tabby wall across the backyard and ruin the view of the marsh!"

Sloan made a brief satphone call. The very substantial ornamental iron gate blocking Spencer's former driveway began to slowly open. After the EMT truck had cleared it, the gate immediately began closing. Sloan parked at the rear of the house and told everyone it was time for them to get out. *Nice prison!* Mark first thought, viewing the ten-foot-high tabby wall that surrounded the entire homesite.

From the EMT truck's window, Sloan announced he and his

partner were going to return to Brunswick, but he'd be keeping in touch by satphone. "Don't worry, our guys here will be taking good care of you," Sloan said in parting.

The exterior of the house still looks the same, Spence thought, surveying his former house in the bright moonlight.

Immediately, another marshal, one with a gray-muzzled tan and black Rottweiler on a leash, appeared in the yellowish wash of light from one of the home's exterior floodlights. "Hi, I'm Tim Ryan, U.S. Marshals Service. Please stay where you are to meet 'Stutz.' He's your friend if I tell him you are. I use the command 'Stutz OK' to let him know you are OK. Always state his name first, then the 'OK.'" The marshal unsnapped the leash, and kept speaking the "Stutz OK" command repeatedly as the dog made his "crotch-sniffing" rounds. Oscar seemed to be the one new arrival the dog accepted most readily, and began vibrating his stump of a tail while Oscar patted the 115-pound male dog's box-like head. For some reason Oscar got tickled, and kept repeatedly saying "Stutz OK" to the dog. Stutz soon stood on his hind legs trying to "kiss" Oscar's face.

Tim Ryan became amused, but managed to sternly say, "Stutz off!" The dog immediately returned to Tim's side and sat. "Don't y'all start spoiling your protection partner here! I know he's getting old now and is due for retirement soon, but he's the only dog we've got at the moment. Let's go inside, and I'll show you your rooms."

After they entered the house, Tim escorted everyone upstairs ... except Spencer. Remaining behind in a daze now, Spence felt the urge to cry, but didn't. He'd frozen in thought: *I'm glad Cathy is not alive to see this ... she put her heart, soul, and her best years, into our home's interior design and its decoration.* Though the exterior of the home was unchanged, its interior had been "institutionalized"; the hardwood floors were now covered with a blue-gray commercial carpet. The same carpet continued up the beautiful curved stairs that led to the second floor. The original interior earth-tone paint colors chosen by Cathy were now changed to a monochromatic off-white; every ceiling sprouted sprinkler heads for a fire-suppression system; video cameras, smoke detectors and motion sensors adorned every room, though in a fairly unobtrusive way.

Spence went to the room that was once his most private place, his study. There, he found the once beautiful heart pine floors now covered with the same institutional carpet. The built-in shelves he once used for his many books were now holding video monitors and electronic panels, ones indicating things like "on," "off," "inop," "armed," "disarmed," and "aux. gen." Spence observed several radios, multiple phones and a computer on his former desk. *They've converted my study into a command and communication center!* he thought.

Upstairs, upon discovering he had a "missing" safe-house occupant, Marshal Tim Ryan quickly descended the stairs to find Dr. Spencer Roberson still standing in his former study: "Sir, it's time to go upstairs," Tim said, gently taking Spencer by the arm and leading him out of the study. "I'm afraid you're going to be staying with us, too. Shortly before you arrived, we received several disturbing radio messages."

"Disturbing?" Spence said to the young buzz-cut brown-eyed marshal.

"Yes, *quite* disturbing. We've just learned your trailer and the office building in the refuge have burned to the ground. Only a fireproof safe remained at the office, but there was no indication anyone even tried to open it. The Marshals Service now has that safe in their possession because we understand it contains a lot of evidence. Is that correct?"

"Yes," Spence replied. "Almost all the original image file evidence related to the drug investigation is in that safe. I sure hope the heat didn't damage the contents, most of which are on CDs. But some of the most important images are backed up off site ... the ones I sent to DEA's website."

"Sir, we've already had the safe opened. The contents are OK, and we're going to transfer the entire contents to the Department of Justice for safe keeping," Tim explained.

"You think Sinaloa did it?" Spence asked.

"Yes. Sinaloa left their mark at both fire scenes. It was spray-painted on the pavement at the office parking lot, and at the RV pad where you had your trailer. They also torched three vehicles. A late model F-150, and old Chevy truck, and a fairly new Ford Explorer that were parked at the refuge office. But I'm gonna let you tell the old fella the really bad news about his home. His name is Oscar Dunham, right?"

"Yes," Spence said.

"Well, it seems Oscar's house has been torched, too ... again by Sinaloa. They left their mark spray-painted on his white mailbox— and that's about the only thing left standing near his property. The heat was so intense, it even melted a stack of crab traps he had in his backyard. I'm sorry we couldn't get a follow-up team there in time to prevent all this. The only good news is the Telfairs' home has not been disturbed. We do have federal agents there now who are staying with that home to protect it, and we'll keep them there in shifts 24/7 as long as necessary."

"Shit! This is *all* my fault! I should never have agreed to work with DEA ... should never have gotten the civilians involved," Spence said, as a tear rolled down his cheek, with guilt and dread dragging at his face. He wiped the tear away with his sleeve, then asked Tim a question: "Would you please go upstairs with me while I tell Oscar the bad news?"

"Certainly. You've got my support. It might be good to have the doctor and his wife there too. I think Oscar will need everyone's support."

With Tim leading the way, Spence followed the marshal up the stairs that once had revealed hand-selected beautiful white oak wooden treads. At the top of the stairs, Spence froze. Apparently the homes entire second floor had been gutted, and rebuilt to resemble a motel's hallway with multiple side rooms.

"Welcome to 'Motel 6,'" Tim joked, hoping to lighten Spencer's spirits. "We've got six rooms with private baths and twin beds. Nothing fancy, but really comfortable. Oscar's in Room 6, the Telfairs are in Room 5, and you'll be in Room 4. We have no other upstairs guests at this time. Another marshal is sleeping in our quarters downstairs. Our quarters used to be the master bedroom for this place, I think."

Standing in the hallway upstairs, Spencer paused a moment to tell Marshal Tim Ryan the circumstances leading to his previous home becoming a government-owned safe house. Tim blushed deeply, and said, "Dr. Roberson, I'm so very sorry. I really put my foot in my mouth, didn't I? I mean that 'Motel 6' comment. But the Service never gave us the *history* of this house, just training on how to use the security and communication provisions it now has. Just knowing that you and your wife once owned it will make this house special to me, too. But I think we now need to get the doctor and his wife, then go to Room 6 and tell the old fella what's happened."

With Mark, Anne, and Spence standing next to him in the hallway, Tim Ryan briskly knocked on the door of Room 6. No response. After a second series of knocks failed to produce a response, Tim cautiously opened the door. Oscar was sound asleep on his bed—with Stutz snuggled tightly against his back! Stutz immediately knew he was in trouble when he saw Tim, and sprang off the bed, jolting Oscar awake in the process. Sheepishly, the dog came to Tim's side in the hall and sat, looking up at him as if to say, "I'm sorry boss, it won't happen again."

Everyone, including Stutz, entered Oscar's room. Sitting on the bedside in his stocking feet, Oscar sensed he was about to receive more bad news. He looked at Spence, then said, "Jus' tell me straight out."

And Spencer did: "Oscar, Sinaloa has burned your house to the ground. They burned your truck, too. They burned the refuge office and my trailer, and my truck and the Telfairs' car."

"De Lawd knows e'zakly who them Sin'loa mens is. An' He fo' sho get 'em! Lawd ain't gonna let 'em get Oscar, you wait an' 'see. An' all 'em Sin'loa mens got was *my things* ... an' *things* what can be replace ... 'cept my *family* ... my pitchers on my wall ... oh Lawd my pitchers ... my pitchers."

Oscar began to steadily weep. Stutz softly whined at Tim's side. "Stutz OK," Tim said. The dog went to Oscar, who bowed his head, wrapped his arms around the dog's massive upper chest, and allowed Stutz to gently lick the tears off his cheeks.

Not a single dry eye in the room, Tim included. He finally spoke: "As one of this dog's handlers, I've broken Service rules ... but somehow I just don't give a damn about that right now! I'll let Stutz stay in your room at night, if it would make you feel any better, Oscar. And nobody here ever heard me say that. But I am required to give you guys some other house rules. We'll do it downstairs at the dining table. I hope frozen pizza cooked in a microwave is OK, because that's about all we've got at the moment. Any volunteer cooks are appreciated. Just make a grocery list, and we'll gladly arrange to have a marshal shop for you."

31

THE SAFE HOUSE

The new arrivals assembled at the dining table eating microwaved pizza and drinking Diet Coke. Tim Ryan sat at the table's head, and began talking to them while they ate and drank. He glanced at several pages of notes as he spoke:

"This is the part of my job I really hate. My shift nominally ends at midnight, and it's only nine o'clock, so I get to do the 'dirty work.' With intelligent adults, it always makes me feel like I'm insulting the intelligence of our house guests by talking to them like children. I'm sorry, but if you elect to remain here, the Marshals Service requires that I give you the rules and conditions of your stay. First, you are here *voluntarily.* You're here for one reason, and one reason only: *your protection* from criminal elements. Secondly, you are not yet in WITSEC, or our Witness Security Program, but that may be a next step for some of you.

"You are not allowed to have any weapons of any kind, and if you have any, you must surrender them to me to be put in our safe. I know you guys have a couple of satphones, but I've got to put those in the safe, too. You are not allowed to use any of our electronic devices; specifically, you may not use our computers, send e-mails, or use house phones. You are free to watch either of the two TVs we have in the lounge area, and we'll provide a daily newspaper, the *Savannah Morning News.* You may write letters, but the content must be reviewed. Your letter may possibly be censored by a marshal before mailing it. The postal address for this house is actually a PO box number and it is kept secret. As house guests, you are not allowed to visit one another in your assigned rooms. An exception is being made here for the Telfairs, who are man and wife; they may remain together in Room 5. Official visits to your room, such as legal counsel, members of the U.S. Marshals Service, representatives from the Attorney General's office, medical doctors et cetera, are permitted in your assigned room with proper prior authorization. If you have any prescription medications, you must turn them over to me. Either myself, or my currently off-duty partner, will administer your medications in a timely manner. We'll have your prescriptions refilled as needed. You may not use or have any illegal drugs in your possession at any time."

Tim turned a page in his notes and continued: "You can't smoke cigarettes, cigars, or anything else, either inside the safe house, or on its grounds. Alcoholic beverages of any type cannot be consumed anywhere on the premises."

Anne raised her hand like a grammar school kid.

"Yes, Anne," Tim said, pointing.

"The only clothes any of us have are what we've got on our backs. How are we going to deal with that?" Anne asked.

"We have several marshals we refer to as 'outside marshals.' Basically, they shop and transport items to and from this and other safe houses. I want each of you to make a shopping list for a week's worth of inexpensive casual clothing that's appropriate for the season. Those items will be bought for you, along with toiletries and other personal items … if you don't mind one of our 'outside marshals' doing your shopping. We do have a washer and dryer at your disposal. You're expected to keep your room clean and uncluttered, and empty your own room's trash downstairs in the central container. For security reasons, there is no maid or laundry service. For a similar reason, the 'outside marshals' assigned to serve this house also keep the grounds. And a word about the grounds: Watch where you step. Stutz uses the lawn as his bathroom, and we've seen an occasional copperhead and rattlesnake inside the wall. The wall that surrounds this house is electrified. So is the gate. Don't touch either of them! Any other questions?" Tim said.

Spencer spoke: "So we're not officially in any program, right?"

"Correct," Tim replied. "I understand the Department of Justice, or DOJ, and some folks from the U.S. Attorney General's office are currently looking at options available to you guys. To keep you abreast regarding the circumstances that put you folks in danger, you will receive at least one daily briefing; either my fellow marshal or I will give the briefing. I've been told all of you here have already signed NDAs, or nondisclosure agreements. Is that correct? "

In unison, the Telfairs, Oscar, and Spencer nodded a "yes."

"You're not to disclose any details you learn about this house, not even its general location. The NDAs apply to any updates I may give you at future briefings. I'm sorry to say, there's going to be more paperwork to sign. I'm going to have all of you sign a document indicating you understand the safe house rules. I just condensed them to give to you verbally. I also have a printed version of the complete house rules for your review before you sign anything. As I said earlier, your stay here is *voluntary*. If you elect not to remain, now is the time to speak up."

For a long moment Tim paused, awaiting answers.

Oscar finally responded: "Well I ain't got no home lef' to go to. Ain't ev'n got no truck to get me there, ev'n if I was to still got a house. I's got a son, what live in Savannah, but I be 'fraid to go there. 'Em Sin'loa mens might know I's went there, an' burn he house, an' he wife an' new grandbaby. Can't take no chance."

Looking down at his half-eaten pizza that was now cold, Spencer said, "I'm in the same boat as Oscar. I have no home either, if you could call my little trailer a 'home.'"

Mark and Anne stared at each other. The fright he saw in Anne's beautiful hazel eyes gave him the confirmation he needed. "Tim, fortunately Anne and I still have a house. I know you said other marshals are now guarding our home at Dunham Point ... but I just wouldn't feel right leaving Oscar and Spence here alone. I know Spencer feels guilty about getting us into this mess, but, truth be known, we all *elected* to get involved. We've *all* had chances to back out a long time ago, but we didn't. I think I can speak for Anne, too. We're in this until those Sinaloa sons of bitches are *permanently* run out of our area on the Georgia coast!"

Tim Ryan smiled broadly. So did Spencer and Oscar. "Doctor Telfair, I know the fine print in the house rules prohibits swearing ... but I hope the courts fry those fucking Sinaloa bastards! And you never heard me say that!"

Tim disappeared a few moments, returning with separate printed copies of "house rules" for them to read and sign. Oscar slowly ran his index finger along each line of the three-page document. Sensing Oscar might be having trouble reading, or unable to read at all, Tim spoke up. "Oscar, are you having any trouble understanding that?"

"Naw suh, Mr. Tim. I know I slow, but I kin sho read *readin'*, jus' can't read no *writin'*."

Spence explained: "Tim, I don't know why it's that way with Oscar. He's had no formal education. He taught himself word recognition from the Bible. He can read the *printed* word just fine ... like in his Bible. He cannot read cursive or script handwriting, but he reads my block-letter handwriting fairly well, if I do it very neatly. Don't worry, if Oscar runs into any words he does not understand, he'll ask me to tell him what they mean."

"Take your time," Tim replied, suppressing a smile. "I'll check on you guys in about an hour."

When Tim returned, he saw everyone had signed. The marshal grinned, but said nothing, when he saw Oscar's standard "signature" in very neat capital block letters: OSCAR DUNHAM.

Tim made an announcement to the group: "Everyone has signed. Welcome to our safe house. I'll be going off duty in about an hour. I plan to give you a briefing about 1:00 p.m. tomorrow afternoon after I come back on duty. Do you have any questions before I change shifts with my partner?" No one had questions, and Tim continued: "My current partner's name is Max Bollinger. He's an older but very capable U.S. Marshal. You guys will like him, I promise. He'll be knocking on your doors at seven for breakfast orders. We'll have our outside marshals deliver the food. I suggest you go with fast food, like something from McDonald's until we establish a meal and cooking routine. Retire when you want, but remember the 7:00 a.m. wake-up is not that far away. And please don't open any of the exterior doors or windows. The intrusion alarm will go off if you do that."

The four "house guests" expressed no interest in TV. They wearily climbed the carpet-clad stairs and literally began crashing into their beds, each thinking this was the most unusual day in their entire lives.

Undressing in Room 5, Anne spoke to Mark. "I'm proud of you, Little Man ... for saying what you did downstairs. For saying we all really *elected* to remain involved. I think that made Spencer feel a lot better."

"I hope it helps relieve Spence's obvious and deep sense of guilt. I'm not changing the subject on you, Anne, but what does our current situation remind you of?"

"That night in Atlanta. Was back in 1968, when you and I were dating and in training at Grady Hospital. They'd put all the house staff under 'house arrest' at the hospital. It was the night right after Martin Luther King was shot ... the night the hospital felt sure there'd be one helluva bloody riot in Atlanta, and they wouldn't let any staff leave the hospital. But at least they relaxed the rules, and they allowed us nurses go to the 14th floor and sleep in the same quarters used by the interns and residents. Even this safe house room looks almost identical to your room at Grady, the one you shared with a trash-mouthed Polack, that Dr. Zack Paslaski."

Mark smiled at Anne's uncanny ability to recall events of almost 30 years ago. "Ya know, I really need to look old Zack up. I think he became an ER doc in Harlem, but we've totally lost contact over the years. When we get to the point where we can use computers and phones, I may try to locate him."

Anne yawned. "Are you as beat as I am?"

"I *know* I am," Mark admitted. "My mind wants to jump your bones, but I don't think my body can follow through."

"Ditto," Anne said. "But at least we've got sex to look forward to, something that the others don't have."

Clad only in their underwear, they elected to cuddle together in just one of the two single beds. Due to the space limitation, they reclined on their sides. Mark kissed the back of her neck, then whispered, "I love you ... we'll get through this, somehow."

* * *

A little after seven the next morning someone knocking on their door awakened them from a dreamless sleep. Mark got out of bed in his Jockey shorts and walked to the door. Clad only in bra and panties, Anne rolled onto her back and pulled the bedspread and sheet up to her chin. Mark cracked the door and a slightly familiar voice spoke to him: "Second-shift U.S. Marshal, here. It's 7:05, sir. The outside marshals are going to make a breakfast run to McDonald's. I need your order."

Where have I heard that voice before, Mark thought before he answered, "We'll take four Egg McMuffins, and two large OJs. Do you have in-house coffee?"

"You bet, 24/7. Including cream and sugar. Anything else?"

"No, that's all I can think of for Room 5. Thanks," Mark said, and closed the door. He noticed Anne was giggling beneath her covers. "What's so darn funny?"

"Oh, it's just something I read a while back: 'You can tell you've been married too long when your spouse orders your food for you, and they order *exactly* what you wanted.'"

238

32

THE FIRST BRIEFING

Mark and Anne took separate showers, resisting the urge to shower together; both knew what that invariably led to, and they didn't want to eat a cold breakfast. The bathroom was nothing fancy, but it was clean and comfortably warm. No accessories or toiletry items were provided, other than a bar of soap, washcloths and towels. It felt odd to be putting back on yesterday's clothes, but both knew Oscar and Spencer were no better off than they.

They descended the stairs and went to the dining area. No one else was there yet, but there was a Styrofoam box in the middle of the dining table. They opened it and removed what they had ordered, leaving the remainder inside the box to keep it warm for their fellow visitors.

Almost immediately, Max Bollinger appeared carrying a tray bearing a pot of coffee and several mugs. When Mark and Max saw each other, they mutually froze and locked eyes.

Anne did the same thing.

"Hey, I know you, Doc! From Grady Hospital, a.k.a. the 'Gradies.' Remember me? Max Bollinger, the Surgical ER cop?"

A broad smile formed on Mark's face before he answered: "I *thought* I recognized a familiar voice when you came to the door of room 5 this morning! You haven't changed a darn bit, Max. Still got the build of a young man, still baldheaded as ever. Still keep it all shaved off, huh?" Mark asked, extending his hand to Max.

Max laughed. "Not necessary anymore, Doc. Mother Nature took care of most of that daily chore for me!" Max explained, then laughed again. "But except for your hair turning gray at the temples, you haven't changed a bit either. And neither has that pretty lady with you. I think you two were dating when I worked the ER, as best I remember."

"Yep, she was formerly Anne Hunt, R.N. She was the night supervisor for the OR at Grady, but now she's my wife of some 25 years. We've both been retired a few years from our private practices located in Statesville, Georgia, but we now live down here on the coast in McIntosh County. At least that's where we *were* living ... until all this stuff happened!"

Anne extended her hand to Max. "It's great to see you again! Just having someone from Grady here in this safe house makes me feel a lot better about our current situation," Anne said, as she poured coffee and offered the first cup to Max.

"Max, when and why did you leave Grady?" Mark asked, while Max took his first sip of coffee.

"Doc, I think it was right after you finished your surgical residency there. I went for some additional training at the Federal Law Enforcement Training Center near Brunswick, then to the U.S. Marshals Service and I've remained with them since. I just got off a detail looking for one of our missing marshals, and now I've been reassigned to this safe house. Anyway, with the Service, the pay's better, and it sure beats risking your life every day in an inner-city hospital ER. But what ever happened to that crazy Polack cohort of yours ... that Dr. Zack Paslaski guy? Crazy, trash-mouthed, brilliant ... that's what I remember about him. I'll never forget that guy! And how he solved the problem of removing a light bulb stuck up some gay guy's butt! It's a small world, Doc."

"Max, I'm not sure what happened to Zack, but I heard he went to work as an ER doc in Harlem, New York. Marshal Tim Ryan gave us the 'house rules' yesterday. I know we can't use the computers or phones. So, for right now, I have no way of tracking Zack down."

"I'll find Zack for you ... after I bring myself up to speed and read all the reports Tim Ryan has about you guys. The file is a couple of inches thick!" Max exclaimed, just as Oscar and Spencer approached the dining table.

Max introduced himself to the new arrivals, and advised them to eat while it was still warm. He then disappeared, apparently into the kitchen, which the new guests had yet to explore.

Oscar and Spencer greeted the Telfairs a "good morning," then took their own food out of the box, poured their coffees and departed to the lounge area to eat while watching the morning TV news. Mark and Anne sat side by side and alone at the long dining table.

"You know Mark, the Gradies still keeps on tracking us down, doesn't it?"

"You said *tracking us down?*" Mark replied.

"Well not literally, Little Man, but figuratively. Just how likely do you think it would be for us to be tucked away in a U.S. Marshals Service safe house in Richmond Hill, Georgia, and there we run into a marshal who just happened to be a former cop in Grady Hospital's Surgical ER? Or, how likely is it that in Statesville we'd run into Cootie Bloodworth, the daughter of your very first patient at Grady? Or Dr. Holton, your partner in Statesville, personally knowing Mrs. Costellanos, who ran the General Admission Clinic at Grady ... where you started your internship?"

Mark never answered Anne's questions because Max reappeared with paper and pencils. "I need your shopping list for clothing and personal-care items. One of our outside marshals will be here in about an hour to go shop." Without further words, Max left to find Oscar and Spencer in the lounge, and instructed them to prepare their own shopping lists.

* * *

At noon, Tim Ryan replaced Max Bollinger. Tim assembled the group in the dining room, and spoke: "First, during my off time, I didn't get a lot of sleep due to incoming information. I've got tons of things to tell you guys. Secondly, we need to place lunch orders now. Again, I suggest fast food until we can go shopping for some real groceries. I'll start today's briefing at 1:00 p.m. I'll do it right here in the dining room at lunchtime. To kill time until then, you guys may want to go outside on the grounds for some fresh air. The intrusion system is now off, but avoid the gate and wall. They're still electrified. Watch out for any 'Stutz land mines.' See you guys at one," Tim said, then promptly went into Spencer's former study, and closed the door.

" 'Tons of things' he said. Wonder what's happened now?" Mark asked Anne.

"God only knows," Anne replied. "As long as our house at Dunham is OK, I think I can take just about any news. Sounds like we're going to need a new car, though. The Explorer had only 18,000 miles on it, but it's insured. And what about our big boat? We certainly don't want to leave *Fanta-Sea* in the water indefinitely, do we?"

"Heck no, Anne! She'd have an inch of barnacles on her bottom if we did that. I'm sure we'll think of hundreds of things that will need to be done in our absence. I guess we need to start making a list ... like paying our utility and credit card bills, insurance bills, getting our mail, and stuff like that. Shit, we may be in more of a pickle than I thought. Do you remember the comment Roberto Gonzales made to us about being in Witness Protection?"

"Yep, I sure do, Mark. It was at that meeting in the DNR building in Brunswick. Roberto said it was a combination of fear and isolation, mostly *isolation,* but right now I don't feel any fear. I think the isolation is what's going to get to me ... and we haven't even been here 24 hours yet! It's our inability to personally deal with day-to-day things in our former lives ... that's what I think will get to us."

"Agreed, Anne. If it gets too bad we'll ask Saint Christopher what to do. Tim did say our stay is *voluntary.* Right? But for now, let's just take it a day at a time."

* * *

At one o'clock their lunch was delivered. More McDonald's. *Wonder if the government gets a kickback from them?* Mark thought. Tim Ryan sat at the head of the dining table, but he was too busy munching his quarter-pounder with cheese to begin speaking right away. In a few minutes he did:

"OK, my hunger pains have subsided enough to begin your first briefing. Feel free to ask questions, but this is the single most important thing: *We've got indictments for all 12!*"

Confusion swirled in Oscar's head. "Mr. Tim, you say we's got what?"

Tim explained: "Oscar, it's a written statement charging folks with the commission of a crime. In this case there are 12 different folks charged with breaking the law. Nine of them were the folks driving those SS boats, and three were the guys driving the pontoon boat to pick up the drugs."

"Is them 12 peoples all lock up, now?" Oscar asked.

"You bet, Oscar. And the prosecuting attorney is ready to begin a trial at the U.S. District Court in Brunswick just as soon as they can get on the calendar. They'll stay locked up until the trials begin, and if found guilty, they'll stay locked up for a long, long time."

Dr. Spencer Roberson also had a question. "Tim, has the immigration status of the nine Hispanics been established?"

"Yes, Spencer, that was going to be my next point. The leaders of Sinaloa are maybe not quite as smart as some of the folks they hired to drive their subs. If the captured SS crews were here illegally, they would likely end up being deported or extradited. At least that's what

242

would happen, eventually, and that's probably what Sinaloa bosses would actually prefer. If deported, the higher-ups in Sinaloa would simply arrange for them to be killed once they got back inside Mexico. But—"

"Are they legal or illegal?" Spencer cut in.

"Spencer, if you'd please allow me to finish, I'll explain! It now seems the SS crew members were perhaps smarter than their Sinaloa bosses; they *all* actually have valid U.S. immigration documents. The subs got entrapped so quickly in the shrimp nets, the crews apparently had neither the functional tools nor the time required to access their documents. The federal guys who interrogated the crew members said they kept swearing they were U.S. citizens, and not illegals. Finally, federal officers working at the port in Brunswick found their papers hidden *inside* their subs' fiberglass bulkheads. They actually had to use power tools to cut through the fiberglass to find them. Each sub did have tools that would have allowed the crew to get at their documents, but the batteries in their cordless saws were all *dead!* They found each set of documents had been carefully waterproofed by sealing them inside triple Ziploc bags. Obviously, this could have allowed the crew to escape using SCUBA, without risk of damage to their documents … if they'd just had the time and tools that worked! Without question, their papers are not counterfeit, and that means *all* the Hispanics are legal residents of the U.S. That makes them subject to *our* laws and *our* penalties for breaking them. On the other hand, if the crew had not been captured, and escaped taking their immigration documents with them, they'd simply blend in with the legal U.S. population."

"OK, Tim. Sorry I butted in. So, you are saying those sub crew members knew the worse they'd face is the U.S. judicial system. But what about the other three guys, the ones using the pontoon?" Spence asked.

"All are from Alabama, born in the U.S. All have prior drug-related felonies. The federal prosecutor's office assures us all the indictments are solid," Tim explained, before taking the final bite of his quarter-pounder.

"Tim," Spence asked, "what about the locals, the McIntosh County Deputies that got caught red-handed?"

"The legal folks are still batting that one around. I think jurisdiction is the issue. But you folks here were not direct witnesses to any part of that event with the local deputies, and I doubt any prosecuting attorney would want your testimony."

"Anne piped in: "Tim, do you have any idea how long we'll be here?"

"No, I don't. All I know is Max Bollinger and I have been assigned to this safe house for 90 days ... with no leave time for either of us. And our assignment 'could be extended,' we've been told. And, I've told you your stay here is voluntary at this time; ours is not. For your safety, I strongly suggest you remain here until more of the details are known."

We might just as well be in jail! the Telfairs simultaneously thought.

33

MORE PIECES OF THE PUZZLE

Days morphed into weeks, weeks into their second month at the safe house. Everyone had an obvious case of "cabin fever," and it was getting more and more difficult to tolerate one another in perfect harmony. When the Telfairs felt they could not tolerate the boredom any longer, they went to their room to consult Saint Christopher, or to have sex. But they lived for the daily briefings, and Tim Ryan was about to give one. He'd earlier indicated today's was going to be "the big one" they'd all been waiting for.

Tim stood at the head of the dining table, a stack of file folders at his side. He cleared his throat, as though preparing to give the most important speech of his life. Mark thought it a little odd that Max Bollinger, though technically off duty, sat at Tim's side.

Tim began: "I know your stay here has been a drag on you emotionally. It gets to the marshals, too. But let me give you the bottom line first, then fill in all the details that made that bottom line possible. Please try to keep separate in your mind those events which you *personally* witnessed, and those events you have learned about through briefings given at this safe house. Reading now, Tim said, "The bottom line is this: *The U.S. Department of Justice has authorized the voluntary admission of Mr. Oscar Dunham, Dr. Spencer Nelson Roberson, Ph.D., Dr. Marcus Milton Telfair, M.D., and Mrs. Anne Hunt Telfair, R.N., for admission to the Federal WITSEC program for protection as noncriminal federal witnesses.*" Tim paused a moment to let his one-sentence bottom line sink in. "I'm sure you'll have questions, but let me fill you in on the latest first. The latest comes from Roberto Gonzales, a U.S. Border Patrol officer who was undercover for DEA in Canada."

Oscar raised his hand for the first question. "Mr. Tim, you say Roberto *who?*"

"His name is Roberto Gonzales, Oscar. In reading Dr. Roberson's reports, I realized you are the only person here who does not know about Roberto. His name has been kept from you because DEA wanted it that way. Also, you never had a real need to know his name. That's not even his original name. In fact, *none* of us here in this room know what 'Roberto's' original name is; he was in the Federal Witness Protection Program, as well as being with Border Patrol and DEA. Spencer, Mark, and Anne all know him by his assumed name, and that's only because they had to arrange for Dr. Telfair and his wife, Anne, to do some secret surgery to change the appearance of Roberto's face. They did that so Roberto would not be recognized by Sinaloa, and killed by them while he was working undercover."

"Lawd, dis here is somethin' else!" Oscar exclaimed. "So what 'Roberto' find out dat we don't knows already?"

"It's a long story, Oscar, and I'm getting to that now. Roberto was able to penetrate Sinaloa, first as a crew member for one of their subs. He actually made several 'runs' with them and learned how they navigate the Atlantic ICW and various rivers on the U.S. East Coast. That includes your Barbour River down there in McIntosh County. In fact, as Sinaloa's trust in Roberto grew, he was subsequently given a 'tour' of the very site where the subs are manufactured."

"Lawd, dis is getting' worser an' worser," Oscar said, looking quite dapper in his new red flannel shirt and unfaded blue bibs the outside marshals had bought for him.

Tim and the others chuckled as Tim continued: "Well it does get 'worser' as you say, Oscar. The Sinaloa even further corrupted the Mohawk Indians, who were already involved in skimming funds from their own casinos, and smuggling black market U.S.-grown tobacco *into* Canada, where all growers must be licensed, and are highly regulated by the Canadian government. Sinaloa even got some of their boat builders to come up to Canada from Columbia, and relocate to one of the Mohawk Indian reservations; there, the Columbians taught the Indians how to build SSs on an island in the St. Lawrence River. Using the 'locate' function on his satphone, Roberto gave us the exact GPS coordinates for the boat-building site."

"Sin'loa ev'n mess up 'em Injuns, too?"

"That's right, Oscar. Even the Indians, too," Tim replied.

"When's the last time Roberto was heard from?" Spence asked.

"I personally talked to him about a week ago, shortly after a joint U.S./Canadian task force shut down the boat-building site completely. While the boat construction site was being raided, Roberto slipped off of the reservation, and a day or two later he even managed to work his way into one of the underground Canadian grow labs."

"*Underground?* Literally or figuratively?" Anne asked.

"Literally," Tim replied.

"Well, why grow the stuff underground?" Anne asked.

"There are several reasons. First, it makes the crop impossible to find using aerial surveillance. Second, it's easier for the growers to guard their crop and prevent theft. And third, as I understand it, the crop grown underground is protected from undesirable crosspollination by plants grown on the surface. In other words, they are trying to protect the purity of a highly modified potent genetic line, and not let their plants get pollinated by low-potency plants produced by other growers in their area. I know Dr. Roberson is a biologist. Have I got that about right, Spence?"

Spence said nothing, but nodded a "yes."

Tim continued: "So, let me tell you how it happened. First Roberto shaved his beard and head to again change his appearance. During numerous prior satphone conversations with Dr. Roberson, Roberto had acquired a vocabulary containing a number of 'genetic buzzwords.' This allowed Roberto to be able to convince folks operating the grow lab that he was a Columbian 'plant genetics specialist,' especially regarding the cannabis family of plants. Roberto said the grow lab is located about 400 feet underground, in an abandoned nickel mine in southeastern Canada. The Canadian growers had their own electrical generators to run their highly filtered ventilation equipment, as well as water pumps, and multiple 1,000-watt metal halide grow lights. They'd cycle the lights to produce 24 hours of light, then 12 hours of darkness. That light cycle forces budding of their genetically modified unpollinated female plants, ones called sinsemilla. Roberto says 'sinsemilla' is Spanish for 'without seeds.' It seems the sinsemilla buds are much more potent than their male counterparts."

Spence cleared his throat, then angrily butted into Tim's briefing: "About *100 times* more potent than the stuff that was around in the 70s! *I* am a plant geneticist, with a Ph.D., and I know what in the hell I'm talking about. But I want to go on the record: I *never* encouraged Roberto to do this! Whoever authorized Roberto's going to a grow lab, may just as well have signed his death certificate! God, what a cockamamie idea! Those growers are far too sophisticated to have Roberto BS them for any period of time. It won't take them very long to figure out Roberto is a mole. And they'll *kill* him!" Spence screamed, his face beet-red.

Tim held his hand up, palm outward, then glanced at Max Bollinger, who was armed beneath his blazer. Tim spoke: "Max, I know tempers are getting short. Since you received the very latest communication regarding Roberto, please see if you can calm Dr. Roberson down."

"Glad to," Max said, staring at Spence who was still red-faced.

"Dr. Roberson," Max began, "we marshals also got uptight about DEA's *apparent* decision to let Roberto try to BS his way into a grow lab. But bottom line, it *worked!* We now not only have the GPS coordinates for the entrance of the abandoned Canadian nickel mine, but Roberto was able to 'steal' some of their sinsemilla buds. They were flown to a plant genetics lab in Atlanta about a week ago. They're being compared to the samples you obtained from the marijuana Oscar found in the Barbour River crab traps. It's also being compared to the pot found inside the subs. Any moment now, we should be hearing from Atlanta, and we'll know for sure if that particular Canadian grow lab is the single source we think it is. But the most important thing is this: At 0615 today, we were notified Roberto Gonzales has been extracted from Canada, and he's now safely in Federal Witness Protection here in the U.S. He is reunited with his family, and has been placed on administrative leave by both the U.S. Border Patrol and DEA. Specifically, DEA did *not* authorize his going to a grow lab. That was all Roberto's idea. I'm sure there will be some token reprimand, maybe in the form of a slap of his hands … followed by a pat on the back," Max said, now chuckling.

Spencer's anger evaporated just as quickly as it had appeared. He began smiling, then slowly clapping; soon he was joined by all in the room. The beeping of Tim's satphone silenced the applause. "That's great!" Tim said, upon hearing the phone's timely message. "But let me put you on with our real expert here, Dr. Spencer Roberson," Tim said, passing the phone to Spence.

Spence identified himself, but then listened for what seemed like five minutes before he spoke: "You're sure? Absolutely positive? Comprehensive protein and DNA and isozyme purity all match?" Whatever the reply had been, it caused Dr. Roberson to grin. Spence thanked the lab technician, then passed the satphone back to Tim, who signed off.

"Well," Spence began, "this *is* the briefing we've all been waiting for!"

Anne still had questions. "OK, so we now know Roberto is safe, we know the exact location of the Canadian grow lab that was producing this stuff, and how they were getting it to market using our East Coast ICW. Their boat-building site has now been shut down completely. So, what's left to do?"

"*Successfully prosecute this case!*" Tim blurted. "That's where you guys come in, Anne."

"Duh," Anne said testily. "But can I ask you about some other things that bug me ... before we talk about more legal stuff?"

"Sure," Tim replied.

"Whatever happened to U.S. Marshal Todd Whitmore?"

Max and Tim stared at each other a brief moment. Both men slightly blushed. Tim finally said, "You tell 'em, Max. You were directly involved, and you're better at this kinda thing than I am."

Max again stood. For some reason his gaze was mostly fixed on Mark Telfair. "This," Max began, "is a rather sensitive subject for the U.S. Marshals Service. I know Dr. Telfair realizes there are bad professionals. He's personally experienced one. In Atlanta at the Grady Hospital ER, he experienced an incompetent cop. In fact, Dr. Telfair experienced a *lousy* cop who allowed a druggie to get inside the ER with a gun and shoot up the place. Fortunately, no one was injured, but the guy could have killed a number of staff and patients. I was the cop that replaced that ineffective Grady ER cop, and that's how I came to know Dr. Telfair, who trained at Grady. I worked there for a couple of years, then transferred to the U.S. Marshals Service. I thought they'd be a 'class act,' with no bad apples."

"So, Max, you're saying Todd Whitmore is a bad apple? Correct?" Anne interrupted.

"Let me finish, Anne. Todd Whitmore's work for the Service was outstanding. He is a very intelligent young man, but his ultimate goal in life was to become a surgeon like your husband. Todd 'arranged' his own disappearance, but as clever as he was, he made one 'fatal' mistake: He booked a flight to Guadalajara on Delta, using his *real* name, and carried an expertly done counterfeit Mexican passport bearing his real name. Under an assumed name, we discovered Todd was attending medical school in Guadalajara, Mexico. The Sinaloa was paying his full tuition, with one proviso: Todd would become a surgeon who worked exclusively for Sinaloa upon completion of his training. Todd has now been extradited to the U.S. for trial. He'll never be able to get a job in law enforcement again, or attend medical school ... ever. I don't need to remind you that you have signed NDAs."

Anne raised her hand like an excited school kid. "Max, who ratted on Spencer and Oscar ... so Sinaloa would know which things to burn?"

Again Tim and Max exchanged glances. Tim gave Max a nod, and Max spoke: "Anne, we think Todd has cleanly confessed to everything. He's even had several voluntary polygraph tests. He swears he didn't rat on either Spencer or Oscar, or you and Mark. We currently think it was possibly local law enforcement who told Sinaloa something that caused them to think you, Mark, and Oscar were involved. They all know Oscar is a crabber and oysterman who's worked the Barbour River for years. They knew his boat and where he lived. Thus Sinaloa, probably acting on information given them by locals, burned Oscar's house and boat in revenge. As far as torching the refuge office goes, and the trailer behind it, and the vehicles parked in front, we think Sinaloa was working purely on the *assumption* that someone in the office was connected to the drug bust. As far as we know, Sinaloa thinks the trailer they burned belonged to the office secretary, a lady named Stella Pacheco. The Sinaloa seems to like *swift* retribution, more so than *accurate* retribution. That's probably the reason they shot and killed a look-alike kid in Nogales ... a kid they thought was Roberto's child. The files indicate you were given that information during a meeting at the DNR building in Brunswick. Do you remember hearing Roberto tell you about that?"

Anne and Mark both nodded a "yes."

"So far, we still believe neither local law enforcement nor Sinaloa has any idea Dr. Roberson was in charge of the investigation at the refuge, and we've no direct evidence that Sinaloa knows of your or Mark's involvement, nor that of Victor Timmons with the DNR."

Anne breathed a sigh of relief, but immediately asked a question of Tim. "Our involvement will all come out at a trial, won't it?"

Tim paused. "Yes, Anne. It's unavoidable. That's the reason we've tried so hard to get you guys into WITSEC. We've rightly convinced the Department of Justice that you guys are credible and essential witnesses for a smooth prosecution. We don't think Sinaloa will foot the bill for fancy defense attorneys. We don't expect appeals. They'll probably let public defenders do the work, just to cut their losses, and run. We think Sinaloa is going broke. Between the loss of their boats, their cargo, the closing of their boat-building site, and the Canadian grow lab, we think they'll give up using the Atlantic ICW. We think they'll consider it a lost cause. We know Sinaloa has lost well over two billion dollars. They were trying to get the jump on their competition by opening up the first successful smuggling operation using the East Coast ICW. And we know Sinaloa is at war with competing Mexican cartels, especially the Juárez Cartel and the Gulf Cartel."

"Tim, how long will the trials go on?" Anne asked, her voice now dispirited.

"I wish I could give you an accurate answer, Anne. But I can't. Maybe up to several years, would be my guess," Tim replied, sympathetically. "But in WITSEC you won't be committed to staying inside the walls that surround this safe house for the rest of your life … you'll have what I call 'controlled freedom.'"

"*Controlled freedom?* Tim, what kind of bullshit answer is that!" Anne yelled, slamming her palm on the tabletop with a loud *pop*. She abruptly stood and screamed: "I'm leaving!" And she would have left, had Mark not caught her hand. Reluctantly, she sat back down. *She's about to crack,* Mark thought, still holding her hand tightly in his own. He pulled her close to him, placing his mouth next to her ear.

"Honey, we'll ask St. Christopher tonight," Mark softly whispered. But she didn't seem any calmer; he could still feel her trembling with anger.

Max sensed the potentially explosive tension now building in the entire group and he stood to speak, with Tim nodding his approval.

Max began, his voice calm and steady. "Anne, I'm not talking to just you alone … I'm now talking to *all six* of us in this meeting, us lawmen included. We've all got to manage any anger we may feel. So, let me have your full attention. Please at least *listen* to what the folks trying to set up your WITSEC have to say. What if I told you they can provide a reasonable job opportunity for you? What if I told you they can provide a lifetime subsistence payment of up to $60,000 per year? What if they could find quite acceptable housing for you? What if they can provide you with every conceivable identity document you might ever need? And, within limits, when you're no longer needed as a witness, allow you to freely travel this country?"

Oscar, who'd been silent for quite awhile, finally said, "Mr. Max, that sound lak a heap of 'what ifs' to me. But rat now I ain't got nothin', 'cept a few clothes an' dis safety house. On my own, I's got no house. No money. No truck, no boat, not ev'n no crab trap to put in the Lawd's river. Ain't ev'n got no pitchers of my family … and no Bible! All I's got lef' is the Lawd, an' las' nite He tol' me to listen to what 'em WITSEC folks is gotta say. So I's at least gonna listen!"

Max leveled a relieved gaze at the old black man. "Oscar, I know you don't have any formal education … but you're a very smart man. You probably have more common sense than all of us combined. I do hope your friends will join you … at least in *listening*.

"I'm with Oscar," Spence said.

"Me too, provided Anne agrees to listen," Mark said, seeing tears in Anne's beautiful hazel eyes.

"Shit," Anne mumbled under her breath, brushing away tears with the backs of her hands. "I know when I'm outnumbered," she loudly announced. "I'll listen, too." Finally, she smiled.

34

WITSEC

Following the briefing, everyone seemed a little more at ease. Anne first apologized to the marshals for her outburst, then to Mark, Spencer, and Oscar. As everyone began scattering, she then told Mark she was going to their room, "To do some serious thinking, alone," she'd said.

After Anne left, Max remained and said, "Mark, I'm glad your wife settled down. I think the whole group feels better now. But do you think she's OK in the room by herself?"

"Yes. She just likes her own personal space when she gets this way. I've been married to her for over 25 years. She rarely has explosive anger, but when it happens, she'll work it out on her own. I promise."

"Well," Max began, "now that we're alone, I have some news for you. Earlier I'd told you I would try to locate your former Grady roommate, Dr. Zack Paslaski."

"Did you find him, Max?"

"I'm afraid so. The news isn't good ... he was killed," Max relayed somberly.

"What! But how?" Mark exclaimed.

Max paused, then talked. "Let me explain. When Zack left Grady, he went to Harlem Hospital Center, or HHC as the locals there call it. It's a big facility, a Level 1 Trauma Center. In that way, it's somewhat like Grady in Atlanta. Their ER treated a whole cross-section of patients, including some of the lowlife types like you and I occasionally saw at Grady. Zack worked exclusively in their ER at HHC. Apparently, Zack was supposed to be a witness at the trial of a mob-connected doctor, one who freely wrote large prescriptions for controlled legal narcotic drugs. Zack had seen numerous overdose patients, their prescription bottles all bearing the same doctor's name. Zack saved the bottles as evidence that was going to be presented at the doctor's upcoming trial. Paslaski was offered police protection. He refused. Needless to say, some mob goon faking an illness got into the

ER, and shot Zack three times in the head. He also killed one patient, and wounded a nurse in the process. That goon is still at large."

Mark was speechless for a full minute. He suddenly felt weak, and sat in a chair. Max pulled up a chair next to Mark, and turned it so they were face to face. *Max is doing this just to scare the shit out of me, and make sure I'll agree to the WITSEC thing,* Mark thought at first. "Max, is this some BS you're telling me to encourage me to get into your program?"

Max let out a long breath, but kept his eyes locked on Mark's. "Doc, have I ever lied to you? Look into my eyes. Do you see any lies there?"

"No, Max. I think you're being straight with me. What about Zack's wife?"

"Her name is Alasia Petroski Paslaski. She's alive, still single, and their male child is premed in college. She works as an X-ray tech at HHC, and the hospital is sending their kid, Zack Paslaski II, to med school."

"God! I sure hate to tell Anne this. She's upset enough as it is," Mark lamented.

"Then *don't!* But if she asks, whatever you do, don't lie to her. I've printed several pages of the information I found on the Internet about Zack. I'll see that you get them after all this is over. You can tell Anne when you think the time is right ... and a right time may never come. And as a heads-up, the marshals working with WITSEC will be starting their interviews with you guys tomorrow morning."

* * *

Following their evening meal, Mark felt there'd be a long night of discussion in the privacy of their room. Both were trying to avoid confronting the WITSEC issue head-on. They started off with small talk.

"You know, Anne, it's really getting a little better here at the safe house. I mean with the outside marshals now checking out library books for us, getting some real groceries in the pantry, and especially allowing Oscar to cook some of the food."

"Yeah, Little Man. Especially that deviled crab Oscar made tonight ... and his made-from-scratch biscuits! I've watched Oscar make them twice now, and he's promised I can make the next batch on my own."

Mark chuckled. "Well, *if* we *ever* get out of here, I'm sure Tim and Max will hate to see us go. Or at least they'll be sorry to see *Oscar* go.

They'll probably just go back to that junk from McDonald's and those horrible TV dinners they can microwave."

"Mark, you just said *if* we *ever* get out of here. Is there doubt in your mind?"

"No, Anne. In fact, we could walk out right now. Our stay is still voluntary. We still have a home to go to. Suppose we did that? Then what?"

"For about an hour after the briefing I thought about our options. I soon discovered I was getting nowhere. I finally decided we should do what we've done in the past—just flip that darn St. Christopher medal when we're undecided about something! But I couldn't do it in the room this afternoon. You had your wallet in your pocket."

"Well, I'm here now," Mark said, reaching for his wallet. He withdrew the medal. "Are the rules still the same? The side with the saint's face means a 'yes,' and 'no' is the blank side?"

"Those are the rules. So do it!"

Mark flipped the medal hoping it would land on the bed: It did ... *with the saint's face showing.*

Both exhaled, then kissed. Then kissed again, long and deep. "Well," Anne said coming up for air, "I guess we need to decide how and where we want them to protect us."

"Anne, I'm not sure that's going to be entirely our choice. After the briefing—after you'd returned to our room—Max said some marshals would be coming to this safe house tomorrow. I think they're supposed to explain things, and begin planning. Maybe we should listen to what they say first. Then you and I can have another discussion."

"Agreed, Little Man," Anne said, as she began stripping her clothing. "But right now I want to have sex with you ... because I love you, and I just flat want to!"

"And this time it won't be just to relieve boredom! Long and slow, the way we both like it," Mark said, slowly removing his clothes, smiling.

* * *

At 7:00 a.m., Marshal Max Bollinger knocked on the door of Room 5. Mark barely cracked the door, but only because he and Anne were still nude from last night's events. Max spoke: "Oscar says breakfast will be at eight, and the marshals will be here at nine to start going over details of WITSEC. This will be done individually and in private, except for you and Anne, who will be first interviewed together as a couple in your room. You may recall your assigned marshal; his name is Sloan Stafford, one of the fellows who escorted you and Anne the nights you two did Roberto's surgeries. Be ready at nine, and be available here in your room."

"Well, I guess its time to shower, eat, and wait," Anne said, standing, wrapped in a sheet because she'd forgotten to put "bathrobe" on her shopping list for the outside marshals.

At nine, the Telfairs sat in their room awaiting the arrival of their assigned marshal. Only a few minutes late, Marshal Sloan Stafford knocked on the door and was promptly let in. Probably through habit, Sloan introduced himself and presented his credentials. Noting the room had no chairs, the marshal asked permission to sit on one of the beds Anne had quickly made up. The Telfairs sat together on the opposing single bed.

"It's nice to know I'm not dealing with total strangers here," Sloan started. "The last time we met, my sole function was to conceal your identity and safely escort you guys aboard a Coast Guard cutter to perform some secret surgery. But my purpose here today is to begin to discuss the Witness Security Program, the one we call WITSEC. To give you a brief history, the program was created by the Organized Crime Control Act of 1970, an Act of Congress, signed by Nixon. It is administered by the U.S. Department of Justice, and operated by the U.S. Marshals Service. The main function of the program is to allow our witnesses to safely testify in cases where there is a possibility of retribution by the criminal elements being prosecuted. We know the Sinaloa drug cartel has the potential to harm the prosecution's witnesses. My job is to see that justice is done, and that our witnesses remain unharmed ... and even have as much after-trial freedom and safety as possible. So far, the Service has scored 100 percent in providing for the safety of our witnesses. Do you have any questions?"

"I hardly know where to begin. Do you mind if we call you by your first name?" Mark asked.

"In this informal setting, just call me 'Sloan,' but in a courtroom refer to me as 'U.S. Marshal Sloan Stafford,' so there'll be no question in the transcription records."

"Sloan," Anne began, "this conversation we're having today will not actually put us in WITSEC, correct?"

"Correct," Sloan replied. "Until you've signed what we call a 'Memorandum of Understanding,' you will not officially be in the program. But we've got a lot of work to do before we get to that point."

"Such as?" Anne immediately asked.

"Such as your *new* names. We'll even let you choose them. That's for use after the trials, when you guys start getting on with your private lives again. Your names will be legally changed through the courts, but those records *will be permanently sealed.*"

"In other words, we'd have a new identity?" Mark asked.

"Correct," Sloan replied. "I'm not going to rush you. You two decide what you want your new names to be. Once that is decided, I can get to work supplying you guys with all the identity documents that will bear your new legal names."

"What kind of documents?" Mark asked.

"Essentially everything you two have now: driver's licenses; social security cards; vehicle and voter registration cards; credit cards; wills and legal documents; bank account checks and financial records; insurance papers; birth certificate and marriage license, et cetera. But first, I've got to have *names* to place on those documents. I'll need all three: a given name, middle name, and a surname. Choosing new names is sometimes the hardest part for some folks entering WITSEC. It may be helpful to keep your first name and initials the same, but that's certainly not essential. However, until you are officially in WITSEC, you cannot disclose your new name to anyone *except me.* You can't share it with the marshals running this safe house, not even between yourselves as husband and wife, or share it with Oscar Dunham or Dr. Spencer Roberson. Likewise, they can't share their new names with you."

"That seems stupid!" Anne immediately blurted. "They are our friends, for God's sake."

"I know, I know," Sloan replied. "But rules are rules. The Service has a definite basis for this rule. It has to do with something that happened 20 years ago, shortly after WITSEC was first set up. After a spat, a wife ratted her husband's new identity, and we almost had a breach in the husband's witness safety."

"I see, I guess," Anne said. "So how long does it take to get these counterfeit documents," Anne asked.

"They're not fake or counterfeit!" Sloan exclaimed. "After the legal name change, they are just as legal as the current documents you two now have."

"And we can stay *legally* married, right?" Anne asked.

Sloan laughed. "Of course! But in your particular case it's entirely up to you. You guys have lived together presenting yourselves as man and wife, both in the states of Georgia and Michigan. You are married by common law anyway, even if your new surnames don't match. I guess it sometimes could be better to have you two *not* married. I see where that could help isolate the new surname identities. By that I mean, if the former identity of either one of you should be discovered, it's less likely your spouse's original identity would be discovered as well. In my 25 years with the Service, we've never had that happen, though."

"What about our professional titles ... like 'Doctor' and 'M.D.,' and 'R.N.'? Can we keep those?" Mark asked.

Sloan paused a moment. "I'd recommend that only if you two are planning to return to active professional practice. Your new legal names would be changed at the appropriate licensure boards anyway. We can have those boards seal your files. But having your professional credentials openly attached to your name does make you easier to find. In other words, it would narrow the computer database for someone seriously trying to track you down."

"Will WITSEC be in effect before the trial?" Mark asked.

"No. At least not in this particular case. During the trials, you'll use your present names. Immediately following the trials, everything will already be in place for your new identity, and you'll be free. In the meantime, U.S. Marshals will pick you up at this or a similar safe house, then escort you to and from all the pretrial and proceedings at trial. You may be transported to court in anything from a helicopter to a U.S. Mail truck, or even an EMS truck. I expect most of the pretrial security to be relatively simple, and we'll probably just escort you two in our unmarked cars. You'll probably be hooded again—just like we did at the port—when you get in or out of the vehicles at the courthouse. In Brunswick, we'll probably use the underground or side entrance to the U.S. District court there."

"Sloan, my head is spinning!" Anne said, but still managed a grin.

The marshal gave her a sympathetic smile, then chuckled. "I'm sure your head is spinning, Anne. I've heard folks joking about 'dizzy blonds' all my life, but you certainly are not one of them! You're a sharp cookie." Sloan studied Anne a long moment. "Ya know, if you had short red hair of just the right shade, it would match your complexion and eye color. Just a suggestion on changing your appearance. And Mark, a beard is an option for you. Think about it. I know you two have had enough for one session, so I'm going to quit for now. I'll be back in three days. At that time, I'll need the new names you've decided upon. Don't tell *anyone* your new name ... not even each other, the house marshals, or the other 'guests' here."

35

MORE WITSEC DETAILS

Sloan stood slowly, then shook the Telfairs' hands while they remained seated, side by side on the bed. Stepping quickly to the door, he paused and turned. "Remember, new names in three days." Closing the door gently, Sloan left the Telfairs alone in a curious blend of bemusement and amusement.

"Anne, do you think the marshals talking to Oscar and Spencer told *them* the same things?" Mark asked.

"Yeah, Mark. I'm betting Oscar and Spence also got that same first-day spiel about new names. And the name-secrecy thing, too. But I'm not about to quit calling you 'Little Man' when I want to. That's been my personal pet name for you—has been forever! I've never called you that when others are around, and I'm not about to quit calling you that in private."

"Anne, I don't think that's the type name Sloan is interested in. It's certainly not a legal name. It's nowhere to be found in any of our legal documents. So, don't slip up and call me 'Little Man,' especially in front of Sloan and the others."

"I don't know about you, Mark, but I'm going to pick only new first and middle names. I'll accept whatever you use as your surname. I only want to always be 'Mrs. whatever-*you*-choose-to-be.'"

* * *

Three days later, Sloan and the other marshals returned to the safe house. As before, Sloan found the Telfairs in Room 5 patiently sitting and waiting for him. He shook their hands but skipped presenting his credentials. This time he carried an attaché case and got right down to business:

"Do not speak them, but have you chosen your new names yet?" Sloan asked.

Silently, the Telfairs nodded an affirmative.

"Sloan, I've picked only a new first and middle name for myself," Anne said. "I've decided to use whatever surname Mark has chosen."

"That's fine, Anne. But I'm going to ask you to step out of the room a few minutes while Mark gives me his new name. He will not speak it aloud, just print his full new name for me on a form I have in my attaché."

Reluctantly, Anne complied, stepping into the hall. She closed the door, and leaned against the wall with her arms crossed over her chest. *This secrecy shit is going to drive me nuts!* she thought.

Inside the room, Sloan quickly withdrew a form from his case, closed it and handed Mark his attaché to serve as a writing surface. Mark glanced at the form: "Petition for Change of Name," it read at the top. "Instructions are on the back of the form. Read them if you like. I only need you to do two things, though. I can fill in the rest for you. In all capital letters, carefully print your chosen new name ... first, middle, and last, in that order. Do it right here," Sloan said, pointing to an "X" he'd previously placed there. Mark accepted the black U.S. Government pen Sloan handed him, and printed his new name on the form. "OK, fine," Sloan commented. "All you've got to do now is sign here in cursive, using your current full legal name," he said, pointing to a second "X" at the bottom of the form. Mark signed as Marcus Milton Telfair. "Doc, you want a 'Dr.' or 'M.D.' attached to your new name?"

"No, I guess not. And I've always hated 'Milton,' my middle name. I won't mind losing that sucker one bit. Anne and I both have decided to drop our professional titles ... for the reasons you discussed during your first visit with us. All she told me is that she's going to use my new surname at the end of her new first and middle names."

"And she hasn't told you what her chosen first and middle names are?" Sloan asked.

"No. Not a word," Mark replied, being totally honest.

"Great!" the marshal replied. "Now I'm going to ask you to step outside while I get Anne to start the same paperwork you and I have just begun. In moments, Anne completed an identical "Petition for Change of Name," but Anne left the new surname space blank, and signed the petition as "Anne Hunt Telfair," her current full legal name. Sloan scribbled something on a yellow Post-it he attached to Anne's form, then stuck her papers back inside his attaché. "Anne, if you don't mind, ask Mark to step back inside the room."

She found him standing in the hall just as she had been: arms crossed over his chest, leaning against the wall and looking bored. "He wants to talk to both of us some more ... inside the room."

The Telfairs sat on the bed as before, with Sloan sitting on the opposite one. "What you both have signed is merely a petition to the court. We'll have to do some background checks on the new names you have chosen before we submit them to the judge. We do that mainly to be sure your new name is not that of a known criminal. We also want to be sure you don't share a new full legal name with someone else in the area. Once those checks are done, the name change is essentially done. I'll tell you if we encounter any problems. Under no circumstances are you to use your new names until I give you the OK, and that won't be until *after* the pretrial and trials. Is that clear?"

Both Mark and Anne nodded a "yes." Mark asked, "Sloan, what else do you have up your sleeve today?"

"Your fingerprints. Mark, yours are already on file with the U.S. Air Force, but I think it best if we get a current set on both of you. Let's go down to the counter in the kitchen. We need a better work surface than we've got here in this room. Plus it gets a little messy sometimes, getting the ink completely off, you know."

"You're treating us like criminals!" Anne exclaimed, but smiled as they followed Sloan to the kitchen.

"Quite the contrary!" Sloan responded. "It's Service rules. If it was up to me, I'd waive the fingerprint and polygraph requirements in your particular case. But actually it's for your protection. If you change your appearance after the trial, we don't want some look-alike committing a crime in your new name. In other words, we need to be able to get a positive ID on you guys for the rest of your lives. We do have a number of felons in WITSEC. Unfortunately, some of them become repeat offenders, and if we can prove they've committed another felony while in WITSEC, they permanently lose their protection status under the program."

"Why do you need to repeat *my* fingerprints if they are already on record?" Mark asked.

Sloan replied, "That's not my area of expertise, but I do know fingerprints change with age. The skin thins, you develop little fissures, and you may pick up a few scars here and there. It's just easier to match if we have current prints. That's what I've been told."

"And why the polygraph?" Anne asked.

"I honestly don't know, other than it's the Service's rules. I don't have much faith in polygraphs myself. I guess it would be like that 'baseline EKG' my doctor insisted on … said it's easier to spot changes if you have a reference point. I do know a polygraph is definitely required if you are a felon entering WITSEC. In your case, I'd personally waive that requirement … but it's the U.S. Attorney General who has to give the final approval. We want to have all our *i*'s and *t*'s dotted and crossed, and give him absolutely no reason for a rejection."

The Telfairs were first fingerprinted by Sloan in the safe house kitchen, then introduced to a female polygraphist who'd apparently accompanied the marshals to the house. She briefly interviewed both Mark and Anne, and indicated she would be back with some equipment in a day or two for the actual polygraph testing.

Sloan asked Mark and Anne to return to their room, "Just to go over a few more points I need to explain," he'd said.

Arriving at Room 5, Mark spoke first. "OK, Sloan, what else are you keeping from us? Mug shots?"

Sloan laughed. "Yeah, that too. We'll do it right before we submit the application to the Attorney General's office. And I'll give you two the details of pretrial and trial security when we get a little closer to that point. I've got a few things to tell you that will apply after the trials, when you'll actually be in WITSEC."

"Such as?" Mark asked.

"Once you're located in your new permanent home, local law enforcement will be informed of your location."

"What! Mark exclaimed. "That's what we fear the most, now. *Local law enforcement.* Like those two McIntosh County Sheriff's Deputies that got busted. It's our understanding they may even be tried locally, because the drug pickup site is technically off federal property. And we read in the *Savannah Morning News* that their trials will not be a part of the federal trials for the sub drivers and those men from Alabama, the ones who picked up drugs in their pontoon boat!"

"Calm down, Mark!" Sloan demanded. "Marshals Tim Ryan, Max Bollinger, and I have discussed your concerns at length. But let me ask you a question?"

"By all means do!" Anne shot back.

Sloan paused a moment. "Just how committed are you to living in the same house you two now own there on the Julienton River in McIntosh County?"

Mark answered: "Aside from being nothing fancy, and the only home we own, and loving its location, we're not otherwise committed! I think I can speak for Anne, too."

Anne nodded agreement.

"Just suppose, if you would," Sloan began, "that WITSEC could give you the ongoing freedom to move your 'home' anywhere in the U.S.? Of course I'm talking about *after* the trials, but you could move your home at your own discretion. Like any day, week, month, or year … at a time of your own choosing? You might be required to report your location to WITSEC, from time to time, though."

"What! And become freaking Gypsies?" Mark asked.

"Not exactly," Sloan countered. "I'm retiring from the U.S. Marshals Service in 18 months, but that's not for publication. The factory notified me they've finished building my 'retirement home.' As we speak, it is in the process of being delivered to me. It's a 1997 Fleetwood Discovery motorhome. It is a diesel pusher, has a slide-out living area, excellent galley and bath, two large bedrooms, and just about every bell and whistle you could possibly hope for. If all remains on schedule, I'll be accepting delivery tomorrow morning. I don't want to bring it to this safe house, but I'd be glad to give you guys a private tour of it at my apartment in Brunswick. I'd have to get special permission to take you guys off site, but I'm going to insist it's 'official business,' in that it's showing you an option for living in WITSEC. You'd have to be hooded when we go to look at it."

"Has anyone else in WITSEC ever chosen to live in a motorhome?" Mark asked Sloan.

"Yes. Off the top of my head I can think of several WITSEC couples that have chosen the 'Gypsy' lifestyle, as you called it. It obviously wouldn't be a good option for young couples with a big family and kids in school, or for folks that can't do their work using mobile-based electronic communication. All I ask is that you consider this as one option. I know my wife and I are both looking forward to retiring in our motorhome. We want to see all this great country, border to border, shore to shore. Just think about it."

* * *

That evening, following an excellent meal of turnip greens, cornbread, and oyster stew prepared by Oscar, the Telfairs retired early to discuss the information Sloan had given them earlier in the day.

"Little Man, this is about the craziest thing that has ever happened to us. Don't you think?"

Mark chuckled, mostly at himself. "I don't *think* it is ... I *know* it is! In my mind, I never thought I could ever live in such a confined space for days on end. But look at how long we have been here. This is now our *third* month of living in just a ten-by-twelve bedroom. Well that, and a few other selected areas of a house that probably has less than 2,500 square feet ... and we're surrounded by a half-acre of grass inside an electrified ten-foot-high wall!"

"You know Little Man, for me it's not so much of a 'claustrophobic thing,' as it is a 'loss-of-freedom thing.' I don't mind tight quarters as long as it's shared with you inside them. And don't you smile at me that way, Little Man ... that's not the 'quarters' I'm talking about!"

Best I say nothing ... and hear her out on this one! Mark immediately thought.

Anne almost laughed, but settled for a smile. "Little Man, I'm talking about the motorhome idea Sloan mentioned today. We could travel, even tow a car or boat with us. We could eliminate our fear of revenge from local law enforcement in McIntosh County. We could move when hurricanes threatened. We could—"

"Look at Sloan's motorhome first," Mark cut in. "I haven't been inside one since college, and that was an old small Winnebago that was cramped and shabby."

The next afternoon, Marshal Sloan Stafford appeared at the safe house to pick up the Telfairs. He was driving a light blue Ford Crown Vic, one that did not bear government plates. Because Sloan's personal car did not have tinted windows, Mark and Anne were again required to wear hoods while they traveled south on U.S. 17. An hour later, Sloan had driven them to the Westminster Apartments in Brunswick, where Sloan and his wife rented a small efficiency unit. His new 1997 Fleetwood Discovery motorhome was parallel-parked at the curb; it dominated at least six parking places in the apartment building's lot. Still hooded, the Telfairs were quickly escorted inside Sloan's Fleetwood.

"Well, whatcha think?" Sloan asked, smiling broadly, after the Telfairs removed their hoods.

"This is certainly not what I expected!" Anne exclaimed, as she examined the galley. "Mark, it's even got a microwave. And look at this fridge. It's as big as the one we have at home! It even has an icemaker!"

Sloan, with child-like enthusiasm, continued showing them every minute interior amenity. "I'd operate the power slide, and show you how the living room expands some eight feet ... but I don't want to risk popping it out here in the parking lot, and have a car run into it. I can show you a picture, though," Sloan said, reaching into a cabinet and withdrawing a handful of brochures.

"I know the photographers who make these interior pictures have a way of making things appear larger than they are ... but this is impressive!" Mark exclaimed.

"I'll want those brochures back, eventually. But why don't you guys take them back to the safe house, and study them over? There are brochures for makes and models other than Fleetwood in there, too. There's a number of floor plans and options," Sloan explained, as he stuffed all of them into a large Manila envelope and handed it to Mark.

"Sloan, can I ask you a personal question?" Anne asked.

"Sure, but I may not answer it," Sloan smiled.

"Other than travel this country, what else do you plan to do with your time in retirement?"

"Write. Write a book," Sloan said. *Inside the U.S. Marshals Service,* or something like that. In my 25 years with the Service, I've had a number of very interesting experiences. Ones that are not classified, I can write about. Maybe the civilian community will find it educational as well as entertaining."

"Sloan," Anne began, "that's *exactly* what Mark and I had planned to do in retirement. Write. But we've yet to write the first word."

"Both of you come here, please. There is a second bedroom I had the factory outfit as my office space. It's got a filing cabinet, desk, shelves, computer, keyboard, monitor, and printer. Everything you need to write is all here in this one private space."

"Sloan, you've really given us a lot to think about," Mark said. "But I don't know how we could ever afford to buy something this nice on our retirement income. What are we talking about cost wise, if you don't mind my asking?"

Sloan didn't hesitate: "I've got about $55,000 invested with this particular make and model. The wife and I sold our home here in Brunswick, and that generated way more than we needed to pay cash for this Fleetwood. We're getting all our financial business set up so we can bank, pay bills, and access cash money as needed while on the road. Whatever you do, if you retire to a motorhome, go with diesel. It's cheaper, safer, and more reliable. Even the electrical generator is diesel, and diesel is running about $1.13 a gallon now."

If Sloan does not write in retirement, he could become a motorhome salesman! Mark thought.

36

THE TRIALS

The Telfairs' ride back to the Richmond Hill safe house was largely silent. While on U.S. 17, they received a few curious stares from occupants of other vehicles that passed Sloan's Crown Vic. *I think it's the black hoods that are causing the stares,* Mark thought.

Sloan finally broke the silence. "I guess I got so excited about showing off my new 'toy,' I forgot to tell you some very important news: The pretrial stuff will all start at 9:00 a.m., two days from now. You'll need to get up a little earlier than usual, and be ready for a departure at 7:00. We've got a couple of young outside marshals who are going to buy you some clothes suitable for your courtroom appearance. And for God's sake, give those young bozos some guidelines and specific sizes. Male witnesses will need a coat, tie, slacks, and dress shoes. Anne will need a tasteful dark dress with a high neckline, and a skirt length that falls at or below her knees. Her shoes should be closed at the toe, and short-heeled. *Conservative* is the word I guess I'm looking for. I know the particular judge conducting the pretrial will not allow uniforms, so even Spence will need new clothes for court, too. Our Service people inside the courtroom will be in dark suits, with white shirt and dark tie. They'll have their top eagle badges on the left lapel of their suits, just like the ones the guys wear at the safe house. We'll also have a marshal, who used to be a licensed barber in his former life; he'll come to the safe house and freshen haircuts."

When Sloan pulled to the gate at the safe house, a quick satphone call told someone inside to open the electronic gate. Oscar was out in the yard walking Stutz on a leash. Forgetting their hoods, the Telfairs exited the Crown Vic. Stutz almost yanked Oscar's arm out of its socket by straining at his leash. "Stutz OK! Stutz OK!" Oscar yelled. "Y'all take 'em socks off yo' heads. Dat's what got he so shook up!"

Anne and Mark immediately removed their hoods. Stutz sat at Oscar's side while Sloan backed the Crown Vic out the drive, the gate immediately closing behind his civilian car. Oscar unsnapped the leash, said another "Stutz OK," and the dog bounded some 50 feet to greet the Telfairs and be petted. *This dog really has an expressive face ... and embarrassment is all I see there now!* Mark thought.

Marshal Tim Ryan stepped out the front door of the safe house. Tim was all smiles. "I've got some great news. You'll be starting pretrial, day after tomorrow."

"Sloan already told us while we were out with him," Anne said. "At least the ball has started rolling, Tim."

"Shoot! That was going to be my surprise topic for your briefing at the evening meal. That Sloan is a 'spoiler' ... just like Oscar is spoiling our guard dog rotten! I've known it was happening, and I aided the process by allowing Oscar to keep Stutz in his room at night. But I've got some news I bet Sloan doesn't have yet. I just got it by phone minutes ago. We're getting a brand new guard dog in about six weeks. A female German Shepherd. She's completing her $5,000 training program at a special K-9 facility the Service uses."

God, no wonder our taxes are so high ... $300 hammers, $600 toilet seats and now $5,000 dogs! Mark thought, but said nothing. And he was glad he didn't.

"And," Tim continued, "the Service has agreed that Oscar can adopt Stutz ... that's if Oscar still wants the dog after we complete the trials."

"Say what now, Mr. Tim? Is you tellin' me I kin keep dis dog?"

Seeing the hopeful look in Oscar's dark brown eyes, Tim beamed. "Yes, Oscar. Stutz can be your dog once you're in WITSEC. That's exactly what I'm saying. Stutz is only eight years old now. I think he's got a lot of lifetime left and the vet says Stutz is in perfect health. The Service requires that we retire his breed at his age, even though they are healthy."

Oscar, a look of utter disbelief on his face, an empty leash still in hand, sat on the grass overcome by emotion. Oscar was crying like a baby. Stutz came to Oscar and gently began licking his tears. "Oh, Lawd! Dis here is too much for a old man lak me. Aside my friends what I's got here at dis safety house, I's now got two mo' things: I's got de Lawd an' now I's got me a dog, too!" Oscar exclaimed, giving the dog a tight hug that was not resisted.

Tim, obviously struggling for composure, said, "Oscar, tell *your* dog to go inside."

Oscar got off the grass, carefully coiled the leash, and stuffed it into the large breast pocket of his bibs. "Stutz inside," Oscar commanded, and the dog immediately bounded to the front door and sat, waiting to be let in.

Oscar is a man of simple wants and simple needs ... but certainly not simpleminded ... and one of the most fascinating people I've ever met, Mark thought, as they entered the house.

* * *

Following Tim's briefing and the group's evening meal, Mark and Anne studied motorhome brochures in the privacy of their room. After two hours of looking at different makes, models, floor plans and options, Mark finally summarized:

"Anne, it's obvious Sloan researched his motorhome choice for months. Out of the dozen different manufacturers he's looked at, it's obvious his selection was not casual."

"Agreed, Mark. The notes Sloan has written on the brochures also give a lot of information, too. Like 'Fleetwood: 72 service centers coast to coast in U.S.,' and 'Most reliable RV Cummins diesel generator and engine on market,' and things like that."

"Anne, I do think we could live in a motorhome like Sloan has chosen to do. But there's a major problem: *money.* There's no way we can plop down $55,000 until we sell our home in Dunham, and the *Fanta-Sea.* The deed and title are both in our current legal names. I can see all kinds of legal entanglements trying to sell our Dunham assets *after* we've changed our names."

Anne felt something thin remaining in the Manila envelope that had not been removed. It was a folded yellow legal-sized worksheet where Sloan had looked at a lease-purchase option offered by Fleetwood. "Better to buy outright, after we sell our home," Sloan had written at the bottom.

"Mark, according to Sloan's worksheet, we've got enough retirement income to lease one at $525 a month, and that includes the insurance. And did you see that mirrored ceiling in the bedroom?"

Anne's sold on the motorhome idea ... at least for a lease. We've never done it with a mirrored ceiling. Sloan, you old rascal! Mark thought.

"I couldn't miss the ceiling, Anne. I didn't mention it when Sloan gave us our tour. Figured it might embarrass him, if I did."

"What say we shower together, then pretend we have a mirrored ceiling in this room," Anne said, wearing a suggestive smile. We'll work out the details of a lease tomorrow ... or next week ... or next month or year ... when all this legal stuff is over."

* * *

Over the next six months, the Richmond Hill safe house witnesses spent many hours at the U.S. District Courthouse in Brunswick, Georgia. As promised by Marshal Sloan Stafford, their going to and from the courthouse became a boredom-breaking adventure unto itself. The Service used a multitude of vehicles, and constantly varied their routes. Anne was disappointed that they never used a helicopter; she'd always wanted a larger-scale view of the coastal area where they lived.

The pretrial proceedings crawled at such a slow pace, Mark had to fight to stay awake at times. *If it took this long to make medical decisions, most patients would be dead of old age by the time a doctor administered treatment!* Mark thought. But he was looking forward to the present day in court: It would be the first day of the actual trials. He knew they'd probably all be called to the stand for testimony. Oscar was one of the first witnesses called. It soon became apparent the defense attorneys felt Oscar, as a key eyewitness, would be very easy to discredit.

When he was called to the stand, Oscar looked like a preacher: dark blue jacket, white shirt, dark tie, black slacks, and black shoes shined to a mirror finish.

"Please state your full name for the record," the young defense attorney requested.

"Where is that record at?" Oscar asked.

A chuckle or two caused the judge to use his gavel. Silence fell.

"Sir, the 'record' is that lady over there who's typing what you say here today. She's called a court recorder. Please state your full name, sir."

"Oscar Dunham."

"That's all? No middle name?"

"Naw suh. When I's born that's all th' name they gimme."

"I see. And *where* were you born?" the attorney asked.

"In my momma's bed at her house," Oscar replied.

"Were you born in the United States?"

"Well I reckon so, on account my momma's bed be in th' United States."

The judge gaveled again.

"Do you have a birth certificate, Mr. Dunham?"

"Naw suh. They ain't be givin' 'em out where I wuz born at."

"I see," the attorney said. "So you can't prove you're a citizen of the United States?"

"Well—"

The judge interrupted: "Counselor, the records regarding this witness have already proven to *my* satisfaction that he is a United States citizen. Stop this line of questioning, and get on with what this witness actually *saw.*"

"Yes, Your Honor. I'm getting there."

"Proceed," the judge said.

"Mr. Dunham, you claim to have seen semisubmersible boats in the Barbour River. In your prior deposition, you have referred to them as 'SS things.' Is that correct?"

"Yes, suh."

"Could you describe for the jury what the SSs look like?"

"They's about six foots longer than my boat was. An' my boat was 24 foots, so that would make 'em 'bout 30 foots long. They be shape and color lak a giant dolphin on they top, an' they got two pipe stickin' out 'em ... 'bout dis size," Oscar said, forming a four-inch circle with his hands. "Pipe on the back be a e'zaust pipe, cause I seen a little black smoke come out, an' could hear motor running. I think de pipe on they front end be suckin' in air fo' they motor, an' fo' 'em mens inside to breathe. An' they's got a hump 'tween 'em two pipe what's got low windows. Hump is got radar thing on de roof. But nothin' stick up much ... maybe not ev'n two foots."

"And exactly where did you see these so-called SSs?"

"Second straightaway 'tween 'em bends when you's goin' upriver from th' Barbour Landin'. Be 'bout a mile up from the landin'."

"Mr. Dunham, what time of day did you see the SSs?"

"'Round three o'clock in de afternoon. Was three different boat."

"Was it foggy that afternoon you claim you saw them?"

"Naw, suh. It be clear."

"And how far away were you from them when you first spotted them?"

"'Bout as long as this court buildin' that we's now in."

"So you'd say you were 100 yards away?"

"Leading the witness, counselor. Restate your question," the judge demanded.

"Yes, Your Honor. I'll accept the distance as being as far away as this court building is long."

"You may proceed," the judge said.

"Mr. Dunham, do you wear eyeglasses?"

"Naw, suh. Ain't never had no need for 'em."

"Assuming the air is clear, Mr. Dunham, just exactly how far away do you think you can see things clearly?"

Oscar paused a very long moment. "Witness will please answer counsel's question," the judge finally butted in.

"Well I can see the moon jus' fine. Now, how far away is dat?" Oscar asked.

The courtroom erupted in raucous laughter. Even the judge was laughing. It took a full five minutes to restore order. The defense attorney sat at the counsel's table with a beet-red face. The judge finally declared a ten-minute recess.

After the recess, the prosecution recalled Oscar to the witness stand. The experienced federal prosecutor had in hand two items: a Snellen eye chart and a 100-foot tape measure. "Your Honor, if I may indulge the court, I ask your permission to conduct a short experiment that will resolve any issues regarding Mr. Oscar Dunham's visual acuity."

"Proceed, but this better be brief," the judge informed the prosecutor.

The Snellen chart was handed to a juror in the back row. The prosecutor instructed the juror: "Please hold this card up so it faces the witness. And please hold this end of the tape measure while I go to the witness stand."

The prosecutor walked to the witness stand, letting tape spool off as he went there. He then began to examine the federal witness:

"Mr. Dunham, do you see the card a member of the jury is holding so that it faces you?"

"Sho does," Oscar replied.

"Have you ever in your life seen such a card as that juror is now holding?"

"Naw, suh. Never. Look lak jus' letters to me."

"You're not wearing contact lenses, are you Mr. Dunham?"

"Not sho what dat is, but I ain't got nothin' but my natchel eyes."

"You see this tape measure I'm holding close to your face?" the prosecutor asked.

"Sho does."

"Can you read the distance the tape indicates you are from that card?"

Oscar studied the tape. "Hit say 67 foots an' some three little marks, too."

"Let the record indicate that Mr. Dunham, verified by me, has indicated he is 67 feet and three-eighths of an inch from the Snellen eye chart. Mr. Dunham, could you read the lowest line of letters, left to right, that you can *clearly* read from where you are now seated?"

Oscar squinted. Anne and Mark held their breath. "Hit say H-E-l-O-P-Z-X-Q," Oscar slowly replied. "But hit ain't no word I's ever seen befo'," Oscar added.

"Your Honor, may I show you this standard Snellen eye chart?" The judge nodded a "yes," and accepted the chart handed him by prosecution counsel. "Your Honor, please note that Mr. Dunham has read down to the 20/20 line at over *three times* the normal 20-foot testing distance. I submit to this court, Mr. Dunham has no visual impairment, despite his being 82 years of age."

* * *

Events like the "challenging of Oscar's eyesight" had made the courtroom boredom tolerable. In just two months, the three Alabama men operating the pontoon, and the nine Hispanics operating the subs, were each convicted on multiple counts. They were subsequently sentenced to prison times varying from 25 to 30 years. Anne squealed (and got gaveled!) when it was announced: The SS driver that had shot Nosy the dolphin got a $20,000 fine, and an additional year added to his 25-year sentence ... for violating the federal Marine Mammals Protection Act.

EPILOGUE

At the safe house, they had a post-trial celebration of sorts. Oscar, with Anne's help, prepared the equivalent of a Thanksgiving meal. At the dining table, an odd combination of elation and sadness filled the air. Despite the crisis that had bound them all so tightly together, each member realized the friendships they had formed were about to be abruptly dissolved. Following their feast, and with tears in their eyes, Oscar, Spencer, Anne, and Mark signed "The Memorandum of Understanding." They were now officially in the WITSEC program.

Prior to the safe house guests losing their former identities in WITSEC, the outside marshals had served as couriers who transported voluminous legal paperwork. The U.S. Marshals Service produced valid real estate deeds, insurance papers, and even title documents bearing the guests' new names. Mark and Anne sold their Dunham Point home (and their two boats) to Spencer. He had insured the purchased home at "replacement value," and did not seem to worry the least about retribution from Sinaloa, or even by local law enforcement as the Telfairs had seemed to fear. Spence said he planned to become a biology teacher, hopefully at Armstrong Atlantic State University in Savannah. Spence was not sure if the WITSEC program would allow him to work that nearby, but it did. He became Professor William Nelson Worthington, Ph.D., at Armstrong State, and ultimately became the Chairman of their Department of Biology. He fell in love with one of his "late-bloomer" graduate students, a Ph.D. in her mid-30s. She was a few years younger than "Spence" when they got married. Both loved their "new" home and their work at the university, and didn't mind the 40-minute commute to Armstrong from the former home of Mark and Anne Telfair.

Though his new name remained unknown to the others at the safe house, Oscar Dunham simply became Oscar Durden. Oscar had indicated he didn't need a middle name: "I's had a birthday an' now lived 83 years without no middle name, an' I don't need one now!" he'd insisted. Along with Stutz, he was relocated to a very nice little low-country home on the water at Daufuskie Island in South Carolina.

A sale of Oscar's charred homesite in McIntosh County was made to one of Oscar's former neighbors. At least the $3,000 Oscar received for his land gave him some cash until the WITSEC subsistence funds started coming in. Those generous funds permitted by the program allowed Oscar to buy himself used replacements for his burned boat and truck. Oscar again resumed work as a waterman using the Cooper River, and its hundreds of tributary creeks. His ever-present canine companion, Stutz, served as his eager "first mate" when out on the water, or as his "copilot" when driving his truck. Calling upon his son in Savannah (in violation of WITSEC rules!), and using a family photo album his son had, Oscar was able to reproduce his entire collection of pictures that had once graced the "pitcher wall" of his home Sinaloa had burned in McIntosh County. He felt his life was complete again, and Oscar now had more money than he'd ever had in his life. But he didn't spend it ... he *gave* it away to poor black kids, ones he hand-selected according to their motivation and need for college money.

On cruise control, and relaxed while he drove their new 37-foot Fleetwood Discovery toward Phoenix on I-10, she spoke to her husband-driver. "I like your new beard, Little Man. Just don't let it get much longer. It kinda tickles when we ... well you know what I mean! But how did you ever come up with your new name?"

"I don't really know. It just sorta popped into my head. I use to know a kid in Atlanta. He lived in Buckhead, where I grew up. His first name was Jon, but everyone called him 'Jonny.' He was sort of a science nerd, but I really liked him anyway. Some of the guys teased him about the spelling ...you know, about someone leaving the *h* out of his name. And I liked another name I'd heard in high school. That kid's last name was Traer. A short and simple name. I don't even remember what that Traer's first name was. And I've always liked the name Wayne. So I guess that's how I came up with my new full name: Jon Wayne Traer."

"Same with me, Jon. 'Mary Kristin' just sorta popped into my head."

"You know, Mary Kristin, you sure look sexy with your new short red hair."

"It's Clairol's 'Paint the Town – Deep Red 044.'"

"Did you paint *everything?*"

"You better believe it, my Little Man. Why go halfway?"

"You want me to pull over at the next I-10 rest stop?"

"Yes ... but no. Let's see if we can practice a little self-discipline. When we get into some RV park tonight, don't you think we could at least *start* writing our books?" Mary Kristin asked.

"Sure! Right *after* we try out that mirrored ceiling again," Jon replied, grinning.

"No, Jon! Not until we write at least *one* paragraph of our first book, the one we are going to call *Going to the Gradies.* That's all I ask, just *one paragraph!* We've gotta learn some self-control. Otherwise, we'll never get it done."

"Why not start with one called *Beyond the Gradies* ... about private practice in Statesville?" Jon asked.

"No! We write them *in order,* just as things actually happened to us," Mary Kristin responded, firmly standing her ground. "And I think one called *Beyond Beyond* should definitely come last. Just think: We're only five years into retirement, and so far it's been one helluva wild ride! No telling what else may happen in our retirement ... something we'll want to put in a final book."

Jon frowned, but then smiled. "OK, we'll do 'em in order. But if you could go back in time, is there anything you would change?"

"I don't think so, Jon. I'm quite content to now be Mrs. Mary Kristin Traer. And you'll always be my Little Man ... but I've got a sneaky feeling that first paragraph of *Going to the Gradies* we'll write tonight is going to be a mighty short one."

And it was!

* * *

Author's final note: The two McIntosh County Sheriff's Deputies alleged to have been involved, were tried locally at the courthouse in Darien. During the second week of their trials, the two deputies mysteriously disappeared. Both men were out on bail, and staying in their local homes at night during the trial. A few years later, the truth would come out: As one of the cartel's final violent acts—before its total collapse on the East Coast—those two deputies had been captured by Sinaloa in their homes at night, taken to Mexico, then executed.

Made in the USA
Charleston, SC
20 August 2010